Exposure

By Aga Lesiewicz

Rebound

Exposure

Aga Lesiewicz

EXPOSURE

MACMILLAN

First published 2017 by Macmillan
an imprint of Pan Macmillan
20 New Wharf Road, London N1 9RR
Associated companies throughout the world
www.panmacmillan.com

ISBN 978-1-4472-8314-0

1 3 5 7 9 8 6 4 2

A CIP catalogue record for this book is available from the British Library.

Typeset by Palimpsest Book Production Ltd, Falkirk, Stirlingshire
Printed and bound by CPI Group (UK) Ltd, Croydon, CR0 4YY

Visit **www.panmacmillan.com** to read more about all our books
and to buy them. You will also find features, author interviews and
news of any author events, and you can sign up for e-newsletters
so that you're always first to hear about our new releases.

Exposure

Prologue

A new email pings in my mailbox and my chest tightens with anxiety. I know I have no reason to react like this any more, but the sound still fills me with dread. I click on the mailbox icon and stare at its contents in disbelief.

'Exposure 5'.

My worst nightmare isn't over, after all.

I could ignore it, I could delete it, but I know it will appear again. And again. I also know there is no point in trying to trace its sender. The person who has sent it doesn't want to be found and isn't interested in my answer.

I take a deep breath and click on the attachment. It's a photograph this time and it's mesmerizing. I've seen something like this before. It seamlessly blends two images, the one of the view outside and that of the inside of a room. The image of the exterior is projected on the back wall of the room and is upside down. I rotate the picture on my computer screen and take a closer look. It's a section of an urban riverbank, a uniform row of solid four- and five-storey houses, perched in a neat line above the dark water. The brown and beige brick mass is interrupted by splashes of colour, marking the developer's frivolous idea of painting some of the tiny balconies white or blue. A modern addition breaks the brick monotony, an incongruous cube of glass and steel crowned with a 'For Sale' sign. Below, the river has left its mark on the mixture of rotting wood and concrete with a vibrant green bloom of algae clinging to the man-made walls. My heart begins to pound when I realize the view looks familiar.

I know where the photo was taken.

I rotate the image back and concentrate on the interior. It's someone's bedroom, dominated by a large bed. The heavy wooden frame fills the picture, its carved antique headboard clashing with the image of the exterior projected over it. The bed is unmade, a mess of pillows and a duvet entangled with sheets that are dark red, almost crimson. A small bedside table on the left, with an unlit brass lamp on top of it. Some books scattered on the floor, mostly large-format, hardcover art albums. I find my eye keeps coming back to one spot in the image, a body on the bed. The woman is partly covered by the crimson sheet, her dark hair spilling over the edge of the mattress. One of her arms is twisted at a weird angle, revealing a small tattoo on the inside of the forearm, just above the wrist. I recognize the image. And I can tell the woman is dead.

I close the attachment and get up from the table, away from the computer. I feel dizzy and faint, my skin clammy, the thin shirt I'm wearing drenched in cold sweat. No, I can't let panic get the better of me. I have to think and act. I go to the sink and pour myself a glass of water from the tap. I drink it greedily, spilling some on the floor. It helps a little, but the choking sensation in my throat persists as I go back to the Mac and click on the attachment. I force myself to look at the image again. Yes, there is no doubt about it. I am the dead woman in the photograph. And I know who my killer is.

1

Three Weeks Earlier

It's an overcast and oppressively hot summer day, so humid everything I touch is damp. We've been filming at Shepperton Studios in Surrey since early morning and I have a feeling the shoot is going to run well into the night. The small space, a tarted-up storage room rented out to low-budget shoots, doesn't have any ventilation to speak of. It's in a deserted part of the film studio complex, tucked away behind the D Stage. Everything happens in slow motion today and everyone seems to be in a foul mood. Even Milo, the motion-control rig we are using, has succumbed to the tropical temperature. Something is over-heating inside, causing the rig to jam, and no one can find the source of the glitch. As the studio guys are trying to fix it, most of the crew lumber to the canteen in search of air-conditioning. When I say 'the crew' I mean Jason, the director, Lucy, the production assistant, a couple of model makers and me, the director of photography, or DOP for short. I do mostly still photography these days and don't normally work on film shoots, but Jason and I go back a long way and I never say no to his little projects. We reach the canteen and stare passively at the locked doors. Of course, it's past 6 p.m. and the cafe is closed. The studio complex, normally buzzing with life, seems deserted. We begin to crawl back to the studio when my iPhone pings. We've been told fixing Milo will take a bit of time, so I fall back behind our group to check my emails. There is a handful of spam offering Ray-Ban glasses and friendship from 'a pretty Russian girl called Irina', a couple of emails from my accountant and an email from an unknown sender titled 'Exposure 1'. My finger hovers over the 'Delete' button, but then I change my mind and open it. It has an attachment that most likely contains a virus, but curiosity gets the better of me. Here's to living dangerously, I think as I click on it.

It's a photograph of a crime scene that instantly takes me back to my early days when I freelanced for the Met police as a forensic photographer. The gig, my first attempt at putting my nose to the grindstone, didn't last long. I quickly realized I simply couldn't hack the mundane brutality of it. And so I tried my hand at concert photography only to end up working in small, dingy clubs and spending a fortune on earplugs. Craving fresh air and open space, I dropped the gigs arena to become a landscape photographer. I took out a small mortgage to fit my Canon 5D with a reasonable selection of wide-angle, medium and telephoto pro-zoom lenses, packed a sturdy tripod into my bag and headed for America. The only thing I brought back from there was a dislike for chipmunks and a growing debt. What else could I do? The thought of putting up with weddings and corporate events sent shivers down my spine. What about travel photography? After my disappointing landscape-chasing stint in America I knew that getting up at 3 a.m. to climb some slippery mountain weighed down by a ton of equipment to catch a perfect sunrise was not my idea of fun. Food photography, my mate Sophie suggested, leafing through the new Jamie Oliver cookbook. It was easy for her to say: she ran a successful catering business. I couldn't tell my parsnip from my carrot. All that was left was taking stock pictures, photographing packshots and praying for an occasional job for an ad agency. And this is what I do today, juggling much-needed but rare advertising shoots with bread-and-butter packshot jobs I can usually do in my little studio in Shoreditch. So much for the ambitious dreams of a bright-eyed art college graduate, who imagined herself with a forty-thousand-dollar Hasselblad DSLR camera round her neck and an entourage of assistants.

But I can't complain. I have paid off my debts. I own a great loft space opposite a sex shop just off Hoxton Square. I have a trusted Canon 5D Mark III with a lovely selection of lenses and a handful of loyal clients.

And I have Anton. I am happy.

Deep in thought, I stare at the photo on my phone screen without seeing it properly. I find that more and more often I tend to drift off into some disconnected reverie, forgetting the world around me. Apparently it's common among people who freelance from home and rely most of the time on their own company. With Anton being away a lot I mostly have Pixel and Voxel as my escorts. But cats, especially ginger cats, tend to be fickle friends, so my working hours are rather lonely. Unless, of course, I have an external shoot like the one today.

'Kris, we're on!'

I close the mailbox on my phone and dash back towards the studio. Jason is waiting for me, holding the heavy door open.

'Milo's back online, it looks like we can start. With a bit of luck we'll be done by midnight.'

I'm used to overtime without extra pay. It's common practice these days, when everyone is scrambling for a decent gig and the competition is fierce. But I don't mind it this time. I like working with Jason, a quiet man with the smile of a happy child and the creative imagination of a teenage genius. We are shooting a trailer for one of the TV crime shows. As the footage from the series isn't available yet, Jason has come up with the idea of using miniature models to re-enact crime scenes.

The model makers are finishing setting up the scene, and Jason excitedly reminds everyone what we're supposed to achieve.

'. . . isolate the central part of the shot in focus, just here, where the woman is standing by the open door, face covered in hands, she's obviously scared, frozen in fear, while we throw the dark figure in the background out of focus and into a nice, silky blur. And then we gradually shift the shallow depth of field . . .'

I tune him out as I concentrate on the image. I instinctively know what he wants. We've always understood each other like this, Jason and I, even before and after our sweet and short fling ages ago. Jason is married and has three great kids who are probably all in secondary school by now. He is devoted to his family, and his occasional infidelities are, according to him, euphoric outlets for his exuberant creativity. It may sound like complete bullshit, but I think I know what he means.

Just as Jason predicted, we are done with ten minutes to spare till midnight. While the guys are packing up, I carefully put away my camera and lenses into a hard case. It may seem overcautious, but the case has saved me a lot of money over the years. There is nothing worse than the sound of an unprotected two-thousand-pound lens hitting the floor.

Everyone is in a hurry to get home. The crew disperses swiftly. I part with Jason and Lucy, who head to the main car park by the reception. I have left my car parked in a small lot behind the A Stage, which is on the other side of the complex, but I don't mind a short walk. It's still very warm, but a slight breeze is moving the air pleasantly. As I pull my case through the deserted alleys, I feel tension leaving my body. I love this feeling, tiredness mixed with satisfaction when a long but productive day is over. It's a cloudless night and the moon is almost full. Actually, I think as I stop and stare at it, it *is* a full moon. How lucky I am to be able to catch that perfect moment, when the world is bathed in silvery light, making everything seem clean and still. Some birds have begun chirping in the distance, poor little bastards clearly confused by the brightness of the night. I can see my old and faithful 1996 MG roadster convertible, the only car left in the whole lot, when my iPhone pings with a new email. At this hour it's either spam or a message from Anton who is working on a project in Buenos Aires. I hope it's from him, it would be a perfect ending to a good day. I squeeze my case onto the back seat of my MG and get in, contemplating whether to put the roof down. I know it may seem rather eccentric in the middle of the night, but the air is warm and inviting. I undo the latches and slowly coax it down. I've had this car for years, it's an old and scratched banger now, but it still gives me a teenage thrill to feel the sky above my head when I'm driving. And there it is, the starlit sky shimmering overhead, peaceful and bucolic. It's an advantage of working in the sticks, miles from home, but also far from the hustle and bustle of the metropolis. And when it comes to hustle and bustle, Shoreditch rules. It will take me a couple of hours to drive home from the Surrey suburbia, but I don't mind. I actually like driving at night, especially with the roof down.

Without turning the engine on I pull out my phone and

check my emails. No message from Anton, but the persistent Russian beauty Irina has sent me another email, together with a couple of offers from an online casino. And there it is again, 'Exposure 1', from a sender whose name doesn't mean anything to me. I open it and go straight to the attachment. It's the same photo, a crime scene in a concrete, urban environment that has already been marked by a forensic team. It looks just like hundreds of forensic photos I have taken, except for one detail: a figure clad in a light-blue uniform covering the whole body, including a tight hood around the head. Blue overshoes, a white face mask and a camera held in both hands, which are protected by blue nitrile gloves. Normally a crime-scene photo would not include a photographer for the simple reason that they would be behind the camera and not in front of it. But in this picture the person seems to be its main focal point, as if the crime scene itself is secondary. A sudden chill goes through my body as I recognize the image.

The nocturnal birds have stopped chirping and I'm surrounded by silence. The temperature has dropped and I feel cold. I jump out of the car and pull the roof up until it clicks into place. Back inside, I slide the windows up and lock the doors. I turn the key in the ignition and drive off so fast something in the case on the back seat rattles worryingly. I hit the brakes right in front of the security barrier at the exit and drum my fingers impatiently on the steering wheel as it goes up slowly. And I'm off, on a narrow road that will take me to the London-bound M3. I drive recklessly above the speed limit, the adrenaline singing in my blood.

2

Taking pictures of dead bodies. I would pack my kit into a white, unmarked Peugeot Expert and drive to the designated police station. There I'd wait for a call-out. Sometimes there were no call-outs at all throughout the whole shift. That would be considered a good day for London. At other times it would be non-stop, especially when there were just the two of us forensic photographers on one shift for the whole of the Met. When I first started my job we'd go out to assaults, to take pictures of victims of violent attacks, as well as to more serious crime scenes. Then our task was narrowed down to serious crimes only, an incessant procession of dead bodies, bloody scenes and cold mortuary slabs.

I used to smoke in those days, inhale deeply and blow the smoke out through my nostrils to get rid of the smell. But it would linger anyway, in my hair, on my skin, inside my mouth, the sweet, sickly smell of decomposing blood. I still can't go into a butcher's shop without getting nauseated by the smell of raw meat. And here's a paradox: as soon as I'd finished my cigarette, I'd be starving. I'd go looking for food, preferably something salty and greasy, to quench my craving. It was as if dealing with death made me hungry for life.

I stop at a 24-hour petrol station to buy a packet of Marlboros and a box of matches. I get back to my car and light up straight away, staring at the 'No Smoking' sign on the wall of the station. I half prepare myself for some fireworks, an explosion that would wipe me off the face of the earth, but nothing happens. The feeling of smoke in my mouth and lungs is unpleasant, but as the nicotine hits my brain I instantly get light-headed. Then the dizzy spell passes, replaced by a wave of serenity. I needed that. I can think calmly now.

'Exposure 1'. I remember the case. It was a cold and wet night, one of those when I'd put my paper suit on even if I didn't have to, because it provided extra warmth. I was called in to the Southbank Centre undercroft. The place was deserted, the concert crowds and skateboarders dispersed hours ago. The officer in charge offered to carry my tripod and led me through the echoing concrete caverns with walls covered in striking art and graffiti. We crossed the second cordon and approached the crime scene, brightly lit and protected from view by nylon screens. There was a palpable tension in the air. When I saw the body I understood why. It was headless and armless, and stuffed into a white double bass hard case.

It was the third murder of the killer dubbed by the media 'The Violinist'. The name was, of course, sensationalist and inaccurate. A human body, even a decapitated and severely maimed one, would not fit into a violin case. The murderer used double bass covers, progressing from a soft padded bag to a hard-shell case. But I suppose 'The Bass Player' doesn't have the same ring as 'The Violinist'. The bizarre way of disposing of the bodies had riveted the media, whipping up a frenzy of speculation. Double bass cases are not exactly easy to come by and are definitely not cheap. But the police were helpless: they had not only failed to find the source of the cases, but also failed to identify the bodies. Despite an Orwellian network of closed-circuit surveillance cameras covering London, they were unable to catch sight of the Violinist delivering his gruesome cargo. Not even a glimpse, a tiny blur of movement, a hunched figure weighed down by a heavy case, nothing. It seemed almost impossible in one of the most watched cities in the world, where one gets caught on CCTV over three hundred times a day, but it was frustratingly true. And there I was, looking at the Violinist's third victim, this time neatly packaged inside a shiny white fibreglass case.

I jump when I hear a knock on my car window. The petrol station's night cashier is pointing at the 'No Smoking' sign on the wall. I mime an apology and drive off. At the first red light, I open the window and throw the cigarette out. But the bad taste in my mouth persists until I get home, greeted by Pixel and Voxel who meow loudly and circle my legs, twitching their tails.

'Sorry, guys, I know, it's very late.'

I go to the fridge and give them double portions of their favourite Lily's Kitchen Organic Lamb dinner. Only the best for my boys. They attack their bowls, instantly ignoring me. The cat pleasantries are over.

My loft is one big space, with areas assigned to the office, consisting of a large glass table with a six-core and dual GPU Mac Pro connected to an Eizo monitor, my photographic stage, the sleeping area – consisting of, well, a large bed and some storage for clothes – the kitchen and the bathroom, which is the only room separate from the rest. All in all, 1,558 sq. feet of what an estate agent would describe as an 'open-plan living/ entertaining space with floor to ceiling windows which allow a wealth of natural light'. I could never afford a place like this, but I inherited it from my aunt Stella. Stella was a trailblazer, so different to my mother, who was her older sister, that I sometimes wondered if one of them was adopted. She moved to Hoxton long before Peter Ind opened the Bass Clef and Jay Jopling turned an old piano factory building in the square into the White Cube. Faithful to the true spirit of the place, Aunt Stella bought the top floor in a derelict warehouse that used to be a carpentry workshop and set up her own business – furniture design. She would make mostly chairs, drawing her inspiration from the early Scandinavian masters Jacobsen and Wegner, combining Modernist shapes with 1950s eclecticism. I still have her wire-mesh chair, probably the first of its kind in London. I adored Stella and the affection was mutual. I never really got on with my parents and as soon as I could make my own choices I left our family house in Southgate and moved in with her. It caused a bit of a stir at the time, as Stella lived with her lover, Veronica. To my mother's horror and disgust, Aunt Vero and I hit it off instantly. It was Vero who encouraged me to go to art college and supported me through my creative and emotional ups and downs. After Stella's death, Vero didn't want to stay in London so she transferred her share of the warehouse lease to me and moved to Whitstable. Now that she's retired, she keeps herself busy by tending to her beehive box and making her own honey, as well as being an active member of a bell-ringing society. I visit her whenever I can and she always insists on taking me out to Wheelers Oyster Bar for lunch. According to her, oysters are good for body and soul, and I don't disagree.

I go to the office area and open a big black filing cabinet. I rummage through the files and folders until I find what I've been looking for: my forensic notebook. I always carried it with me and made meticulous notes, from the first call from the ops room describing the nature and location of the job, through a detailed description of the crime scene, to the final notes for the photo album I made by the duplication unit at the back of my van. And here it is, looking worn and faded, but still full of vital information. I flip through it and find the pages about the Violinist's crime scenes. It turns out I only photographed two of them, the second body found in a black hard-shell case left by the entrance to one of the towers at the Barbican Estate and the Southbank undercroft one, which was his third.

I sit down on the floor by the filing cabinet and read through my notes. It's the usual dry description of the location and the crime, with a detailed list of all the shots I took. There is nothing in it that makes me jump up and scream *eureka*. But one thing is clear: I was the *only* forensic photographer at the scene and no one else in the team took pictures. What the hell . . . ?

I put the notebook down and switch on my Mac. I scan through the long list of unread emails and find 'Exposure 1'. There are, in fact, three emails titled 'Exposure 1' and they are all identical. I click on the picture and it fills the screen with stunning clarity. The first thing I notice is that it's not as grainy as I would have expected a night shot to be. The scene was of course well lit, but still . . . It was probably shot in a RAW format that captures uncompressed data and gives the highest image quality, and probably from a tripod, to avoid the blurry picture so common at slower shutter speeds. It's not the work of an amateur. There is a nice little touch, a starburst effect on the lights in the background, usually achieved by using a narrow aperture, which also gives you a deeper depth of field. It was definitely taken by a professional. There were no other forensic photographers at the scene, so who could have snapped it? A paparazzo? I'm pretty sure there were no photojournalists at the scene. My journo-radar usually spots them a mile away. Could this be the work of an accidental shutterbug, a passing photo-tourist? No, it looks too well prepared and executed. Who took it then? And why is it popping up on my screen now, so many years later? What is it supposed to mean? And, most importantly, why is it freaking me out? It's just a picture after all.

I get up from the floor, go to the kitchen counter and pour myself a glass of wine from an open bottle. I move to the window and take a sip. The lit-up high-rises clustered around the Gherkin look almost ornamental against the purple-black sky. Long gone are the days when no building taller than a fireman's ladder was allowed to be constructed in the City. The newest architectural additions have a strange culinary flavour, with the Can of Ham being built between the Gherkin and the Cheese-grater. But I love the view, the elegant multitude of lights that make the city look clean and benevolent. Nothing bad can possibly happen in a world that looks like this.

My gaze wanders down to the building opposite. It's similar to the one I'm in, a Victorian workshop converted by a developer into a 'unique and quirky collection of live/work units'. All the large windows are dark, except for one on the top floor, almost level with mine. It's a big space, sparsely furnished, with high ceilings, exposed brickwork and stripped-wood flooring. Backlit by dim lighting, there is a man standing motionlessly by the window. He is looking at me.

I instinctively step back away from the window to hide in the shadows of my studio. I have never noticed the man before. Was he really staring at me? I move forward until I catch a glimpse of him again. He hasn't moved, his face in the shade, his silhouette looking almost two-dimensional. Impulsively I pull down the blackout blind that covers the whole window. There. He's gone.

I pour myself another glass and take it to bed. I feel wired, exhausted but wide awake, and I hope the wine will slow me down. I check my phone and there are still no messages from Anton. I text him –

Where are you? I want you back

– and put the phone down. Almost immediately my phone pings with a new message. I pick it up, expecting something short from Anton. But the message is not from him.

Great to see you today. Must catch up soon. Xx

It's from Jason. Jason? I know we've had a long day, but texting me at 3 a.m.? I delete the message, putting its sentiment down to a mild case of midlife crisis.

3

I drag myself out of bed at 10 a.m., knowing that there is a stack of toys on my studio floor waiting to be photographed. Being the master, or mistress, of one's time is a curse and a blessing of freelance life. It's a blessing to be able to stay in bed till noon because no one is breathing down your neck and you'll be fine as long as you work till midnight. But it's a curse to have to be your own slave driver, to crack the whip over your own shoulders. This bit is acquired knowledge: if you don't work, you don't get paid and your accountant will be disappointed in you.

I make a pact with myself to start the shoot at 11 a.m. and stumble to Curious Yellow Kafé down the road for a chai latte and a croissant. My phone pings as soon as I sit down at a table outside. This time it *is* Anton.

Back soon. Hang on in there.

Succinct and unsentimental, that's my Anton. Or Savage, as he calls himself. His surname is, in fact, Sauvage, which in a funny way suits him. The untamed but gentle giant who swept me off my feet, or to be precise, chatted me up at a late-night movie show at the Queen of Hoxton's rooftop cinema. I don't remember the film, it might have been *Trainspotting* or *Pulp Fiction*, I'm not sure. What I remember is sitting in a director's chair, wrapped in a blanket, with wireless headphones round my neck, because I wasn't listening to the soundtrack. I was listening to a rugged-looking French guy who was telling me that his name was an aptronym.

'Carl Jung was convinced there was a connection between a surname and the man himself.' Anton shifted in his chair to murmur straight into my ear. 'A grotesque coincidence, he called it. I mean, it goes back to the old days when a butcher would be called Mr Butcher and a baker – Mr Baker. Take my name, Sauvage. My dad was a rude bastard, my granddad a brute . . .'

'And you, what are you?' I murmured back, aware of an undercurrent of heavy flirting going on between us.

'Me?' He looked straight at me with his innocent, blue-eyed stare and I knew I was falling for him. 'I am a gentle barbarian. And your name must be . . .' He paused for effect. 'Ocean Dream – just like your blue-green eyes . . .'

I made a face.

'Flattery won't get you far.'

'You don't know what the Ocean Dream is, do you?'

I raised my eyebrows.

'It's the only natural deep blue-green diamond in the world.'

And that was it.

We left the show early, stopped for a drink at the Electricity Showrooms and ended up at mine after midnight. It was seven years ago, when I still thought I was the chosen one, a bona fide artist.

A lot has happened in those seven years. Our fortunes have ebbed and flowed, but we've stuck together. We travelled from the east to the west coast of the US, spent months in Argentina, half a year in Brazil, visited Australia, island hopped in Thailand and whizzed around Eastern Europe. No, Anton is not a travel agent. He is a street artist on a mission to paste the whole world up with his art. He's getting there – his work is beginning to appear in street-art anthologies and his prints are selling quite well in a couple of galleries in Paris and London. His fame hasn't quite reached its peak yet, but I reckon in a few years' time he'll be up there with Banksy, ROA and JR. In the meantime he has to take on paid assignments from city councils and art foundations all over the world and I stick to my packshots. Which reminds me . . . I pay for my chai and croissant and head back home.

As I stop at the lights, a voice behind me says, 'You have to be *careful.*'

I turn round and see an older woman berating two small kids, a boy and a girl.

'If you run out in front of a bus, it'll hit you and you'll die,' she says drily.

'Oh no,' corrects the little boy. 'You don't *always* die when you're hit by a bus. My mum's friend was hit by a bus and she didn't die. You just – you just –' he searches for the right expression – 'you just have to spend a long time in hospital.'

The light changes to green and we all cross cautiously, safe in the knowledge that nothing bad will happen to us right now.

I get back home and wave Voxel's snake catnip toy in front of him for a few minutes. Pixel is watching us from his vantage point on the bookshelf, pretending he's not interested. Playtime over, I reluctantly begin setting up the lighting for the shoot. I'm supposed to photograph a selection of early learning wooden toys for a catalogue. I take them out of their boxes and marvel at the ingenuity of the puzzles, workbenches and activity cubes.

Things have moved on since I was a child. I decide to start with alphabet blocks and set about building a tower out of them, careful not to create any rude words accidentally. You can't be too careful in the commercial graphics trade. I remember a designer friend of mine inadvertently creating a logo for 'Minge Pies', all because of the flowery font he chose. The pies flew off the shelves at Christmas.

By the afternoon coffee break I'm done with a toddler truck, a push-along pram and a train. All that's left is a rocking horse, a set of ducks on wheels and a Noah's ark, complete with twelve pairs of animals and Mr & Mrs Noah themselves. I hope if I keep the rhythm up I should be done by the end of the day. But as I get into the groove of arranging the sets, lighting and snapping them, my mind drifts back to 'Exposure 1'. I leave Mr Noah to his ark and wake my computer up.

The screen lights up with the image of the Southbank undercroft. I close my eyes and try to recreate the crime scene in my head. We were never allowed to hold on to any of the forensic photographs, so all I have left to rely on is my old notebook and my memory. It all begins to come back to me now. The smell of damp mixed with a lingering whiff of hot dogs. Almost complete silence, interrupted by the hushed voices of the forensic team. The quiet sound of the river lapping at the bank. The low rumble of an MSU patrol boat. Someone whistling. *Whistling?* I open my eyes. Was there really someone whistling in the undercroft or is my mind fabricating a new, distorted reality? I simply can't remember. I look at the photo again. If it *is* genuine, where was it taken from? A passing boat? Impossible, the water level is far too low. Waterloo Bridge? The angle is wrong. The Savoy? It would have to be one hell of a telephoto lens. Festival Pier? It is just possible that someone was hiding in the shadows of the ugly glass and blue steel construction. But wouldn't it be shut at night? Something on a pillar above the case containing the mutilated body catches my attention. I blow up the picture and take a closer look. It's blood-red, chunky graffiti: big bold letters with huge drops of red paint dripping off all the 'O's dramatically. 'OFF TO VIOLIN-LAND'. I don't remember seeing it. I would've noticed it for sure if it had been there when I was processing the scene. I grab my notebook and go through the list of photographs again. There is no mention of the graffiti. Is it possible I'd missed it? If I had, I may have omitted a vital piece of evidence. No, it simply wasn't there. I get up from the desk and go to the window. I need a cigarette.

You quit smoking ages ago, I tell myself, and go back to Mr Noah and his ark. Setting up the wooden toys calms me down. For all I know the picture is a fake. A good one, I must admit, but nothing that someone with a working knowledge of Photoshop wouldn't be able to do. I should know better. How many times has Photoshop saved my skin when something has gone wrong during a shoot and the only way to fix it is to fake it? The problem with Photoshop reality is that it can be so perfect no one can tell the difference between it and the real thing. Well, almost no one. Cubic Zirconia, I think, and it makes me smile even now. 'Fake diamond', the name of a collaborative duo I started at college with my best friend, Erin. We saw ourselves as the female version of Gilbert and George, destined to conquer the world of visual art. We had it all worked out, from our anti-elitist manifesto to the vision of creating a modified reality that would become the ultimate work of art. We had the talent, we had the skill and we had the looks – slim, tall and dark-haired. We both dressed in cheap Vivienne Westwood knock-offs and looked so alike people often mistook us for each other. Encouraged by our tutor at the digital art faculty, we lived the Augmented Reality dream before it became a buzzword. Our first installation was a massive six-foot-tall glass test-tube combined with an interactive optical projection system. Inside the tube was a digitally manipulable 3D holographic projection of fetal development, from conception to birth. Thanks to video-tracking, the spectators could interfere with the development cycle by simply flapping their arms in front of the tube. They could create a hybrid, a monster or bring on a miscarriage. Needless to say the installation caused a stir. The windows of the gallery got smashed, there were raving and scathing reviews, there were death threats. Fame was knocking on our door. A controversial exhibition under our belt, a few feet away from making a splash in New York's art world, on the verge of becoming a household name, and all this before we even turned twenty-five. We were Cubic Zirconia.

And then real life intervened and we realized there were things that could not be augmented. Bank accounts, debts, responsibilities, other people's expectations, the boring stuff. And, above all, the pressure of the budding celebrity status. Nothing had prepared us for the brutality of fame, the cut-throat competitiveness of the art world. I was the weaker part of our duo and it was me who began to crumble under the weight of it all. It was then I met Anton and fell in love with his anti-establishment stance, his earthiness, his sense of freedom. Not to mention his knowledge of natural diamonds . . . I bailed out of Cubic Zirconia, dropped my 'arty' friends, immersed myself in Anton's world. Erin fought for a while longer but she had no chance on her own. Part of me thinks she has never forgiven me for shattering our beautiful dream and for talking her into swapping the life of an artist for the daily grind of a forensic photographer. I reasoned that if the job was there we should take it. And so we did. We couldn't have ended up further away from the fantasy of Cubic Zirconia. Lucky for Erin, the crime-scene gig didn't last long, and before I knew it, she got catapulted into the glamorous world of portrait photography. She's the one with a forty-thousand-dollar Hasselblad round her neck and an entourage of assistants. She spends most of her life in airport executive lounges and on first-class flights, travelling between London, New York, Los Angeles and occasionally some exotic location. Everyone who is anyone wants to have their essence captured by Erin Perdue.

Would Erin be able to shed some light on 'Exposure 1'? If I remember correctly, she was the photographer who got called out to the Violinist's first crime scene, the one at the Albert Hall. Should I ask her about it? But what could she tell me? She's probably too busy to even answer my call anyway. She's moved on and you haven't, I think, and the familiar feeling of inadequacy kicks in. It's funny, I'm normally quite content with my life, proud even of what I've managed to achieve. But when it comes to comparing myself with Erin, everything I've worked so hard for fades to pitiful insignificance.

My phone rings and I twitch, knocking down the carefully arranged animal queue to Noah's ark. It's from a long number beginning with +54.

'Anton!'

'Hi, babe. Missed me?'

'Like a hole in the head. When are you back?'

'Soon, babe. Maybe even next week. Wrapping some stuff up, not sure how much longer it'll take.'

'You better get your arse back here *toot sweet*.'

'That bad, eh?' He laughs. 'What's up?'

'Oh, nothing, it's silly . . .'

'What's wrong?' He knows my 'in-distress' tone by now.

'I've been getting these emails, an email actually, with a photo of a crime scene, you know, from the time when I used to work for the Met.'

'Who is it from?'

'I don't know . . .'

'Did you try asking what it's about?'

'No . . . Maybe I should.'

'You could try speaking to the police, if it's one of their pictures.'

'No, it's just a photo of me, with my camera, at the scene. It was the Violinist case – remember, I told you about it?'

'Oh, yeah. They caught the guy, right?'

'I think so . . .'

'It's probably just a stupid prank. As long as they are not blackmailing you over anything, don't worry about it.' He laughs, but I don't find it funny. 'Anyway, babe, I have a favour to ask. You know the big black art portfolio case, the A2 one, that stands by my desk? It's got some signed prints of my Prague project, I think about ten artist's proofs. Could you take them to a gallery just off Brick Lane? The Fugitives Gallery, in Sclater Street. If you could get it to them by the end of the week, it would be perfect.'

'I'm a bit busy, but I'll try.' I'm peeved he dismissed my worry so easily.

'You are a star. Gotta go now. But will be back real soon, promise. OK, babe?'

'OK. Love you.' I don't get an answer to that because he's already disconnected.

That's my Anton, fierce, formidable and hopelessly un-romantic. But he's probably right when it comes to that stupid email, I think as I put the phone down. I go back to the computer, bring 'Exposure 1' back on the screen and hit 'Reply'.

Who are you and what do you want?

I click 'Send'.

It instantly makes me feel better. I google 'The Violinist' next. I trawl through a handful of violin discussion boards, ads for musicians, a few sites about Paganini and an IMDB entry for a 2009 movie, until I come across a Wikipedia entry.

> Known as 'The Violinist' Karel Balek was a Czech national based in the UK who kidnapped and killed four women in London between January 2009 and March 2011. He would decapitate his victims and sever their arms, before putting their bodies in double bass cases. He dumped the cases in public places in the vicinity of famous concert hall venues.

Tell me something I don't know, I think, scrolling down the page.

> None of his female victims have been identified, although it was widely assumed they were illegal immigrants trafficked from ex-Soviet republics by gangs specializing in forced sexual exploitation. Balek was a professional contrabassist who began his

career with the Ostrava Philharmonic
Orchestra, before moving to the UK where
he briefly performed with a few of the
leading London orchestras. He was forced to
abandon his music career in 2008, after a
freak accident in which he lost two fingers
of his right hand. He famously evaded
capture on CCTV despite disposing of the
bodies in heavily monitored public places.
He was arrested in 2011, following an
anonymous tip-off. He hanged himself in
his cell while awaiting trial.

This I didn't know. During my short career as a crime-scene photographer, I quickly adopted a 'disengage or die' philosophy. You take the pictures, produce all the necessary evidence, do the paperwork, sign a statement, turn it in and forget about it. Unless you were required to go to court and testify, in which case disengagement was delayed. It may sound cold and thick-skinned, but it was a simple survival mechanism. If you allowed yourself to feel sorry for the victims, to empathize or, God forbid, follow the case, you were finished. A girl whose place I took over got fixated on a case, started playing at being a detective and ended up at the Maudsley suffering from paranoid anxiety. Faithful to my disengagement method, I never followed any of my cases once I was done with them. I didn't google them, didn't discuss them with anyone and stayed away from any headlines even remotely related to them. It kept me sane, but it also kept me in the dark.

So, the Violinist is dead. He has not escaped from a high-security unit to stalk me, hasn't been released because of some freak miscarriage of justice – he is gone, buried, six feet under. What is 'Exposure 1' about then? My mailbox pings with a new email. My heartbeat quickens as I click on the 'Exposure 1' reply.

Error 553. Inactive/invalid user.

Was I seriously expecting anything else? A friendly apology? A shame-faced explanation? No.

A stupid prank, said Anton. Why does it *feel* so real then? I wish there was someone else I could talk to about it, just to convince myself that I'm fretting over nothing. But Sophie's away in Brittany, sourcing some crêpes and galettes for her catering business. And most of my other friends have entered the phase of spawning and are busy fighting for a place at the best nursery in town or moving house to be in a catchment area for a good school. Erin – my mind helpfully supplies her name again. OK, I'll ring her, even though I haven't spoken to her in ages. If she's too busy, she'll simply ignore my call.

I rummage through IKEA storage boxes until I find my old phone. I plug it in and after a few minutes it springs to life. Yes, Erin's number is there. I dial it, expecting to hear her voicemail. But she picks up almost instantly.

'Erin, it's Kristin Ryder . . .'

'Ryder!' She calls me by my surname and I'm instantly transported to our Cubic Zirconia days. Everyone called me Ryder then.

Without going into details I awkwardly explain that I need her help with something really silly. I expect her to say she's too busy to meet up, but she surprises me. She's doing a photo shoot on the top floor of the Shard. But she should be free by

9 p.m. and we can meet at the Oblix there, if it's OK with me. The table will be reserved in her name.

Of course it will, I think as I put the phone down. One of her minions is probably booking it right now, making sure Ms Perdue has a secluded table by the window. A photo shoot on the seventy-second floor of the Shard, in one of those amazing spaces for hire at thirty thousand pounds per hour. Wow. I imagine Erin with a gaggle of waif-like models or perhaps a moody pop star, snapping pictures against the backdrop of the London skyline. Creating a cover for the *Rolling Stone* magazine. Or a feature for *Wallpaper*.

I look at Mr Noah's animals inside the lighting cube and decide I'm done for the day. I don't have to deliver the job till the end of the week anyway. I switch off the lights and take the camera off its tripod. Everything needs to be put away, no matter what. I know from painful and costly experience that Pixel and Voxel are attracted to the most fragile pieces of my equipment. They simply can't resist a shiny reflector, a delicate softbox or a loose spigot. Every bit of kit is a potential enemy that needs to be attacked and destroyed. I pack away Mr Noah's zoo and the rest of the toys. They rattle dully inside their cheap cardboard packaging. And to think it could be me, rubbing shoulders with the beautiful and famous on the seventy-second floor of the Shard.

4

Ms Perdue is running late but our table is ready. A beautiful hostess of immaculate complexion and impossibly full lips leads me through the open kitchen to a discreetly lit dining room. I was right, our table is in the best spot, in a quiet corner right by the glass wall of the window. Although the restaurant is on the less dizzying height of the thirty-second floor, the view is still breathtaking. London lights shimmer below, constant, but somehow alive. The river looks unusually peaceful tonight, a smooth and reflective ribbon of water illuminated in red, yellow, green and blue. It divides the panorama into two parts: the clean and orderly lines of the City and the urban mess of Southwark and Borough, with slow worms of trains crawling in and out of London Bridge. I ignore the menu and the wine list, staring at the view. If only Cubic Zirconia had ever gone beyond the idealistic fantasy . . . My phone pings with a new text message, interrupting my reverie. Guess who it's from: Jason. I put my phone down, annoyed.

'A message from a secret admirer?' Her voice makes me smile.

'Erin!'

'Ryder!'

There she is, standing right in front of me, elegant, slim and long-limbed, with a mass of black hair over her pale face. I jump up without a word and we hug, discreetly observed by our waiter.

'You smell nice.' I blurt out the first thing that comes to my mind.

'After a ten-hour shoot? I doubt it.' She sniffs at her armpit unceremoniously and we both chuckle. It feels like we're picking up exactly where we left off, the gap of nearly six years disappearing without a trace.

'I mean the perfume.'

'Patchouli Absolut by Tom Ford. It hits the spot, doesn't it?'

She doesn't sit down straight away, but goes to the window and presses the palms of her hands to the glass pane, fingers splayed open.

'I love this view, even after seeing it all day. I love the river.'

'How was the shoot?'

She shrugs. 'Run-of-the-mill glitz.'

She sits down and picks up the drinks menu. I watch her as she orders a bottle of Veuve Clicquot that costs more than I earn in a day. She has changed. She is thinner and rougher, the harsh lines around her mouth giving her a slightly mean, cynical look. She's no longer the angelic beauty she used to be in our college days, but is stunning nevertheless. And the outfit she's wearing is probably *genuine* Vivienne Westwood.

We order a random selection of starters because we are both too excited to think about food. We have a lot of catching up to do. A bottle of Veuve Clicquot and a couple of Habanero cocktails later I remember why I called Erin in the first place.

'Remember the Violinist?'

'That limp dick Nikolai?'

29

'You slept with Nikolai *Verenich?*' I let the gossip distract me.

'I dumped him after a couple of weeks. What about him?'

'No, not Nikolai, I meant the serial killer.'

'Oh, *him*. It's not something you easily forget.'

'I know. I processed two of his crime scenes.'

'Yeah, I remember being relieved at the time it was you who got called out to them. Having seen his first was enough—' She shakes her head as if to get rid of the memory. It's the first silence since we sat down at the table.

'I've been getting these emails . . .' I lean down to my bag and get my iPad out. I tap the screen to retrieve 'Exposure 1', then show it to Erin.

'God . . . You've been getting them recently?'

I nod.

'Last night. Three identical emails with the same picture.'

'Weird.' She picks up the iPad to have a closer look.

'You haven't been getting any of these?'

'Me?' She looks at me, her striking light-green eyes wide with surprise. 'No. No, I haven't. You think it's something to do with the Violinist?'

'I don't know. The guy's been dead for years.' I debate whether to tell her about the Violin-Land graffiti in the photo but decide against it.

'Could it be one of the anti-Zirconia nutters?'

'I hadn't thought of that . . . But why now, after all these years?'

'You're probably right. They wouldn't be interested in the Violinist, anyway. Why bother with real evil if you can attack art . . .'

'Anton says it's a stupid prank.'

'Anton!' Erin puts down the iPad. 'You guys still together?'

'We are.' I don't elaborate, remembering she's never been keen on him.

'Good for you.' Erin's waving at the waiter again.

'Well, he's been away quite a lot, so it's just been me and my boys lately . . .'

'Your *boys*? You have kids?'

'Cats.' I make a self-deprecating face. 'Pixel and Voxel.'

'Voxel? As in "a point in three-dimensional space"?'

'Oh, yes, he's definitely 3D. Pixel's a much more two-dimensional character . . .'

She laughs and shakes her head. 'Once a geek . . . Another Habanero?'

The waiter's arrived and is looking at us expectantly.

'Not for me, thank you.' I realize I'm quite drunk and tired.

'Oh, come on, just one, don't be a party pooper . . .'

'Go on, then.' I've always let Erin lead me astray. And I know I'll regret it later.

The rest of the evening disappears in a blur of gossip followed by alcohol-fuelled teary reminiscing. By the time we leave the Oblix, we've promised each other to keep in touch and never again to neglect our friendship so badly. Erin has an account with Addison Lee and she books a cab for me, ignoring my weak protests. To be honest, I'm grateful, because the world is spinning like the London Eye. By the time the cab reaches Hoxton I've sobered enough to direct the driver around the maze of narrow streets.

Pixel and Voxel greet me with loud meowing as I open the front door. I dish their food out for them, deciding to ignore the fact they did try to get into Mr Noah's box when I was out. No real damage has been done anyway. Forget the glitzy life of a celebrity photographer and welcome to my world, I think as I pick up the box and put it together with the other toys. But would I really want to swap Mr Noah and company for a shoot with David Beckham or Rihanna? Of course, I wouldn't mind the creative challenge, not to mention the fee, but the honest answer would have to be *no*. I learnt my lesson with Cubic Zirconia. I love the buzz of creativity but the truth is I'm an introvert. My studio is my kingdom and I like it this way. And I like the view from my kingdom, I think as I go to the window. My self-satisfaction disappears as soon as I look out. He's there again, the man in the building opposite, standing in exactly the same spot as last night, staring at me. The widow Clicquot plus a triple Habanero still flowing in my veins, I fling the window open in a sudden fit of rage.

'Oi! You out there! Seen enough or want a bit more?'

I rip my blouse open, pull off my bra and flash my tits at him. He doesn't move, just keeps staring.

'Like the view? You fucking wanker!'

Very slowly, he turns away from the window and disappears inside his dark apartment. Disappointed, I slam my window shut. I was itching for a confrontation.

5

I wake up with a well-deserved hangover. Sunshine is flooding the loft, making everything look warm and cheerful. I carefully roll out of bed, shading my eyes with my arm. I shuffle barefoot to Anton's coffee machine and sway by it brainlessly as it splurts out a double espresso. Its rich smell tickles my synapses and they begin to fire randomly: *It was good to see Erin. She's changed. What a night.* Followed by, *Oh God,* when I remember my Peeping Tom rage. Coffee cup in hand, I shuffle to the window and look out. There is no one in the flat opposite today. The guy might be a pest, but my behaviour was perhaps a touch excessive. Well, maybe it has taught him a lesson.

Mr Noah beckons and I hop in the shower, hoping the hot water will spur me on. But my head is heavy and my hands shake when I pull the blinds down and begin setting up the shoot. It's going to be a slow day. By noon I'm barely finished with Mr Noah and his biblical friends. But then I pick up speed and I'm done with the rest of the toys by teatime. I copy the picture files onto my Mac and I'm cleaning the images when my phone rings.

'Ryder, how are you?'

'Erin!' I groan. 'What was in those Habaneros?'

'That bad, eh?' She laughs.

'It wouldn't be so bad if I didn't have a date with Mr Noah . . .'

'Noah?'

I tell her about my shoot and the publisher's deadline. She laughs at my description of the toys, but I know she isn't really interested in my mundane job.

'I had this weird dream last night.' She changes the subject.

'See? I told you the Habaneros were dodgy.'

'We were in this tall building, you and I, and it felt like Zirconia days, except we were both older . . . The building was a bit like the Shard, all steel and glass, very cold and windy because some of the windowpanes were missing. You said you were going to fly and I was trying to stop you. It was getting quite scary, you were determined to do it and I was struggling with you to keep you inside . . . and then . . . and then you slipped out of my reach and you were gone, just stepped out through the missing window and disappeared . . . I started screaming and I realized I wasn't alone, there was this guy who'd been watching us and for some reason I knew he was dangerous – and then I woke up screaming . . .'

She falls silent and I don't know what to say.

'I know it's all nonsense, but I just got worried and I had to call you to check if you're OK . . .'

'Erin, I'm fine . . . Nothing a good night's sleep won't cure.'

'You sure?'

'Yes!' I find her insistence a bit annoying. 'I'm perfectly fine and I'm certainly not planning to take up flying.'

'Well, I better let you get back to Mr Noah then . . .' I can hear relief in her voice.

We agree to meet up again once Erin is back from a shoot in New York and I hang up.

I go back to the images on my Mac, thinking about the

phone call. It was totally out of character for Erin to get shaken up by a dream and project her worry on to me. Since when has she started believing in nightmares? Has she changed that much? And why should she care about me all of a sudden? Yes, we were close once, but a lot of water had gone under many bridges since then. On the other hand, her nightmare did sound freaky. The mere thought of jumping off a building gives me shivers. How far would one have to be pushed to even consider ending one's life like that? When I was a teenager I found the theoretical possibility of suicide reassuring, because in my mind it gave me the ultimate way out of any situation. I must say I haven't entertained that thought for years.

Back to the photos for KiddyKraze. All arranged neatly in folders and zipped, I upload the project into my client's FTP site. My client is Serpens Media, a company that provides marketing solutions in the form of publications, online catalogues and directories for mid-range businesses. It also provides me, Kristin Ryder Productions Ltd, with a lot of work. KiddyKraze is their client this time, 'a small but robust toys manufacturer' according to Serpens' blurb.

All done and dusted, I feel I deserve an evening off. I wish Sophie was back from her crêpe-finding mission in France. I long for a quiet chinwag with my sweet best friend, right in the middle of my comfort zone. Being outside of it seems totally overrated tonight. Resisting the pull of 'Exposure 1', I go to Mubi's website and scroll through their updated daily viewing offer, but there is nothing in their thirty films for tonight that grabs my fancy. Shall I check Torrent Butler to see what the movie pirates have to offer? Nah. I pour myself a glass of wine and go to the window. The apartment opposite is dark and empty. A tiny prickle of disappointment creeps in. Am I developing an attachment to my Peeping Tom? I think of Erin's dream and the strange man who was watching me fall to my death. I look down at the cobbled street below our warehouse and imagine a blur of movement, the horrible sound of a body hitting the ground, the silence as blood starts to seep from under my shattered head. Whoa, stop! What is happening to me tonight?

I take the wine glass back to the desk and wake up my computer. If I can't resist it, I might as well try to crack it, I think as I click on 'Exposure 1'. OFF TO VIOLIN-LAND. I actually know where the words come from: Conan Doyle's *Sherlock Holmes*. I probably still have a battered copy of it somewhere in one of the IKEA boxes. It went 'off to violin-land, where all is sweetness and . . .' Sweetness and what? Delicacy. That's it. 'Sweetness and delicacy and harmony'. It used to be my favourite book. Recalling the escapades into violin-land makes me smile. But what has it got to do with the crime scene? Sherlock Holmes used to play the violin, but it's such a tenuous link. I take a closer look at the picture. It is actually an unusually large attachment, nearly 1MB in size, much bigger than a standard email JPEG. I enlarge the section of the image around the graffiti, looking for signs of tampering. There are ways of telling a Photoshop fake. Leaning close to the screen, I search for a difference in the quality of grain or a subtle change in the saturation of blacks in the photo. Sometimes it's the way the edges of an added element blend in with the background that gives away a fake. But this picture is still too small to detect anything unusual. I'd have to break into the police photo records and look for the original RAW-quality photograph to know for sure if I've been duped. Disappointed, I turn away from the screen.

6

I'm up at the crack of dawn, ready for my next assignment from Serpens. Today I'll be filming a revolutionary Bluetooth bike helmet, a 'commuter product' designed by a small company up north. Helmets are usually not the most graceful objects to shoot, they are essentially round, shiny and devoid of personality. Perhaps this one will be an exception. I need to set up a turn-table and decide whether I'll be using a glass display head to perch the helmet on or attempt something more exciting. The first email of the day pings in my mailbox. It's from Zoe, my contact at Serpens, who is letting me know that the helmet delivery has been delayed and they'll bike it to me as soon as it arrives, probably after lunch. I look at the clock. Good, it gives me time to catch up on my VAT receipts. But do I really want to spend the next few hours sweating over an Excel spread-sheet? I look around the loft for inspiration. Anton's prints! I'm supposed to drop them off somewhere near Brick Lane. Anything to avoid doing the VAT return.

Half an hour later I'm on my bike, Anton's art portfolio attached precariously to the luggage rack, heading down the backstreets towards Bethnal Green. It's just past the rush hour on a sunny, still morning and the traffic is unusually light. Things rarely get better for a London cyclist. I cut through the

Boundary Estate, going round Arnold Circus with its spruced-up bandstand, and emerge in Bethnal Green Road just at the end of Brick Lane. Can I resist a hot salt beef bagel from Beigel Bake? No, I can't, I decide, tying my bike to a lamppost outside and keeping an eye on Anton's portfolio while I'm in the bakery. From there it's just a short ride to Sclater Street, where a crowd of onlookers takes pictures of a street artist painting a wall above the car park from a cherry picker. I'm sure I met the guy some time ago with Anton, but I can't think of his name.

The Fugitives Gallery is a bit further on, in a new concrete, steel and glass building. It's surprisingly spacious and there is some decent artwork on the walls. Good on you, Anton. A fat chocolate Labrador with a cute face waddles towards me to greet me. It is followed by a handsome, athletic-looking woman in her late thirties, who turns out to be the owner.

'Anna Wright,' she introduces herself and her handshake is strong.

She looks through Anton's prints appreciatively.

'They are quite decorative. I might want to frame a couple of them and put them in the window. The tourist traffic here is phenomenal. Are you just dropping them off for Anton?'

'What do you mean?'

'Are you his friend? Or merely a messenger?'

'I'm his partner.' It comes out more uptight than I wanted it to sound but I'm annoyed by her brusque manner.

'Oh.' She throws me a quick appraising glance. 'Let's do the paperwork then.'

She leads me to a large desk at the back of the gallery.

'As I've explained to Anton, I take fifty per cent of the price. We agreed on the sum of £700 per piece.'

'Sounds good to me,' I shrug. I know that a fifty per cent

gallery cut is standard but it still shocks me every time I encounter it.

She goes through the prints efficiently, filling in a form. She writes down my phone number and email address, promising to get in touch if there's interest.

'Are you an artist too?' she asks, handing me a copy of the agreement.

'Yes . . . no . . .' I'm fazed by her question. 'Well, I used to be.'

'Street art as well?' Now that the formalities are over, she seems more chatty.

'I'm a photographer. You probably haven't heard of Cubic Zirconia?'

'It rings a bell . . . I'm interested in photographic prints as well,' she adds with a smile. 'I'd be happy to look at your work if you drop by again.'

I leave the gallery feeling strangely thrown by the conversation. Am I an artist? If she'd asked me the question a few years ago, I'd have answered *yes* without any hesitation. What has changed then?

My phone vibrates as I'm unchaining my bike. It's Zoe from Serpens, sounding unusually formal. Something's cropped up. Could I come into the office, preferably as soon as possible? It's a strange request as I deal with Serpens almost entirely via phone and email, but as I'm on my wheels I offer to come by in twenty minutes. Their office is only up the road in King's Cross.

I arrive at Serpens Media covered in sweat, regretting having agreed to come in straight away. I should've gone home, taken a shower and changed into something more professional, instead of turning up on their doorstep in my cycling gear. Thankfully I'm not part of the Lycra brigade, but even so the clothes I'm wearing are not very 'office'.

Zoe greets me briefly and leads me to a small glass office on the first floor. Peter, her manager, and a woman from HR who I don't know are already there, a laptop in front of them on the table. Peter clears his throat.

'Thank you for coming in at such short notice, it's much appreciated.' He takes a sip of water from a plastic cup. 'We have a bit of a problem.'

He looks at the HR woman, as if waiting for her to continue, but she just nods at him.

'It's regarding your KiddyKraze artwork, which we received last night.' He falls silent again and I feel compelled to react in some way.

'You can't open the files? It happens sometimes. I can resend them as soon as I—'

'No, no,' he interrupts me. 'They open fine. It's just . . . they are not what we've been expecting from you . . .'

'What's wrong?' I wish he would get to the point faster.

He throws me a weird glance and pushes the laptop my way, so I can see the screen. He clicks on the folder I recognize. KiddyKraze. I can swear I hear a sharp intake of breath from Zoe and the HR woman as the folder opens. And there they are. The KiddyKraze pictures. Except they are not.

I feel a wave of heat enveloping my body, a rush of blood that seems to fill my head until my eyes want to pop out of their sockets. I unzip my jacket, suddenly aware of the strong smell of sweat surrounding me. I force myself to look closely at the screen. The pictures are not of Mr Noah and his animals.

There is no toddler truck, no push-along pram, no ducks on wheels. Instead there are photographs of Anton and myself having sex. They are sharp, well-lit, and the overall composition is, I have to admit, pleasing to the eye. Of course it is, I took them myself.

I can feel the tension in the room. Everyone's eyes are on me as they lap up my embarrassment, waiting for my reaction. I delay the moment, taking my time looking at the photos. They were taken early on in our relationship, when we couldn't keep our hands off each other. I find that lust fires me up creatively, makes me want to cross new boundaries, taunt and provoke. This was as much an extreme sexual experience as an aesthetic experiment. I lit our bed beautifully with three-point lighting, positioned three cameras at different angles around it, set them all on time-lapse of four-second intervals, and fucked Anton's brains out.

I look up from the screen. Peter, Zoe and the HR flunky watch me expectantly.

'Well . . .' I pause for effect. 'It appears I have sent you the wrong project.'

There is no point in grovelling, pretending to be mortified, offering to rectify the problem. I know they've already buried me. I will not work for Serpens ever again. Peter breathes a quiet sigh of relief.

'You have to understand . . . if these files went straight to KiddyKraze . . .'

'But they haven't, have they?' I smile at him.

'No, they haven't, thanks to Zoe's diligence –'

Out of the corner of my eye I see Zoe shrink in her chair.

'– thanks to her diligence we have managed to avert a major disaster. KiddyKraze are one of our most valued clients. Under the circumstances . . .' He opens his hands in an insincerely helpless gesture. I have a feeling he's never liked me and now he resents me for having a good sex life. It's personal and you can't really argue with that.

'I know, I should go.' I push my chair back as I get up, so its legs scrape the floor.

'Thank you, Kristin.' Peter's on his feet as well. 'Thank you for your understanding. It's been a pleasure working with you.'

'Don't mention it, Peter.' I turn and leave.

As I walk through their open-plan office, I can feel everyone staring at me. They've all seen the photographs. It's probably the highlight of their career.

'Kristin!' Zoe catches up with me by the entrance. 'I'm so sorry it had to end like this . . . if it was up to me —' She grabs my hand and squeezes it. 'Good luck with everything . . . Take care.'

'Thanks.' I smile at her. 'Good luck to you too.'

I notice her cheeks are flushed as she shyly smiles back at me. There is something in her eyes. Apology? Respect? I'll be damned, she actually envies me!

By the time I cycle back home, my bravado has disappeared. I have just lost my main job. Every freelancer relies on that one bread-and-butter-and-occasional-jam client. It's like an anchor that always brings you back home from choppy waters, calms your nausea when things become too rough. It gets rid of that awful tight feeling in your stomach when you realize your work diary for the next few weeks is empty. Because you know exactly what to expect from your regular client, the job is also numbingly easy. It's something you can do in your sleep.

So, no more KiddyKraze for me. I'm beginning to miss that little fellow Noah already. And I won't be shooting the revolutionary helmet this afternoon. It's over. As I lock my bike in the hallway downstairs, my freelance brain begins to scan for alternatives.

Once upstairs I go straight to my computer. I find the folder for the KiddyKraze job and click on it. All the photos I took over the past two days are there: the toddler truck, the push-along pram, ducks on wheels and, of course, Mr Noah and Co. I then go to Serpens FTP site and try to log on. ACCESS DENIED. They've cut me off pretty fast. I look at the KiddyKraze folder again. It's clearly marked and neatly stored in the partition called WORK. No mistake here. So how on earth did I manage to send them my sex photos? They would be in a different partition called ART. Yes, there they are, labelled 'In Bed With Anton'. How could they have got mixed up with the KiddyKraze pictures? In my whole career as a photographer this has never happened to me before. What's going on?

I feel I'm quickly losing the guts that so impressed Zoe. The little coward inside me is beginning to whimper. 'Miss Lily Liver', Aunt Stella used to call me when I didn't stand up for myself as a kid. And now Miss Lily Liver is starting to quiver. Should I try to resend the correct pictures to Serpens? Ask them to reconsider? Beg Peter to hire me back? Email Zoe and try to weasel my way in through the back door? Half-heartedly I check my mailbox. 784 messages. 126 unread. Well, I'll have plenty of time to read them now. As I slowly scroll through them searching for inspiration, a new message arrives with a ping. I lean closer to the screen, disbelieving my eyes. 'Exposure 2'. My hands begin to shake so badly I barely manage to move the cursor over it. Click.

7

It's another photograph. But this time it's not from the Violinist's crime scene. It's from a different batch altogether. Uncomprehending, I stare at the entangled limbs and naked bodies shining with sweat. *Two* naked bodies. Anton's and mine. It's the most explicit image from 'In Bed With Anton', the one, I'm pretty sure, which was not included in the folder that got sent to Serpens. I remember removing it from the project and stashing it away among other files marked PRIVATE. It *was* too private, even for the daring artist in me, the ex-Cubic Zirconia rebel. Imagine Tracy Emin's bed but with its occupants still in it, surrounded by coital detritus. It was raw, shameless and unguarded, so intimate that even looking at it now turns me on.

I jump up from the chair, go to the window and open it wide. I inhale the hot and polluted London air as if it was a calming nectar. In and out, in and out, until my breathing slows down and I'm able to think more clearly. Someone has gained access to my computer and has been rummaging through my files, picking up the juiciest bits. God only knows what else they have managed to unearth. But why? Who is this person? And what is this 'Exposure' game about? I pick up my phone and ring Sophie. I still get the French ringtone, so I end the call without leaving a message. I go back to the computer, turn on Skype and call Anton's Argentine number. It goes straight to his voicemail.

'Babe, where are you? Please call me. Something bad is happening, some really bad shit, and I need you here. Please call me. I need you. Call me.'

I click on the little red phone icon to disconnect. I feel weepy and scared. Even my own home doesn't seem safe any more. On an impulse, I pull the electricity plug out from my fibre broadband router. I sit on the bed, picking at my cuticles until they bleed. I get up and go to the window. I look out. The view is dull and flattened by smog. The loft opposite seems deserted. An image from Erin's dream flashes through my mind, a dead body splayed on the cobblestones below. I move away from the window with a shiver. I stop in front of the fridge and pull out a yoghurt pot. What am I doing? I don't even want yoghurt. This is ridiculous, I decide, and power up the broadband router again. I go back to the computer and patiently wait for it to find the right wireless connection. When it's back online, I open 'Exposure 2' and click 'Reply'.

Who the fuck are you and what's your problem?

My email bounces back after a short while.

Error 553. Inactive/invalid user.

Well, no surprises there. Fucking coward. He doesn't even have the guts to show his face.

Restless, I pick up the phone again and dial Vero's number. After my aunt Stella's death, Vero has become my surrogate mother, father, the whole lot. She answers on the fourth ring, her voice husky from years of smoking. With Vero I don't need to go through the superficial phone pleasantries. I go straight to my story. As she listens, I can hear her inhaling and blowing the smoke out.

'Someone's really pissed off with you,' she says when I'm finished.

'No kidding. But I don't know who or why. And the weasel's hiding behind some no-reply email address. I can't even get into a slanging match with him.'

'So it's nothing to do with the Violinist?'

'I don't think so. The guy's been dead for years anyway.'

'Any of your friends?'

'I think they'd come clean by now. They're not psychos. At least . . . most of them aren't . . .'

I love Vero's laugh, deep, throaty and contagious.

'I've read somewhere about this new online service. Shit-express or Shitcouriers, something like that. They deliver horse manure, beautifully wrapped, straight to your enemy's door, anywhere in the world. Ten quid a box, and that includes a personalized message. And you can pay for it with Bitcoins – you know, cryptocurrency – so no one will ever know you've sent it.'

'What's the point of it then?'

'That is what today's world is about, honey. You pay someone to deliver your shit.'

'I think I'd prefer to get a box of manure instead of all these emails.'

'I know. Shitexpress is actually quite funny. Ingenious even. It forces the recipient to evaluate his or her actions. It makes you ask yourself why did someone think you deserve to receive a pile of shit? But what's worrying these days is a new phenomenon, *toxic disinhibition*. The internet gives you total anonymity, and when the normal social barriers are removed, some people go too far. Anonymity seems to bring out the worst behaviour in us.'

'You know a lot about it.'

Vero laughs again. 'I have a lot of time on my hands. You'll see for yourself when you retire one day. One can't talk to one's bees forever. So I read, I surf the net a bit . . .'

I can't help but laugh with her.

'But when it comes to your troll, honey,' she sounds serious again, 'I bet that sooner or later he'll come out of the woodwork. He'll get bored of having no response. And eventually he'll leave you alone.'

'You think so?'

'I do. And in the meantime, since you have no work, why don't you come and visit your old aunt so we can feast on some oysters? I have a jar of fresh honey for you.'

'I will visit soon, I promise.'

I put the phone down, feeling less anxious. Talking to Vero always helps. An email pings in my mailbox. It's from the Fugitives Gallery.

> Good news. Sold two of Anton's prints. His work
> is generating a lot of interest.
> Regards,
> Anna

As if on cue, my Skype is chiming. It's Anton.

'What's up, babe?'

'I got another email. This time it's a photo of us having sex. You remember the session we did . . .'

'Yeah, I do. I've always known it was a bad idea, I told you.'

'I know . . .'

'It's just asking for trouble. Once you have a photo like this, sooner or later it will crop up somewhere.'

'But that picture has never left my computer. I didn't even keep it on iCloud. I thought it was safe.'

'Obviously it wasn't.' He sounds angry.

'Babe, let's not start an argument now. It's really freaked me out. I need you here. When are you coming back?'

He sighs and I can hear some weird Skype noises in the background.

'Soon. I'll be back soon. Tuesday or Wednesday if all goes well.'

'That's great! You have no idea how much I've missed you.'

'Try to hang on in there, yeah? I'll email you with my flight details once I have them.'

He's gone. I stare at the Skype screen. *Call ended 2 minutes 14 seconds.* So much for a chat with a supportive boyfriend. I forgot to tell him the good news from the gallery, but I don't care. I'm welling up again. I make myself a cup of tea and force the hot liquid down my constricted throat. It burns.

But I have to give it to Anton: he never wanted those pictures to be taken. He'd warned me from the start that documenting 'the bare arse stuff', as he called it, was asking for trouble. I talked him into it. No, actually, I didn't *talk* him into it, I just grabbed his dick at the right moment, knowing he wouldn't be able to resist it. He didn't object in the end, even though he saw the lights and the cameras. But I can see why he's pissed off with me now.

OK, the damage's been done. Let's just hope 'Exposure 2' doesn't end up on some dodgy porn site. So how do I protect myself against someone rooting around my computer? As usual, I try Google as my source of knowledge. Here we go. *Regular software updates.* Done. *Antivirus software.* Got it. *Turn on Firewall.* It's turned on. *Make regular backups.* I'm quite obsessive about backing everything up and I use TimeMachine. *Disable auto login and lock your screen when away from computer.* Frankly, I never thought it was necessary, but I'll think about it. *Use your administrator password cautiously.* I do. *Never open files from unknown sources.* Duh. *Encrypt your files.* Ah . . . that's something I should definitely consider. But looking into the technical side of things doesn't make me feel any better. Deep down I know the real question is not *how* my troll did it, but *why*. How did Vero put it? Ask yourself why you deserve to receive a pile of shit. And this is where I get stuck. I really don't know. The 'Exposure 2' sender is most likely also responsible for swapping the KiddyKraze files for 'In Bed With Anton'. *Why* is he doing this to me? What is the link between 'Exposure 1'and 'Exposure 2'? Was the Violinist just a ruse? What is it all about?

Overwhelmed by questions, I get up from the computer and go to the window again. I look across the street at the building opposite and freeze. The Peeping Tom is back. And he's looking straight at me. I turn round and grab the house keys from the kitchen counter, scaring Voxel who's been sitting next to a pile of unwashed dishes licking his front paw. I rush down the stairs, buzz the front door open and run across the street. The building opposite is almost an exact mirror image of our house. I try their front door. It's locked, of course. I look at the entryphone, which is identical to ours. Five floors, five apartments, five names. I push the top buzzer, next to the name 'Ewer'. No answer. I keep the buzzer pressed in, banging on the door with my free hand. Nothing. I try all the other buzzers, swearing to myself. *Come on, I know you're in there!* Silence. I kick the closed door and slide down onto its stone steps, sobbing.

'You all right?' A brightly dressed woman with turquoise hair is looking at me with concern.

'Yeah, I'm fine.' I wave her away.

'Kristin, isn't it?'

I look at her again.

'It's Heather, from Discreet.'

Ah, the sex shop. I recognize Heather, the owner, who is smiling at me as if sobbing on your neighbour's doorstep was the most natural thing in the world.

'Oh, hi, Heather. I'm sorry, I'm just having a bit of a meltdown here . . .'

'Do you want to come in?' She points at the inconspicuous door to her shop. She looks friendly and calm.

Actually, why not?

'Thank you.'

I follow her inside. She leads me through brightly lit displays of colourful sex toys to a small office at the back. She points to a red velvet armchair and goes to a small fridge that stands right by her desk.

'Water? Or something stronger?'

'Water's fine, thank you.'

I take a few long sips while she busies herself with some papers on the desk. I can feel my blood pressure dropping and my breathing gradually returns to normal.

'Sorry I made a scene outside.'

'That's OK.' She smiles at me. 'Were you looking for someone in particular?'

'The guy who lives on the top floor.'

'That would be Mr Ewer, the composer. He's hardly ever there. He travels a lot—'

A pretty girl with pink hair pops her head through the door.

'Heather, can I borrow you for a moment?'

'Excuse me.' She leaves and I can hear her casually telling someone about a bondage workshop, as if she was talking to them about a pottery class. She comes back a few minutes later.

'So, what's the story?'

I'm thrown by her question, but then I take a deep breath.

'Well, I have a cyber stalker. Someone's broken into my computer and stolen some compromising pictures. And I have lost my job. That just about sums it up.'

'Wow.' She nods. 'A triple whammy. You're a photographer, aren't you?'

'How do you know?'

'Oh, a wild guess. Almost everyone in this street is a photographer.' Seeing my raised eyebrows, she cracks a smile. 'I've seen you loading your car with equipment. Nothing escapes our spycam.' She points at a CCTV screen with a view of the street outside. 'What kind of stuff do you do?'

I blow air through my lips in a French mannerism I've picked up from Anton. 'Anything, really . . . anything that pays the bills.'

'I might have a job for you, if you're interested. We're rebranding our website and need a complete set of photos of our new range of toys. The photographer I had lined up for the shoot has just pulled out. She was a bit weird anyway. So, the job is yours if you want it. I'll pay the going rate.'

I resist the temptation to repeat the French pout, this time the impressed one.

Half an hour later I leave Heather's office with a new job, starting on Monday. Ta-ra KiddyKraze, welcome Discreet Playthingz.

8

My phone is vibrating somewhere under a pile of clothes on the floor and I try to ignore the sound until I can't stand it any longer. What kind of a moron is ringing me at 8 a.m.?

'Am I speaking to Miss Kristin Ryder?' A woman's voice, sounding uptight.

'Ms, yeah.'

'I'm calling from Queen Elizabeth the Queen Mother Hospital in Margate.'

'Oh?'

'Your name and number have been given to us as the next of kin of Mrs Veronica Diaz.'

'Aunt Vero! Has something happened to Aunt Vero?'

'She's had a nasty fall.' The woman sounds less uptight and more human now. 'She's quite shaken, but stable.'

'Can I come and see her?' I'm already out of bed, looking for some clothes.

'I think you should.'

The woman gives me her name and a contact number, then proceeds to explain how to get there. I interrupt her, telling her I'm on my way.

* * *

I boom along the M2 as fast as my old banger can take me. I arrive in Margate in just over an hour. The Waze application on my phone chooses a scenic route round the town avoiding all the traffic jams and gets me to St Peter's Road in good time. I find Nurse Benedict, the woman who rang me, in A&E and she takes me to Aunt Vero's bed. The ward is hushed, filled only with regular beeps and swooshes of medical equipment. Aunt Vero is in the bed by the door, a tiny figure almost invisible under a blue hospital blanket. A multitude of tubes connects her to two monitors and various machines. Her head is bandaged and there is a shocking red bruise on her face, her right eye practically hidden under the swelling.

'She's conscious, but we had to give her a strong painkiller and a mild sedative. She might be a bit woozy,' Nurse Benedict whispers to me.

'Aunt Vero!' I touch her frail hand with a drip attached to it.

Her left eye opens, bloodshot, but alert.

'Lily Liver.'

Tears instantly blur my vision.

'You've had a nasty fall.'

Her eye stares at me with defiance.

'I don't do falls,' she croaks. 'I was pushed.'

'Neighbours found her unconscious in the driveway this morning,' whispers Nurse Benedict.

'Bridget and Midget,' Aunt Vero butts in. 'What fusspots.'

Nurse Benedict and I exchange glances.

'I'll leave you alone for a few minutes.'

I nod at the nurse and take a chair by the bed.

'Damn, I'll miss a bell-ringing competition in Devon next week.' Vero grumbles about being a 'useless old cripple' for a while, then closes her eye. She's asleep.

I stay with Vero till lunch, holding her hand. I think of the day I officially moved in with Stella and Vero, a gangly and rebellious sixteen-year-old with an axe to grind on almost any subject. They gradually taught me patience and tolerance, respect for the opinions and behaviour of others. They taught me love. Please don't leave me, I think, squeezing her hand gently, don't leave me now.

'Hey, Lily Liver.' I can feel her hand squeezing mine back. 'Don't you worry. Remember that saying about worrying and a rocking horse? It keeps you busy, but it gets you nowhere.'

This makes me want to cry even more. Sweet, sweet Vero. She tells me to go and get on with my life and eventually I relent, promising her I'll be back tomorrow. Having seen her suddenly frail but still full of spirit puts all my little dramas into perspective.

On the way back I get stuck in a traffic jam on the approach to Blackwall Tunnel and by the time I reach home it's nearly four o'clock. A small group of neighbours has gathered outside our building. I recognize Ben the DJ from the flat below and Susan from the ground floor, a florist, who insists on keeping her stock inside her flat, making our hallway smell like a funeral parlour.

'Gas leak,' she informs me reproachfully. 'In your flat. You could've blown us up.'

I run upstairs, taking two steps at a time, until I reach my landing. There is, indeed, a Gas Board engineer in a blue uniform pushing a thin tube attached to a portable box through the keyhole in my front door. The red light in the box begins to flash madly.

'High concentration of gas inside,' he says. 'Are you the owner?'

When I nod, he asks me to unlock the door. The sulphuric smell hits me instantly. He swiftly goes to the cooker and turns one of the knobs off.

'My boys!' I shout and the guy looks at me, startled. 'My cats,' I explain.

'Please open all the windows,' he instructs me, not in the slightest bit concerned about the cats.

Holding my breath, I rush to open the windows, calling the boys. There's no reply.

Searching Pixel and Voxel's usual hiding places, I barely listen to the engineer as he gives me a short lecture about the dangers of leaving your appliances on unattended.

'. . . an emergency in Enfield Cloisters, you know, off Fanshaw Street, where a cat jumped on a gas stove and managed to turn all the knobs on—'

'Vox!' I interrupt the engineer's monologue, seeing Voxel's white and ginger paw sticking out from his favourite nook on the kitchen shelf. 'Voxie!'

I touch him, but he doesn't move.

'Voxel?'

I tug at his paw, but there's no response. I slide my hands into his hiding place and gently pull him out. He feels heavy and limp. His head is lolling about and his eyes are half closed, showing the white third eyelid.

'Oh God, Voxie . . .'

I lay him down on the kitchen table and blow into his face. Still nothing. I massage his hairy tummy, desperately searching for a sign of life.

'Voxie, wake up!'

I lift him up again and put my ear against his chest, listening for his heartbeat. Nothing.

'I need to call the vet,' I whisper to the engineer, who's staring at me in silence.

He clears his throat. 'I'm no paramedic, ma'am, but if you don't mind me saying so, I think your cat is dead.'

I hug Voxel's lifeless body as the engineer's monotonous voice seeps through my daze.

'. . . severe exposure . . . natural gas . . . carbon monoxide . . . preventing oxygen from being absorbed . . . damage to internal organs . . . report the incident . . .'

I bury my nose in Voxel's fur and rock backwards and forwards, tears rolling down my cheeks. My sweet little kitten, what has happened to you . . .

'Ma'am?' I recoil when the engineer touches my arm. 'The gas levels have gone down to neutral.' He shows me the reading on his machine. 'We'll need to follow up the incident, but your flat is safe now. I'll be off then . . .'

He leaves without closing the door behind him.

'Sorry about the cat . . .' I notice Sarah the florist hovering in the doorway. 'If you leave him outside in the street, the council should clean it up. You know, like road kill. I can give them a call if you like . . .'

Without a word I put Voxel's body down on the table, go to the front door and shut it in her face.

'Didn't you have *two* cats?' Her shrill voice penetrates the closed door.

Oh my God, Pixel! Where are you? I call out his name, frantically dashing around the loft.

A faint sound at the back of the loft makes me stop. Pixel!

Yes, I can hear meowing again and it's coming from the bathroom. I open the door.

'Kitty, kitty . . .'

The litter box is empty. He's not hiding among the towels either.

'Pixie, where are you?'

Meow

'There you are.'

For once I'm grateful that Anton hasn't kept his promise of installing a new ventilation fan above the shower cubicle. In a hole in the exposed brick wall, high up by the ceiling, I see Pixel's ginger ears.

'Pixie, how did you get up there?'

I put a chair inside the shower cubicle, climb it and grab him. He starts purring instantly, rubbing his nose against my neck.

'Oh, Pixie . . . thank goodness you're OK . . .'

I carry him out of the bathroom and sit down on the bed, holding him tightly in my arms.

What has happened here? Why was the gas on? I don't remember using the stove this morning – in fact, I'm positive I didn't touch it. I rushed out, grabbing a latte from a cafe on the way to the car. I look around the loft. Is it possible one of the cats had accidentally turned the gas on? Or has someone been here when I was gone? A shiver runs through me. What is going on in my life?

I wake up the following morning with a throbbing headache and a mouthful of Pixel's fur. I cried myself to sleep last night, making his fur wet with my tears. He is sitting by the Mac now, licking himself ferociously. He seems to be ignoring Voxel's body, still lying on the kitchen table, just as I left it. I remember leaving tearful messages for Anton, Sophie and Vero and then being too tired to answer when my phone started ringing later in the evening. Anton calls again when I'm forcing down a coffee, more concerned about Pixel than Voxel and myself. Hurt by his lack of empathy, I cut our conversation short. I feel battered and weepy, but I know I'll have to deal with Voxel today. I'm not going to dump him in the street for the council to pick him up. Just thinking about Susan's suggestion makes my blood boil. Heartless cow. And to think she sells flowers . . . I'm not going to take him to the vet to be cremated, either.

Stifling the tears, I put Voxel's stiff little body into a blue IKEA bag. I pile a double portion of Pixel's favourite Meowing Heads Purr-Nickety cat nibbles into his bowl and make sure he has no access to the kitchen stove. I check and double-check the gas is off and leave the loft, locking the door carefully behind me.

The traffic on the M2 is moving smoothly. I get to Margate just for the start of the hospital visiting time. Aunt Vero has improved and has been moved to a different ward. When I arrive she's busy lecturing the other patients in her room about the importance of keeping your body and mind agile in your 'golden years', but stops mid-sentence when she sees me.

'Kristin! Are you all right?'

I shake my head and tearfully tell her about Voxel. She holds my hand and listens in silence.

'He was the most egotistical and manipulative cat I've ever known. Actually, I think he was a sociopath, but I loved him. He had that wonderful skill of making me feel generous and forgiving, much better than I really am.'

'What about Pixel? Is he OK?'

'He seems fine. He's Anton's cat. I've never really been able to understand him.'

'He'll miss his brother. You'll have to be kind to him.'

'I'm always kind to him!'

Talking to Vero helps to clear this awful heaviness in my chest, the daunting feeling that an animal that has relied on me all his life is gone and maybe in some way I'm to blame for his death.

Vero, as if reading my mind, asks me if I want to bury Voxel in her garden. I haven't told her there is an IKEA bag with his body in the boot of my car, but somehow she knows.

'Use your keys, let yourself in, you'll find a spade in the shed. There's an empty spot at the back of the garden. I want to put some tulip bulbs in there in the autumn, I think it'll be perfect for him. I'll call Bridget and Midget to let them know you'll be in the garden, so they don't think you're an intruder. They've been very protective, those two.'

She reaches out to her bedside table to retrieve her phone and finds its battery flat.

'That's why I didn't hear you call last night. Can you tell Bridget to bring my charger next time she visits?'

I thank her and leave, still aching with sadness, but more at peace. It's started to drizzle and by the time I reach Vero's house in Whitstable it's pouring down. It somehow feels appropriate to bury Voxel in the rain.

9

Monday morning and I'm sore from yesterday's exertions. I coax Pixel out of his hiding place under the bed and play with him for a while. He seems skittish and distracted, his mood matching my own restlessness. I can't stop thinking about Voxel and the gas leak. How did it happen? Was it really an accident? Aware of my anxiety levels rising, I force myself to concentrate on something else. Fighting back the tears I scrub the kitchen table with hot, soapy water, then spray it with Dettox and wipe it dry. When there is nothing left to clean in the kitchen I focus on the first batch of Discreet Playthingz.

It's amazing how much sex toys have changed since I had a fleeting interest in them. I remember rather hideous-looking, clunky objects whose purpose was crudely obvious. Now they are sleek, intelligent and aesthetically pleasing. If they were cars, they would've evolved from a Ford Escort into the new Aston Martin. I'm fascinated by a Swedish vibrator with a purple silicone body. It has seven speeds and three patterns of vibration: still, escalating and pulsating. It is a technical wonder and its design is exquisite. It comes, wait for it, with a display stand in case you wanted to add a nice touch to your bedroom.

I look at the selection of toys and debate the best way to photograph them. I reject the simplest solution of using a white background with the infinity curve. Instead I decide to shoot them against a dark background with rim lighting to define their edges. As Professor Stein, our digital art and photography tutor, used to say, 'Good photography is all about light. And about what not to light.' I set out to create my stage: a black cloth screen at the back, about five feet behind a square piece of black Perspex, which will serve as a reflective surface on which I'll place my toys. Next, the lights: the main flash inside a white bounce umbrella and two rim lights with blue and red gels on the sides. It's nearly three o'clock when I'm finally happy with my lighting set-up.

A phone call makes me jump. It's a number I don't recognize.

'Kristin? It's Anna Wright from the Fugitives Gallery.'

'Oh, hi, Anna. I'm so sorry, I haven't had a chance to let Anton know about the sold prints. It's brilliant news!'

'Yes, he's definitely tapped into the zeitgeist. I sold another one of his today.'

'I can't wait to tell him.' A little white lie.

'But I'm ringing about your work . . .'

'*My* work?'

'The photos you've sent me. There are some really powerful images there, really strong stuff. Personally, I love them, but I'm not sure our clients are ready for them.'

'Anna, I haven't sent you any of my photos,' I say slowly. It feels as if all the blood has suddenly left my head. I sit down heavily on the bed.

'Oh,' says Anna after a brief silence.

I know exactly which photographs she's received.

'Perhaps I should come over to see you.'

'Yes . . . perhaps you should.'

'I'll be with you as soon as I can.'

'I'm at the gallery till six.'

I get to the Fugitives a few minutes after five and I'm greeted again by the chocolate Labrador, whose name, Anna tells me, is Wispa, as in the chocolate bar. Sergey, a waif-like young man with a bushy hipster beard and 'bed-look' hair, is left minding the gallery while Anna takes me to her office, shuts the glass door and points to a reclining armchair, clearly a Robin Day. Thanks to Aunt Stella, I know my designer chairs. It's surprisingly comfortable.

'You all right?' She throws me a curious glance as I settle into the armchair.

'Not really. My cat's just died.'

'That's so sad. I know how painful it is. Wispa ate rat poison some time ago and it was touch and go for a few days. I don't know what I'd do without her . . . I'm sorry – rattling on about myself . . .'

'It's fine.' I force a little smile. 'You said you received my photographs?'

She nods, opens her laptop, clicks on a folder and pushes it across her desk towards me. I look at the screen. Yep, it's 'In Bed With Anton', including the photo I'd kept out of it.

'They *are* yours?'

'Yes, but I have never intended them for commercial use. And I definitely haven't sent them to you.'

'They *were* sent from your address.'

'Do you mind if I see the email?'

'Not at all.' She goes to her mailbox and finds the email.

Yes, it's come from my address. The message is short.

EXPOSURE

Dear Anna,
I trust you'll find the attached of interest.
Yours,
Kristin

It was sent as a reply to Anna's email to me about the sale of Anton's prints.

'To be honest, I got quite excited when I received it.' Anna smiles. 'The images are so bold, they are . . . intense and mischievous at the same time. They actually remind me of Mapplethorpe's nudes, balancing classical aesthetics with raw, sexual charge.'

'Wow, thank you.' Despite the weird circumstances, I am tickled by the comparison. 'But they're not for sale.'

'I realize that. What's going on, Kristin?'

I sigh and shake my head. 'If only I knew . . .'

Anna opens a filing cabinet and takes out a bottle of wine and two glasses. 'Patagonian Malbec?' She starts pouring even before I say yes.

I'm not a wine expert but this is exceptional, slightly smoky, smooth and rich.

Anna is a good listener, and before I know it, my stalker story comes out, encouraged by a generous amount of Malbec.

'So, we are looking at "Exposure 2"?' she says when I'm done.

'Exactly.' Having told the story to a relative stranger feels surprisingly liberating. Probably because I instinctively know Anna's on my side.

'Do you have any idea who is doing it?'

'No.'

'No?' She looks at me questioningly. 'An ex-boyfriend, an ex-colleague, a pissed-off friend?'

'I really don't know.'

She keeps looking at me, deep in thought.

'There's one thing I don't understand. Substituting the toys catalogue for your intimate photos was meant to hurt you, and it did cost you your job. But sending them to me? It's almost doing you a favour.'

I laugh. 'You might have found them offensive. Reported me for distributing porn.'

Anna makes a face. 'Highly unlikely. I think we should give your stalker more credit. Maybe he wanted you to know he appreciated your art?'

'That would be the most twisted praise I have ever received.'

'Maybe he is a twisted man.'

'No.' I put the empty wine glass on Anna's desk. 'I don't buy it. The guy wants to hurt me. And I can't figure out why.'

'Why do people want to hurt other people?' Darkness passes across Anna's face, as if she's pulled back into some painful memory.

There is a gentle knock on the glass door and Sergey pops his hairy head in.

'Anna, darling, I'm going. Shall I lock the front door?'

'No, leave it unlocked, hon. I'm nearly done here.'

I get the message and stand up hastily. Anna notices it.

'Oh, no, I didn't mean it that way.' She puts her hand on my arm. 'I'd like to go on talking, but I have an appointment tonight. Promise you'll drop by again. Soon, yes?'

I promise Anna I'll come back then leave, turning left towards Brick Lane. As I walk through the crowds of hipsters I think about our conversation. Is it possible that Anna's right and sending my photos to the gallery was a twisted gesture of appreciation? No, it just doesn't make sense. I stop at the window of Brick Lane Gallery and peek in. What did she say about my photographs? That they reminded her of Mapplethorpe's nudes. I must say I found her comment very gratifying. As any artist, I'm a sucker for praise. Am I an artist? I remember my college discussions with Erin about the nature of art. We actually had time and energy to argue about such things, to feel passionate about abstract ideas. And then we lost that creative hunger, that youthful affectation, and became grown-ups. I pass a young guy sitting with a white Staffie on the pavement outside a closed shop, holding a cardboard sign in his dirty hands. 'A KISS FOR £1' it says. I dig a coin out of my pocket and throw it into his hat. He smiles at me and blows me a kiss.

I grab a Bun Xiao takeaway from a Vietnamese in Kingsland Road and head home, fired-up about my photography. I can't get the Mapplethorpe comparison out of my head. I unlock my front door, push Pixel with his twitching tail out of the way, and go straight to my bookshelf. Andy, a pre-Anton ex-boyfriend with an OCD streak, rearranged all my art albums according to their size and cover colour, so it takes me a while to find what I'm looking for. But there it is, right at the top, the first 1990 edition of Mapplethorpe's *Flowers* with an introduction by Patti Smith. A present from Vero. I open it and flick through the pictures greedily. They are stunning in their simplicity. I go through the book page by page, feeling the same thrill I felt when I looked at the photographs for the first time. *Tulips, Calla Lily, Anemone, Orchids,* and my favourite, *Poppy,* with its bristled stem and bulbous bud. While I find the precision of composition comforting, its intense eroticism excites and challenges. As with most of Mapplethorpe's images, its power

lies in the contradiction, the conflict between the stylized calm-
ness of still life and its unsettling sexual charge. I put the book
down. An idea is forming in my head, but will I be able to pull
it off?

I feel a pang of hunger and remember the Bun Xiao. It's
cold by now, but I devour it straight from the takeaway box,
pacing the loft as I eat. I pour myself a large glass of wine and
drink it in big gulps. I haven't felt so excited about a possible
project in a long time. I have to give it a go. I crouch by the
batch of sex toys I received from Heather this morning. Straight
away I reject those that seem unphotogenic. A leather corset
strap-on harness with a matching dildo, stretchy cock rings that
resemble doughnuts and a hideous pink vibrating thong. But a
few of the toys are perfect for what I have in mind. The purple
Swedish vibrator. A black and silver wand massager. Turquoise
vibrating beads. A couple of dildos will do as well, especially
the glass ones. My plan is to create a series of beautifully lit,
highly stylized close-ups that would desexualize the toys, but
enhance their sensual quality. I'm thinking bold, elegant images
that even the most discerning collectors wouldn't mind displaying
on their walls. I'm going to do with dildos what Mapplethorpe
did with flowers. In my mind I'm already at the opening of my
exhibition at the Fugitives Gallery.

I grab my phone wanting to call Vero then remember she's
still in hospital. I dial Sophie's number and get the monotonous
European ringtone, just like the last time, when I left her a
message about Voxel. I call Anton and listen to a network
announcement in Spanish. My finger hovers above Jason's
number, then moves on. I know, Erin! *This is Erin Perdue.
Leave me a message. If it's urgent call my agent Tim on 078—'*
I throw my phone on the bed. Suddenly my idea seems

ridiculous. I'm no Mapplethorpe and it'll never work. I lost my creative flair ages ago. KiddyKraze catalogue is at my level now. Discreet Playthingz with a bit of rim lighting at a push. How pathetic.

I go to the window and there he is, my Peeping Tom, looking at me. For once I don't let it upset me, just look back at him. Let's pretend we're two lonely people in a big city, looking at each other. I go to my desk, rummage for a thick marker pen and scribble a message on a piece of paper. I take it to the window. 'A KISS FOR £1?' For a long while he doesn't move, just stares, then, very slowly, turns and disappears inside his loft.

I wake up in the middle of the night with a start. Anton's T-shirt I've been wearing is drenched with sweat. I've been dreaming. Just like Erin's nightmare, I was lying on the cobbled street below the warehouse, eyes open, blood seeping from under my shattered head. But it was Voxel, sitting on the shiny cobbles next to my body, lapping up blood from the growing maroon puddle by my head, that scared me most.

10

Thank God I didn't get through to anyone last night, I think, sipping my morning latte from Anton's coffee maker. My Mapplethorpe idea seems ludicrous in the cold light of day. How much did I have to drink yesterday? Not enough to justify such a flight of fancy. I put the empty mug down and look at the sex toys scattered on the floor. Mapplethorpe my arse.

Let's do something sensible instead. I ring my Internet Service Provider and let them know my account has been hacked. It's obviously a commonplace occurrence for them. They advise me to virus-sweep my computer and change my password. Choose a *strong* password, says the young man I'm talking to. When I ask him what it actually means, he gives me a short but useful lecture. Don't use *iloveyou, 123456* or cute names like *princess*. Don't use addresses or birthdays. Use eight characters or more and mix letters with symbols. But common substitutions like *p4ssw0rd* are still vulnerable. So instead I should use a passphrase or try to create a password from a sentence. I do what he says, feeling smug. *Try2h4kMen0w.*

Now, work. I decide to do a trial run of photographs on a black background with contour lighting and see what Heather says. She may find it too fancy, in which case I'll revert back to simple shots on white. I'm enjoying this. The weird shapes and textures of the sex toys make the shoot more challenging. I struggle for a while with a pair of shiny love balls that reflect light and everything around them with the tenacity of a disco ball. Eventually I settle for a large light softbox right above the camera to get the feathering effect. I'm pleased with the result.

My mobile rings. It's Sophie at last.

'I thought you were going to stay in France for good!'

'I thought so too. The food there is amazing.'

'I'm so glad you're back.'

'What are you doing tonight?'

'Nothing . . . unless Aunt Vero needs me.' I briefly tell her about Vero's fall.

'Give my love to Vero and let me know how things go. But come over for dinner if you're free. We have *masses* of food for you to try.'

'Did you get my message about Voxel?'

'No, what happened?'

I tell her about the gas leak and my trip to Whitstable to bury Voxel. Her warm-hearted reaction makes me realize how much I've missed her. It's good to know she's back. Next I ring Vero. Good news, she'll be discharged later today and her neighbours Bridget and Midget (I don't even know the poor guy's real name) are picking her up. Bridget, who is a natural carer, has been insisting Vero stays with them for a few days and Vero's reluctantly agreed.

'Don't come and visit though,' she says. 'They'd bore you to death. I'll let you know when I'm back at my place.'

She never beats around the bush, my aunt Vero.

* * *

I'm done with the first batch of Playthingz by late afternoon. I create small JPEGs of the images and email them to Heather for approval. Fingers crossed she likes them. I confirm with Sophie I'm coming over for dinner, take a quick shower, throw some comfortable clothes on and head for the City Beverage Company. What can I get a couple who have just returned from a gourmet trip to France? Obviously not wine. I pick a nice-looking box of Fairtrade tea, then get advice regarding local London beers. I end up going for a few bottles from the Redchurch Brewery, Great Eastern IPA, the Shoreditch Blonde and Bethnal Pale Ale. Let's welcome them home in style.

Sophie and Marcus live in a terraced house just off Roman Road, a stone's throw from Victoria Park. To call it a 'terraced house' would be the understatement of the century. The only thing remaining from the old Victorian house is its facade – the rest has been ripped out and replaced with a modern glass-and-steel design marvel. Its conversion cost a fortune, probably more than buying a new house, but Sophie and Marcus didn't mind. They love the East End. And they had the money to spend. Marcus used to be a musician but retrained as a chef. Sophie studied fashion at St Martin's but dropped out when she met Marcus. They travelled the world together, propelled by their shared passion for food. It was that passion that helped them make their fortune. They started small, running food stalls at various London markets. Marcus did most of the kitchen duties, while Sophie took care of the business side of things. Soon they were opening an online gourmet food delivery business that established them as serious players on the London catering scene.

The food they serve tonight is amazing. It all comes from Brittany, where they have spent the last few weeks sourcing new products. We have the traditional fish soup with a garlicky saffron sauce, a pork sausage to die for, a selection of crêpes and galettes, and finish it off with Far Breton, a prune pudding. Not to mention the cheeses . . . Marcus, having very politely cooed over the beer bottles I brought, stashed them away in their larder and put a couple of litre bottles of red wine on the table. The bottles have no labels but the wine is divine.

A true gentleman, Marcus lets us retire to the sitting room while he stays 'in his kingdom' washing up. Sophie tells me about their trip and a house they found near Nantes.

'You're not going to abandon me here!' I'm only half joking.

'Oh, come on. EasyJet flies from Gatwick to Nantes and from there it's just a half-hour drive. You could practically live with us there. The house is huge. It needs work, but . . . Kris, what's the matter?'

I don't quite know what has hit me but I find myself sobbing into my wine glass. Sophie puts her arm round me, which makes my sobbing worse.

'How about a drop of Jurançon with your coffees?' Marcus stops when he sees us huddled on the sofa and quietly retreats to the kitchen.

'What's going on?' Sophie pushes my fringe from my eyes. 'Is it Voxel?'

'I felt so lonely when you two were gone.'

'When is Anton back?'

'Soon . . . he says . . .'

'When did you speak to him last?'

'Yesterday . . . or the day before . . . I don't remember.'

'Did you two fall out over something?'

'No. No, it's not Anton.' I wipe my nose on the sleeve of my shirt.

'What is it then?'

Sophie knows me well enough to want to dig for the truth. She knows I don't have a habit of bursting into tears for no reason. And so I tell her about 'Exposure 1' and 'Exposure 2', about the KiddyKraze mess and the fake email to the Fugitives.

'Bloody hell. Maybe you should report it to the police?'

'And tell them what? That someone is having fun with my porn? Or trying to scare me with Photoshop?'

'Do you have any idea who could be doing this?'

I shake my head.

'Could it be fallout from Cubic Zirconia?'

'I don't think so. No one cares about Cubic Zirconia any more.'

'A mad ex? You've had your share of weirdo boyfriends . . .'

I shake my head again.

'What about that creepy guy who stalked you when you worked for the Met?'

'Which one?'

'Oh, you know, the Frankenstein guy.'

'Oh, Walter. No, he was harmless.'

'Harmless? I nearly had a heart attack when you showed me his picture. In those white wellies and overalls splattered with blood . . .'

'He was an APT at the mortuary, Sophie. It was his work uniform.'

'He used to tie his apron with a chain. A *chain*. Does that sound normal to you?'

'He was eccentric but the guy was OK. Asked me to go out with him, I said no, end of story. There was never any bad feeling between us.'

'If you say so . . . but I wouldn't be so sure.'

'I'm sure. I haven't seen him for years.'

'Maybe you're right. If it was him you'd be hanging off a hook in some freezer by now.'

'Sophie!' I punch her playfully. Her sense of humour can be very dark sometimes.

My tearful moment has passed and I don't feel like talking about it any more.

'How about that coffee Marcus has been promising?'

'And some Jurançon. You have to try it.'

We join Marcus back in the kitchen. I tell them about my Discreet Playthingz gig and they reciprocate with stories of Bretons who carry magnets in their pockets to protect themselves from bad vibes.

'Maybe I should get a magnet . . .'

As we all laugh I feel tension leaving my body at last.

But when I get home around midnight, my anxiety is back. Everything seems to be fine – there are no new emails in my mailbox, Pixel is asleep in his bed, the Peeping Tom's vantage point across the street is empty. No one has been to my loft when I was out and yet there is a palpable menace in the air, a quiet hum as if the electricity current creeping along the wires has been flipped to produce a harmful field. Perhaps those magnets are not such a bad idea after all . . .

11

Anton is coming back tonight. He's arriving at Heathrow at 5 p.m. on an Iberia flight from Buenos Aires via Madrid. As usual, he doesn't want me to meet him at the airport. He'll hop on the tube and will be home for dinner, he tells me. I rarely cook, so in my excitement I book a table at St John's in Spital-fields. He'll probably be totally beefed-out after his long stay in Argentina so let's treat him to something quintessentially British – a whole suckling pig, a roast wood pigeon or a Stinking Bishop.

Sophie's back and I'll have Anton with me by tonight – things are looking up! In a burst of jubilant energy I tidy up the loft, wash a pile of dirty dishes that has accumulated over the last few days, change the bedding and shave my legs. Straight from the shower, I tiptoe naked through the loft and fling the wardrobe door open. I fancy wearing something sexy today, something that will reflect my mood. As I go through my summer dresses, Spotify web player, which has been quietly piping out my favourite tunes through the iMac speakers, decides to play Emilia Mitiku's 'So Wonderful'. I drop the dress I was looking at, crank up the volume and do a little dance, watched by a perplexed Pixel. Life suddenly does feel wonderful. At the end I choose the Superdry sleeveless skater dress with the crochet top and the flowy jersey skirt. It's black and it makes me feel damn sexy.

An email pings in my mailbox, its sound magnified by the speakers. It's from Heather. She loves the pictures! Perhaps I should try my Mapplethorpe idea after all. Her email confirms my theory: if you put positive energy out into the universe, it instantly pays you back in kind. I got myself into a rut these past few days but the dark mood is definitely over.

My mailbox pings again. Another email, this time from someone called R. B. Stein. *Professor* Stein? I haven't heard from him since my college days. I click on the email, unsure what to expect.

> Dear Kristin,
> I am putting together a show based on works created in the photographic medium by some of my former students. It will launch at the Light Vault Gallery, a visual project I am the curator of. Its aim is to introduce cutting-edge works of lesser-known artists to a wider audience, culminating in taking the show to this year's Paris Photo and next year's Paris Photo Los Angeles, the US edition of the world's most celebrated fine art photography fair.
>
> Kristin, you are probably aware I consider you one of my most gifted students. I have followed your development with great interest and am somewhat dismayed by your recent creative silence. Please do reassure me you are not wasting your talent on easy mediocrity. I want you to be part of the Light Vault.
> Yours,
> Robert B. Stein

Is this another internet prank? Incredulously, I reread the email. I can almost hear Professor Stein's voice: *wasting your talent on easy mediocrity*. It has to be from him, as baffling as it seems. One of his most gifted students? I am amazed he remembers me at all. It's true, Erin and I used to hang out at his beautiful riverside flat with a bunch of other students, talking art and philosophy while depleting his impressive wine collection. But I'd never noticed him paying me any more attention than others. He says he's been 'following my development'. What was there to follow? After the brief success of Cubic Zirconia, I more or less disappeared from the art scene. Perhaps he's mixed me up with Erin? It would make sense, everyone knows her stuff. But me? If it *is* me, what could I offer him for his show?

I get up from my computer table and go to Anton's coffee machine. As it splurts out an espresso I think of how to respond to Professor Stein's email. First of all, check discreetly if he's not confusing me with someone else. That would be highly embarrassing. Secondly, find out if I have something worth submitting to the Light Vault. I can't think of anything apart from a project I did when I was a forensic photographer. With the help of Walter, the anatomical pathology technologist Sophie mentioned only yesterday, I documented the job of an APT and the process of reconstruction of the dead body after a post-mortem. It was a series of gruesome but beautiful pictures, so intimate in their starkness that I abandoned the idea of ever making them public. It was probably the right decision, so I shouldn't be thinking of rehashing them now. If you discount 'In Bed With Anton', a handful of concert photographs and my landscape portfolio from California, I really don't have anything to show for myself. How sad. Unless . . . I look at the sex toys scattered on my light stage . . . unless I have a go at the Mapplethorpe idea.

Fired up, I inspect the toys closely. I pick up the purple vibrator. It's beautifully designed, the flowing lines of its body resembling an exotic plant or flower. How would it look in extreme close-up? I position it on the black Perspex display stand and set up the lighting. I choose an EF 100mm macro lens, which will give me a great close-up with a blurred background thanks to its large aperture. I try various angles and distances, monitoring the photos on my iPad as I go along. The effect is nice, but 'nice' is not enough. I swap the reflective Perspex surface for black cloth. I like the change, but something is still missing. I persevere, trying out different lighting combinations and different lenses. When I look at the time, it's already 5 p.m. I still haven't come up with an image that would capture my imagination. I feel disappointed and annoyed. It's ridiculous, this sudden urge to find a new form of expression. It doesn't happen just like that, because Professor Stein said so. It's a process that should take years to master. I'm going to write back to him and say I have nothing to offer. Easy mediocrity is my field of expertise.

Five o'clock. I check Heathrow Live Arrivals. There it is: Iberia flight from Madrid, landed at Terminal Five at 17.10. Anton should be home in a couple of hours. I try his mobile but it's still switched off. I can feel excitement building inside me, pushing out the depressive musings of a failed artist. He'll be here soon, loud, passionate, irresistible. Without him the loft seems cavernous and dull, with dark shadows and cold echoes lurking in the corners. But when he's here the place shrinks, it almost becomes too small, filled to the brim with his voice, his smell, his nervous energy.

My phone rings.

'Got your boy back?' It's Sophie and I feel a slight stab of disappointment that it's not Anton.

'Not yet, but his plane landed on time. He should be here soon.'

'You can have a few days to yourselves, but then we want you two over for dinner.'

'Great. I'll be in touch as soon as I know what his plans are.'

'Enjoy your boy!' She disconnects.

She always calls him 'boy'. She couldn't be further from the truth. Anton is a man, a mate, an irritatingly macho male sometimes, but never a boy.

I pace around, unable to concentrate on anything. It's quarter past six and he still hasn't rung. He's probably on the tube by now. I find an old yellow duster under the sink and wipe Anton's desk, which hasn't been touched since he left for Argentina. Dusting, that's an activity I hardly ever do unless I don't know what to do with myself. In a sudden outburst of domesticity, I stuff another load of dirty laundry into the washing machine and set it on 'Easy Care'. Then I go to the bathroom and apply a bit of mascara and some Nude Lips lipstick. A splash of perfume? I reach for a bottle of Escentric Molecules and squirt it on my neck. That's it, improvements done.

Next I go to the fridge and open it expectantly. Thank goodness I had the foresight to stash a bottle of Prosecco away. I take it out, pop the cork and pour myself a glass. Let the party begin early.

Two glasses on and still no sign of him. The washing machine has already reached its rinse phase. It's half past seven and he should definitely be home by now. Maybe he missed his connection in Madrid? He would've texted me, for sure. The Prosecco glass in hand, I go to the computer and check emails. There's nothing of interest. I click on the folder with the photographs I took earlier. They all seem very static, lifeless. But what if I were to play with movement in a longer exposure time, to create a semi-transparent blur of motion? Most of these toys vibrate or pulse, why not use their energy then? I feel I'm getting somewhere here. I pour myself a third glass and debate whether to have another go at photographing the vibrator right now. What about Anton? Sod Anton, his being late is beginning to annoy me. As I reach for the purple vibrator I hear a key in the front-door lock.

'Anton!'

And there he is, tall, tanned and tired. His eyes are blood-shot, his combat trousers rumpled and smeared with paint, his hair long and wild. He drops his heavy rucksack on the floor and grabs me in his arms. He smells of sweat, cigarette smoke and long-haul travel. I hug him tightly, my ear pressed against his chest. I can hear his heartbeat.

'Good to be home, baby.' His voice rumbles in his chest.

'Good to have you back.'

With a kick of his foot he shuts the door behind him. I stand on my tiptoes and raise my chin, looking for his mouth. As we kiss, his stubble scratches my skin, sending needles of lust along my body. There's alcohol on his breath, a slight nicotine bitter-ness and a hint of garlic, a combination that I normally find uninviting, but today it turns me on. The fact that he stinks after his long trip works like some strange aphrodisiac, his pheromone-laden smell triggering an unmistakable reaction in me. I push my hand under the front of his T-shirt and pull at the short hair on his chest. His fingers slide up my thighs and under the flowy skirt. I've anticipated this, so I'm wearing no knickers tonight. He sighs with approval and cups my bare buttocks. I tug at his heavy belt. We peel away from the door and I doubt whether we'll make it as far as the bed. We don't. Combat trousers at his ankles, he clutches my waist and lifts me onto the first piece of furniture we stumble upon. The washing machine. I grab his cock and guide him in as the machine goes into its final spin.

The clock by the bed says it's half past ten, our reservation at St John's long gone. We're both tipsy and starving. Despite my weak protests, Anton orders a takeaway from Red Dog in the square. An insane amount of Bar-B-Q wings, plus a stack of fries, onion rings, mozzarella sticks, coleslaw and a pecan pie if there's still any space left for it. Oh yes, the man is definitely back. I'm glad I've stocked up on his favourite Leffe Blonde.

It's a lucky day for the delivery guy who gets tipped ten quid for the short stroll from Hoxton Square to our place.

'We're celebrating, mate,' Anton tells him, opening the door wearing just a towel round his waist.

We take the food straight back to bed, gorging ourselves on the wings and fries, the sheets smeared with Red Dog sauce. Ecstatic, Pixel dances between us as Anton feeds him tiny bits of chicken, normally a forbidden food. I feel light-headed and heavy-limbed, in a state of perfect post-coital bliss where nothing matters except the here and now. Eating the pecan pie is a mistake, albeit a delicious one. We both roll onto our backs, unable to move, replete, burping and happy.

I wake up in the middle of the night, enveloped by the smell of sex and Bar-B-Q sauce. Anton is snoring quietly beside me. I rest my head on my arm and watch him dreaming, his eyelids fluttering. I feel so close to him and yet I have no idea what his dream is about. And he doesn't even know I'm looking at him.

12

Over breakfast at Ruby Café in the square, I tell Anton about his sales at the Fugitives Gallery and we catch up on what's been going on in our lives. Or, to be precise, he mostly talks and I mostly listen. I sip orange juice and nibble on a croissant while he wolfs down a plate of scrambled eggs with chorizo and rocket, telling me about his new project. He's going to make a massive, 180-metre-square paste-up on a whole house in Doel in Belgium.

'It's ultimate kudos, babe. Doel is a total street-art mecca. Some twenty years ago, when Antwerp's docks were expanding, it was earmarked for demolition. It's almost completely deserted now, there's a handful of residents left and they are super cool about street art. So it's become this amazing open-air art gallery. You should see the pictures. Everyone's done a piece there, ROA, Resto, Psoman, Luc Tuymans . . .' He's listing the names with awe. 'And wait for this, it's going to be a BBC documentary. They'll follow me with a proper film crew! It'll keep me busy for a few weeks,' he says, wiping his plate with a piece of bread. 'Not to mention all the stuff that may come out of it. I'm telling you, babe, I'm on a roll.'

I'm happy for him, mainly because he's a nightmare to be around when idle and bored. Not that it happens very often.

'What about those stolen photos? Have you managed to sort it out?' He switches his attention to me at last.

'You don't know the half of it . . .' I take a deep breath, unsure where to start, when Anton looks at his phone.

'Shit! I was supposed to be in Soho fifteen minutes ago!' He grabs his phone and his cigarettes and jumps up from the table. 'Sorry, babe, gotta run, meeting up with the Beeb producer. We'll catch up tonight, yeah?'

He pecks me on the cheek and is gone. I finish off my juice, pretending I'm not upset by his sudden departure. The waitress has been watching me, so I shrug and signal for the bill. She brings it straight away.

'Anton's in a hurry today, isn't he?'

Anton? She knows his name? Even though he's been away for three months and the waiting staff here changes like the weather?

'So he is,' I say noncommittally. I don't leave her a tip.

Back at the loft, I throw the house keys on the kitchen worktop and they clatter loudly, startling Pixel. Last night's bliss is gone, replaced by annoyance. I'm pissed off he left me at the cafe to pay the bill, pissed off he didn't listen to my story, pissed off he always thinks of himself first. Well, I suppose that's what you get for having an artist for your partner. Wait a minute, *I* am an artist too, but I'm not as self-absorbed and narcissistic as he is. Is it because I am a woman?

I look at the washing machine and notice that yesterday's washing is still in it. Its stale smell hits me as I open the door but I can't be bothered with running the cycle again. As I start pulling the damp clothes out, flashes of last night's shag start flooding in. It was, I must say, pretty amazing. I don't think I've ever felt such unrestrained abandon. I remember my heels digging into his tight arse as his thrusts got faster and faster, syncopating with the vibrations of the washing machine, and I suddenly go weak at the knees. I drop the laundry on the floor and slide down next to it. Damn you, Anton. It's hard to be angry with you for a long time. And the problem is that you know it and rely on your charm to get away with murder.

I put the washing in the dryer and look at the pile of dirty clothes Anton peeled off himself last night. Somehow they've lost their pheromone potency and they just stink now. As much as I resent doing the housewife chores, I'll feel better without the smelly heap in the middle of my floor. I pick up his T-shirt, underwear, socks, his cargo pants and the light jacket. If I throw a few of my things in I'll have another full load for the washing machine. Out of force of habit, I go through Anton's pockets. I started doing it after I found two hundred pounds' worth of notes rolled up in the pocket of his jeans. There were other things I used to find in his pockets too, squashed roll-ups, little chunks of Moroccan hash in tiny plastic bags, lighters, sticks of chewing gum, loose change. This time I find a boarding pass stub in his cargo pants and a folded piece of paper in the inside pocket of his jacket. Not bad for having travelled halfway across the world. I load the machine and set it on 'Intensive Stains' at 60 degrees. This stuff needs a good wash. I throw his boarding pass away. I'm just about to do the same with the piece of paper I found in his jacket when it crosses my mind to see what it is. It's a hotel bill.

I sit down on the stool by the breakfast counter, focusing on the printout in my hand. Only You Hotel, Calle Barquillo 21, 28004 Madrid, Spain. Two nights in a Deluxe Room, bed and breakfast, plus some bar charges. A total of 576 euros. Guests' names: Mr & Mrs Sauvage. Check-out date: yesterday.

I put the bill on the counter and flatten it with my hand. I sit motionlessly staring at the printout, listening to the washing machine going through its cycle. *Chug-chug-chug.* Silence. *Chug-chug-chug.* Silence. *Chug-chug-chug.* Anton didn't just catch a connecting flight in Madrid. He's spent the last three days there. In a Deluxe Room with Mrs Sauvage. And I don't think it was his mother.

In fact, I am certain Anton's mother didn't join him in Madrid. Madame Carinne Sauvage suffers from severe dementia and has been in an expensive care home just outside Aix-en-Provence for five years. The Sauvage family, which consists of Madame Carinne, Anton and his brother, Lionel, who works as a banker in New York, is very rich. Papa Sauvage, from what I know, used to run a successful import–export business bringing cheap goods from China and selling them for a lot of money in Europe. The fortune he accumulated he then reinvested in the most rare artefacts smuggled out of China during the Cultural Revolution. I have seen a small part of his collection in the vault of their huge house in the Quartier Mazarin of the city of a thousand fountains, called by the locals simply Aix. Papa Sauvage died of a heart attack ten years ago, leaving his riches to Lionel and Anton. So, as much as he hates to admit it, Anton is a wealthy man. A man who prides himself on surviving on the proceeds from his street-art gigs but who wouldn't bat an eyelid at spending over five hundred euros on a two-night stay in Madrid. I have to give it to him though, he could've splashed out on the Ritz or Westin Palace but instead opted for a more humble four-star hotel, 'offering great beds, a buzzing bar and excellent service, close to the Prado Museum'. It's the 'great beds' I'm upset about most, for I don't think he chose Only You Hotel for its proximity to the Prado.

So, Anton's playing around, shamelessly cheating on me with some *bombón* he probably picked up in Buenos Aires. I wonder if he's brought her with him to London. I get up and go to the window. The loft opposite is dark and empty, my Peeping Tom probably busy doing whatever Peeping Toms do for a living. As hard as it is to believe, my boyfriend is having an affair. Anton and I have never discussed the issue of infidelity, never opted for an open relationship, a notion I find oxymoronic anyway. We walked into our coupledom bright-eyed and bushy-tailed, not bothering to read the small print. But perhaps his small print has been different to mine? Perhaps having an affair is well within the boundaries of his definition of being in a relationship? Which leads on to my next question: how long has this been going on? Is it a one-off, a holiday fling, or does he have a string of *bombóns* in tow? And, most importantly, what am I supposed to do about it?

The flash of anger I felt a moment ago has gone, replaced by a cheerless heaviness of heart. I so wish this wasn't happening. I hate confrontations and usually go out of my way to avoid them. But I can't bury my head in the sand and pretend everything is all right. Can I? No, I can't. I have to react, to *do* something. I hate myself for it, but the only thing I feel like doing right now is retreating. I pick up my phone and press one of the speed-dial buttons.

'Are you still at Bridget and Midget's?'

'Yes . . .' Aunt Vero answers diplomatically. 'But it could be easily rectified.'

'Great. I'm coming over to pick you up then. I'll stay with you for a couple of days if that's OK.'

'I think I can manage that.' Aunt Vero is careful not to show too much enthusiasm and I can just imagine Bridget and Midget hanging on her every word while she's on the phone to me.

I grab my overnight bag and throw a handful of essentials in. I dish out an extra-large portion of Pixel's lamb dinner and check if his water bowl is full. I pack my Mac Air, pick up the car key and head for the door. I stop, then go back to the kitchen counter to fetch a vital piece of evidence. Anton's hotel bill. I fold it carefully and slide it into the side pocket of my bag.

It takes Anton until nine at night to send me a text message.

Where are you?

He obviously hasn't got a clue what has happened.

At Aunt Vero's. She's had a fall. Will stay with her for a couple of days.

Followed by Anton's succinct

OK.

Not even 'How is she?' or 'Give her my regards'. He is digging himself deeper and deeper into my bad books.

Aunt Vero assures me she feels better than she looks. The bruise on her face has turned yellowy-blue but the swelling has gone down. She's annoyed she won't be able to have fun with her bell-ringing society for a while, but otherwise she seems fine. We've had a takeaway pizza for dinner and have retired to her living room with a cup of tea and Bridget's lemon drizzle cake, which Vero calls 'saccharine squidgy'. It sounds like she's had enough of Bridget's baking for a while. She's unusually quiet when I tell her about Anton's fling and show her the hotel bill.

'Were you and Stella ever unfaithful to each other?' Something in her pensive look prompts me to ask this impudent question.

'Well . . .' She takes a sip of her tea. 'We were together for thirty years. That's an awfully long time.'

'You *didn't*!' Her evasiveness is telling.

'We were a very good couple. A match made in heaven. The sex at the beginning was amazing. She was my first lover, you know. I was this naive, starry-eyed Portuguese girl, transplanted from tiny Monsaraz to mind-blowing London, head full of women's lib ideas, *Spare Rib* under my arm . . . And Stella . . . she was much older, sophisticated, with a bit of a reputation . . . Suave Stella they used to call her. She was a real charmer.'

'Where did you two meet?' I can't contain my curiosity. Stella and Vero rarely talked about their early years together, so this is an opportunity I can't miss.

'At Gateways – you must have heard of it.'

I nod, vaguely recalling reading somewhere about the iconic gay club.

'Actually, I'm lying, we didn't meet at the club, we met *outside* of it. I was quite radical in those days. So there I was, protesting outside Gateways . . . We were shouting at the women going in to "come out". And suddenly this gorgeous, tall woman approached me and kissed me on the lips.'

'Aunt Stella? She *didn't*!'

'Oh yes, she did . . .' Vero falls silent, immersed in her memories.

'And that was it?' I prompt her again, because I want to know more.

'Well, not quite. She gave me her phone number and asked me to call her. It took me weeks to pluck up the courage. I lived in Brixton at the time and I kept hovering around the phone box in my street for so long the locals thought I was a prostitute. Eventually I call her and she answers the phone and says, "Please call me later, I'm having sex now."'

'*No!*' I nearly drop my cup of tea on the floor.

She laughs and for a moment I see the young Vero, happy and in love.

'I never rang her back. But we bumped into each other at Foyles some time later. I moved in with her two weeks after that.'

Vero gets up slowly from her armchair and goes to the drinks cabinet.

'Eighteen-year-old Macallan, Stella's favourite. Fancy a wee dram?'

I'm not a great whisky enthusiast but I know the stuff Aunt Stella used to drink is good. Vero pours two generous glasses and adds a splash of water to both. She settles back in her chair and raises her dram, as she calls it.

'Here's to Stella, the light of my life.'

As the whisky burns my throat, its delicately smoky toffee taste brings back memories of our evenings together back at the loft.

'I cheated on her once.' Vero holds her glass in both hands, as if trying to warm herself on it. 'We'd been together for years and we were going through a rough patch. I lost my job, her business was suffering because of the recession, and on top of that, she started an early menopause. Her hot flushes became so bad we had to stop sharing the bed. She couldn't sleep, was always tired and irritable. To be honest, I began avoiding her, hung around with a crowd of younger women, one of whom I knew fancied me. One night I got home really late and Stella was waiting for me, drunk but lucid. She told me to go and have an affair. "Go and do it," she said, "just don't tell me about it." And so a few days later, I went and did it.' Vero takes a sip of her whisky. 'So, that's my story.'

'Did she know?'

'Of course she did. I told her about it as soon as it happened. And begged her forgiveness.'

'Did she forgive you?'

'Yes. But I have never been able to forgive myself.'

'But you stayed together . . .'

'Oh yes, and we had many happy years after that. You see, life is never black and white. It's monochromatic, with occasional splashes of colour.'

As we sip Aunt Stella's favourite whisky in silence, I'm beginning to think rationally about Anton's infidelity.

'Do you think I should forgive him?'

Aunt Vero produces a silver E-cig out of the breast pocket of her loose shirt and takes a couple of puffs.

'I think it's up to him to come clean.'

'And if he doesn't? Should I confront him?'

'Do you feel like pretending you don't know he's been unfaithful to you?'

'No.'

'Then you two should talk.'

13

The next day, after lunch with Vero at Wheelers, I'm heading back to London. Vero has convinced me I should stop dodging the issue and confront Anton. There's no point in delaying the inevitable, whatever it may be, she said.

As soon as I get onto the M2, my phone rings. I fumble with my headphones, but manage to answer it before it goes to voicemail. It's Heather, asking when she could send someone over with the next box of toys to be photographed.

'I'll pop round tonight before you close to pick up the next batch. I should've done it earlier but Anton, my boyfriend, is back and I got a bit distracted . . .'

'No worries, tonight is perfect. It's good you have your man back. I thought I saw you two on my spycam last night. You must bring him over next Saturday for drinks. We're doing a couples' evening, Bubbles and Browse.' I thank her for the invitation and disconnect.

She saw us last night on her CCTV? Last night I was at Vero's. So unless she was mistaken . . . No, he wouldn't *dare* bring his floozie to my loft. I notice I'm doing ninety and take my foot off the accelerator. No, that's impossible. Heather probably mistook someone else for us, or saw us together in the morning and got her times mixed up. There must be an innocent explanation for this. My phone rings again. It's Sophie and I let it go to voicemail. I know I'd have to tell her about Anton and I simply have no energy to get worked up about it again. Take it easy, said Vero when I was leaving, and that's exactly what I intend to do.

My resolve lasts as far as the Blackwall Tunnel. As I hit the East London traffic on the other side of it, my nerves begin to jangle. Why is this happening to me? The Violinist picture, the Serpens sabotage and the Fugitives, and now Anton's screwing around. What on earth is going on? I haven't had any job offers apart from the sex toys gig and it's beginning to worry me too. It seems that every part of my life has been infected with a malicious virus. I feel I'm slipping into a full-blown panic. I leave my car on a meter off Roman Road and trot to Victoria Park, hoping I won't bump into Sophie and Marcus. I'm sure I'll need Sophie's shoulder to cry on later, but at the moment I have to deal with my shit on my own. I head straight for the Pavilion cafe but it's too crowded, buzzing with mums and kids. Clutching my takeaway cup, I find a secluded bench away from all the noise and sip my latte, planning my next move. Being in the park helps, and by the time I finish my coffee a half-baked plan is beginning to form in my head and I feel calmer.

I even manage to remain calm when I get back to the car and see that someone has scratched it. A long gash of scraped paint along the driver's side door and the front-wheel panel. Well, that's driving in London for you. I'll have to take it to my car mechanic, Elvis (yes, he's alive and he's Croatian). He'll probably say it's not worth fixing. Strangely, the fact that someone's keyed my car has a cathartic effect on my mood. I have probably subconsciously decided that the car damage is the ultimate bad news for today, and as it's already happened, there's no point in continuing to feel anxious.

He's in and he's surprised to see me.

'Hey, I thought you were staying with your aunt a bit longer. How is she?'

'She's fine. She's made of sturdy stuff, Aunt Vero. So I decided to come back early and spend some quality time with you.' I drop my bag on the floor.

'That's great, babe.' It doesn't sound convincing.

He hasn't moved from his computer, so I walk over to him and push the chair round so he's facing me. I straddle him, put my arms round his neck and kiss him hard on the lips. As expected, he responds immediately, kissing me back. He is a good kisser and I'm getting turned on, even though that's not part of the plan. I can also feel his arousal, which is something I've been counting on. I place the palms of my hands on his chest and push him away gently, interrupting our kiss.

'I've been thinking, maybe we could go away for a few days somewhere nice . . . to celebrate you being back?'

He grunts amicably because he doesn't want this to stop.

'How about Spain? Some nice hotel in Madrid . . . perhaps this one?'

I reach to the back pocket of my jeans and pull out his hotel bill. I slap it on his chest. As I get up from his lap, I let my knee graze his crotch. Not too hard but enough for him to wince in pain.

'What's this?' He looks at the bill and I swear I can see him lose colour under his tan.

'I was hoping *you* could tell me what it is.' I'm controlling my anger well, sounding cool and matter-of-fact.

'Where did you find it?' He's up on his feet, reaching for my hand, but I move back. 'It's not what you think. I can explain.'

'Please do.'

I turn my back to him, go to the kitchen counter and switch the kettle on. Let's deal with the whole thing as civilized people would do, over a cup of tea.

'Babe, it's nothing . . . It *meant* nothing . . .'

He is smart enough not to deny it.

'It was a really stupid thing to do . . .' His French accent gets more pronounced when he's nervous.

'You want me to believe it was nothing?'

'It wasn't even a fling! It was just . . . *un coup d'un soir!*'

The kettle has boiled but I don't fancy tea any more.

'For a one-night stand it lasted a long time.' I'm desperately trying to keep my conversational tone up. 'Two nights? Were there any interruptions or did you fuck her non-stop for forty-eight hours?'

'Babe, please, stop.' Anton pulls me towards him but I push him away.

'You cheated on me! And you *lied* to me!' My composure is slipping but there's nothing I can do about it.

'I'm so sorry . . .' He puts his arms round me and holds me tightly.

'Let me go!' I struggle to free myself but he's stronger. I can feel his muscles tensing up as he locks me in his embrace. Bloody hell, and he *dares* to have a hard-on! Fuming, I reach behind with my free arm and grab the first thing off the kitchen counter that comes to hand. With all my strength, I whack him with it on the side of his head. He yelps and releases me. I drop my weapon and it clatters onto the floor. I move away from Anton, who is kneeling down, holding his head in his hands. The object on the floor keeps moving, rattling on the kitchen tiles. It's a big, black, vibrating dildo. My anger gone, I keep watching it doing its strange dance on the floor. I'd find it funny if I didn't feel like crying.

Anton is by the sink, a paper towel by the side of his face. It looks like my blow has managed to split the skin just below his eyebrow. He is actually bleeding. I pick up the dancing dildo, turn it off and put it back on the kitchen counter. I wonder what it was doing there in the first place. I switch the kettle on again, wait for it to boil and make two mugs of tea, a milky one for me and a black, sweet one for Anton. I carry the mugs to the table.

'Come and sit down, we need to talk.'

'I'm bleeding.' There is a hint of reproach in his voice.

'Oh, come on, it's just a scratch. Don't be such a wuss.'

He sits down, the bloody paper towel still pressed to his face.

'I don't know if I'll be able to forgive you, Anton. Not sure I want to.'

'Do you want me to move out?'

I sigh and take a sip of my tea. 'I don't know.'

'I'll go if you want me to.'

As much as I hate him right now, I'm taken aback by his readiness to bow out.

'That's it?'

'What is it that you want me to say?' He scrunches the paper towel and throws it on the table. 'I've done something I shouldn't have. My bad. I said I'm sorry. And I truly am.

But if you can't forgive me, if you can't stand me, then I'm offering to go. I don't *want* to go and I don't want to lose you, but if that's the only solution, then I have no choice. Have I?' He gives me a fierce look and I realize I'm scared he's actually going to get up and leave. The truth is I don't want him to go.

'You can sleep on the sofa.' I get up, praying that this is what he'll choose to do.

I go to the bathroom, lock the door and sit down on the closed loo. I listen out for the sound of the front door being slammed shut but it's quiet.

Meow.

'Pixel!'

I can see his ginger ears sticking out from the ventilation hole above the shower cubicle. How did he manage to get up there again? I coax him out of his hiding place with cat-language sweet nothings and eventually he lets me catch him as he makes a tentative move down.

When Pixel and I emerge from the bathroom, the lights in the loft are dimmed and Anton's gone. A cheat *and* a coward. I feel deflated, hurt and desperately lonely. Despite his faults, Anton is, on many levels, the closest I'll ever get to having a true soulmate. OK, he is self-absorbed and unromantic, but he can be charming, funny and warm. When he focuses on you, he makes the whole world disappear. But what attracted me to him most was his daredevil nature and his insatiable creative drive. That and his smoky, rugged sexiness.

I curl up on the bed and let Pixel knead my pillow for a while with his soft paws until he settles by my side. Well, at least he's remained faithful to me, through thick and thin. It's just you and me, Pix, I think as I hug him closer, taking comfort from his purring.

I'm woken up by a strange sound. I open my eyes, frozen with fear, my heart pounding. It's already light outside. There it is again, a quiet tap as if something hard was hitting glass. Is someone trying to break in? I grab a heavy torch I keep on the floor by the bed, tiptoe barefoot to the door and put my ear to it. Silence. There's no one behind it. But then I hear it again, the weird sound. It's coming from the window. I creep towards it, looking at the building opposite. The Peeping Tom's loft is dark and empty. *Clink!* A small stone hits the glass pane right in front of my face. I crack the window open and cautiously look down.

Anton. He is standing in the middle of the street, his arms spread wide, staring right at me. The cobblestones beneath his feet are sprayed with bold white and red graffiti letters stretching across the whole width of the lane.

I AM AN ASSHOLE. PLEASE FORGIVE ME.

14

I have forgiven him. Not enough to let him straight back into my bed, but sufficiently to share the coffee and crodoughs he's brought from Rinkoff Bakery in Whitechapel. Apparently he waited for them to open at 7 a.m. Their hybrid half-croissants and half-doughnuts are divine. He's brought a selection of flavours, which I nibble on indulgently at the kitchen table, trying all, dismissing those I'm less keen on and gorging myself on those I like. The winner is salted caramel with pistachio.

Anton has turned his charm on and it feels like the good old days. It's amazing how quickly we've slipped back into blissful domesticity. No, it feels better than the usual domestic bliss, because of the undercurrent of sexual tension that happens after a blazing row. I realize I want him but I don't trust him. Isn't that what we feel when we've just met someone new? Is it the lack of trust that works as an aphrodisiac?

'Kristin?'

'Mmm?' Licking the icing off my fingers, I throw him a glance.

He hesitates, looking apprehensive all of a sudden.

'What is it?' I'm instantly on my guard, the feeling of blissful togetherness gone in a flash. *Please don't tell me you've had more affairs.*

'Kristin.' He approaches and reaches out for my hand. I instinctively pull it away.

'Give me your hand.' He seems dead serious. What the hell does he want?

'It's all sticky.'

'It doesn't matter.'

He drops to his knees in front of me.

'Kristin Ryder, will you marry me?'

I stare at him, wide-eyed, disbelieving my ears. Is this a joke?

'Will you marry me?' He says it with such intensity I feel my disbelief evaporate. *I'll be damned, he means it!*

'Well . . . yes . . .' I mumble.

He grabs my hand and pushes a ring on my finger. It's made out of thin silver wire, interwoven in so many layers it's surprisingly heavy and thick.

'It's the best I could do . . . at such short notice . . .'

'Short notice?'

'I made it last night.'

'You *made* it?'

'I crashed at Doyle's place last night.' Ah, Doyle, his Australian mate with a workshop at the Rag Factory. 'I really wanted to *make* something for you . . . and I found this reel of wire lying about . . .'

Trust Anton's ability to make everything sound so unromantic.

'So you haven't actually been planning to propose . . .'

'No . . . yes . . .' He gets up from his knees and wipes his face with his hands in exasperation. 'Look, babe, I know I'm a selfish bastard. I don't do the lovey-dovey stuff. I disappoint you. I know you deserve better. But I want to *be* with you. Give me a chance. I'll try to change. We've got so much going for us – don't throw it away . . .'

There are tears in his eyes. Despite myself, I'm beginning to well up.

'I love you, babe.'

I know he means it. And I know how much I *want* him to mean it.

'I love you too.' Big fat tears are rolling down my cheeks now.

He whisks me from my chair and locks me in his bear embrace. He smells of a sleepless night in a damp workshop and there is nothing I have ever found sexier than this.

He carries me to the bed and throws me onto it, scaring Pixel who jumps out from under the duvet with a hiss. Shall I let him do what he's evidently planning to do? Despite his proposal and our mutual declaration of love, part of me still wants to punish him, disgusted with his infidelity. This should not be happening. Or rather, this should not be happening *yet*. But my resolve weakens as he pulls down my Uniqlo track bottoms and starts kissing the inside of my thighs, his stubble brushing the delicate skin, making it tingle. He knows what he's doing. I'm annoyed with myself for being unable to resist him. And then it's too late to try to stop him.

'Have you had any more of those dodgy emails?' Anton lights a post-coital cigarette and inhales deeply.

'No, thank God, not since the bare arse one . . .'

He shakes his head and I can see he's making an effort not to tell me again that 'In Bed With Anton' shouldn't have happened.

'Do you have any idea who might have sent it?' he asks instead.

'No.'

'Any weirdos giving you grief lately?'

'No . . . well, there's Peeping Tom but he's harmless, I think.'

'Who?'

'The neighbour opposite.' I gesture at the window. 'I call him Peeping Tom because he stares at me sometimes . . .'

'What . . . ogles you and wanks off?'

'No, no, I don't think so . . . He just stares . . .'

Anton gets up from the bed and swaggers naked to the window. He has a beautiful body, I think as he looks at the dark and empty loft opposite, his shoulders squared aggressively. I know this pose well. I call it Anton the Protector.

'Let me know if he does it again, yeah?'

'OK, hon.'

He goes to the kitchen table and picks up another crodough, a raspberry one.

'The Fugitives Gallery have offered me a solo exhibition space next month. For two weeks it'll be totally mine.' Anton takes a bite of the sweet pastry and I feel a stab of envy.

Come on, bitch, I think to myself, he really deserves it and you should be pleased for him. He is your fiancé, for God's sake. *Fiancé* – I bounce the word around in my head, trying to get used to its implications.

I *am* pleased, really, but a tiny part of me feels sidelined, forgotten. Is success ever going to come to *me*? Or is my role always going to be waiting in the wings, clapping for someone else? It felt like this with Erin after the fiasco of Cubic Zirconia, when I watched her come into her own, become confident and then famous. I didn't mind it much then – perhaps I was secretly hoping it would eventually happen to me as well. With Anton it's more painful because I'm more aware of my limitations. Am I destined to become Mrs Anton Sauvage? The artist's *wife*? Yes, Professor Stein, mediocrity. I've become a plodder with no chance of success. I'm also peeved that Anna from the Fugitives kept the news to herself when I saw her at the gallery. She must've known then that she'd offer the space to Anton. But why should she tell me about it? Is envy making me unreasonable?

As if to test my generosity of spirit, Anton goes on, chewing on the crodough.

'And guess what? This woman emailed me yesterday, from some architects' company that has been commissioned to develop an urban design study for the King's Cross something-or-other partnership, basically the guys who are in charge of the whole regeneration project at King's Cross. They deal specifically with the area adjacent to the railtracks, you know, all those new buildings you can see from the Eurostar trains as you come into St Pancras.'

I nod as he pauses for effect.

'They want me to do this big-ass mural on the *whole* side of their main building!'

'Wow!' It does seem impressive, even through the fog of envy.

'We're talking a seven-storey construction!'

'They want you to do a paste-up?' Paste-ups, made of paper and stuck to a wall with wheat-paste glue, are by their nature very ephemeral, sometimes lasting just a few days, especially in English weather.

'No, here's the best part. They've offered to work with me

on developing a new medium that will be more durable, some-thing semi-permanent.'

'That's fantastic, babe.' For as long as I've known him, Anton's been tirelessly experimenting with different types of glue, vinyl, PVC, even Perspex, only to be defeated by the elements or human hand each time.

'We're going to be famous, babe!'

Anton's enthusiasm and joy are so infectious, I reluctantly let go of my green-eyed monster. He did say 'we', after all.

It's eleven by the time we're eventually up. Anton dashes off to yet another of his meetings and I go down to Discreet. Heather's in her office but she's busy with a customer, her pink-haired assistant informs me. I wait for her in the shop, browsing. By the looks of it, there's still plenty of stock left to be photo-graphed. As I contemplate the toys, the Mapplethorpe idea starts to niggle again. Perhaps I should persevere with it after all.

A red-faced and bald-headed man in a suit storms out of Heather's office, heading straight for the door. The Pink Girl and I watch him, startled. Once he's gone, Heather appears in the shop, calm and composed.

'What was that about?' we ask in unison.

Heather shrugs. 'A disappointed slave.' She sees my perplexed expression and goes on. 'The guy was looking lost and when I offered help he said his "lady" had sent him to get a special toy for her. He couldn't make up his mind so he asked me to call her for him. It turns out his "lady" is an S&M mistress and next thing she wants is for me to "discipline" her boy for her.'

'And did you?'

She looks at me, her eyes round and innocent. 'We don't

offer that service.' She keeps her face straight. 'That's what I told her and she put the phone down on me. However, I did invite her hapless slave, as politely as I could, to our bondage workshop.'

The Pink Girl lets out a giggle and Heather and I join in.

'You get all sorts in this business.' Heather checks her make-up in the ornate cheval mirror by the door. 'Kristin, I have the next batch of toys for you in my office.'

The box waiting for me by her desk is even bigger than the first one. Heather insists on paying me 'an advance' as she calls it and we agree I'll send her my first invoice today.

'How is your man? Anton, is it?'

'A rascal, as always.'

'Aren't they all?' Heather shakes her head, smiling. 'But we still love 'em.'

'He proposed this morning.' I touch the ring on my finger as if to check the whole thing wasn't a figment of my imagination.

'And did you say "yes"?'

'I did . . . At least I think I did.'

'You don't sound very convinced!'

'It all came out of the blue, really . . .'

'Do you want to get hitched?'

'I do!' My sudden certainty takes me by surprise.

'Congratulations, then!'

'Thank you.' I'm unable to contain a happy grin.

I dash back to the loft, spurred on by a buzz of creative energy. I unpack the box and look through the toys. Then I go to my Mac, find Professor Stein's email and click 'Reply'.

Dear Professor Stein,
I was surprised and delighted in equal measure to receive your email.

I am currently working on a photographic project entitled Macro Perceptions. Its aim is to decontextualize everyday objects in extreme close-up. By relinquishing their original meaning, I want to achieve freedom to appreciate them from a purely aesthetic perspective. I aim to demonstrate that once we swap meaning for feeling, we are able to achieve unadulterated, true perception.

I would be delighted for Macro Perceptions to become part of your Light Vault project and will submit a sample of my work for your consideration shortly.
Kind regards,
Kristin Ryder

I read through the email and smile at the slightly pompous style I've always adopted in my communications with the professor. It takes me back to my student days. But I hope it's sufficiently enigmatic and highbrow to pique the old codger's interest.

I pick up my phone and dial Sophie's number. It goes straight to voicemail and I decide not to leave her a message. Instead, I text her.

I said YES!

Let's see if she gets it. I call Vero next and she answers on the first ring.

'Anton proposed to me!'

'Wow! You guys move fast! Wasn't he unfaithful to you last time we spoke?'

'Yes, and that was part of the reason . . . No, let me rephrase it . . . It has forced us to be really honest with each other and we both realized we want to be together. He said he'll change and I believe him.'

'You do . . .'

'Yes. You should've seen him . . . He brought me doughnuts and he *made* me a ring.'

'As long as it makes you happy.'

'It does, Vero, it really does.'

'Then I'm really happy for you.'

I promise to come and visit her with Anton soon, and then disconnect, feeling slightly annoyed by her underwhelmed response. But she did say she was happy for me . . .

My phone buzzes with a new message. I open it, expecting Sophie's reply to my text. It's from Anton.

LET'S GET MARRIED IN DUBROVNIK!

Dubrovnik? Why not Dubrovnik?

Hell yeah

I text back, my heart fluttering with excitement.

And now it's time to do some work. I check the lighting stage and all the lights, put a new memory card in the camera and reach for the first Plaything. It happens to be a black leather spanking crop, stylish-looking but not the most photogenic of objects. I adjust the lighting to make sure there are no unsightly shadows or reflections and snap a few pictures. I'll correct anything I've missed in Photoshop. The next Plaything is much more interesting. In fact, it's a thing of beauty. It's a cat-o-nine-tails whip with a heavy handle, which I suspect is silver-plated, and nine elegant braided leather tails. Each of the thin tails is crowned with a delicate white suede petal. It brings to mind a Mapplethorpe flower. Yes, there it is, in the album I grab from the bookshelf, the photograph of the calla lily, with its sturdy, masculine stalk and the exquisite waxy white head. Whoever made the whip was a true artist. I lovingly position it on the dark background and light it sparingly, bringing out just a few essential details. It responds to the camera lens like a sexy model. Light Vault, here I come!

I break for a late lunch and check my emails. No answer from the professor, yet. But the Russian beauty Irina still wants to be friends and the online supply of Vicodin and Viagra seems to be boundless. I'm just about to go back to my shoot when a new email pops up in the inbox. As soon as my brain registers its title, I'm hit by an instant wave of cold sweat. On an impulse I click 'Delete', get up from the computer and go to the window. I look at the sun-drenched view and take a few deep breaths. There's nothing that calms your nerves better than the exhaust-fumes-heavy hot London air. Eventually I force myself to go back to the Mac. I pick up the stylus I use instead of a mouse and drag it along the tablet until the cursor hovers above the 'Trash' mailbox. Tap. And there it is, sitting at the very top of a long list of deleted emails. 'Exposure 3'.

15

The attachment is a movie this time, an innocuous-looking MPEG waiting to be clicked on. Could it contain a virus that will wreak havoc in my computer? Well, my antivirus software is scanning it and, having utilized the knowledge collated from 230 million devices protected worldwide that act as its sensors and are updated every six minutes, declares it safe. So, I click on it and let it play.

At first I'm confused, because what I'm seeing seems familiar. It's a mirror – not any old mirror but Aunt Stella's pride and joy, a huge art deco fan-shaped mirror, with its large central panel and six slimmer, bevelled ones, three on each side. I pause the movie, turn away from the computer screen and there it is, right behind me, hanging on the main wall of the loft, facing the windows. Someone has filmed *my* mirror in *my* house. As the initial shock subsides, it dawns on me it was done through the webcam of my Mac. I quickly turn back and look at the tiny pinhole eye above the computer screen. It's dark and probably no one is looking at me right now, but on an impulse I grab a roll of gaffer tape from the desk, cut a small piece off and stick it over the webcam eye. I smooth the unsightly piece of tape over the glass surface of the screen, noticing that my hands are shaking.

I go back to the movie and click 'Play' again. As my eyes become accustomed to the images, I realize I'm seeing a series of reflections within reflections, a sort of visual layer cake. The first, top layer of the cake is the mirror. But then there is something in it. The mirror reflects the loft's windows and the view behind them. I zoom into the picture and, although it gets more pixelated, it also gives me more detail. A dark silhouette in the loft opposite. The Peeping bloody Tom! I throw the stylus on the desk and get up. I don't believe it! Someone has sent me a movie of *my own* loft, with *my own* stalker staring at it. Is it him? What is he playing at? I move to the window and look out. The loft opposite is dark and empty, of course. Wait until I set Anton on you, you gutless freak. But as the sudden wave of anger passes, doubt creeps in. What if it wasn't Peeping Tom who sent me the video?

I go back to the computer and play the movie from the beginning again, putting my face close to the screen, looking out for details, anything that would solve its mystery. And there it is, some movement, reflected in the side panels of the mirror that are bevelled at a different angle to the main one. As my eyes begin to make sense of the fragmented images, my mind refuses to accept it. Multiplied by three and reflected by the side panels on the mirror's right, there is an image of someone's naked back, moving rhythmically. Anton, and there is no doubt what he's doing. Someone has filmed us having sex. Oh God. I let the movie play on, unable to take my eyes off it. Subconsciously, I register a jump in the continuity, as if something has been edited out. A new image appears. Yes, it's Anton all right but now he's leaning over the edge of the bed, his naked body truncated by the mirror's angled panels. There is a blur of movement and it takes me a while to realize that the person standing behind him isn't me. The woman, who has her back turned to the mirror, is naked except for a few straps criss-crossing her buttocks. As she turns sideways it becomes clear she's wearing a strap-on harness. I can just about make out the shape of a small dildo as she leans over Anton's bare back. And then the image fades to black. Frozen with shock, I stare at the blank screen.

It seems that eons have passed until I'm capable of any action again. I get up from the computer chair, go to the fridge, get a bottle of Absolut from the freezer and pour some into a mug. I swallow a few mouthfuls, until the burning sensation in my throat takes my breath away. Gasping, I slide down along the side of the fridge to the floor. I should be upset, I should be angry, but I'm just numb. And then I'm numb *and* drunk. The vodka hasn't helped. Instead of the usual fuzzy euphoria, I'm overwhelmed by heavy sadness. So this is how it feels to be totally and utterly betrayed. Not only did Anton cheat on me but also he's shown a side I wasn't even aware existed. I have just watched a man I thought I knew engaged in behaviour that is so out of character for him it seems unimaginable. Yes, we experiment a bit but Anton has always presented himself as a straightforward and uncomplicated lover. Passionate – yes. Kinky – hardly ever. Anal intercourse, either way, is certainly something that has never entered our sexual vocabulary and it suited us both. That is, I *assumed* it did.

I get up from the floor and shuffle back to my computer. I plop heavily onto the chair and watch the screen saver tirelessly hurtling through wormholes and starbursts. The smooth and monotonous transitions on the screen are all I can handle at the moment. I don't want to see anything else. After a while the screen goes dark and I still stare at it as the unwanted images from 'Exposure 3' begin to replay in my head. I'm reeling but I don't know what has shocked me more: the fact that Anton has cheated on me in my own bed or the fact I've just said 'yes' to him, that I've entertained the notion of being married to him. And then there is another layer to all this: the movie. I realize its very existence disturbs me even more than its contents. Why is someone doing this to me? And who is it? Anton? As it turns out, I don't know him at all, but judging by the grief he's given me over 'In Bed With Anton', the idea of him filming himself in such a compromising situation is totally implausible. He wouldn't send the video to me. Not now, anyway, not a few hours after proposing to me. Unless he's a complete freak, a sadistic psycho taking pleasure in making me suffer. No, not Anton. He might be an irresponsible idiot, but he's not a freak. What about the woman? Is she the *bombón* from Madrid? What is she doing in London? Has Anton been so infatuated with her he was prepared to break the cardinal rule of our relationship and bring her here? Some knocking shop in Madrid is bad enough, but *my* bed, in *my* house? Fucking idiot. I stomp back to the fridge, get the bottle of Absolut out again and take a swig straight from it. And another one. In a flash of drunken clarity, I suddenly know why seeing the woman in the video has disturbed me so much. She looks just like me.

I go back to the computer and, gritting my teeth, I play the video again. Anton's naked back, pumping away, and the shadow of a woman underneath him. Dark hair, slim body, nothing distinctive. Cut. In the second part she's behind him, much more discernible. Her face is turned away from the camera, but the way she moves seems familiar. Who the hell is it? The video stops on the last frame of black and I keep staring at it until the screen saver kicks in again.

What if she isn't just an accidental bit of fluff picked up on a trip abroad? What if Anton has been having a long-term affair right under my nose? What if he's known her for months, even years? What if she *pre-dates* me? No, it's impossible, I would have noticed something. Would I really? I'm beginning to doubt everything I know about Anton. Why has he proposed to me? My mind keeps relentlessly throwing up new scenarios. She could be a prostitute. Maybe he's addicted to sex with strangers. I jump up from the chair and go to Anton's computer bag lying on the floor by the door. I unzip it and pull his battered laptop out. It's locked with a password but I decide to try my luck. I may not know this man's sexual habits but I do know the name of his first dog. *Corto.* Wrong password. I let my finger hover above the mouse pad, trying to remember what he told me about the dog. It was a cute Maltese, named after his favourite comic book about a rogue sea captain with a heart of gold. *CortoMaltese.* Wrong again. *MalteseCorto.* Nope. So much for my hacking attempt. I put his laptop back in its bag and return to my desk.

I click on the 'Exposure 3' MPEG and let it play again. And again. I keep clicking the 'Play' icon, driven by an irrepressible compulsion. I don't want to watch it but I'm unable to stop. And there it is, for the umpteenth time, Anton fucking the stranger and then the stranger fucking him. I stare at the woman wearing the strap-on, her body multiplied by the mirror's panels, moving confidently, without a shade of inhibition. She's done it before, this is not some improvised escapade into the unknown. She must've come prepared or . . . A wave of nausea rises in my throat as I look at the box of Discreet Playthingz standing by my desk. No, they wouldn't dare. And then again, why not? They didn't seem to have any problem with crossing the other lines. I open the box and focus on its contents. There is nothing in it that would set alarm bells ringing. Then I remember the rest of the toys, scattered around my lighting stage. One of them stands out immediately: a slim, silicone baby-blue dildo with a leather strap-on harness. If I remember correctly, it came as part of a 'Pegging Kit' that also contained some lubricant, which seems to be missing now. I go to the bathroom, put on a pair of yellow Marigold gloves I use for cleaning the toilet and return to the stage. The kit goes straight into a black rubbish bag and I scrub the Perspex and all the surrounding areas with a disinfectant spray. I'll worry about how to explain the missing Plaything to Heather later. I can always pay for it, no big deal, I'm sure it wasn't a prototype. Next I strip the bed and stuff the bedding into the washing machine, setting it on the 'Heavy Stains' 90°C cycle. It'll probably ruin the delicate Egyptian cotton percale but I don't care. I throw all the bath towels in as well and turn the machine on. I scrub the gloves with an antibacterial hand-wash and return them to the bathroom. I know my 'blitzing the crime scene' borders on OCD, but when I go back to my computer, I'm surprisingly energized by the cleansing outburst. The feeling of elation dissipates as soon as I hear the key in the front-door lock. Anton is back.

'Wow, it smells clean in here. Clinical.' He wrinkles his nose.

I don't reply, watching him curiously. The man who has just walked into my loft, the man I've spent the last seven years of my life with, the man who could've been my husband, is a total stranger.

'What's up?' He notices my inquisitive look.

'This.' I point at my computer screen. I've decided I won't try to elicit some 'guilty' response from him. I have no energy for playing emotional games. I want this thing over in the shortest possible time.

He comes to my desk and leans over, looking at the screen. His smell hits me, the usual mixture of cigarette smoke, sweat and aftershave. Normally it turns me on; now I find it repulsive. I swallow hard to contain my growing nausea as I click the 'Play' icon. He watches the video and I can tell he's not seeing what I want him to see, just as I didn't see it when I looked at it for the first time.

'What about it?' He shrugs.

'Have another look.' I play it from the beginning.

This time he notices the Peeping Tom, just as I did.

'That wanker! I'm gonna break his fucking neck!' Anton straightens, ready to deliver his threat immediately.

'Wait!' I raise my voice and he looks at me, surprised. 'Watch it again.'

'I've seen enough.'

'No, you haven't.'

He lets his breath out in irritation but looks at the screen. As the video plays out again, I feel his body tense up. He's seen it this time.

'Fuck!' He walks away and stops by the window, his back to me.

The video fades to black.

'I want you to move out right now,' I say quietly.

'Babe, let me explain.' He turns to face me.

'I don't want to hear any more of your lies.'

'Babe, please . . .' He takes a few steps towards me.

'Don't! Don't come near me.'

'This is . . . this is all so fucked up . . .'

'You can say that again.' I feel anger and resentment bubbling inside me.

'I . . . I don't want to lose you—' His voice cracks with emotion.

I let out a bitter chuckle.

'Kristin, please . . .'

He drops to his knees in front of me, silently pleading. There are tears in his eyes. I slip his ring off and put it on the table next to the Mac's keyboard.

'Kristin . . .' He reaches out for my hand.

I get up from the chair to get away from him. I go to the window and look at the dark loft opposite.

'I'm going out this afternoon for a few hours. When I get back I don't want to find you or any of your things here. I don't want to see you ever again.' I'm shocked by the harshness of my own words. Anton stares at me, speechless. Dismay in his eyes slowly turns into rage. He gets up from his knees with a furious grunt and, for a split second, I'm afraid he's going to hit me. And then he's out of the door, stomping down the stairs. I realize I've been holding my breath and I let it out slowly.

The door downstairs bangs loudly and I can see Anton crossing the cobbled street. He's heading straight for the Peeping Tom's building. He presses all the buttons on the entryphone, then starts kicking the door, shouting something I don't quite catch. His ranting goes on until the door cracks open and he throws himself at it, ramming it with his shoulder. He pulls someone outside – a short, skinny man who is trying to block his way in – punches him in the face and disappears inside the building. The man reels back but doesn't fall. Heather's turquoise head appears in the Discreet entrance. She says something, pointing at the shop, but the man waves her away and pulls a mobile phone out of his pocket.

It takes the police three or four minutes to arrive. Two officers in black vests talk to the man, then enter the building. What a mess. He's going to get himself arrested. I realize my legs are shaking but I continue to lean on the windowsill, unable to tear myself away from the drama downstairs. It feels as if hours have passed before the policemen appear back in the street. They are leading Anton away between them and I think he might be handcuffed. Good grief, what has he done? Just as he's about to be bundled into the back seat of the police car, he looks up at my windows. I instinctively step back, hiding from view. I don't want him to see me now. I don't want him to know that I still care.

I look around the loft. It suddenly feels empty, almost uninhabited, as if its soul has been taken out. Come on, get a grip, nothing has changed except you're single again. You survived it before and you'll survive it now. I reach for my phone, thinking of calling Sophie, then change my mind. I feel a fool texting her about saying 'yes' earlier. I don't think I could bear spilling my guts right into Soph's and Marcus's cosy coupledom at the moment. Perhaps I could ring Erin? Nah, she's probably busy jet-setting, doesn't have time for yet another misery saga from a loser like me. I'll call Vero later I decide, as I pick up Anton's rucksack from the floor and throw some of his clothes into it. In a stash of flattened cardboard packs behind the wardrobe, I find a big box and fill it with his street-art gear, packets of wheat-paste glue, brushes, bits of sandpaper, spray cans and paint-stiffened rags. In one big swipe, I gather all his stuff from the bathroom, then put the box together with his rucksack by the front door next to his computer bag. On top of the pile lands the black rubbish bag with the strap-on. There, all done. Of course, there are more of his things strewn all over the loft but putting his essentials by the door feels cathartic. He can look for the rest himself when I'm not here.

16

Where do you go to lick your wounds in a big city? How do you get away from it all? I usually do one of three things: pick a random film show, look for a cemetery or head for water. Cinemas are good, especially on Mondays and in the afternoons, when only sad souls with too much time on their hands are willing to spend two hours in the dark. The Rio in Dalston and the Hackney Picturehouse are the obvious choices but it's too hot and bright today to even consider a stint in a dungeon. The weather is conspiring against me: it should be a miserable, drizzly day that would enhance my gloomy mood. Instead the glorious afternoon sunshine is asserting life and vitality, nudging me to keep going.

A cemetery would be a fitting choice but the thought of schlepping all the way to my favourite Abney Park in this heat is off-putting. There is, of course, Bunhill Fields close by but that would mean negotiating the Old Street roundabout night-mare. I might as well choose water. I stride across Shoreditch Park, along Bridport Place, past Rosemary Works on the corner, until I reach the entrance to the Regent's Canal towpath. Left towards Victoria Park or right towards Islington? Islington wins, tempting me with the promise of a glass of chilled white wine at the Narrow Boat pub. I march along the water's edge, jumping out of the way of mean-machine cyclists, inhaling the smoke of disposable barbecue sets and trying to fall in step with the beats of some jazzy tune emanating from one of the moored boats. Sturt's Lock is heaving with couples picnicking on the hot concrete, their pale-skinned backs turned greedily to the sun, bottles of cheap rosé and cans of lager cooking in the heat. Coming here was a mistake. But the thought of that chilled wine keeps me going.

Predictably, the Narrow Boat is packed. I manage to elbow my way to the bar and order a large glass of unoaked Chardonnay. I slip the change from a tenner into my pocket and shuffle outside, holding the precious glass as if it were the Olympic torch. I spot a place on a bench further on, just before the bridge, and hurry towards it, overtaking a couple of hipsters who are heading that way as well. And next I'm flying in the air, desperately trying to hold on to my glass. I hit the ground with a yelp, my cheek grazing the concrete, the filthy water of the canal suddenly close to my face. Someone shouts behind me, someone else screams in the distance and then I can feel myself being hoisted up.

'Are you all right?'

One of the hipsters I was racing a moment ago is gently touching my shoulder, propping me up.

'I think so . . .'

'He didn't even stop!' The other hipster is shaking his head, outraged.

'Would you like to sit down?'

They are leading me back towards the pub where a small crowd is staring in our direction. Someone brings out a chair and I'm being parked on it like a broken doll.

'You're bleeding . . .' Hipster One rushes into the pub, while

Two stays with me, hovering protectively as if he's expecting me to keel over.

I look down at my knees. Indeed, the left one is a mess.

'That bastard just rammed into you and pedalled away as if nothing happened!'

'I didn't even see him coming . . .'

'He was tearing down the towpath like a maniac. All Lycra-wrapped, flashy helmet, Oakley sunglasses and one of those Respro face masks that make you look like Hannibal Lecter. Obviously thinks that "Share the Space, Drop the Pace" doesn't apply to him. You know, the "entitled" kind' – he makes quotation marks in the air.

'I was actually trying to race you to that bench over there. Oh, my wine . . .' I remember the expensive glass of Chardonnay. 'I've lost my wine.'

'It went flying into the canal. Don't worry, we'll get you another one. What are you drinking?'

Rupert and Daniel, for these are the names of my hipster rescue duo, turn out to be delightful companions. While Rupert tends to my grazed knee, Daniel plies me with white wine. Rupert is a graphic designer and Daniel works for a cyber security company. They have just moved into one of the Grand Canal Apartments.

'We absolutely love it. Dark wood flooring, semi open-plan kitchen, two luxury bathrooms and of course a *private* balcony overlooking the canal. This has always been our dream . . .'

Before I know it, we're opening a bottle of Prosecco at R&D's canal-view apartment and I'm getting acquainted with their pet, Matilda. Matilda is a two-foot-long African *Python regius*, otherwise known as a ball python, the name reflecting its penchant for curling into a ball when stressed or frightened, a habit I can relate to totally. She isn't any old ball python, Daniel explains, she is a *granite* ball python, which means her skin is black with beautiful golden linear markings along her back and an intricate dorsal pattern that resembles ancient hieroglyphic writings. I'm told her belly is equally stunning, white with scattered black dots, but I have to take Daniel's word for it because Matilda is asleep, coiled into a perfect ball, inside her designer vivarium with a thermostat-controlled heating pad under it, and is not to be disturbed.

'Cleopatra used to wear a ball python just like Matilda round her wrist as a bracelet.' Rupert sounds like a proud father of a particularly gifted child and I know he expects me to be impressed.

Our conversation smoothly transitions from snakes to ex-boyfriends and I find myself telling them the story of my very short engagement and break-up with Anton.

'You're probably much better off without him, honey,' declares Rupert, the one with oversized glasses and a sleeve tattoo of a Hokusai-style wave.

'Come on, give her a break, the girl is still in mourning. We need to support her, offer sympathy . . .' Daniel is smaller and hairier, with a bushy beard and a discreet septum piercing.

Their light-hearted banter does help a bit, and when I'm leaving their place a few hours later, I'm melancholy drunk. They insist on walking me back all the way to Hoxton, and having delivered me to my front door, go on for a pint at the George & Dragon in Hackney Road. But by the time I climb the stairs and unlock my door, my heart is pounding. Will he be waiting for me or is he gone?

The loft is dark and I'm greeted by Pixel, who sniffs at my bandaged knee and does his tail-twitching dance around his empty bowl. I turn the light on and dish out his food. The pile of Anton's things I've left by the door is gone. His set of keys is lying on the kitchen counter next to a rotting apple. How symbolic.

17

The sunshine is too bright and it's already too hot when I wake up, regretting last night's alcoholic binge. I lie in bed staring at the ceiling, trying to make sense of yesterday's events. I feel devastated by Anton's betrayal and I know it wouldn't hurt so much if I hadn't let my guard down with his stupid proposal. I can't believe I actually allowed myself to imagine our future together. Silly, silly me. Then I remember 'Exposure 3' and my life seems even worse. I drag myself out of bed and spend the next half hour in the shower. My bruised knee is swollen and it stings under the stream of hot water. And there is a red patch on my face where I grazed it against the pavement. I tend to my battered body, wishing it was equally easy to fix a soul.

Anton's things are gone, which means he was released by the police almost immediately, probably without charge, and had enough time to come here and gather his stuff before I got back from my drunken evening with Rupert and Daniel. The thought of my new hipster friends cheers me up a little. Meeting them was the only good thing that has come out of yesterday. The 'Exposure 3' day. My mind seems to be going round in circles, relentlessly going back to the same two questions: who is doing it and why? I can't shake off the feeling that someone's watching me. Am I being paranoid?

By the time I get out of the shower, there are a couple of texts, a message from Sophie and two missed calls from a number I don't recognize on my phone. Sophie's message is ecstatic, congratulating me on my engagement. I'll have to bite the bullet and ring her today. I'm not looking forward to telling her about the break-up with Anton. Not that she ever gets on the 'I told you so' high horse. But admitting yet another defeat in my personal life to someone who seems to have got it right a long time ago is never much fun. She's always been supportive and understanding but I know that deep down she doubts my ability to sustain lasting relationships. I check the texts. An automated one about my bill being 'ready to view' and a short one from Jason:

Please call me.

His timing is uncanny. It's as if he somehow got wind of my break-up. But maybe I'm reading too much into it. I delete his message anyway. I won't be calling him back straight away.

A new email catches my eye when I sit down at the computer.

Dear Kristin,
Lovely to hear from you.
I would like to find out more about your Macro Perceptions.
Please come to see me at the Light Vault Gallery in Leonard Street EC2A. I'm there every day this week 10 am–5 pm.
Yours,
Robert B. Stein

Short and sweet. He doesn't seem overly excited about my project but hasn't said 'no' either. Not yet, anyway. Macro Perceptions moves to the top of my 'to do' list for this week. I'll need something to show Professor Stein when I go to see him at the gallery. But first things first. Playthingz. I have to have the next batch of photographs ready when I call Heather tomorrow morning. I force myself to set up the lights and start shooting.

I find the physicality of the shoot cathartic. It makes me concentrate on the technical details, blocking all the other thoughts out. By midday I'm done with most of the strap-ons, minus the one that ended up in the rubbish bag, and move on to bondage Playthingz. Collars and leads prove a bit of a challenge; how do you photograph a loop and a piece of string? I briefly consider using a wire-frame vintage mannequin I keep in storage, but decide against it. It doesn't have arms so it wouldn't solve the problem of displaying handcuffs.

I'm arranging a bondage set on the lighting stage, when the piercing sound of the entryphone buzzer interrupts me. Annoyed, I pick up the receiver. A male voice introduces himself as 'the police' and asks if he can come up. The police? On a Sunday? Whatever next? I hesitate briefly, then buzz him in. I hope it's not some stupid prank. I go to the door and look through the peephole. After a while two figures appear in the fisheye lens. One of them, the taller one, is wearing a police uniform. Let's give them the benefit of the doubt, I think, as I unlock the door and crack it open.

'Miss Ryder?' The guy who does the talking has three down-pointed chevrons on his epaulettes and introduces himself as 'Sergeant Graves'. He does have a grave aura about him. A plain-clothes woman who accompanies him, petite and friendly-looking, is apparently PC Singh. They are both keen to get inside and I open the door wider for them. They do seem genuine.

I point to the kitchen table, realizing I'm waving a pair of pink leather cuffs with fluffy lining.

'I'm in the middle of a photo shoot,' I say, aware of how ridiculous it may sound. But Sergeant Graves and PC Singh don't look amused as we all settle at the table.

'From what we understand, this is the address for Mr Anthony Sauvage.' Sergeant Graves pronounces his name 'savage'.

'Yes, *Anton Sauvage*. What has he done now?'

'And you are his . . . partner?'

'Well, *ex*-partner. As of yesterday.'

Sergeant Graves nods solemnly and I'm annoyed by his stiff manner.

'What is it about? The fight yesterday?'

'I'm afraid there's been an accident.'

'Oh God, has he hurt someone? Hot-headed idiot . . .'

'Miss Ryder . . .' Sergeant Graves clears his throat. 'I'm very sorry to say Mr Sauvage is dead.'

I stare at him, uncomprehending.

'What do you mean *dead*?'

I search for a flicker of a smile, some sign that this is some kind of horrible joke, but his features are set, his eyes stern.

'He *can't* be dead.' I look at the woman. 'Not Anton. You must be mistaken.'

'I'm afraid it's true,' she says quietly.

'But he was here yesterday . . . He *proposed* to me . . . We were supposed to get married. In Dubrovnik. He made me a ring—'

The woman shakes her head. 'I'm so sorry.'

'No, wait, who are you again? Can I see your ID?'

They glance at each other and then the woman pulls a warrant card out of her bag and puts it on the table without a word. I look at it, then push it back towards her.

'This doesn't prove anything.'

'He died at 7 a.m. this morning,' says Sergeant Graves quietly.

'No, no, no, you've got it all wrong. Anton doesn't even get up that early. How did you find me anyway?'

'He had his identification on him. With this address. And we found your name.'

'Maybe it's someone else. Maybe his wallet got stolen . . .'

'I'm afraid it is Mr Sauvage.'

'How can you be so sure? How can you fucking sit at *my* table so flippantly certain . . . ? How can you do this to me . . . ?'

They say nothing, just stare at me, two quiet harbingers of doom. Their sad determination erodes my denial.

'Oh God . . .'

'Would you like me to make you a cup of tea?' the policewoman pipes up and it sounds as if she's miles away. The surface of the table in front of me is swaying and I drop my hands palms down, trying to steady it.

'Take a few deep breaths, love.' The policewoman is suddenly beside me, touching my shoulder. I try to do what she tells me but there is no air in the loft. Everything around me goes very dark.

'I'd like you to put your head between your legs for me.' She is gently pushing me and I lean forward. Gradually my vision comes back and I'm able to breathe. I straighten myself in the chair. There is a mug of tea on the table right in front of me.

'How . . . What happened?'

'He fell from the fifth floor of a building in King's Cross.'

'King's Cross? I don't understand.'

'It appears he fell through a guard rail in the peripheral safety barrier. The building is under construction and there are safety panels on all the floors instead of external walls and windows.'

'What was he doing there?'

'We're still establishing all the facts, checking the CCTV footage, interviewing the site security staff . . . The thing is, it's a restricted access area and he shouldn't have been there at all.'

No, I think, he should've been home with me. I pick up the mug and notice my hands are shaking.

'Is it OK if I ask you a few questions?'

I nod, swallowing a sip of tea. It's hot, milky and very sweet.

'Is there any family . . . apart from you, that is?'

'He has a brother, Lionel.'

'Do you have his contact details?'

'No. I know he lives in New York. But I haven't met him.'

Sergeant Graves scribbles something in his little notebook, then looks up at me.

'Would you mind telling me what happened yesterday? You mentioned a fight . . .'

'Oh, that. It was nothing – I mean, it was silly. He got annoyed at someone in the building opposite. Tried to speak to the guy and lost his temper . . . Your colleagues picked him up.'

How come he doesn't know about it? I throw Sergeant Graves a suspicious glance but he doesn't seem to notice.

'Did he use to lose his temper a lot?'

'Why do you ask?' I don't like his tone.

He clears his throat again. 'You said he was your ex-partner. May I ask what happened between you?'

The question hits me right in the stomach. My hand automatically goes up to the bruise on my cheek. I force it down, trying to regain composure.

'We got engaged . . . and . . . and then we split up. And he moved out.'

'Right.'

'Is that why he's dead? Tell me! Is that what you think? That he's dead because I kicked him out?' I'm shaking and I know I sound hysterical.

'There, love.' PC Singh puts her hand gently on my shoulder. 'It's all right.'

'No, it *isn't!*' I push her hand off and get up. 'It's *my fault*, isn't it?'

I go to the window and put my forehead against the cool glass. I close my eyes, trying to tune out Sergeant Graves's voice, willing the time to rewind to yesterday. If only I'd stopped him before he stormed out . . .

'No one is suggesting . . . blame . . . need to ask questions . . . understand what happened.'

My own words ring in my head: *I don't want to see you ever again.* The last thing I said to him. *I don't want to see you ever again. Ever again.*

The monotone of Sergeant Graves's voice has stopped and the sudden silence brings me back to the present. I turn round and see both of them staring at me expectantly.

'I'm sorry?'

For a split second I see impatience in Sergeant Graves's eyes, then he blinks and repeats what he has just said in a measured voice. 'We were wondering if we could ask you to formally identify the deceased.'

The deceased. The word I heard hundreds of times as a

forensic photographer cuts to the quick. I swallow hard, trying to get rid of the metallic taste in my mouth. I stagger back to the table and sit down heavily.

'It's entirely up to you. We'll understand if you—'

'No, I'll do it,' I interrupt him.

'Thank you.' He sounds relieved. 'PC Singh here is your FLO.' He nods almost imperceptibly at her and she takes over.

'Kristin, my name is Anu and, as Sergeant Graves has just said, I'm your Family Liaison Officer. I'll be looking after you from now on. Is there anyone you'd like us to get in touch with for you? Anyone who could be with you right now?'

'No, thank you. I'll be fine.'

'Are you sure?' There's genuine concern in her voice. Or perhaps she's just a better actor than Sergeant Graves.

'Yes, I am.'

'Just in case you need anything—' WPC Singh slides a card with her details towards me. 'I'll come back tomorrow morning to pick you up for the identification, if that's OK with you. Would nine a.m. suit you?'

I nod, barely listening as she reels off the sympathy mantra.

I lock the door behind them and go straight to bed. I curl up, holding a pillow in front of me. Am I imagining that it smells of Anton? I inhale the faint scent, a mixture of aftershave, greasy hair and dust, trying to bring back the image of him. But he's gone and I feel desperately lonely. No, not lonely, alone. I chose to be alone when I told him to go, but this is not how it was supposed to happen. I thought I'd be raging at his betrayal, at his easy desertion. I wanted to despise him. His death has deprived me of all this, of being able to feel hurt and self-righteous. Instead, I feel guilty. Guilty about pushing him away, about being unforgiving.

Is it possible that he killed himself? The thought goes through my body like an electric current. No, no, no, he wouldn't have done it. Not him. He would've ploughed on, bumbling haplessly forward, always hopeful, always believing that everything was going to be just fine. No, our engagement wasn't *that* important to him. He wouldn't have fucked someone else if I was. I welcome a tiny stab of anger. He betrayed me and I pushed him away. I had every reason to do so.

An accident, they said. They must know what they are saying. It was an accident. What was he doing at some building site at 7 a.m. on a Sunday morning? At King's Cross? Something stirs in my memory and then I know. He did say someone had emailed him regarding a mural in King's Cross. Some regeneration project, something-or-other partnership. I wish I'd listened to him more carefully when he was telling me. *That's* what he was doing in King's Cross. I can picture him climbing over a fence, breaking and entering, as he always did when it came to casing places for his paste-ups. 'Recce' he called it. Why wait for legal access if you can do it right now, on the sly? I must tell the police this is what he was doing there. I stagger out of bed and pick up PC Singh's card, looking for my phone. But then I put it down. What difference does it make now? He's dead and they said it was an accident. He's dead and it's not going to change anything. He's dead. I crawl back to bed and reach for Anton's pillow again.

I fall asleep, breathing in his smell. In my dream Anton and I are in a small plane, just like the tiny yellow Piper we once took in Argentina, flying over Iguazu Falls. Anton is in the pilot's seat, wearing an old-fashioned aviator's cap and a red scarf, straight from *Dastardly and Muttley*. Next, I'm holding the control stick, screaming at Anton who is crouching on the wing of the plane, smearing it with wheat-paste glue. He looks up at me, shouting, *'We're on a roll, babe!'* I try to grab his leg but can't reach him without letting go of the controls. He smiles at me and steps off the wing, spreading his arms like a skydiver.

18

I wake up with a start, covered in sweat, Anton's words still ringing in my head. *We're on a roll, babe, we're on a roll.* For one blissful moment I'm annoyed with him for being his usual carefree self, then the reality hits me. Anton is dead. I close my eyes, trying to shut out the brightness of the day. It's unbearably hot and stuffy in the loft. Pixel is sitting right next to my face, kneading the pillow rhythmically, his claws catching on the pillowcase.

'All right, all right, I get the message.' I drag myself out of bed and fill his bowl with Lily's Kitchen chicken dinner. It'll do for breakfast.

This is the best thing about pets. They won't let you wallow in misery for too long, they'll drag you meowing or barking straight back to life. OK, I'm up, what now?

I let the cold water run in the kitchen sink, lean over and drink greedily from the tap, then splash water on my face, wetting my hair. Do I dare to face the world?

Reluctantly, I switch the computer on and go to the BBC news page. I scroll all the way down to UK & Local News, and there it is, the second item in the England section.

'Man dies after falling from fifth floor in Central London.'

No, I don't want to read this. I get up and go to the window.

It's wide open and it's hotter outside than it is in the loft. I look down as I reach out to shut it and see a police car stopping in front of my building. Shit, it must be nine o'clock. A moment later my entryphone buzzer is screeching. My FLO is here.

'Thank you so much for agreeing to do this,' says PC Singh as I settle in the back seat of the car.

I nod, unsure what to say. She sits at the front, next to the driver, turning towards me with a reassuring expression on her face.

'We're going to St Pancras mortuary, it's not very far. And it shouldn't take long . . .' She hesitates, before continuing. 'But there is something I need to tell you before we get there. When Mr Sauvage – when Anton fell, he hit some steel fencing. He . . . We had to get the fire brigade to help us to remove him. What I'm saying is he sustained some serious injuries in the fall. There might be some disfigurement and it may not be that easy to identify him . . .'

I feel a wave of nausea rise in my throat. 'Can you stop the car, please? Now?'

We're surrounded by traffic right in the middle of Old Street roundabout, but the driver turns the blues and twos on in a short blast and nudges the car towards the kerb in City Road. As soon as we stop I'm out, throwing up on the pavement. I haven't eaten much today, so all that is coming out is yellow streaks of bile and white froth. I lean against the car, waiting for the retching to subside. PC Singh appears by my side, a bottle of Evian and a packet of tissues in her hands. Eventually I'm able to take a few sips of water. We've stopped right in front of Sainsbury's Local and a handful of shoppers are watching us curiously.

'Miss Singh . . .'

'Anu, please.' She hands me the tissues.

'Anu . . . I can't do it. Can you please take me back home?'

'Of course.' She opens the car door for me and says something to the driver.

Back at the loft, PC Singh busies herself with the kettle. She rinses out two mugs and makes fresh tea, as milky and sweet as the one before.

'I'm so sorry, Anu. I just couldn't do it.'

'Don't worry, it's fine. I understand.'

'But I've let you down, wasted your time . . .'

'Don't worry, really. There are other ways.'

'I just . . . couldn't face seeing him . . .'

'I understand. It's a very traumatic experience. It's tough.'

We sip the tea in silence.

'You know, I used to work crime scenes.'

'You were a SOCO?'

'No, a photographer.'

'Ah, yes.' She looks at my equipment at the back of the loft.

'I've seen so many dead bodies . . . victims of traffic accidents, fire, domestic violence, murder . . . mutilated, bruised, decaying . . . missing limbs—' I break off and look at Anu apologetically. 'I don't know why I'm telling you this.'

'No, go on, please.'

'I don't even know what I'm trying to say.'

I take a sip of my tea and Anu surprises me by producing a

packet of cigarettes out of her bag. She offers me one and I take it, leaning towards her lighter and inhaling deeply.

'I used to smoke then. I'd arrive at the scene, meet the officer in charge, put my overshoes on, suit up, get my kit through the door, walk the scene, make mental notes of what had to be done, photograph it, film it, write it all down, all on automatic, like a robot, so it wouldn't affect me. And then I'd go back to my van and have a smoke. That cigarette at the end of the job was like a beacon guiding me back to the land of the living. I'd take that first drag and wake up. Back to being human again. Back to life.'

I'm suddenly fighting back the tears and the cigarette is not helping. I stub it out and grab one of Anu's tissues, blowing my nose loudly. She watches me patiently, a quiet companion, a listener.

'You take pictures?' I ask her.

She shakes her head.

'You look through the viewfinder and it's like being inside this dark tunnel. Everything else is shut out, nothing exists outside of it. You just see what's in front of you, with that intense clarity, uninterrupted, pure. You become the eye. It's a strange feeling, like some kind of a trance. And then you snap out of it and become you again.'

I fall silent, searching for words, and Anu waits for me to continue.

'I'm expecting to snap out of it now, and I know it's not going to happen. Because *this* is life. Anton in the mortuary. And I can't face it. I can't face death without the protection of a camera lens.'

Anu reaches out to touch my hand and I burst into tears. It's all coming out now, the grief, the pain, the shock of it all.

The feeble barrier of self-restraint that has helped me to hold it all in is crumbling and I'm sobbing like a lost child.

Eventually I feel calm enough for Anu to decide she can leave, promising she'll call later. Out of habit I check my phone. There are eleven new messages. I'll deal with them later. I can't face talking to people just yet. I sit at the kitchen table, trying to collect my thoughts. It's not easy.

He's dead. He'll never walk in through the door, never whisk me off my feet in his bear embrace. He'll never smile, never snore, never annoy me with strewing his things everywhere around the loft. I'll never say 'yes' to him, never call myself Mrs Sauvage. Hold on, aren't you being hypocritical? You threw him out two days ago. You were prepared to spend the rest of your life without him. So where is this melodrama coming from? Come on, get over it. He was a bastard and a cheat. But he's dead.

A rattle of the old brass letter box that hasn't been used since they installed a row of ugly metal pigeonholes downstairs makes me jump. I get up heavily and go to the door. A rolled-up newspaper is sticking out of the letter box. I yank the door open. There's no one outside. I close the door and pull the paper out. It's the *Daily Mail*. The *Daily Mail*? Why would anyone in their right mind stick the *Daily Mail* through *my* door? I unroll it as I take it to my recycling bin and the headline on the front page catches my eye.

FRENCH ARTIST DIES IN 70ft FALL
IN KING'S CROSS

Fuck. I spread the paper on the kitchen table and sit down.

There is a picture of a smiling Anton next to a wide, single-column article, with a bold line of type below the title.

**Anton Sauvage, 37, impaled on steel
fencing after falling from a building
next to St Pancras station.**

I swallow to get rid of the tightness in my throat and force myself to read on.

An urban artist, dubbed by many 'the French Banksy', has died after falling from the fifth level of a building under construction in a newly developed area of King's Cross next to St Pancras International. Police were called to the building site at about 7 a.m. yesterday, but were unable to save him.

The site's security guard told the *Daily Mail*: 'I had just arrived for my Sunday morning shift when I saw the man's body. He was impaled on the steel palisade fencing fixed in concrete at ground level. It was quite gruesome. Police arrived very quickly and covered the body, but everybody who saw it was really shaken. I have never seen anything so horrific in my entire life.' Metropolitan Police have confirmed the death is not being treated as suspicious but enquiries are being carried out into the

circumstances surrounding the accident. Turn
to page 5.

Against my better judgement I turn to page 5. There is
another picture of Anton, this time on scaffolding by one of his
murals. It's his *Beaubourg* piece on one of the air vents outside
Centre Pompidou in Paris. I know because I was there with
him when he was pasting it up.

> The French artist who died in King's Cross
> yesterday was known for his characteristic
> murals that would crop up in cities all over
> the world, from Brazilian *favelas* to the
> *banlieues* of Paris. Friends of Anton Sauvage
> expressed their utter shock at his sudden
> death. His brother, Lionel, a prominent
> New York investment banker, said in a brief
> statement read out by his lawyer, 'I am
> devastated by the loss of my brother. He was
> an inspiration to many people and his death
> is both tragic and unexpected. I ask the
> media to respect our privacy so our family
> can grieve in peace.' A friend of Mr Sauvage
> said, 'Anton never hesitated to risk his life for
> his art. No building was too high for him and
> no project too dangerous. He always pushed
> himself to the limits both in his art and his
> private life.' Another friend added . . .

I grab the paper and throw it across the loft, startling Pixel.
A *friend?* And *another* friend? Who are these people? Where

did they dig them up from? A statement from Lionel's lawyer? Lionel, who hadn't spoken to his brother for ten years? Who despised him for being 'a leftie loser' and accused him of squandering their father's fortune?

Shaking with anger, I pick up my phone and dial PC Singh's number from the card she's left on the table. She answers on the first ring.

'Anu, it's Kristin Ryder.'

'Kristin, are you OK?'

'Not really, I've just read today's *Daily Mail*.'

'Oh, I see.'

'All that nonsense they wrote about Anton—' I can't contain my outrage.

'Unfortunately these kind of headline stories are quite common . . .'

'But it's all lies! Those quotes from the so-called friends!'

'I'm afraid there isn't much we can do about it.'

I hear a distance in her voice. She doesn't sound like the caring FLO who was in my loft an hour ago.

'The statement from his brother he hasn't seen since they both left home . . . it's all some kind of hideous fabrication!'

'Actually, that bit is true.'

'Sorry?'

'Mr Sauvage's lawyer has just been in touch. He's taking care of all the arrangements on behalf of the family.'

'The *family*? You've got to be kidding me . . .' I can't believe what I'm hearing. Anton hated the very notion of 'the family'.

'I believe the funeral is going to take place next week in the south of France.'

Well, of course, they'll put him in the *family* grave in

Aix-en-Provence. I'm so taken aback by what I've heard I need to sit down.

'What about his stuff?'

'His stuff?'

'You know, the things he had with him when he died.'

'You mean his clothes and the contents of his pockets? All that will go to his family once we're done with it.'

I think she's using the word 'family' over and over again just to spite me.

'Once you're done? What are you doing with it?'

'Nothing unusual. It's all standard procedure in a case like this. We're not treating his death as suspicious.'

'I know. I've read it in the *Daily Mail*.' I hope I sound sarcastic enough.

'Kristin, I'm very sorry it has turned out like this. Obviously, I'll keep you in the loop if you'd like me to—'

I hear the quiet bleep of another call waiting and interrupt Anu.

'Actually, Anu, I have to go. Bye.' I press the button before she has a chance to reply.

'Yes?' I bark into the phone, still shaking from the shock of Anu's revelations.

'Is this Miss Kristin Ryder?' A polite female voice.

'Ms, actually.'

'Ah, of course, Ms Ryder. So sorry to bother you at such a sad time . . .'

'Who's this?'

'My name is Mindy Nygard and I'm a journalist with the *Daily*—'

'You've got to be kidding me!'

'I'm sorry?'

'Go to hell!' Without turning it off, I throw my phone across the room. It bounces off the wall and clatters to the floor.

This is unbelievable. First they print all that hogwash about Anton and now they try to get to me! How did this Mindy person get my name and number anyway? From some weasel at the police station, probably. Talk about adding insult to injury . . . I'm being sidelined by Anton's family as if his death is none of my business and now I'm being pestered by some hack. Perhaps I should've spoken to her. Given her my version of his relationship with his family. *His family.* There are only two people I can think of who fit this collective noun: his dementia-riddled mother and his brother Lionel. *Lionel.* It has to be him behind all this. His hateful older brother, obsessed with the family's reputation, trying to remove all trace of the sibling who never fitted the bill, who in his mind disgraced them even in his death. Lionel is trying to sweep Anton under the rug. To give him his due, he probably doesn't even know I exist. I doubt Anton would've told him about our engagement. But what about those self-proclaimed 'friends' with their fake dirges? They have probably never existed and are a product of Mindy's overactive imagination.

My anger subsides, giving way to gloom again. I force myself to get up and fetch the phone. The screen is cracked, a wonky spider web of broken glass obscuring the icons. But it seems to be working. For one needy moment I consider calling my parents, but quickly dismiss the thought. That relationship went beyond repair a long time ago. I might as well stick to my friends, not that I have many of them. Being basically a self-sufficient geek, I used to leave the socializing thing to Anton. I check my voicemails and listen to the messages, deleting them as I go along. Sophie and Marcus, shocked, caring, desperately trying to get hold of me. Vero, offering to come over straight away. Anna from the Fugitives, politely sympathetic. Heather, asking how I'm getting on with Playthingz. Rupert and Daniel, chirpily unaware, inviting me to a 'vinyl party'. I realize that none of Anton's mates have called me. All those guys who used to populate our busy social life have suddenly gone AWOL. I don't matter to them. Only a handful of people, none of them connected to my life with Anton, have bothered to pick up the phone. And they deserve to be called back at some point. I can't hide with my grief forever.

I have to lie down again. I feel an almost palpable heaviness weighing me down, as if anxiety and grief have parked themselves on my chest, unwilling to shift. Snippets of the *Daily Mail* article, my conversation with PC Singh and Mindy's call keep churning in my head in a relentless cacophony of meaningless phrases.

Wait! I sit up abruptly, knocking Pixel off the bed. When I asked PC Singh about Anton's stuff, she mentioned only his clothes and the contents of his pockets. What about his rucksack and his computer bag? Where are they? Where did he go when I kicked him out? Did he crash with Doyle again? I should give him a call. I must have his number somewhere. But what if . . . A disturbing thought buzzes in my head like a mosquito. What if he went to *that* woman? The woman from 'Exposure 3'?

I rush to the computer and, ignoring hundreds of new messages in my mailbox, look for 'Exposure 3'. I can't find it. I scroll up and down the endless stacks of emails but it's not there. Not even one of the three identical 'Exposure 3' messages I received. I go to the 'Trash' folder but it's not there either. I go back to my inbox and sort my emails by name rather than date. As I look at the alphabetical list, it slowly dawns on me: not only is 'Exposure 3' missing but also 'Exposure 1' and 'Exposure 2'. They should all be there, somewhere between 'Fwd:' and 'Expedia Travel Information', but they are all gone. I realize I'm hunched over the table, practically touching the screen with my nose. I lean back in my swivel chair and let my breath out, subconsciously imitating Anton's mannerism. All the 'Exposure' emails have vanished and I have no record of them ever existing. *Time Machine*, I think with a flicker of hope. Yes, they'd all be there if only I'd bothered to back up my Time Machine in the last few weeks. But I hadn't.

Have they all been somehow linked to Anton? And now that Anton's dead, they are gone too? A shiver runs through me. What does it all mean? Let's not panic, let's try to think about it rationally. The latter two *were* connected to Anton, but the first one? The Violinist crime scene? How is that supposed to be related to him? I didn't even know him then. But maybe *he* knew me? Perhaps he'd been stalking me and then made sure our paths crossed so he could wiggle his way into my bed and my life? *Really?* He'd do that to then go off and kill himself, erasing all the emails while he was at it? No, Ryder, you're getting seriously paranoid. There is no connection between Anton and all the 'Exposure' emails except for an obvious one: *me*. I've been the target of the emails and Anton's just got in the cross hairs because he was involved with me. His death and the disappearance of the emails must be an awful, and scary, coincidence. But . . . if only I still had those emails, if I could have another look at them, perhaps I'd find some little detail, some snippet of incriminating evidence that would explain it all. As if on cue, a message pops up on the screen: 'Time Machine could not complete the backup.' Yes, I know, and unless I plug my backup disk in, it won't be able to. I click 'OK', making a mental note to do it later.

Frustration is welling up inside me. The fact that Lionel has muscled in on the funeral arrangements and somehow usurped the right to be the only official grieving relative is making me feel abandoned and hurt. I should be there doing it all, acknowledged in my grief as his partner. But am I not forgetting something? He *betrayed* me, *lied* to me and then *walked out* on me. No, I threw him out. It was *my* decision. Was it really? Did I have any choice in the matter? Anton chose to be unfaithful to me and showed no respect for our relationship. He had left me emotionally even before I kicked him out. So I can't start playing the grieving widow now. He isn't *mine* to mourn.

He isn't mine to mourn – this hurts almost as much as his death. We were a force of nature for seven years. But now I feel that by letting go of him I've relinquished any right to lament his death. Isn't it ironic? I detested him when he was alive and now I want to claim him back for myself. Too late, honey, too late . . . You should've hung on to him while he was still alive. I get up abruptly from the computer, wiping away the tears that seem to be flowing freely down my face. Oh, what have you done, Anton?

I make myself a cup of tea and force the hot liquid down my throat. It burns my swollen-from-crying lips, but relaxes me. As I take small sips, an idea begins to form in my head. Let Lionel have Anton's body, let him go through with all that family bullshit. I pick up the ring that's been sitting next to the Mac's keyboard and close it in the palm of my hand. I'm going to say goodbye to Anton my way.

19

There is a small church tucked away in the village of Tudeley, not far from Tonbridge, in the Kentish countryside. It's nothing much to look at from the outside, its medieval structure rebuilt in red Flemish bond brick in the eighteenth century, its roof topped with blue slate tiles. But this is where Anton brought me seven years ago. And this is where I'm parking my MG now, its tyres crunching on the gravel of the empty car park carved out from an adjacent field.

It was supposed to be a surprise, with Anton refusing to tell me anything about our destination. And it was. An unwavering non-believer, I was bewildered by my new lover, the cosmopolitan French urbanite, bringing me to what I thought was a rather nondescript religious location in the back of the Kentish beyond. My bafflement dissipated as soon as we entered the church.

I push the heavy, wooden side door and step inside.

It's like walking inside a diamond – Anton's words ring in my ears.

I perch myself on the pew at the back of the empty church and soak in its atmosphere.

'It is all about light and colour, and Chagall was the master of both,' he said.

The church's story, he told me, was extraordinary. Its stained-glass windows were indeed made by Marc Chagall. The artist had been approached by a local couple whose twenty-one-year-old daughter died in a sailing accident off the East Sussex coast. They wanted him to turn the east window of the chapel into a memorial tribute for her. Reluctant at first, he came to see the church, was enchanted by it and offered to make not one, but all twelve windows. The project took fifteen years to complete and was finished in 1985, the year Chagall died at the age of ninety-eight.

As I watched Anton pointing out details of each window to me, the marks of Chagall's hands, scratches and smudges of light, I tuned in to his excitement. I understood his passion for visual art and his relentless drive to create. I felt I had found a soulmate.

The heavy side door creaks open and a woman with an Osprey backpack and a Canon camera bag walks in. She makes a beeline for the visitors' book, her Gore-Tex boots squeaking on the stone floor. A tourist. It's time to go. I take one last look at the stunning interior and leave. Outside I turn left and go towards the graveyard at the back of the church. I pick the oldest-looking gravestone, the name on it half-eaten by lichen, and crouch next to it, pulling Anton's ring out of the pocket of my jeans. I push it deep into the moss covering the grave then smooth down the surface until any sign of disturbance is gone.

Bye, Anton.

Tears blur my vision and when I blink they run down my cheeks, stinging.

I remain crouching until my legs go numb and my face is dry again.

As I eventually get up and turn to go back, I notice the

woman from the church hovering by a distant gravestone. Her long-lensed Canon is pointing at me.

'Oi, you!' My grief flicks into fury. 'What do you think you're doing?'

She turns and heads for the car park, disappearing behind the hedge. I follow her, skipping between the graves.

She's just about to get into a white Ford Focus when I catch up with her. I push the car's door shut, blocking her escape route.

'Mindy, is it? I'll have my pictures back!'

'Excuse me?' Her eyes are round with fear.

'Your memory card!' I snap at her.

'Why?' Her confusion seems genuine.

'Because you've been taking pictures of me.'

'No, I haven't! This is preposterous! Let me go!' She's recovered her composure now. 'Step back! Or I'll call the police!'

'I know who you are. And if I see *any* of these photos *anywhere*, I'll come and kill you,' I whisper into her ear and then I move away.

She jumps into her car, slams the door and drives away without putting her seat belt on.

I lean against my MG, shaking. What the hell has just happened? Was she really a paparazzo? She didn't look like one.

I trot back to the church and check the visitors' book. The last entry, dated today, is by Sandy Farmer from Atlanta, who thought the church was 'totally awesome'. Good grief. Have I just attacked some gormless American tourist? Her white Ford Focus could've been a rental . . .

Back in the car, I stare out of the windscreen, trying to gather my thoughts. This was supposed to be a spiritual farewell to

Anton. Instead it's turned into a hideous confrontation with someone who was most likely an innocent stranger. I need to get a grip . . .

I throw a parting glance towards the church and slowly drive out, turning right onto the main road. Once in the village, I follow signs for the Poacher & Partridge, the pub I'd discovered with Anton.

I perch myself on the stool at the bar and order his favourite strong ale. I'm not really an ale person, but it seems like a fitting tribute to his tastes. It's actually not bad. As the alcohol hits my stomach, the chaos in my head begins to subside.

I dig my mobile out of my bag. I google 'Mindy Nygard' and get pages of photos of an immaculately coiffed and lipsticked blonde woman in various glam poses. It's definitely *not* the woman from the church. But Mindy Nygard wouldn't be running around the muddy countryside with a camera. She'd send her freelance flunkey in Gore-Tex boots.

I'm getting paranoid. This trip is about Anton, not some unsavoury hack. I have to find a way of saying goodbye to him. Burying his ring felt good, wholesome, but a part of our relationship still remains unresolved. I take another sip of Anton's ale. And suddenly I know. I pick up my phone again.

Anna answers on the first ring.

'Kristin! I'm so sorry . . . What a shock, I'm still recovering from the news. How awful . . . How are you coping with all this?'

'Not terribly well . . .'

'When is the funeral?'

'Sometime next week, probably. Arranged by his family in the south of France.'

'Will you be going?'

'No.'

'Oh . . .' There is a long pause. 'I know it may not be appropriate to mention this now but all his pictures have sold . . .'

'Actually, that's the reason I'm calling you. The exhibition you were planning? I think it should still go ahead.'

'The exhibition?'

'The solo show you offered Anton. He was so excited about it. I think it should happen, especially now. To celebrate his art, his creative free spirit, his life . . .'

'The solo show . . .'

'Yes, let's do it, Anna! I have some of his pieces at the loft. And there's more in storage. I'm sure we'll have enough. Don't you think it'll work?'

'Sure,' she says slowly, but she doesn't sound sure at all. 'Kristin, would you be able to pop in and see me today?'

'Well, I'm not in London at the moment, but you know what? Give me a couple of hours and I'll be there.' There's nothing like the present. I should discuss the details with her while she seems interested.

'Great, I'll see you shortly then.'

I rush out of the pub, taking a good look round the pub's car park. There is no sign of a white Ford Focus. Sandy is nowhere to be seen. The coast is clear.

The prospect of organizing the exhibition is propelling me back to London as I boom along the A13, checking my rear-view mirror more often than normally. I'm a bit disappointed Anna didn't show more enthusiasm for my idea, but perhaps she's concerned about the copyright issues. That's probably it. Oh well, we'll cross that bridge when we get there. There is no doubt in my mind: a solo show will be the most apt tribute to Anton, his life and his art.

Anna greets me warmly and gives me a proper hug, which surprises me but feels nice. Her dog wags its tail at me as if I'm an old friend. There are no clients in the gallery and she takes me straight to her office where I park myself in the Robin Day armchair.

'How are you?' Her concern seems genuine.

'Fragile. Confused. Shocked . . .' I shrug when I run out of adjectives.

She nods. 'I know how it feels to lose someone close.'

'Oh.' I look at her, puzzled by her willingness to share something so personal.

'People I really cared about died because of me.'

Unsure how to react, I wait for her to continue.

'I was selfish and reckless and they paid the highest price for my moment of madness. I thought I would never be able to forgive myself . . .' She lets out a slow breath.

'I'm sorry.' I regret saying it as soon as the words come out of my mouth. But Anna doesn't seem to mind my knee-jerk expression of sympathy.

'You know what the most ironic thing was about it? It seemed like the end of the world then, and it was in a way because it changed my life completely, but it also pushed me in a new direction, forced me to change. Perhaps I'm a better person now . . . but at what price . . . ?' She suddenly looks much older, her expressive face tired and pale under her make-up. She pinches the bridge of her nose with her fingers. 'God, how insensitive . . . rattling on about myself like this . . .'

'No, it's fine.' I'm moved by her sincerity.

'Let's talk about Anton's work.' She pauses and looks at me expectantly.

'Yes . . . I thought we could still go ahead with the solo show you offered him . . .'

'Kristin –' she hesitates – 'I don't quite know how to say it . . . I have never offered him a solo show.'

I stare at her, my mind suddenly gone blank.

'You haven't?'

'No.'

'But he told me . . .' I pause, frantically trying to recall what he had actually said. 'It was supposed to be next month, for two weeks. I'm pretty sure that's what he said.'

'Really? The gallery's fully booked up till next April.' Anna turns to her computer, clicks on something and a colourful schedule unfolds on the screen. 'Next month we're having a retrospective, the forerunners of modern street art, you know, people like Thierry Noir who did a lot of influential stuff in the eighties. It's going to run for the whole month.'

'I don't understand . . . Maybe he misunderstood you?'

'I haven't spoken to him about a solo show, Kristin.' She lets out a nervous laugh, almost a giggle. 'I'm getting a twisted sense of déjà vu. First your photos that mysteriously ended up in my mailbox and now the exhibition that wasn't meant to happen . . .'

A hot wave of sickly sweat hits me; even my eyelids seem clammy.

'You think I've been inventing all this . . . ?'

'Oh, no, not at all.'

'God, you must think I'm a psycho.'

'No, Kristin, I don't. I *believe* you.'

'You know, sometimes I don't believe *myself*. It's as if I'm going mad . . . These weird emails, Anton's death, and now this . . . You know, this morning I went to bury a ring he'd given me. I hoped it would give me some closure. And instead I ended up chasing some woman around a graveyard because I thought she might be a journo spying on me. I feel I'm getting paranoid. My life seems distorted, it's lost its normal dimensions. Everything is warped, unreal, evil somehow. I feel threatened . . . exposed . . .' I break off, choking back the tears.

Anna reaches into her filing cabinet, pulls out her bottle of wine and shows it to me. I shake my head. She opens a small glass fridge next to her desk and offers me a bottle of Evian instead. I grab it as if it were a lifebuoy and drink greedily, as she pours herself a glass of wine.

'I'm so sorry, Anna,' I say at last, 'these last few days have been hard core.'

'No need to apologize. You've been under a lot of stress. Have you spoken to the police about it?'

'Anton's death? They said they are not treating it as suspicious.'

'No, I meant the other stuff. The emails, your photos that got hacked into . . .'

'Oh, that. Somehow I doubt they'd treat it seriously.'

'They should. Cybercrime is an offence.'

I shrug. 'Judging by the way they acted after Anton's death, I don't think they'd be very helpful.' I feel a stab of anger as I'm reminded of my conversation with PC Singh. Anna leans down to pat her dog, who has curled up by her feet, its cute brown snout parked comfortably on her shoe as if it were a pillow.

'About Anton's work . . .' She throws me a quick look as if

to check I'm not going to burst into tears again. Reassured, she goes on. 'Do you know if he's left a will?'

'I don't think so.' I hesitate. 'I don't think the idea of writing a will would even have crossed his mind. He was . . . so much about life.'

'Too young to die.' Anna nods sadly. 'A lot of people think that. And then it's too late for some.' She takes a sip of her wine. 'Dealing with art works after the artist's death can be complicated. There's copyright that lasts for seventy years and there's also the artist's resale right, which lasts for as long. An artist can choose to leave either of them to whomever he or she wishes – a lover, a museum, a charity. But if there is no will . . . If there's no will then all the assets go to the next of kin.'

It slowly dawns on me.

'His mother and his brother.'

'Yes, if they are his only family. It's all based on strict rules, which may not necessarily seem fair to those who are left behind. It may not be what he would've wished for either.'

Now I understand what Lionel's doing.

'His wolf-of-Wall-Street brother's lawyer is dealing with it . . .'

'Well, that's what lawyers are for.'

Bye-bye Anton's solo show. Forget the celebration of his art. My own naivety clashes painfully with the reality of the situation. And loses.

'But listen, let's wait and see what happens next. Let me know if you hear from the lawyer. All right?'

She puts her wine glass down and I have a feeling I'm being dismissed.

* * *

As I walk back along Brick Lane I think about Anna. A strange woman, blowing hot and cold, touchy-feely one minute and strictly business the next. I wonder if she really hadn't offered Anton the solo show or if she has changed her mind now that he's dead. Having heard the copyright lecture I wouldn't blame her if she did. On the other hand, would Anton lie to me about the show if it weren't on offer? No, he wouldn't, not him. So what really happened? Was he duped? Perhaps the same person who sent Anna my photographs led him to believe he had a show coming at the Fugitives? A cold shiver runs through me even though I'm sweating in the heat. Who on earth is doing all this? Can I trust Anna? That story about some people dying because of her, it seemed weird. If they really died because of her, why isn't she in prison? Why would she suddenly open up to me like that? What's her agenda? I think back to how I met her. Anton asked me to take some of his pictures to her gallery. And immediately after, 'In Bed With Anton' got hacked into and ended up on Anna's computer. Not to mention the computers of the whole Serpens Media. Anna and Anton. Anton and Anna. No! I stop in the middle of the street. It can't be. No, it's not true. A white van honks and passes dangerously close to me. I step back onto the pavement. My legs are shaking and I feel faint. I need to sit down. I realize I'm right in front of Craftti House, opposite the Beigel Bake. I used to come here a lot with Anton. As I walk into the cool urban space, Kieran at the bar notices me straight away and makes a cappuccino for me even before I ask for it. I settle at the table by a striking mural of an elderly couple in love. It's peaceful here and the aroma of coffee soothes my jangling nerves.

Anton and Anna. Is that at all plausible? Was it *Anna* who filmed herself having sex with Anton and then emailed

'Exposure 3' to me? She does strike me as a woman who wouldn't shrink away from stealing someone's man or engaging in a bit of rough sex. She's got that sensuality about her, a physical openness that seems inviting and curious. It's attractive, I have to admit. When I turned up at her gallery for the first time, I thought for a moment she was flirting with me. Then I realized it was her way of breaking the ice and making the other person feel welcomed and at ease. Anton and *Anna*? Although the woman in the video looked familiar, it was definitely *not* Anna. There might be a tenuous connection between her and 'Exposure 2' and '3', but what about the crime scene photo, 'Exposure 1'? There is absolutely nothing that links her to that part of my life. Or is there? She did mention the death of her lover and a friend . . . What if I was the photographer at their crime scene? But even if I was, why would she hold a grudge against me? And what would be her connection to the Violinist? He was hardly lover material. Or a friend for that matter. The longer I think about it the more far-fetched it becomes. I put my cappuccino cup down with a loud clonk. I must be going crazy. There is absolutely *no way* Anna is involved in all this.

20

I've rung Sophie. I've spoken to Vero. I called Heather and apologized for the delay in delivering the Playthingz pictures. It's another day and I'm dealing with life. I'm holding up. But I'm not returning PC Singh's calls. Whatever she has to tell me can wait. I put the phone down on the kitchen table. Just those few phone calls seem to have sucked out all the energy I had left in me. What if I sit here quietly and wait for something to happen? No, I don't want anything to happen. Nothing at all. I'll just sit here until I get so tired I'll have to rest my head on the table and fall asleep. Perhaps I'll never wake up.

Pixel pulls me out of my stupor. He keeps nudging me with his nose, purring loudly.

'What do you want?'

I open a fresh tray of his cat food but he ignores it, weaving in and out around my legs, meowing. I check his water bowl. It's full.

'What is it?'

He stares at me with his striking green eyes, twitching his tail.

'I hate it when you're so demanding,' I tell him and playfully ruffle the fur on his back, which I know he dislikes. But he purrs even louder, pushing his head under my hand.

And then I know. He misses Anton. He never behaved like this when Anton was gone for months on end but today he's grieving over his death because somehow his sixth sense has told him that Anton's not coming back. I scoop him off the floor and hold him tightly, much too tightly, but he doesn't mind. He seems tiny, somehow much smaller now than he appears when he's prowling the loft like a miniature tiger, and I find comfort in holding his delicate, warm body next to my chest. I rock back and forth with the purring bundle in my arms, and for the first time since Anton's death, I feel pure, absolute grief, unadulterated by the residual anger caused by his betrayal.

Holding up is not that easy after all. Now that Anna has shattered my illusion about organizing a show for Anton, I can't even throw myself into some displacement activity that would make me feel I'm doing something meaningful. But I know that if I keep sitting on my own in the loft feeling sorry for myself, I will self-destruct, implode with all that grief pent up inside me. I have to do *something*.

I look at the box of Playthingz sitting abandoned by the lighting stage. Perhaps I could have another go at the Mapplethorpe idea? I put Pixel gently down on the floor and get up heavily. I force myself to look through the contents of the box but nothing grabs my imagination. The toys have lost their sensuous, quirky power, they just look like cheap pieces of PVC, silicone and rubber. It's not going to work. I was deluding myself when I thought I could breathe some magic into them, create something worthwhile. I will not break onto the art scene by photographing bits of plastic. It's simply not going to happen.

The sharp sound of the entryphone buzzer interrupts my

creative brooding. It's PC Singh and I buzz her in even though she's uninvited. I need some distraction. Anything will do, as long as it pulls me out of myself. She arrives at my door short of breath, which makes me wonder about the police fitness requirements.

'I'm sorry I've come unannounced but I did leave a couple of messages on your phone . . . How are you?'

'Surviving.'

'I know. It's hard.'

She looks at me with her sad puppy eyes but this time I don't fall for her 'supportive' act. I shrug and let the silence drag on until she clears her throat.

'May I?' She gestures at the kitchen and I nod.

She goes to the kitchen table, pulls out a chair and sits down. She points at the chair opposite. Taken aback but curious, I sit down, facing her.

'Why are you here, Anu?'

Without a word she reaches down into a big TKMaxx bag she's brought with her. She pulls a green carrier bag out of it and places it on the table.

'These are Anton's possessions. His brother didn't want them.'

Anu pushes the bag towards me. I stare at it, speechless.

'His lawyer requested we dispose of them. As far as he knows, we have done just that.'

'Why are you doing this? Why are you being so nice to me all of a sudden?'

'I know you don't trust me. You feel sidelined, ignored, and you blame me for it. But you're wrong. I'm on your side. I'm very sorry you've lost your boyfriend. I do know what you're going through.'

She sounds sincere and I believe her. She has managed to break through my defences.

'Thank you,' I croak through tears. 'Thank you for bringing it here.'

She nods. 'Shall we have a cup of tea?'

'Yes, tea . . .'

She fills the kettle and turns it on.

'You know what they call me at work? Teacup to my face and Teabag behind my back. Because I'm always making tea.' She smiles at me. 'My mother used to say that a nice cup of tea is the key to good health, happiness and calm. And she was right. There's plenty of scientific evidence that it reduces the risk of heart attack and lung cancer, helps prevent Alzheimer's, provides protection from—'

'I'm sorry I was a bit of an arse earlier. I do appreciate you dropping by.'

'That's all right, you're welcome.'

She places the mug in front of me and sits down.

'Do you mind if I ask you about Anton?'

I instantly tense up but have no reason to say no.

'Go on.'

'Was he prone to mood swings, depression?'

'Anton?'

'You said you'd split up . . . he must've been upset.'

'Upset enough to kill himself, is that what you're saying? Anton was the most resilient, headstrong, gutsy person I've ever known. OK, he was a bit volatile, but he'd never take his own life . . . Never.'

'Men tend to hide these things quite well. They keep ploughing on until they reach breaking point. Statistically, suicide is the biggest cause of death among men under fifty—'

'No.' I shake my head. 'Not Anton.'

'The reason I'm asking is that we've checked all the CCTV footage from the building site. As you can imagine, the whole area is pretty well covered and there's absolutely no evidence of anyone else being there with him.'

'Of course, Anton always did his recces on his own.'

'His what?'

'He was there on a recce, it's obvious. He'd been offered a street-art project in the area and he was doing his research. You know, taking pictures of the site, measuring the walls. He must've had his G15 with him.'

'G15?'

'His camera, Canon G15. Similar to this one, just a bit newer.' I point at my G12 sitting on a bookshelf next to some travel guides. 'He always carried it with him on a recce.'

'We didn't find a camera at the scene. But please, tell me more about his recces.'

'Well, he'd go to the site in advance to get the feel of the place and to get all the measurements. He had one of those laser measuring things. With paste-ups you have to be precise about the size of the artwork. Every piece gets printed in advance and on the day you just glue it to the wall.'

'Do you know who offered him the job in King's Cross?'

'That I don't know.' I pause, trying to remember. 'He mentioned a regeneration project or partnership, something like that . . .'

'Yes, there's a lot of it still going on in the area.' She finishes her tea and puts the mug down. 'Oh well, I'd better get back to the station before they run out of tea.' She smiles at me.

'Thanks for bringing this over.' I gesture at the green bag.

'Don't mention it.'

She walks to the door, then stops as if she's remembered something.

'Oh, one more thing. Was Anton a user?'

'What, drugs? No. He was a heavy smoker, like most French guys. But that's it.'

'They've found Ketamine in his system.'

'That's impossible.'

'These tests are usually quite conclusive.'

'I've never seen him take drugs. Apart from an occasional joint . . .'

'That's fine. Forget I asked, it's nothing to worry about. Take care of yourself, Kristin.'

Anu smiles at me reassuringly and then she's gone, the front door clicking shut behind her. I sit motionlessly, trying to process everything she's said. Depression, suicide, drugs – they all contradict the image I've always had of Anton. It's as if she was talking about someone else, a complete stranger, not him. I look at the bag she's left on the table, with a green PATIENT PROPERTY sign emblazoned on it, and I'm scared to open it. I'm scared of what I'll find inside.

I get up and wander aimlessly around the loft. I stand for ages by the window, staring at the dark building opposite. Eventually I turn away and look around. It strikes me how chaotic and untidy the loft has become. A stack of unopened mail by the front door, a messy pile of tangled T-shirts by the bed, dirty plates and mugs in the sink, pellets of Pixel's cat litter crunching underfoot. I sweep the floor and tidy up, stopping short of hoovering the whole place. This will have to do for now. I can't ignore the plastic bag sitting on the kitchen table any longer.

I pick it up and turn it gently upside down, its contents

spilling onto the table with a rattle. I sit down and stare at it, without touching anything.

A black matte Zippo lighter.

A packet of Marlboros.

Blue Powerbeats earphones.

A titanium money clip with three twenty-pound notes.

A half-full blister pack of Nicorette gum.

A Surefire tactical flashlight.

A driving licence.

A Staedtler Pigment Liner.

A Kryptonite bicycle lock key.

A Durex condom in its blue wrapper.

Two one-pound coins.

A strangely shaped thin piece of wood.

That's it. I double-check the hospital bag but it's empty. No phone. No camera. No wallet with his cards. Nothing else. My throat constricts with grief and I have to bite on my knuckles to stop myself from crying again. Nothing else is left of Anton. I take a few deep breaths and force myself to go through the objects on the table, one by one, slowly and deliberately.

The lighter: I remember Anton always playing with it, turning it in his fingers. Hands are one of the first things I notice about people and his were exceptionally beautiful, big and strong, with long fingers and neatly trimmed nails. The earphones: I got them for him last Christmas. The flashlight: last year's birthday present from me. The Staedtler liner: it's mine, actually. The tiny flat piece of wood: it's smooth and so thin it's almost weightless, with elaborate symmetrical shapes cut into it. I raise it against the light, trying to guess its purpose. And then it strikes me; it resembles space invaders, the tiny pixelated baddies from the seventies arcade game. More to the point, it looks just like the street art by Invader, the French urban artist who'd been Anton's idol and inspiration for years. I remember our first trip to Paris and Anton pointing out a colourful shape made of tiny square ceramic tiles stuck to the facade of a Beaubourg building, while he told me excitedly about the elusive guy who 'invaded' cities around the world with his art. I place the tiny wooden shape in the palm of my hand. This must be one of Invader's pieces of art and it must've meant a lot to Anton for him to carry it around in his pocket. I open my wallet and drop it in. There, little guy, you'll be travelling with me from now on.

I go back to Anton's things scattered on the table. I choose to ignore the condom and poke at the Nicorette gum. I didn't know he was trying to quit. Feeling a sudden urge to smoke, I pick up the packet of Marlboros. There are two cigarettes left, and as I pull one out, I notice something else inside the packet. A USB flash drive in a rubberized silicone casing. I grab it and head straight for my Mac. Typical Anton, hiding something like this inside the most disposable of containers. I wonder if the police had found it.

Instant disappointment. The drive is password-protected. You and your bloody passwords, Anton. I try *Corto*, *CortoMaltese* and *MalteseCorto*, getting a 'wrong password' message each time. How about *Pixel*? Wrong again. *Savage*, his street-art name. Nope. Maybe *Invader*? The drive does something weird, as if trying to reset itself, but I'm still not getting access to any files. So much for playing the digital detective. I return to the kitchen table and look at the objects.

The bicycle lock key. I pick it up. *His bike*. I'd completely forgotten about it. Where is it? He hardly ever used public transport so he must've cycled to King's Cross. There is a remote chance that his bicycle is still there, chained to some railing.

If it hasn't been nicked by now that is . . . I turn the key in my fingers. Would I be able to recognize his bike among the hundreds of bicycles that are probably left at King's Cross every day? Then again, would anyone in their right mind leave their bike in KX? I must find it. I jump up from the table, a woman on a mission.

21

I'm on my bike, pedalling along City Road towards Angel. Normally I'd weave in and out of small streets to avoid the main thoroughfare but today I'm in a hurry. The traffic is surprisingly light and I reach Pentonville Road in record time. Soon the majestic two-arch facade of King's Cross station is looming in front of me. I go around it, along the side of St Pancras International, spotting a row of bicycle racks on the pavement right by the taxi rank in Battle Bridge Place. I lock my bike, surreptitiously inspecting all the other bicycles parked there. Anton's Budnitz No. 3 isn't among them. He loved that bike, with its beautifully engineered frame, all titanium and steel, and large Kojak tyres. I thought he was crazy spending a fortune on such a nickable pair of wheels but he was adamant. He called it his 'fun machine' and treated it better than he'd ever treated me.

I look around, seeing the area with fresh eyes. King's Cross has always seemed like a place you pass through, holding your breath, on the way somewhere else. Now I see it for the first time as a destination. It's changed. It's no longer preening itself to attract money. The money has arrived. I look at the elegant building of the Great Northern Hotel with its Plum and Spilt Milk restaurant advertising champagne dinners, the swanky German Gymnasium where instead of losing pounds you can gain them on their Mittel-European dishes, and the 'industrial chic' of Vinoteca. As I watch travellers rushing by with their expensive rolling suitcases I wonder when was the last time I bothered to notice the changes. A couple of office girls pass me, one of them talking loudly about her new boyfriend who apparently isn't used to being in a long-term relationship. What am I doing here? I've come chasing Anton's shadow and now I'm not sure it was such a good idea. But the place has drawn me in and is not letting me go. I cast a glance towards King's Boulevard. Is this where he went that morning?

I follow the wide pedestrianized alley, cross the canal and reach Granary Square. There are too many people here, tourists, office workers, St Martin's students, milling around the sun-drenched space, captivated by the choreographed jets of the fountain in the middle. The fountain makes its own sound, resembling the clapping of many hands. But it's too bright here, too noisy and cheerful. Something pulls me towards the derelict remains of an old warehouse flanking the square from the left, its rickety wall propped up by sleek scaffolding. Just in front of the cavernous Grain Store restaurant on the corner, I spot more bike rails, packed with flashy urban two-wheelers. There is a Budnitz among them but it has a honey-leather saddle and white wheels. It's not Anton's.

I walk along a steel fence in Stable Street and soon reach another open space with modern, angular solid wood benches and ridiculously cheerful yellow metal tables and chairs. Obviously the money has reached this corner too. And there they are, the dark steel and green-tinted windows of the new buildings still under construction. I instantly know that this is where he'd come that morning, drawn by these unfinished, huge structures filling the horizon. These are the concrete behemoths that greet the Eurostar passengers just before their train pulls in to the station. This is exactly where Anton would want to put his art up. But there is nothing that would suggest a tragedy has happened here, no police tape, no tarps shielding the scene. The whole site is neat, tidy and well protected. In fact, it strikes me as being too well protected, with a tasteful green fence, bright orange gates and a security booth. How did he manage to get inside? I certainly won't be able to scale the fence now and I wouldn't be able to do it at 7 a.m. either. Did someone let him in? Was someone else with him when he died, despite what the CCTV footage seems to suggest? I sit down heavily on a bench, staring at the unreachable construction site sprawling in front of me. I know I will never be able to find the spot where he died, I won't find his bike, won't come across even the tiniest trace of Anton. He is gone.

I stagger back towards the station, enclosed in a tight bubble of grief, not seeing the crowds around me. Coming here was a bad idea. It hasn't helped in any way, it has only made me feel worse. What was I hoping to find anyway? Even if I did manage to come across his bike, what would it tell me?

It's the beginning of the rush hour and Battle Bridge Place is filled with urban hustle and bustle. I dart out of the noise and heat into the new departures concourse. The semi-circular steel-and-glass structure is stunning and its elegant beauty manages to penetrate my private gloom. The concourse is packed with commuters but there is a strange stillness about them as they all stare at the departure boards. For a moment I'm convinced I've stumbled upon a flash mob, but as I walk among them I realize they are simply waiting, their eyes glued to the information boards, ready to make a dash for the right platform. Maybe I could hop on some train, go somewhere, no matter where, just to get away from the here and now? But wouldn't the 'here and now' follow me wherever I go?

All the ticket barriers are open for some reason and I continue on to the platforms. This has always been my favourite part of any station. The comforting low hum of the train engines greets me as I move along the fronts of the trains, from Platform 8 down to Platform 1 at the other end. The glazed arched roof lets in the warm shades of the afternoon sun, bathing everything that is normally greyish-blue in persimmon reds. I'm drawn to an old clock hanging above Platform 1, and once I reach it, I'm surprised to find one more platform beyond it. Platform 0. It's empty. How appropriate. A train to Nowhere from Platform Zero, this is what I seem to be catching at the moment.

I'm about to turn back when I spot a neat bicycle rack further along Platform 1. Despite a security camera perched right above it, there is an official notice advising the owners to lock both frame and wheels to the rack. What are the chances of finding his bike here, I think, as I throw a cursory glance at the rack. And there it is, right in front of me, a graceful Budnitz No. 3 with black Kojak tyres. I reach out and touch its frame. It's his bike, it must be. It looks so familiar. I fish Anton's key out of my pocket and bend over towards the lock.

A sudden touch on the shoulder gives me a jolt. I straighten up, letting out a scream that gets drowned by the rumble of a departing train. There is a man standing behind me, tall and wiry, with a long, weathered face and closely cropped ginger hair.

'I'm sorry if I startled you.' He grins, showing a gap between his front teeth.

'It's OK,' I mumble, willing my heart to slow down.

'I noticed you were admiring my bike.'

'Your bike?'

'My fun machine.' He points at the Budnitz.

I stare at the bike as if I'm seeing it for the first time. Why has he called it 'fun machine'? Why is he using Anton's expression? He is looking at me with his light-blue eyes, clearly waiting for me to answer.

'Oh, yes, sorry.' I'm struggling to find something to say. 'It's a beauty.'

'Yes, it is. A very *expensive* beauty.'

Is he accusing me of trying to steal it? Is this what he's thinking?

'It's a Budnitz, isn't it?' I'm squeezing the key so hard it cuts into my skin. 'My boyfriend has one of those.'

'Has he? Good for him.'

He doesn't sound friendly any more. He casts a glance towards the front of the platform and I suspect he's looking for a guard to report an attempted theft. I need to leave, right now.

'Well, I'd better be going.' I make a move to go but he blocks my way.

'You're leaving already?' He sounds sarcastic now. 'But it's so nice to meet someone who admires your property.'

'Let me go!' I scream hysterically and some people at the end of the platform look in our direction. He raises his hands and steps back.

I run along the platform and don't slow down until I'm back in the departures concourse, surrounded by the benign indifference of strangers. I quickly make my way out of the station and find my bike chained to the rail at Battle Bridge Place. My hands tremble when I try to unlock it, drops of sweat running down my forehead, stinging my eyes. At last the lock snaps open and two seconds later I'm on my bike, joining the traffic to the irate honking of a cab behind me. My heart hammers away in my chest but no one is chasing me, no one pays attention to my frantic departure.

I get home shaken and sticky with sweat. I strip my clothes off, dropping them on the floor as I head straight for the shower. It takes half of the Thames to cool me down and make me feel human again. I wrap myself in Anton's navy towelling robe and lie down on the bed.

What a complete disaster that was. The whole escapade has only succeeded in making me even more anxious and paranoid. King's Cross station has morphed into a hostile monstrosity in my head. And that man, that awful man with his vicious grin and his bloody bike. I try to block the memory of the encounter but my thoughts keep going back to it, replaying it as if on a loop. *My fun machine*, he said. I have never, ever heard anyone use that expression. Except for Anton. It was as if he *knew* I'd be there looking for Anton's bike. But how? There is no way he'd know that. Unless . . . Unless he is Anton's killer.

I'm covered in cold sweat again. No, no, no, it can't be true. It's just a crazy coincidence. There are probably hundreds of Budnitz bicycles in London. Let's try to think about it logically. A man sees a woman attempting to unlock his very expensive bike. To him it's obvious she's trying to steal it. He gets pissed off. Understandably so. He tries to remain civil as he considers his options for catching the thief. In the end he lets her go. There. The most likely scenario. *But . . .*

Why did he call it his 'fun machine'? Is it part of some secret vocabulary used by Budnitz owners? Is this what hipsters call their bikes these days? Or did he *hear* Anton call his bike just that? A quick Google search convinces me that it isn't a unique expression, after all. There are plenty of two-wheeled fun machines in the world. *But . . .*

I never actually saw the man unlock the bike. As far as I remember he didn't have a bike-lock key in his hand, he didn't make a move to claim his property. What if it *wasn't* his bike at all? What if he was staking the place out, knowing that sooner or later I'd come looking for Anton's bike? But why? Why would he do that?

This is unbearable. I'm trapped in a spiral of endless questions that wind tighter and tighter around me. I feel the familiar throbbing of a stress migraine. I go to the bathroom and rummage through the medicine box until I find what I've been looking for. *Amitriptyline.* The antidepressant I used to take for migraines that plagued me in the Cubic Zirconia days. It's past its 'use by' date but I don't care. I need something to knock me out, to give me a break, albeit a chemically induced one, from this nightmare. I swallow a tiny tablet with some tap water and return to bed. I lie there with my eyes closed, waiting for blissful heaviness to descend on me. But I know it won't come for at least another hour.

I can't stop thinking about the King's Cross encounter. The man's face and his sarcastic grin are flickering under my eyelids, changing colours like Andy Warhol's *Marilyn*. I should've taken a photo of him. I'm up again, rummaging around for a sketchpad and a soft pencil. I settle back in bed and, leaning the pad against my knees, begin to sketch his face. There was something attractive and at the same time haggard about his features. Tanned, but tired, almost gaunt, with the deep wrinkles of someone who's spent a lot of time in the sun. Full mouth, gingery stubble, deep-set eyes. Did he have a small scar above his left eyebrow? I've never been great at sketching people's faces but my final drawing does resemble the King's Cross man. I feel a stab of anxiety looking at the picture. There is something familiar about his features. Was he the cyclist who knocked me over on the towpath by the canal? According to Rupert and Daniel the guy wore sunglasses and a Respro face mask, but it could've been him. Would they be able to recognize him? I must show them the picture . . .

All of a sudden my eyelids feel like lead. A familiar heaviness floods my body. I push the sketchpad off the bed and curl up, hugging Anton's pillow. A curtain of sleep falls with merciful finality.

22

The beauty of Amitriptyline, apart from its amazing ability to combat neuropathic pain, lies in its power to knock you out swiftly and completely, like a skilful executioner. The dark side of it presents itself upon waking up. Or should I say, *attempting* to wake up.

My mouth is dry, my body weighs a ton and my limbs are refusing to move. But a tiny, persistent voice keeps drilling into my ears, forcing me to open my eyes. Pixel. He is sitting in his usual spot on my pillow, about two inches from my face, staring at me.

'Hello, Kitster.' I call him by the name Anton had given him. He stretches and jumps off the bed, probably disgusted by my bad breath. But he's succeeded in bringing me back to life and I'm up, sort of. I shuffle to the kitchen to dish out his food for him and make a double espresso for myself. Once caffeine enters my bloodstream, the world becomes a more bearable place. It seems like a nice day outside. The street below looks peaceful and clean, the Peeping Tom's loft is empty and life's usual sharp edges feel smooth and curvilinear. It's also very early, barely past 6.30 a.m.

'Thank you, Pixel.' I shuffle back to bed, noticing the sketch of the cyclist lying on the floor by the Mac. A shiver runs through me when I look at his face again, handsome but with a cruel streak. I'll scan the drawing in and email it to Rupert and Daniel. Maybe they'll recognize him from the towpath incident. But even if they do, then what? It'll only prove there's a link between my towpath accident and the KX encounter. But who is he?

I pick up my Mac, forcing myself to stop thinking about him. As soon as I open my mailbox, everything else is forgotten. There are *hundreds* of new messages. The only good thing is the absence of any new 'Exposure' emails.

I need to get back to Heather today. And I should finish the Playthingz shoot, ASAP. There is a short message from Jason, asking me to call him. Not now, Jason. Some agency I've never heard of is asking me to send them my portfolio. Potential work, good news. A couple of emails from my accountant. It can only be bad news. There is a sweet note from Aunt Vero, simply letting me know that she's thinking of me. I *must* visit her soon. Sophie wants me to get in touch. She knows that when she can't get through on my mobile, the best way to elicit a response from me is an email. Surprisingly, there is also a cryptic message from Marcus, who almost never emails me. Surely they should be better at coordinating their digital communications. Linked-In announces proudly that people are looking at my profile. Good, perhaps someone will give me a job. The rest of it seems to be junk. It takes me a while to weed out all the spam and deal with the genuine messages.

I force myself to have a go at the Playthingz and by midday I'm done with the next batch. Encouraged by getting things done, I decide to have another go at Macro Perceptions. The result isn't mind-blowing, but I feel it's going in the right direction. With Mapplethorpe flowers in mind, I take an extreme close-up of a dildo, avoiding the titillating aspect of its shape and going for a classical, black-and-white look. It's not bad. And it takes me back to an exhibition I saw with Anton some time ago at the Musée Rodin in Paris. It was a bold and impressive collection, combining sculpture and photography, and two great artists, Rodin and Mapplethorpe. I remember watching Anton, who spent ages at each piece, enthralled and awed, talking to me excitedly about movement, tension and the play of light and shadow within them. It felt pure and erotic at the same time and by the time we left the museum we were both so fired up we barely made it back to our room, ripping the clothes off each other in the hotel lift. It was one of those intense, sensual fucks that leaves you open and vulnerable, and totally in love. Oh well, let's not get melodramatic again . . . You've got some nice momentum going here, Ryder, don't waste it on histrionics. I dump the new photograph, together with some earlier attempts at Macro Perceptions, on my iPad, and head out of the door. Professor Stein, here I come.

After the King's Cross experience I'm dreading going anywhere near my bike. I'll walk to Leonard Street, it'll do me good. It has cooled down a little and the afternoon air feels pleasant. As I don't remember the street number for the gallery, I decide to start at the Great Eastern Street end and walk towards City Road. As far as I know, most of the galleries are clustered on that side anyway. I pass Pure Evil and ICN galleries and get a whiff of real-smelling coffee from the Book Club cafe. There is some impressive street art on the derelict buildings on the right and it instantly makes me think of Anton. I resist the temptation of stopping by at Westland London, an amazing antique dealers' warehouse in the former Church of St Michael's. It's a dangerous place that convinces you suavely you're in desperate need of an antique fire basket or a nineteenth-century Italian gilt bronze chandelier, even if you have to remortgage the house they're meant for to get them. I push on, stopping briefly at the junction with Paul Street, by an ugly building with a beautiful name, Telephone House. A bit further on, Whitefield's Tabernacle at the corner of Tabernacle Street offers some needed respite from the boredom of casual modernity. And that's it, I emerge onto City Road, right by Pret a Manger. Where the hell is the Light Vault Gallery? Have I missed it? I retrace my steps, studying every doorway and peeking into each window display. Nothing. No one at Pure Evil or ICN has heard of the Light Vault either. Maybe it's one of the pop-up places further on, suggests a friendly Australian at the Book Club. I turn back, angry with myself for not double-checking the address with the professor. He did say Leonard Street in his email, didn't he? When I reach City Road again I'm convinced the gallery isn't there. This is bizarre.

Perplexed, I cross the road and turn towards Bunhill Fields cemetery, a tiny scrap of peace and quiet in the middle of urban commotion. Have I got the address wrong? Is the whole Light Vault thing a ruse? Is it possible that Professor Stein is going senile? Or is there something more sinister behind all this? Oh God, please no. A shiver runs through me as I cross the gate to the cemetery. Please, please, let it not be another hoax email. I don't think I could bear another 'Exposure'. Propelled by the anxiety building up inside me, I walk briskly along the narrow, long pathway, heading towards the wide paved alley in the middle of the grounds. Perhaps one of the wooden benches there will be free and I can gather my thoughts in the company of Bunyan, Defoe and Blake. Is it possible that someone has been impersonating Professor Stein and sending me on a wild goose chase in Leonard Street? But what would be the purpose of it? I can't think of any, except perhaps damaging my already fragile artistic ego. This seems far too subtle to be the work of some cyber troll. The name 'troll' conjures up an image of a grunting, hairy beast, slobbering over a sticky, dirty keyboard. Not someone who could effortlessly imitate Professor Stein's lofty style.

I jump at a noise behind me. I turn and see a flash of movement. A cyclist is hurtling by. A blur of face, blue helmet, sunglasses, Respro mask. The King's Cross man – the split-second thought flashes through my brain. On an impulse I reach out and grab hold of the hi-vis rucksack on his back. His impetus pulls me behind him as he loses balance and hits the ground with a grunt, the bike scraping the pavement. I fall on top of him. The bike's handlebar hits my ribs, knocking the breath out of me. I bounce back, landing heavily against the pathway's iron railing. As soon as I get my breath back I'm on my feet, lunging myself at the prostrate cyclist.

'You fucking bastard, LEAVE ME ALONE!'

I lean over him and grab his Respro mask, trying to pull it off his face.

'Show me your face, you coward!'

He pushes me off him, makes a move to get up. I reach for his mask again.

'Oi, lady, cool it!'

I turn round, furious at the interruption. The man who stands behind me is short and skinny, with the battered face of a wino and a shiny, scarred bald scalp.

'What was that for?' He shakes his head in disapproval and crouches down by the cyclist, a distinct whiff of unwashed clothes and stale urine hitting me as he moves.

'You all right, mate?'

The cyclist mumbles something as he slowly pulls his mask off.

It's not the man I saw at King's Cross.

The other guy was tall, sinewy, with a ginger complexion. This one is stocky, with pale olive skin and dark hair. He looks nothing like him. I'm sure I've never seen him before.

'You need a doctor?' asks the wino.

'No, thanks. I think I'll be fine.' The cyclist touches his shoulder with his gloved hand and winces.

I feel a pang of guilt as I watch the wino help the cyclist pick up his bike.

'I saw her push you, mate. You wanna call the cops?'

Now, wait a minute. I'm a victim here as well!

'You were going too fast.' My voice is trembling.

They both turn and look at me. The wino shakes his head reproachfully. 'You're lucky the gentleman here is OK. Otherwise you'd be in trouble.'

'He shouldn't be riding here. Cycling is not permitted on these grounds.' I know I sound like a stuck-up cow. The long and the short of it is I pushed him.

They keep staring at me, and after a brief pause, the wino snorts. 'Just clear off, bitch.' He waves me away dismissively.

Humiliated by his contempt, I turn on my heel and walk quickly back towards the gate.

Once in City Road, I remember to breathe. I draw in a lungful of heavy city air and double up in pain. The whole right side of my ribcage is on fire. Someone stops by me, asking if I'm OK, and I raise my hand in a reassuring gesture. Gradually the pain subsides enough for me to draw in a few shallow breaths. I'll be fine, I'll be fine, I keep repeating to myself, as long as I can get home.

The short walk back to Hoxton takes ages. I have to stop every few steps just to breathe. Climbing up the stairs is a monumental struggle. Once in the loft, I pull off my dirty jeans and crawl into bed. I lie on my left side, hoping it's just a bad bruise and my ribs aren't broken. I feel like crying but have to stifle the sobs because of the pain. I probably should take some painkillers but the thought of moving off the bed, of moving at all, is too much to even consider. I think I need help.

I slowly reach down to my bag which I dropped by the bed and fish out my phone. I speed-dial Sophie. The call goes straight to voicemail. I hang up and put the phone down. Marcus. I wouldn't normally ring him – I've always communicated with Sophie, Marcus hovering on the peripheries of our friendship – but he did send me that email this morning, asking me to call him.

He answers on the first ring.

'Kristin! I'm so sorry about Anton.'

'Marcus, I've tried calling Sophie—'

'Are you OK?'

'Yes . . . no, actually.' I'm holding back the tears. 'I've had an accident.'

'Oh my God, what happened? Where are you?' He sounds over the top in his concern.

'I got knocked over by a bike. I'm at home now . . .'

'Have you called an ambulance?'

'I don't need an ambulance. I just need some painkillers.'

'I'm coming over. Will you be able to let me in?'

'I think so.'

'I'm on my way.'

He hangs up and I lie back on the bed, trying to breathe normally. A sudden chill goes through me and I pull a sheet over my bare legs, finding comfort in its lightweight cocoon.

I must've dozed off because it seems only a couple of minutes have passed when he rings the bell. Wrapped in the sheet, I shuffle to the entryphone to buzz him in.

'Shit, Krissy, you look awful.'

'Thank you.' I attempt a smile as I crawl back to bed.

'We should really go to the hospital, have you X-rayed. You could have some broken ribs.'

'I don't fancy spending the next ten hours at A&E. I want to be home, Marcus.'

Marcus lets out a sigh of disapproval.

'At least let me have a look at it.'

'Suit yourself, doctor.'

'Believe it or not, I do have the St John Ambulance first-aid certificate. A *valid* one.'

'You do?'

'Yep. There is a lot that you don't know about me, young lady. May I?'

He perches himself beside me on the bed and gestures at my T-shirt. I nod. Gently, he pulls up my T-shirt, stopping just below my breasts. He sucks his breath in, looking at my ribs.

'Ouch. It does look nasty. You sure you don't want to go to A&E?'

'Positive.'

I pull the T-shirt down, suddenly uncomfortable with his closeness. He must've picked up on my discomfort, because he jumps up and begins to rummage through his canvas bag.

'Ta-dah!' He pulls out a couple of blister packs. 'The old faithful, Paracetamol, plus Ibuprofen. Take two of each, with water, right now. Just in case this doesn't work, I've brought Tramadol as well.'

He brings me a glass of tap water and watches me swallow the pills. 'Oh, and for later' – he reaches into his bag again – 'some Arnica cream.'

He moves one of the kitchen chairs closer to the bed and sits down.

'Tell me what happened.'

Reluctantly, I start telling him about my unsuccessful escapade to Leonard Street. But he seems to be listening with such undivided attention that I get into my story. When I reach the encounter with the cyclist I make it sound like a collision, too embarrassed to admit I pushed him.

'Bloody hell. How awful.'

I nod in silence.

'I wonder if there are any cameras over there. Maybe we should report it.'

'No, it's OK.'

'It's not! Let me call the police.'

'No, Marcus, drop it, please. I've had my share of dealing with them . . .'

'Oh God, how stupid of me, I'm so sorry . . . It was such a shock . . . If there's anything we can – I can . . .'

I take a deep breath and regret it instantly, the sharp pain from my bruised ribcage shooting up my arm.

'Thanks. It's been pretty awful. And I'm not coping well, to be honest . . . I still don't want to accept that he's . . . I mean – that it's happened . . .'

I bite my lip, fighting back the tears. Marcus reaches out and touches my hand.

'How can I help?' he asks quietly.

'You can't bring him back, can you?' I try to smile through the tears.

He looks at me in silence, then lowers his head.

'Let me make you a cup of tea.' He jumps up and begins to fuss around with the kettle, his back to me. He brings a mug over, then settles down on the floor by the bed, his back against the mattress.

'We're splitting up,' he says quietly and I'm convinced I've misheard him.

'Sorry?'

He puts his face in his hands, exhaling loudly.

'Marcus?'

Eventually he lowers his hands, staring ahead.

'Yes, you've heard me right, we're splitting up.'

'But why?' Sophie and Marcus are the happiest, best-matched couple I've ever known.

'I'm sorry, Krissy, I shouldn't be telling you this, you're Sophie's friend . . . She'll tell you when she's ready . . .'

He makes a move to get up.

'No, wait! Tell me, what on earth is going on?'

He leans back against the bed, still not looking at me.

'We just . . . can't be together any more.'

'Have you met someone else?'

'Who, me?' He chuckles joylessly. 'No.'

'Sophie?' The disbelief is evident in my tone.

'No, no. It's not that.'

'What then? I don't understand.'

He just sits there and I'm too shocked to say anything. Eventually he starts talking, in a quiet, dispassionate monotone.

'Remember we tried for a baby a few years ago?'

Yes, I do remember, it was a very traumatic time in their

relationship, the period during which, I thought, they became even closer to each other.

'It turns out I have a very low sperm count. We tried all sorts of treatments, but as you know . . .' He sighs. 'I tried to convince her we could use donor's sperm, but she wouldn't hear of it. She nearly bit my head off when I suggested adoption. She got it into her head that it's nature's way of telling us we're incompatible. She believes in this theory . . . *histocompatibility*, it's quite complicated, but she's latched on to one aspect of it, scent attractiveness . . . that we're basically drawn to our potential mates by sense of smell. She told me she never liked my smell, that she actually detests it. And that's why, according to her, we can't have children . . .'

He falls silent and I'm trying to get my head around what I've just heard. Marcus clears his throat and goes on.

'And suddenly children became a taboo subject and she threw herself into the catering business. You know the company is hers? I'm just . . . an employee.'

I didn't know.

'I thought it was her way of healing, you know, distracting herself with work, so tried to help as much as I could, got up at six every day, made breakfast for her, cooked, cleaned, took her suits to the dry-cleaners, waited for her with dinner on the table every night, while she built her career. The company has become . . . an extension of her personality. Every morning she leaves me a list of things to do. And there's hell if something on the list doesn't get done.'

'But the house in France . . .'

'Oh, that was her idea. I think she genuinely thought it would somehow salvage our relationship, give us both an equal footing. But it never would've worked. Things have gone too far . . .' His voice cracks with emotion. 'I'm so sorry, Krissy, I shouldn't be telling you any of this . . . You're her best friend. It's just . . . I lost touch with all my mates a long time ago. All our friends are Sophie's friends. I have no one to talk to . . .' he ends in a whisper.

'God, Marcus . . .' I reach out and touch the top of his head, his thinning black curls surprisingly soft under my fingers. He lets out a quiet sob.

We sit like this for a long time, my hand on his head, a reassuring gesture a mother would soothe a distressed child with. Eventually I feel I have to break the silence.

'I don't know what to say . . . I had no idea . . .'

'But you do believe me?' There's pleading, almost desperation, in his voice.

'Of course I do.'

Do I? Even as I reassure him, my mind is throwing up a series of questions. Is it really possible I have never noticed that things were so bad between them? How could I not have been aware my sweet best friend has turned into some kind of harridan?

Marcus turns and looks up at me. I notice how much he's aged. His skin is pasty and there are deep wrinkles around his mouth. He sees my doubt.

'You don't, do you?'

'I do, Marcus, it's just – crazy . . .'

'You think I'm crazy?'

'No, not at all. You're one of the sanest people I've ever known . . .' So is Sophie, for that matter.

'I should go.' He is scrambling to his feet.

'No, wait.' I don't want him to leave while mistrust still hangs in the air. As I reach out, trying to catch his hand, I knock over the untouched mug of tea he'd put on the bed beside me. The lukewarm brown liquid spills on the sheets, making everything wet.

'Shit!'

'No, don't move, I've got it!'

He picks up the mug and dashes to the kitchen. He returns with a big wad of paper towels and starts mopping up the tea. I feel ridiculous just sitting here, watching him fuss about.

'I'm sorry Krissy, I'm such a clumsy oaf.'

'No, you're not. It was my fault anyway.'

'I leave a trail of disasters behind me, wherever I go . . .'

'You don't, Marcus. You are a sweet and considerate man.' His helplessness is making me want to reassure and comfort him.

'You really think so?' There is something needy in his question.

He drops to his knees by the bed and reaches out to touch my thigh. His hand feels scorching on the damp sheet clinging to my bare skin. I remember I've taken my jeans off and I'm practically naked under the sheet, apart from a pair of low-rise M&S bikini knickers. He throws me a quick glance, half challenging, half asking my permission. I close my eyes.

I haven't been expecting this. A shiver runs through my body as he slowly pulls the sheet off me. We shouldn't be doing this. But a part of me wants it, the feeling of total abandon that would dull the pain, the desperate sense of loneliness. My eyes shut and my heart pounding, I wait for his next move. And there it is, a light caress to start, his fingers sliding underneath the bikini elastic, his hot breath on my skin, the stubble on his chin grazing the inside of my thigh. I gasp at the first touch of his tongue, then grab his hair and pull him closer, raising my hips.

I've always found cunnilingus a bit of a let-down, ranging from perfunctorily clumsy to downright awful. Most of my male lovers have been hopeless fumblers in that respect, Anton being the only notable exception. Marcus is definitely trying. But my initial arousal has evaporated under his touch. The relentless persistence of his tongue is, well, relentless. I let him go on for a bit longer and then fake something that could pass for a half-hearted orgasm. And then he's gone. The bathroom door slams shut. Self-consciously, I reach for the crumpled sheet to cover myself. The sudden movement brings back the pain in my ribs, dulled for a while by the painkillers. Marcus spends a long time in the bathroom and I choose not to dwell on what he's doing there. When he eventually emerges, his hair is wet and there are damp patches on his shirt and trousers. Without looking at me he picks up his bag and heads for the door. He stops, runs his hand through his hair, clears his throat.

'I'll be off then . . .'

'Bye, Marcus.'

This time he closes the door quietly and I hear him charging down the stairs.

I lie under the damp sheet, disgusted with myself. What has just happened? Why did I let him touch me? I should've stopped him, I should've diffused the tension, laughed it off. But I didn't. I could say I felt sorry for myself, that grieving for Anton had made me needy and reckless. I could blame the accident, say I was dazed by painkillers, but I know deep down there's no excuse for my behaviour. No matter how pitiful the fumble was, it was also selfish, sleazy and stupid. Unbelievably stupid.

23

I wake up with a heavy head. When I try to get up, the pain in my side knocks the breath out of me. I remember staggering out of bed in the middle of the night to take one of Marcus's Tramadol tablets. And then I remember what happened yesterday and drop back on the pillow with a moan. A wave of self-loathing makes me hot and sweaty.

Oh, Anton, none of it would've happened if you were still here . . .

I'm suddenly aware of how disgusting I feel, wrapped in stained sheets, sticky and reeking of BO. Gritting my teeth, I push myself up and put my feet on the floor. The loft spins round me. I wait for the wave of nausea to subside, then slowly get up. My ribs pulsate with a dull ache and my legs are trembling, but at least I'm up. I wrap myself in the crumpled sheet and shuffle towards the kitchen counter, honing in on the coffee machine. With clumsy fingers, I drop a fresh coffee pod into it and press the button. I swallow the first sip of Pure Arabica and close my eyes, waiting for it to do its job. After a while the shaky feeling inside subsides and the synapses in my brain begin to fire lazily. The first coherent thought of the day is not reassuring. What have I done? I sit down heavily on the bar stool by the kitchen counter. If only I could undo what happened last night. And more to the point – what should I do now? Own up and atone? Bury my head in the sand and wait? Do nothing? No, I can't. I owe it to Sophie. I have to tell her. But how? I can't even begin to imagine the confrontation. What will be the fallout from that stupid lapse of judgement? Will Marcus confess and beg Sophie's forgiveness? Perhaps he's done so already and she's sitting in their cosy kitchen right now devastated by the double betrayal, by her partner and her best friend. Or perhaps she's fuming with anger, smashing up their Mikasa dinnerware? Maybe she doesn't care. Maybe he hasn't told her. None of the scenarios dispel the heavy feeling of guilt lodged in my ribcage, just below the sternum.

The coffee has done nothing to get rid of the relentless buzzing in my head. I lean forward until my burning forehead touches the cool surface of the marble worktop. The cold compress brings some comfort but the buzzing is still there, a persistent high-pitched whine like a swarm of furious bees. I straighten up, massaging the back of my neck.

The buzzing.

It's not in my head, it's coming from the outside. I slowly turn on the stool to face the window. My eyes take a while to adjust to the sunny brightness and then I see it. A shiny white, crab-like object with four arms, each crowned with a small rotor, hovering outside. Transfixed, I approach the window. The object shifts its position, as if aware of my presence. I know exactly what it is. It's the most covetable item on Anton's wish list of digital toys. A DJI Phantom 3 Quadcopter. In other words, a drone. Not any old drone, but one of the most intelligent, powerful and sexy flying machines with its own integrated, stabilized camera, which both Anton and I drooled over at the Photo & Imaging Exhibition last year. We didn't buy it in the end, but Anton kept fantasizing for months about a street-art project that would involve the use of a Phantom drone. And there it is, right outside my window, almost within arm's reach.

I take a step towards it and it shifts again, in a quick, insect-like jerk. The black eye of its camera is trained on me and I'm suddenly aware that it's watching me. OK, I know, *it* is just a sophisticated digital device without will or curiosity, but whoever is flying it through their iPad or mobile phone *is* definitely watching me. Would Mindy be so persistent? Or technologically savvy? I wrap the sheet tighter around myself and quickly scan the windows in the building opposite. They all seem dark and empty. Where is its pilot?

The drone is on the move again, this time rising higher, and I notice a strange contraption attached to the bottom of it, below its camera. This is not part of the standard drone equip-ment. I narrow my eyes, trying to work out what it is, when it suddenly squirts some red liquid in my direction. Instinctively I jolt back, trip over the edge of the sheet I'm wrapped in and fall backwards with a cry. My ribcage seizes in a vice of pain. I can't breathe. I desperately fight for some air, but all I can manage is a horrible wheezing sound in my throat. I force myself to lie still, the sound of my frantic heart pounding in my head. Gradually my airways open up and I take the first cautious breath in. Then another one. And the next.

But the drone is still there, outside my window, buzzing up and down, spraying the glass with a red substance I hope is only paint. I'm still dizzy and weak, but my survival instinct makes me pull myself along towards the only hiding space in my loft. The bathroom. I reach its door after what seems like eternity, crawl in and slam it shut behind me. I lie on the cold tiles until my breathing gets back to normal.

Silence.

I crack open the bathroom door. The drone is gone. I cautiously venture out.

The heady smell of synthetic graffiti spray paint lingers in the air. The windows are covered in thick red lines criss-crossing in an intricate pattern resembling a spider's web. What the hell? My heart begins to pound and my breathing becomes shallow again. My whole body is shaking and I have to sit down on the bed because I don't trust my legs to carry me. Calm down, it's only a bit of paint. It's probably just some silly prank. Calm down. I force myself to take a few deep breaths. The paint fumes are making me lightheaded. Let's not panic, let's try to think. Someone has sprayed my windows, or perhaps even the whole building, with red paint. Definitely not Mindy. But it could be . . . Drone Guerrillas. I remember Anton telling me about a bunch of guys, Italian or maybe Croatian, who'd use drones to paint on government buildings. And then there is Katsu, another of Anton's street-art heroes, who used a hacked Phantom drone to spray graffiti on a giant billboard in New York. Compared with New York this building is a trifle. I exhale a cautious sigh of relief. It's just possible that one of his street-art mates, perhaps even Katsu himself, has decided to celebrate Anton's memory by creating drone graffiti on the building he used to live in. That must be it. This is Hoxton, after all.

The red paint on the windows doesn't look so ominous any more. I slowly get up, propelled by a sudden pang of hunger. I'll have some muesli, pop some more painkillers and deal with the damage on a full stomach. The damage. Shit. Marcus and Sophie. The memory of last night, blissfully pushed aside by the drone attack, comes back with a vengeance. I'll have *that* to deal with as well. My phone pings with a new email but I ignore it, rummaging through the kitchen cabinets in search of muesli. Yes, I shake the box of Anton's favourite Rude Health Granola triumphantly. It tastes surprisingly fresh and crunchy. My blood-sugar level up, I feel ready to take on the new day. I'll call the building's managing agent and see what can be done about the graffiti. And then maybe I'll have enough courage to call Sophie. Well, we'll see. Another email pings in my phone. It's time to start the day. Too lazy to fire the computer up, I touch the 'Mail' icon on the phone and wait for it to update the inbox. And I freeze.

On top of the list of new emails sits 'Exposure 4'.

Compelled by a mixture of apprehension and curiosity, I touch the phone screen again to open it. It's an MPEG and it starts playing immediately. Chaotic, jerky images fill the screen, but then the footage stabilizes enough for me to realize what I'm seeing.

A woman wrapped in a stained white sheet is staring straight into the lens. Her face is pale, her hair a mess, her eyes blood-shot and swollen. Swaying slightly, she takes a step forward, then another one. In a self-conscious gesture, she pulls the dirty sheet tighter around herself. There is something distracted, almost deranged in the way she glares at the camera.

I look away from the screen with a groan. I don't want to watch myself wriggling on the floor like a lunatic, trying to catch my breath. What I've seen so far is bad enough.

But the movie keeps playing and I'm drawn to it, despite myself. It's a wider shot, a mass of red lines filling the screen. The camera moves away in a mechanical, jerky way, character-istic of drone footage. I can see the whole expanse of my windows, sprayed with red paint. And what I see makes me gasp in surprise. It's not the random jumble of criss-crossing lines

I'd thought it was. It's a precise and intricate design that forms two words:

Wake up

I drop the phone and it clatters on the kitchen floor. I turn towards the window, trying to decipher the words in the red labyrinth of lines. And yes, there they are, clearly visible if you know what you're looking for.

It isn't a street-art tribute for Anton. It's not about him. It's about *me*.

But what am I supposed to wake up from?

What does it mean?

Suddenly the loft feels hot and stuffy, with the smell of paint still lingering in the air. Well, of course, all the windows are shut. But the thought of having to struggle with the thick layer of red paint in order to crack them open makes me go weak at the knees.

I have to leave this place, right now. I quickly throw a T-shirt and a pair of old jeans on, stuff my wallet, my phone and my car keys into my bag, grab Pixel and head for the door.

24

Taking the cat with me was a mistake. He hates being in the car on a good day, and today he's picking up on my anxiety, meowing and scratching the upholstery. He should be in a cage but, well, he isn't. At one point, just as I'm negotiating a busy junction, he jumps onto the headrest behind me and bites the top of my head. I swat him with the back of my hand and he hides under the passenger seat, growling. At least he doesn't try to climb under my feet.

Soon I leave the congested streets of East London and find myself cruising along the A13. The traffic isn't bad. The sun is streaming into my eyes, making everything look bleached out. Pixel has fallen silent in his hideaway and Vanessa Feltz is discussing dementia with the Lovely Listeners. I'm driving fast, without a purpose or a map. The speed helps to clear my head and gives me a sense of freedom. I can go anywhere I like. Yes, I should do just that, disappear from my world. Wouldn't that be nice . . . A large truck overtaking me on the inside blasts its horn and I instinctively hit the brakes. The seat belt digs into my sore ribcage. The car behind me flashes its headlights as it hovers dangerously close to my rear bumper. It's a white Ford Focus. I cling to the steering wheel with clammy hands and swerve sharply to the left, taking the exit. The white Ford Focus stays on the A13 and disappears into the distance. I take a few cautious deep breaths. Was it following me? In my panic I didn't notice whether the driver was male or female. But seriously, was I really expecting Mindy/Sandy behind the wheel?

I don't know exactly where I am, but I'm hoping that if I drive along the smaller country roads for long enough, I'll eventually reach the coastline. That's the beauty of living on an island: if you keep driving in more or less one direction, you're bound to hit the water sooner or later. Unless you're going round in circles, which is exactly what my life feels like at the moment.

But I'm evidently in luck and after a while the little villages I drive through become quainter and the pubs I pass gain vaguely nautical names. I know I've arrived when I see the Plough and Sail. I leave the car off the road by the pub, stuff Pixel into my bag and follow the sign for the boatyard.

The boatyard is a ramshackle collection of dilapidated work-shops, rusting shipping containers and geriatric boats. The boat shed along the slipway probably saw its better days a century ago. The whole place smells of neglect and is completely deserted. I decide to skip the crumbling jetty and turn right to follow the edge of the water along a sea wall overgrown with grass. From here I get a clear view of the mudflats and salt marshes. The nagging pain in my side reminds me of my bruised ribcage. I don't think I'll be able to walk far, not with Pixel's weight in my bag. In the distance I see a small hut resembling a tepee. A *tepee* in Essex? Whatever it is, I'm hoping it'll offer some respite for my aching body.

It turns out to be a boat, or rather the top half of one, perched upright, its bow pointing at the sky. Its truncated hull forms a cosy shelter, complete with a wide wooden bench. It's equipped with an old sleeping bag and a rusty kettle resting on two bricks. Just what I've been looking for. I sit down with a sigh and release Pixel from the bag. He takes a couple of steps, his body low to the ground, sniffing the air suspiciously. No need to worry he'll run away. A typical urban cat, out of his element in the countryside, he'll stick to me like glue. I shake the sleeping bag and check it for unwelcome beasties. It looks remarkably clean. I make a cushion out of it and lie down on the bench. There, perfect. They say the best way to find oneself is to get lost in the wilderness. In the absence of the wilderness, Essex will do nicely.

I stare at the scattered white clouds rolling above me, enjoying the distant cries of shore birds. I realize that for the first time in ages I feel safe. It's time to reassess the situation in the clear light of day. I force myself to go through recent events. Anton's death. The 'Exposure' emails. Professor Stein's sudden interest in me. The screw-up with Marcus. Oh God . . .

And the weird *wake up* message . . . What was that about?

It's dark and I'm stumbling through mudflats, my feet sinking into black, smelly silt. Each step is a gigantic effort, my shoes making disgusting, smacking sounds in the mud. There is a black bird hovering right above me, its huge wings almost touching me. It shrieks and cackles, flexing its talons like a demented witch. I can't breathe and I'm running out of steam, I know I won't be able to fend it off for much longer. It senses my weakness. It lands in the mud in front of me and opens its beak, letting out a bright plume of fire. I brace myself for the scorching heat, but the mud suddenly turns into water and I plunge down. I try to find the bottom with my feet, but it's deeper than I thought. The water floods my mouth, runs up my nostrils, enveloping me in complete darkness. No, the darkness isn't complete, there's a wedge of light somewhere high above me and it scares me even more than the murkiness around me. I know it's the bird, hovering above the surface of the water, searching for me with its fiery eyes. Except it's not a bird, it's a drone sweeping the area with its powerful laser beams. The light shines straight onto me and I know it has found me. There is no point in hiding any more.

'Wake up!' I hear a voice.

I choke and open my eyes. It takes me a while to figure out where I am. The smell of sea breeze. The sound of shore birds. The blue sky above my head. I shade my eyes with my forearm and look around. I must've slept for quite a while because the sun has moved and the colours are not as bleached out as before. Pixel is sitting at my feet, licking his paw. Right behind him, leaning against the side of the boat that forms one of the walls of the shelter, stands a man. I sit up with a stifled scream, scaring Pixel, who dives off the bench into the bushes. The man stares at me in silence, one of his eyes wandering to the side. I slide along the bench as far as I can away from him, trying to look in control.

'Can I help you?' My voice seems tiny and scared.

The man keeps looking at me without a word, scratching his thick, greasy hair. I jump up, hastily gathering my belongings.

'What do you want?' I'm hoping to sound in control, but it comes out as a whimper.

He nods and screws up his ruddy face, revealing pink gums flanked by two rotting canines. He stretches his hand out towards me, his fingers gnarled and his nails black.

'Mine,' he says and licks his lips.

'No!' I move back, pressing the bag against my chest. 'Leave me alone!'

He nods his head again and takes a step forward.

Out of the corner of my eye I see Pixel's tail twitching in the bush not far from the boat. I lunge in his direction, grab him and run. I reach the end of the sea wall at full speed and turn towards the boatyard. It's deserted. I cast a quick glance back and am relieved the man isn't following me. I slow down, trying to catch my breath. My bruised ribcage is on fire again. I manage a few tiny, shallow breaths as I trot towards civilization. After a while I have to stop. I look back but the man has gone.

It takes me ages to reach the Plough and Sail. But I'm in luck, it's open, and I rush in, winded and sweaty. There is a woman behind the bar unloading a dishwasher and she throws me a curious glance.

'You all right, love?'

'Yes . . . No . . . Actually – I've just had a bad experience at the boatyard . . .'

'You one of them then?' Her friendliness is gone.

'Sorry?'

'Developers,' she hisses.

'No, I'm not.' I look at her with wounded innocence.

'Is that right?' She eyes me suspiciously.

'Positive. Why do you ask?'

No one has ever accused me of being an estate agent.

'The place's been crawling with them iffy types since they put it up for sale.'

'The boatyard's for sale?'

'Yep.' She inspects a glass she's taken out of the dishwasher and begins to polish it fiercely with a tea towel.

'Oh.' I sit down on one of the bar stools, unsure whether I should react with outrage or approval.

'You can say that again.' She puts the glass on the shelf decisively. 'So what happened to you down there?'

'This weird man came up to me . . .'

'Weird how?'

'Oh, I don't know.' I shrug. 'A bit scary . . .'

'Lazy eye, missing front choppers, a thatch on top of his head?'

'Yes! Do you know him?'

'It's Boatyard John. He's always there. Totally harmless. He's built himself a shelter out of an old boat turned on its stern. A cosy place, with a proper sleeping bag and all. I gave him me old kettle, so he can make a cuppa for himself there. I don't know what'll happen to him once they sell the place.' She shakes her head sadly.

I say nothing, trying to hide my embarrassment. I appropriated the poor man's shelter and screamed at him when all he was doing was trying to claim it back.

'He gave you a proper fright, didn't he?' She doesn't try to hide her amusement.

'Nah,' I wave dismissively. 'It was just a bit . . . unexpected.'

'So you're not a developer?'

'I wasn't last time I checked.'

I feel movement in my bag sitting on the floor by my feet. Pixel is trying to get out. It's time to go.

I get in the car, release Pixel and watch him in the rear-view mirror as he sets out making a nest for himself on the back seat. So much for my road movie experience. Instead of beginning to get a grip on my life I feel even more shaken and lost. There's only one safe place left, one person I can turn to.

Thank goodness for Waze on my phone. The brilliant app circumvents all the bottlenecks and gets me to Whitstable in record time. I haven't announced my visit, but I know Aunt Vero will be home at this hour and she'll be pleased to see me.

And yes, she's in. She opens her arms and I fold into them, relishing the warmth of her embrace.

'So sorry about Anton,' she whispers into my hair and I let my tears flow freely into her linen top. 'You've been through the wars, Lily Liver . . .'

We stand still for a long time.

Eventually she leads me into her kitchen. It turns out I'm not her only visitor. At the kitchen table, eating her coffee and walnut cake, sits a young man. The fact that she's baked her pièce de résistance cake for him is significant. As far as I know she's only ever baked it for three people in her life: her mother, Estefania, her lover Stella and her honorary niece – me. As I see him I have a spoilt-brat moment of feeling jealous and disappointed that she's made the effort for someone other than me. It's quickly replaced by the joy of seeing her and the thrill of having a slice of C&W, as she calls it, on my plate.

The young man is Aunt Vero's first ever lodger. His name is Fly, he comes from Shanghai and is doing a post-grad course at Canterbury. He moved to Aunt Vero's spare room only five days ago but I can tell they are already very fond of each other. I sense a deep bond between them and it doesn't take me long to discover what it's about. *Star Trek*. Or to be precise, *Star Trek: Voyager*, all 172 episodes of it. Aunt Vero has never hidden her addiction to the adventures of Captain Janeway and her crew. She even got me on board for a while, until I discovered other pastimes. It turns out that Fly (at least he doesn't call himself

Paris or Tuvok) is equally passionate about the series. I suspect they'll be spending many hours in the Delta Quadrant together.

We gorge ourselves on the cake, chatting amiably, while Pixel makes himself at home in Vero's lap. I'm grateful she hasn't mentioned Anton again. After a while Fly excuses himself and disappears into his room.

'Why didn't you tell me?' I turn to Aunt Vero with gentle reproach.

'Tell you what?'

'That you need *money*!'

'Oh, you mean the lodger.' Aunt Vero chuckles with relief. 'It's not about money. I have plenty, no need to worry about me.'

'What is it about then?'

'Company. Connection with the modern world. I realized I was becoming a bit of a fuddy-duddy lately. There's only so much you can talk about with Bridget and Midget. I wanted some young energy in my life. You know, a fellow geek. Someone to swap new apps with, to check out what's trending. I have you' – she reaches out and pats my hand – 'but I know you're busy and London is a bit far. So I got myself Fly.'

'Is that his real name?'

'Of course not. But he was fed up with us butchering his Chinese name. You know Chinese is tonal and each syllable can have four different vocalizations. Not to mention all the different meanings. So he decided to go for something easy for our tone-deaf European ears.'

'You like him.'

'I do, he is an absolute darling. And what a breath of fresh air in my life. And he helps me with my bees.' She pauses, looking at me with her bright, sparkling eyes. 'You're not upset, are you?'

'About Fly? No. I'm glad you've found him.'

I try to sound cheerful but I'm suddenly overwhelmed by tears. She fishes a beautifully starched handkerchief out of her pocket and puts it on the table in front of me. And then she waits patiently for me to blow my nose and compose myself.

'Do you want to talk about it?'

'No.' I weave the wet handkerchief in between my fingers. 'I can't . . . I can't keep thinking about Anton . . . it's been destroying me. I have to find a way of moving forward. Living . . . without him . . . But it's so *painful*.'

She nods.

'The pain. I wish I could tell you it'll go away. But it never really does. It sits inside you and every time you touch it, it stings. Every time you try to remove it, it burrows itself deeper. But with time you'll learn how to handle it, gently, on its terms. You'll learn how to live with it. I promise you that, Lily Liver.'

She gently pushes Pixel off her lap, gets up and leaves the kitchen. She comes back with two generous glasses of Macallan with a splash of water. She places one in front of me and sits down with a sigh.

'To Anton. To Stella. And to life.' She raises her glass.

I take a few sips, the strong whisky burning my throat. But as it starts warming up my stomach, I find myself relaxing. My mind leaves Anton and wanders off in other directions. I tell Vero about my wild-goose chase for Professor Stein's gallery, the collision at Bunhill Fields, the drone attack and the 'Exposure 4' email. But I'm too ashamed to tell her about the episode with Marcus.

When I eventually fall silent, she nods. 'We need to do something about it.'

I'm grateful she said 'we'. It implies shared responsibility and it makes me feel less alone.

'Not sure we can help you with *who*, but we can certainly have a go at *how*.'

I look at her, uncomprehending. She winks at me and points at the door. I see Fly hovering in the doorway, a glass of whisky in his hand. She gestures at him to sit down at the table.

'Fly is doing an MSc in Forensic Computing,' she announces triumphantly.

He nods and smiles at me. 'Vero tells me you have a small problem.'

'Well . . .'

'I was just telling Fly about your "Exposure" pest before you turned up. I hope you don't mind.'

Knowing that Vero discussed my private hell with a stranger makes me feel exposed and vulnerable. But I've always trusted her judgement.

'Well . . . I could use all the help I can get.'

'That's exactly what I thought.' Vero makes her voice deeper for effect. 'Fly used to be a hacker.'

Fly clears his throat. 'You make it sound as if I was a pirate or something. I've never been a black hat, Vero.'

'Sorry, a *hacktivist*, do forgive me.' Vero pats his hand. 'And he's been working on something very interesting. Go on, tell us.'

'OK.' He swallows his whisky in one big gulp. 'Back at home I used to play with rootkits a lot. They are a spyware that infects the deepest level of a computer's operating system. In other words, they break into your computer through the back door and leave that door open for someone to gain total control of the computer. Like, literally everything, from accessing logs or executing files to monitoring what you do.'

'Executing?' A cold shiver runs through me.

'Some files are executable, which means they contain a program. In other words, they can be executed or run as a program. They are different from source files that can be read by humans.'

Did he actually say *humans*?

'Do you think those . . . rootkits are inside my computer?'

'It's possible.'

'But I have a Mac. Macs are supposed to be immune to such things.'

'Unfortunately they are not. It's quite easy to bypass the cryptographic signature checks in Apple's EFI firmware update routines.'

'Sorry?'

He looks at me, as if surprised by my ignorance. 'You can infect a Mac with a nasty rootkit using the Thunderbolt interface. You must've heard of Thunderstrike?'

'No.' I have a feeling I'm becoming a digital dinosaur in Fly's eyes. 'But what I'm interested in is – can you find those rootkits and get rid of them?'

He makes a face and looks inside his empty whisky glass. 'Well, it depends on the level of their sophistication. You can track down a simple user-mode rootkit with a special anti-spyware application, but it's not so easy with kernel-mode ones that work on the same level as the computer's operating system. So essentially your own OS becomes your enemy. And then there are *virtual* rootkits and they are practically invisible.'

'You've lost me, Fly.'

'OK. Remember *The Matrix*, the Wachowski movie?'

Both Vero and I nod.

'Imagine that your computer lives inside its own matrix.' He enunciates carefully, as if talking to a group of preschool kids. 'So, instead of putting the spyware *inside* your computer, someone has created a virtual environment *around* it. If the entire operating system of your computer has been moved into such a virtual machine, your hacker gains total control over everything you do on it. You become a fish inside a fishbowl, with no chance in hell of ever breaking out of it.'

Vero and I stare at him, dumbfounded.

'But . . .' Vero says after a long pause, 'you do know how to detect it?'

Fly sighs. 'Well, that's what I'm working on at the moment.'

'So you'll be able to help Kristin?'

'I can try. But I can't promise it'll work.'

'Thank you. Shall I bring my Mac next time I come?'

'I can access it remotely.'

'You can?'

'You'll just have to enable the function.'

'Oh, OK.'

'Great, let's drink to that.' Vero jumps up with surprising agility and gets the Macallan bottle from the lounge.

'So, you've been to China.' Fly smiles at me as we appreciatively sip Vero's whisky.

'I haven't actually, though I've always wanted to go.'

'But your tattoo . . .' He points at my left arm.

'Ah, yes, one of the mistakes of my youth.' I look at the four small, dark-grey strokes just above my wrist. 'A celebration of a present moment that's long gone.'

'It's *hu* , it means fire.'

'So it does.'

'It's a very powerful symbol. Its attributes are enthusiasm and creativity, but in excess it brings restlessness and aggression. Just like real fire, it provides heat and warmth, but it can also burn. How did you get it?'

'Oh, it was a silly pact I made with a friend. We were supposed to conquer the world, bring everyone to their knees with our art . . . Well, it's better than the word "bacon" or "minge" on your foot . . .' I shrug.

'It carries other meanings too. Burn. Anger. Rage.'

'I suppose the fire's burnt out.'

'Maybe it's just on the other side of the river.'

'Enough of your Chinese wisdom.' Vero pours some more whisky into our glasses. 'I can barely understand it when I'm sober.'

Two refills later, the conversation evolves into gentle reminiscing. Vero talks about her wild early days with Stella, I entertain them with a story of Anton who, after too many bottles of Leffe Blonde, insisted on Tippexing all the pigeons in Trafalgar Square. But our anecdotes fade into insignificance when Fly reveals that he is a sapiosexual.

'I fancy clever people. Intelligence is sexy and it's much longer lasting than physical attractiveness. For me a challenging philosophical conversation is a far better turn-on than looking at a pair of boobs. After all, the brain is the largest sex organ.'

Straight-faced, Vero asks Fly whether it's hard to meet other sapiosexuals. Apparently not, he reassures her, as long as one knows where to look for them. My IQ plummets rapidly after yet another whisky refill and soon I find myself on an ancient sofa in Vero's study convinced that all my life I've been looking for the wrong thing in a man.

25

I wake up in what feels like the middle of the night, my heart pumping madly. I check the time on my phone. It's 7 a.m. and the house is quiet. Vero and Fly are still sleeping off our Macallan binge. But I can't sleep. Fly's lecture did nothing to alleviate my fears. In fact, it has made me feel even more vulnerable. Knowing that a hacker can worm his way into my life without me realizing it and with total impunity is terrifying.

I gather my clothes which are scattered across Vero's antique Kashan rug, throw them hastily on and head for the kitchen. It turns out I'm not the first up after all. Fly sits at the kitchen table with a cup of coffee next to his MacBook. He is immaculately groomed and smells of some oriental, woody aftershave. His neat appearance makes me feel slovenly in yesterday's clothes. I self-consciously realize that I haven't had a shower in a while and I'm beginning to smell. But Fly doesn't seem to notice as he offers me a mug of fresh coffee. I sit opposite him at the table and watch him type something quickly, his fingers barely touching the keyboard. Obviously sapiosexuals don't engage in futile chit-chat. There is a small USB stick in designer steel casing plugged into one of the ports in his Mac. Which makes me remember –

Anton's flash drive!

I put down my mug abruptly and dash out into the hallway in search of my bag. I grab my wallet and return to the kitchen. I spill its contents on the table. Where is it? I do remember slipping it into my wallet when I was tidying up my desk.

'Yes!' I spot it among loose change, old receipts and Invader's little wooden gadget, which I've been carrying around as a street-art memento.

I pick the drive up and show it to Fly, who's been watching me in bewilderment.

'It belonged to Anton,' I declare.

'I see.' Fly seems to be taking my strange behaviour in his stride.

'Would you be able to check what's on it?' I put it on the table in front of him.

'Integral crypto-drive. They are usually password-protected.' He studies the stick without touching it.

'Yes, I know, I've tried to break into it.'

'How many times?'

'What do you mean?'

'How many times have you tried to unlock it?'

'Oh, I don't know.' I shrug. 'A few. I've tried all his favourite words.'

He picks it up and plugs it into his Mac, stares at the screen for a while, then shakes his head.

'Six times. You've tried at least six times.'

'How do you know?'

'It automatically erases all data after six failed access attempts.'

'You're kidding me.'

'I'm not. The data and encryption key have been destroyed. It's empty.' He ejects it and gives it back to me. 'Sorry.'

'Damn.'

I put my face in my hands with a sigh. Every way I turn seems to be a dead end. Even the stupid USB drive.

'I didn't know you were a musician.'

'Sorry?' I lower my hands.

Fly is turning Invader's wooden gadget in his slim fingers.

'Vero said you were a photographer.'

'I am.'

'But this . . . oh, did it belong to your boyfriend as well?'

'It did as a matter of fact.'

'Was he a violinist?'

'A *what*?'

'A violinist,' he mumbles, looking at me with round eyes. 'I thought . . . this is . . . I mean, this is a violin bridge . . .'

I stare at the delicate object in his fingers, mortified.

'A violin bridge,' I say at last.

So this is *not* a replica of a mosaic by the French street artist.

'Invader, my arse,' I whisper and Fly's eyes get even rounder. 'I'm sorry, Fly. It's nothing to do with you. It's me . . . I'm . . . I'm an absolute idiot.'

I grab it from his hand, slide the scattered coins back to my wallet and get up.

'I have to go. I've just remembered I have something on in London this morning. Will you tell Vero I said thanks and goodbye? I'll give her a call later.'

Fly nods without a word. I grab my bag on the way out and close the door quietly behind me.

I reach Junction 7 on the M2 before realizing I've left Pixel at Vero's. It's probably the first sensible thing I've done for ages. Vero likes cats and he'll enjoy a break at her little cottage. I'll have some of his food delivered to her address as soon as I get home. It's only temporary, I reassure myself. I'll have him back as soon as . . . as soon as *what*?

As soon as I find out what's going on.

As soon as I feel safe.

As soon as I get my life back.

The engine in my old MG is wailing with effort as I push the pedal to the metal, nudging 80 mph. What's the rush? Where am I going? Slow down. Think. I ease my foot off the accelerator and move to the left lane.

The violin bridge. It was among Anton's things that PC Singh brought to my place after his death. How did it get there? Anton wasn't a musical type. He'd probably never held a violin in his life and he certainly wouldn't know what a violin bridge was. Just as I didn't. So how did it end up in his pocket?

Scenario One: he picked it up somewhere, without even realizing what it was. But he hated classical music, never went to concerts, and as far as I know didn't hang out with musicians. Scenario Two: someone gave it to him. The image of the mysterious woman who had sex with him in my loft pops up in my head. She could've been a musician. Perhaps it was a post-coital gift. Scenario Three: someone slipped it into his pocket. But why? And who? I shiver as Scenario Four slowly formulates in my mind: someone could've put it in his pocket *after* his death.

A violin bridge.

A message.

A message from the Violinist.

I can't breathe. I have to get off the motorway right now. I hit the hazard lights' button and veer off onto the hard shoulder. I'm out of the car as soon as it stops, forcing myself to take deep breaths. A pain in my side reminds me instantly of my bruised ribcage.

I'm still leaning forward, my hands on my knees, waiting for the wooziness to subside when I hear a voice behind me.

'You all right, madam?'

I straighten up and turn. There is a police car parked behind my MG, its lights flashing. The policeman is big and stony-faced and he means business.

'The hard shoulder is a dangerous place to stop. Are you aware . . .'

'I'm so sorry. I felt sick, I had to stop.'

He glares at me. 'Are you fit to drive now, madam?'

'I think so.'

He suggests I take a break at Medway service station and follows me all the way there.

Stopping at the service station isn't such a bad idea. I head straight for Costa Coffee and order a mint infusion. It soothes my nerves and helps me think clearly.

Could the violin bridge *really* be a message from the Violinist? The idea seems far-fetched, now that I think about it rationally. The Violinist is dead. There's no way he's been sending messages from beyond the grave. A vengeful relative? From what I remember reading about him, he was a loner with no family in this country. And even if there *was* a grudge-bearing relation somewhere in the world, why would they choose *me* as the recipient of their angry missives? And why *now*, after such a long time?

No, there *must* be another explanation for its presence among Anton's things, probably a totally innocuous one. He used to carry all sorts of weird things with him. Screws, bolts, washers, earplugs, sticky bonbons, why not a violin bridge? He must've slipped it into his pocket because he liked the look of it. Maybe he was planning to use it in his art. I take a sip of my mint tea, trying to convince myself that this is the most plausible explanation. Of course it is.

I hadn't realized how tense my body is. I stretch and square my shoulders, studying the other travellers lounging in service station bliss: a handful of guys in suits poring over their mobile phones, a smattering of elderly couples working through their daily intake of sugar and a group of surprisingly quiet teenage kids, their noses in iPads. I feel a yawn coming and I turn to cover my mouth, when something black on a solitary armchair by the milk and sugar station catches my eye. The yawn instantly dies in my throat.

Perched on the armchair, all slimline and shiny, sits a brand-new violin case. Where is its owner? I look around. I should tell someone. There must be a security guard on the premises. Speak to the staff at the bar. They'll know what to do. The case is too small to hold a body, but there could be a bomb in it. I have to warn everybody. The girl who served me earlier approaches the station to replenish the milk thermos. Just as I open my mouth to alert her, a young boy appears by the armchair, casually picks up the case and shouts something in French to the group of teenagers. They are getting up, chatting and collecting their scattered belongings. I can see now that they all carry various instrument cases. The boy with the violin case joins them and they pile out through the door to the car park. A white coach pulls up and opens its doors, an *Orchestre Symphonique des Jeunes de Haute-Marne* logo on its side.

A wave of relief washes over me. Thankfully no one has noticed my little flap, the guys in suits are still staring at their phones and the elderly couples keep devouring their cakes. The barista girl has returned to her position behind the counter. Life goes on as normal.

'You gonna answer it, love, or shall I do it for you?' The guy at the next table sounds annoyed.

My phone is ringing.

'Kristin! It's Rupert. As in Rupert and Daniel?'

I hesitate for a moment, trying to place the voice and the names. Ah, my hipster friends from the Grand Canal Apartments. I've forgotten to email them the drawing of the King's Cross man. But it doesn't matter anyway. I don't think there's a cyclists' plot to kill me.

'Sorry not to have called you sooner, darling,' he rattles on. 'We meant to ring you, but we've been so busy. Life just takes over, doesn't it? Anyway, how have you been keeping?'

He doesn't wait for my answer.

'The reason I'm calling, do forgive me for getting straight to the point, darling, but we have a bit of an emergency . . . We're going away tomorrow morning, two weeks in Santorini. It's absolute heaven, we've been going there for years. The problem is our friend who normally looks after Matilda was taken to hospital today with a burst appendix and our other friends . . . well, let's face it, they are all herpetophobic. In case you're wondering, it's an aversion to reptiles, not the fear of catching herpes. How can you *not* like Matilda?'

Ah, Matilda the snake, it all suddenly clicks into place.

'Would you like me to look after Matilda?'

'Oh, sweetheart, would you mind? You'd be an absolute lifesaver.'

Everything else in my life has been turned upside down, so why not add a python to the mix?

'I should be home in an hour. Do you want to drop her off at my place?'

Thank goodness I've left Pixel at Vero's. I wouldn't want him to end up as Matilda's snack.

'Oh no, she's quite comfortable in her vivarium. She doesn't mind being on her own, so don't worry about having to keep her company. All you'll need to do is pop in once, in about a week, and feed her.'

'OK.' I instantly have an image of myself filling up Matilda's bowl with Pixel's dry food. 'What do I feed her with?'

'Peach fuzzies.'

'Peach fuzzies? I didn't know snakes ate fruit.'

'They are feeder mice, darling. We've left a whole bag of them in the freezer, just in case. She used to eat pinkies until recently, you know, neonatal mice without a coat of hair, but now that she's grown she can handle juveniles.'

The whole talk of fuzzies and pinkies is beginning to make me a bit queasy, but I bravely soldier on.

'OK, so what do I do with it?'

'Here's the catch: you have to defrost it at room temperature before you can give it to her. Please, don't do it in the microwave. Just put it between two sheets of kitchen towel and wait. It shouldn't take long, an hour at most. It may have a nosebleed as it thaws, but it's nothing to worry about, it's quite normal. And once the fuzzie is nice and soft, you just pop it into Matilda's vivarium and she'll do the rest. She's quite shy, but if you're lucky she might eat it while you're there.'

Now, there's a lovely thought.

'Do you think you can handle it, darling?' Rupert sounds quite concerned and I have no heart to tell him to stuff his fuzzies and leave me alone.

'I'll give it a go . . . Don't worry, I'll be fine.'

'You are a star! We'll bring a nice bottle of Metaxa Private Reserve back for you!'

I have no heart to tell him I hate Metaxa.

We agree that Rupert will drop off the keys to their flat tonight and we disconnect.

26

The loft with its sprayed-on windows has a dark, almost derelict
feel. It's also very stuffy and there is a whiff of graffiti paint still
hanging in the air. This needs to be sorted out as soon as
possible. After a long wait, I get through to the building's
managing agent who clearly doesn't want to tell me if our
insurance covers vandalism. In the end, he reluctantly agrees
to send someone to assess the damage. Having dealt with them
before, I know it'll take days, if not weeks, before they spring
into action. I decide to bypass them and call the insurance
company directly. They sound more sympathetic and give me
some generic advice on what I should do. Call the police.
Document the damage with photographs and provide notes as
to how and when the incident happened. One thing is clear
though: the damage needs to be assessed before 'vandalism
removal specialists' can be called. Great, it means I'll have to
live in this dungeon for weeks, unless I pay for the removal of
the graffiti myself. It would probably take a team of guys with
specialist equipment on a cherry picker to clean off the paint
and it would cost a fortune. As things stand at the moment I
have barely enough money to live on, so forking out anything
over a hundred quid is out of the question. A life in a dungeon,
then. As a temporary measure I kick open one of the windows

sealed with paint and breathe in the nitrogen-dioxide-rich Hoxton air.

The shaft of light from the open window falls directly onto my desk and the Mac. I look at the big black screen, remembering Fly's lecture. Part of me wants to dash out to the Apple store in Covent Garden straight away. But I really can't afford a new Mac at the moment. Not even a refurbished one.

Is it really possible that someone has planted rootkits inside it? Or worse, locked it inside its own virtual world? In the cold light of day it seems far-fetched, almost absurd. I'm not rich and famous nor do I have any terrorist connections, so why would anyone bother to monitor my digital activity with such a level of sophistication? I resist the temptation to power up the Mac and google 'rootkits'. Instead I resort to pen and paper. It's time to look at my life and separate fact from fiction. I draw a line down a sheet of paper, dividing it into two parts: 'Facts' on the left and 'Speculation' on the right. I start on the left.

– Anton's death
– 'Exposures'
– Loss of job
– Messages from Professor Stein

I go back to the top of my list and add 'Anton's fling/unknown lover?'. Then I draw four arrows growing out of the 'Exposures' line:

Ex 1 – The Violinist's crime scene (forensic job connection?)
Ex 2 – 'In Bed With Anton' (art connection? Anna?)
Ex 3 – Anton's fling (personal life?)
Ex 4 – Drone attack (loft, my past?)

Underneath the fourth arrow I print WAKE UP in capital letters and underline it. Damn . . . I add another item to the list:

– Blip with Marcus

I wish it wasn't a 'Fact'. But let's move on to 'Speculation':

– I've been hacked
– Bike connection

Bike connection gets three arrows:

– Where is Anton's bike?
– King's Cross encounter – who is the guy?
– My two collisions with cyclists – link? (unlikely)

I add two more items to the right column:

– Violinist connection/Violin bridge?
– Street art?

Actually, Professor Stein's emails have to be moved to the right as they might be fakes. The same goes for 'Anton's fling/unknown lover?'. The hotel receipt could've been planted on him and the video of him having sex at the loft faked. Well, maybe.

I read through both lists, swap the black pen for a red marker and begin to draw more lines. The hacking speculation could be connected to almost everything on the list except for Anton's death, the blip with Marcus and the bike. 'Loss of job' seems to be a direct result of 'In Bed With Anton', which could be related to Professor Stein and my art. The Violinist might be linked to Anton through the violin bridge, which would, in turn, tie Anton to the 'Exposures'. The 'Exposures' may have something to do with him anyway, as he appears in two of them. Street art links him to the fourth 'Exposure' through the drone attack. He might have fallen to his death while on a street-art recce. There's also Anna from the Fugitives, who is associated with Anton's street art, but also was an unintended recipient of 'In Bed With Anton'. Unless she herself was the hacker with access to my memory drives. And what about Rupert and Daniel, who just happened to be on the towpath to pick me up after my collision with the cyclist? Doesn't Daniel work for some cyber security company?

I drop the red marker with a groan. This is useless. The piece of paper in front of me, covered with arrows and red doodles, looks like the work of a paranoid maniac. It hasn't helped me clarify anything. On the contrary, it's made me even more confused and suspicious than before. One thing is obvious though – most of the 'Facts' seem to point to my past. I'm supposed to wake up from something, but I have no idea what. But as I dwell on it, my present life is coming apart at the seams.

My present life.

I need to get a grip on it. Talk to Heather about the Playthingz project. Look for a proper job. Face the music with Sophie and Marcus. Sort out the windows. Get Pixel back. Forget about Professor Stein and my unfulfilled artistic ambition.

Job first. I check in with my usual agencies and get in touch with the new one that wanted my portfolio. The job's already gone, but they'll keep my name on file. I reluctantly power up my computer and browse through TV Watercooler, Grapevine, the Unit List and LinkedIn. You never know what might pop up on any of the websites. But it's slim pickings today. Playthingz then. I call Heather and she tells me there are no more batches of sex toys to be photographed. But she is working on a new project she'd like to discuss with me in person. I hop into the shower, throw some clean clothes on, and twenty minutes later I'm sitting in the red velvet armchair in Heather's office.

'We're launching a small and exclusive Discreet fashion range aiming to bridge the gap between designer and alternative clothing. It's influenced by various subcultures, you know, Gothic, Punk, Heavy Metal, but with a softer, more traditional twist.'

I don't need much convincing to agree to do a fashion shoot for her. What else have I got to do, anyway?

'I don't want boring white-screen photos. I'm thinking a more urban setting, full of character, edgy. You know, Shore-ditch fifteen years ago, something like—'

'Hackney Wick?'

'That's exactly what I was going to say. Do you know it well?'

'I haven't been there for a while, but I know a lot of great spaces there . . . Let me have a look around and I'll get back to you.'

'Fantastic. How soon can you do it? I'd like to have something ready for London Fashion Week in September.'

'I can start pretty much straight away.' There's no point pretending to Heather that I'm mega-busy. She radiates positive energy and seems to be genuinely pleased I'm available. 'And the models?'

'I've got that covered.' She's grinning mischievously and I have a feeling it's going to be a hoot.

'OK, I'll just wrap a few things up and then do a location recce. I should have some pictures for you soon.'

'I'm really glad you can do it.' Our meeting is over and Heather opens the office door for me. 'Oh, by the way, do you fancy going to a concert tonight? Patrick Ewer is playing at the Union Chapel in Islington. You know, the composer from upstairs.' She points at the ceiling. 'It's sold out, but I have a spare ticket.'

Ah, my Peeping Tom. I'd nearly forgotten about him.

'Sure, why not.'

It actually might be interesting to watch him instead of being watched for a change.

We arrange to meet outside the chapel before the gig and I leave Discreet, my head already buzzing with location ideas for Heather's project. A fashion shoot for a sex shop isn't going to be the pinnacle of my professional career but, given a free rein, I might be able to produce something I won't be ashamed of.

I dash across the street back to the loft, put my G12 camera in my bag and head out of the door again. There's no better time than now, as Aunt Stella used to say. I catch a bus to Dalston Kingsland, and from there, the North London Line overground train. It's one of the new trains with walk-through carriages and air-conditioning which has long lost the battle with a whole range of urban odours. It's outside the rush hour, so there are quite a few empty seats and I squeeze myself in between a pale Goth boy and a chubby woman who shouts into her mobile phone in a language that sounds like Polish or maybe Russian. I watch the landscape behind the window change from the tightly packed inner-city clutter to a more sprawling and derelict industrial scenery. It feels familiar – I used to come here a lot as a fledgling artist. I remember getting drunk on cheap booze with Erin as we searched for an affordable studio space in our pre-Cubic Zirconia days. We ended up breaking into one of the ramshackle canal boats and sleeping off our hangovers in someone's mildewed bed.

Soon I'm arriving at Hackney Wick station, flaunting its post-London-Olympics modernity against the crumbling remains of the old East End life. I swipe my Oyster Card and walk down the ramp to street level. Sharp left into White Post Lane, past the Lord Napier pub, a ghost of a building with a stunning street-art-decorated facade, and along a row of small warehouses still occupied by wholesalers. Bold graffiti sprayed on a wall – WAKE UP NEOLIBERAL ARTY-FARTY IDIOTS FASHION IS FAKE – announces the arrival of new enterprises, pop-up rave places hiding behind metal gates firmly shut in the daytime. Past a couple of odd burger shacks, the closed shutters of the Celestial Church of Christ, a recycled clothes manufacturer and an MOT garage and I arrive at Queen's Yard. Flanked by the Crate craft brewery on one side and the White Building, an art centre in a converted factory, on the other, this is where I'm hoping to find the location for my shoot. I don't have to look far: the riverside Crate pizzeria, with its industrial interior made from reclaimed local flotsam, looks like a dream film set. I order a pint of Crate Wheat and settle at a table outside, watching an occasional boat pass almost noiselessly along the River Lee Navigation.

The citrusy beer, with its delicious notes of orange peel and coriander, goes straight to my head in a mellow wave. This is it, I think, I could just sit here forever, sipping beer, watching the alternative world go by, far away from my life, far from the craziness of it all. The woman at the table next to mine looks like Tilda Swinton. Bleached hair with shaved sides, strong arms, splashes of paint in different colours on her sleeveless vest. Probably a painter. She's immersed in a conversation with a slim, nervous man with a *Peaky Blinders* haircut and tortoise-shell glasses. An artist for sure. I soak in the coolness of the couple and the place. I could fit in here, I could be their friend. I could reinvent myself and disappear from my present life. The longing for that free-spirited feel of the early Cubic Zirconia days overwhelms me. If only I could have it again, go through the reckless exhilaration of those days once more . . .

I put down the empty beer mug on the table with a loud clonk. The couple interrupt their conversation and look at me with round, aghast eyes. Yep, nothing *nice* lasts forever. I throw Tilda an apologetic smile and get up. Enough of this self-indulgence, I have a job to do. Even if the job is a budget shoot for a sex shop.

I hurry up the steps to street level and cross the bridge over the river. The instant change in the landscape is ruthless. To the right the imposing disc of the Olympic Stadium sits in the middle of an asphalt desert with colour-coordinated signs and immaculate street furniture. To the left hums the rusty giant of the Olympic energy substation. Ahead, in the distance, looms the glass and concrete mass of the Stratford shopping centre. Right in front of me the engineered expanse is empty – there are no people here, no movement, no life. I turn round in disgust and walk back towards the other side of the river.

I spot a narrow alleyway on the left, a messy pathway between tired buildings. Old pipes running up and down the walls are painted red, blue and yellow, and every accessible flat surface is covered in tags, stencils and graffiti. PUNK RUINED MY LIFE. CHADD IS A RACIST. A.CE IS THE NEW KATE MOSS. As I walk further in, the buildings become more derelict and the street art better. It reminds me of the narrow lanes of the Mission in

San Francisco, where Anton and I spent weeks gorging ourselves on the most beautiful murals and the best burritos. The alley continues under the arch of one of the buildings, a short, dark tunnel with aptly dark art on its walls. I emerge from the tunnel into a square yard and I'm dazzled by bright light. The building at the back of the yard has been pulled down and the sunlight is cascading over the remaining pile of rubble, illuminating the cavernous space. Despite the brightness, the houses that still surround the yard on three sides resemble Victorian brick tenements, except their walls are not blackened with soot: they are all covered with stunning, vibrantly coloured murals. On the entire facade of one of them there is an elaborate design composed of many smaller details, in black, yellow, green and various shades of red, from magenta through crimson to deep rust. It looks like a huge, fiery bird, but as I stare at it, I begin to notice a different pattern, and I suddenly know where I've seen something similar before: *Constellations* at the Miró Retrospective. I remember standing in front of a particular painting, totally in awe. It was small, one of twenty-three works Miró painted on paper during the war, a tangle of lines and geometrical shapes representing women surrounded by flying birds. The mural on the wall is not a copy of Miró's image, but a variation on the theme, transformed and developed. I stare at the mural, unable to take my eyes off it. This is clearly the best art I've seen in a long time. But who painted it? Thanks to Anton, I'm familiar with most of the big street-art names, but I don't recognize anyone's style on this wall. I rummage in my bag for the camera and take a picture of it, then another. This is it, this place is perfect for Heather's shoot. The artwork, juxtaposed against the pile of rubble, will be an ideal backdrop for the models. I slowly turn round, snapping photos of the remaining buildings in the yard at different angles, trying to capture the beauty of the place. And then I freeze.

I slowly lower my G12 and look at the wall I was just about to photograph. It's dominated by a large black-and-white paste-up that stretches across three floors, covering all the windows, wrapping itself over every crack in the facade of the building. It's a photograph of a face, in extreme close-up, created in different shades of grey out of a multitude of dots on a white background. The further one gets away from the picture, the clearer it becomes. I'm familiar with the technique. It's digital halftoning, something Anton used a lot in his art. And I know whose face it is.

Mine.

I stumble backwards and, feeling my legs wanting to give out, sit down heavily on a remnant of an old brick wall. I greedily absorb the image in front of me, recognizing Anton's way of running wheat paste over the image in a transparent layer of glue, his signature at the bottom right-hand side of the paste-up. *Savage*. It's Anton's work, I have no doubt about it. I even remember when and where he took the picture of me. It was in Argentina and I was furious with him because instead of travelling all the way down to Patagonia, he wanted to stay in Buenos Aires and do a massive paste-up with his Argentine mates. I was telling him that his bloody street art spoiled our every holiday and he just pulled out his camera and started taking pictures of me. There is something about looking straight at the camera lens that makes you instantly aware of yourself. I saw my anger and I immediately realized how petty it was. He kept snapping away, recording the transition from rage to truce in my face. We never went to Patagonia, instead we had a great time in BA.

In his paste-up, Anton has used a few different photographs from the series, superimposing them on top of each other. In a single image he's captured the whole range of emotions and the effect is striking. It's still my face, but it's also a sublimation of the most universal of human expressions. It's beautiful.

I don't know how long I've been staring at the wall, but eventually I notice my face is wet and my eyes are burning. I didn't even realize I'd been crying. Seeing Anton's mural has brought up so many feelings, feelings I thought I'd managed to put a lid on. Anger. Love. Hope.

Is it possible he's alive? Was his death a dramatic disappearing act? The mural looks untouched by time and the elements. I'm trying to remember whether it has rained in the past few days. Just like any wallpaper, paste-ups hate damp walls, need dry weather for the glue to set, and get washed off when fresh by anything stronger than a passing shower. Well, it's been exceptionally dry and hot lately, but still . . . I approach the wall and touch the paper. It feels dry, the glue underneath it solid. It could've been done some time ago. But it looks so clean and immaculate, as if it's been sitting in a gallery and not a Hackney Wick alleyway. They say the usual lifespan of a London paste-up is a couple of weeks. If the weather doesn't get it, taggers or the council cleaners do. The mural in front of me hasn't been defaced or damaged in any way, it doesn't even have a single tag on it. It looks brand new, as if it was pasted up only yesterday. As if *Anton* pasted it up yesterday.

Is it possible? Is it possible he faked his death and hasn't even bothered to let me know he is alive? Could he be so cruel? OK, we did have a bust-up, but to punish me like this? No, I *know* Anton, he wouldn't be capable of such malice. I'm trying to extinguish the tiny flicker of hope, but it keeps coming back.

I didn't *see* him in the mortuary. For all I know it was Lionel's lawyer who identified the body. Was there an autopsy? An inquest? I don't even know. What if he's alive . . . ?

All's forgiven, babe, just let me know you're OK.

Maybe, just maybe, it's his way of telling me he *is* OK. But he had no way of knowing I'd be here. Even *I* didn't know I'd be here until a few hours ago. This is crazy.

The sound of a door slamming shut gives me a start. A skinny guy in a grey hoodie is crossing the yard, a dirty red rucksack on his back.

'Excuse me!' I'm up and marching purposefully towards him.

He ignores me and keeps walking.

'Excuse me, can I ask you a question?'

He throws me an anxious glance. 'Yeah?'

'Do you live here?'

'Why?'

'This mural.' I point at the wall. 'Has it been here long?'

He looks at the paste-up as if noticing it for the first time. 'I don't know.'

'Please, it's important . . .'

'Not sure . . . maybe a few weeks.'

'Not days?'

He shrugs. 'Maybe.'

I sigh in exasperation and nod at him. 'Thanks.'

I suddenly feel ridiculous, flailing around, accosting strangers. I can't hang about here forever, I won't get any answers just staring at the wall. I take a few pictures of the paste-up and leave, throwing one last glance behind me.

* * *

By the time I get back to Hoxton my hopeful elation seems to have evaporated. I realize there is a perfectly logical explanation for how Anton's mural ended up in the Wick. He could've pasted it up after he got back from his travels and before his death. Perhaps he was planning to show it to me in a reconciliatory gesture, a 'big reveal', Anton-style.

I really shouldn't get my hopes up, I know he's dead. But a tiny part of me is feeding on doubt now, making me restless and raw. On the train back from Hackney Wick I caught myself scanning people's faces looking for his familiar features, listening out for his French accent, searching for him. I can feel an obsession take root, and I know that if I'm not careful it'll monopolize everything I think and do. I have to stop it now, I have to nip it in the bud before it takes over my life.

Distraction. The best weapon against any obsession is distraction.

I force myself to turn my computer on and upload the photos I took at the Wick. I quickly run them through Photoshop, cropping and resizing them to a smaller format. I make a folder for Heather, purposefully ignoring the images of Anton's mural, and email it to her, titled 'Proposed Shoot Location'. There, job done. I'm just about to check my phone messages when I look at the clock. Damn, I'm supposed to meet Heather at the Union Chapel in half an hour. A quick sprint to a bus stop in New North Road just in time to catch a crowded 271, which gets me to Highbury Corner.

I make it with five minutes to spare. There is an orderly queue already formed on the pavement in front of the chapel. I walk along it looking for Heather, catching snippets of conversations about Glyndebourne Festival and the Summer Exhibition. I didn't realize Mr Ewer drew such a posh crowd.

I reach the beginning of the queue without finding Heather. On the heavy wooden doors to the chapel there is a board with the running order for tonight's performance. A quartet called Feather Cerebrum is doing the warm-up act before the main attraction of the evening: the London premiere of Patrick Ewer's chamber piece.

It's called 'Violin-Land'.

'I'm so sorry I'm late.' Heather's voice pulls me out of a shocked daze. I don't know how long I've been standing here. The chapel is open, the queue has disappeared and the usher at the door is gesturing for us to hurry up.

It's packed inside, but Heather manages to negotiate some space for us in the last pew. Feather Cerebrum are already on stage, tuning their instruments and fiddling with the microphones.

'I can't wait to hear Patrick's piece,' Heather whispers. 'He's such a great violinist.'

I nod, trying to hide the panic building up inside me. A violinist.

The guy who's been watching my loft for weeks. The guy who saw Anton being fucked by a stranger in my bed. The guy who caused Anton to get himself arrested. My Peeping Tom is a violinist. And he's composed 'Violin-Land'.

Feather Cerebrum have started playing; melancholy piano riffs overlaid with string cords and delicate percussion fill the neo-Gothic vaulted interior, but I'm unable to enjoy the music. Although it's hot outside, the chapel seems chilly and damp, making me shiver in my thin T-shirt. I suddenly feel pins and needles in my hands and feet and begin to flex my fingers, drawing a strange look from the man next to me. I'm sweating, despite the chill in the air.

Peeping Tom is a violinist. What kind of bizarre coincidence is this? Perhaps it's not a coincidence. Maybe there is a connection between the guy whose victim's dead body I photographed all those years ago and the man who lives opposite and seems to have a penchant for watching me. But what on earth could they have in common? Why is this happening to me? Why do I keep stumbling upon violinists everywhere? Why is Ewer's piece called 'Violin-Land'? What does it all *mean*?

I can't stand being squashed among all these people, I can't stand the loud music, the oppressive damp smell, the glaring lights. I have to get out of here. I mumble something about the loo to Heather and climb over people's legs towards the exit. I spot the 'Toilets' sign pointing at the transept to the right and trot that way, my head lowered, trying to make myself invisible.

Thankfully there is no one inside. I lock myself in the furthest cubicle and sit down on the closed loo, ignoring my usual aversion to public toilet germs. The tiny, dingy space feels like a sanctuary. I take a few deep breaths, the smell of bleach cleaner filling my lungs. There, a bit better. Feather Cerebrum's music trickles in through the closed doors, soothing and gentle.

I'll be fine. There's nothing to be worked up about. Even if there is a sinister side to Mr Ewer, I'm safe here, surrounded by hundreds of people. This is the best place to confront him, to show him I'm not scared. Yes, that's what I'm going to do. I'll walk up to him and look him straight in the eye. Challenge him. The boot is on the other foot, Mr Peeping Tom.

I can hear muted applause – Feather Cerebrum must've finished playing. A couple of women come into the toilet, talking loudly about their daughters who have apparently just got into the Camden School for Girls. Good for them. I wait until they leave and open the cubicle door. One more lungful of bleached air and it's time to face the devil.

The lights are dimmed in the chapel and the compère is introducing the big star of the evening.

'. . . one of the most popular and prolific London composers, whose distinctive contemporary classical style is recognizable to music fans all over the world. He's been composing for stage and screen and has received many awards, including the prestigious SOLO Music Award. His brand new album, *Violin-Land*, will be available for sale in our shop after the concert . . . Ladies and Gentlemen – Patrick Ewer!'

Applause erupts as a spotlight searches out a tall figure, a narrow electronic violin under his arm, standing in the wings. I recognize my Peeping Tom and my heart begins to pound. What shall I do? Jump on stage and confront him now? Wait until the concert is over? Sit in the front row and glare at him? I edge closer to the empty stage. Why is he making everyone wait? Is he stalling? Perhaps he's seen me already . . .

Applause grows stronger as he slowly makes his way up to the stage, accompanied by a slim, blonde woman. She leads him gently towards the music console with its various mixers and keyboards. As I watch him shuffle forward, I take in his stooping, hesitant gait, his self-conscious smile, his dark glasses, and it slowly dawns on me.

Patrick Ewer is blind.

27

I don't remember much of the concert, apart from the fact that the music was haunting and beautiful. What I do remember is being utterly mortified by my own thick-headedness. How could I have *not* noticed the man was blind? As I sat there watching Ewer create the most mesmerizing and lyrical sound, my mind kept replaying the image of me, hanging off the windowsill completely drunk, flashing my tits and shouting obscenities at him. My self-inflicted humiliation couldn't be more complete.

Having excused myself from post-gig drinks with Heather, I half walk, half trot home, wanting to bury myself in the darkest corner of the loft. It *is* dark there, thanks to the painted-over windows, and before I turn the light on I manage to slip on something lying on the floor by the front door. A small padded envelope. I pick it up, my heart racing, not knowing what to expect. It's a set of keys with a small grey fob, accompanied by an art nouveau notecard from Liberty.

> *Dear Kristin,*
> *Thank you so much for agreeing to look after Matilda.*
> *You are an absolute darling. The fob is for the alarm,*
> *which will start bleeping as you open the door. Touch*
> *it against the padlock sign on the keyboard and the*

bleeping will stop. Do the same when leaving and the
alarm will arm itself. You'll have plenty of time to leave
and lock the door. Eternally grateful,
  Rupert, Daniel and Matilda
  PS The address is on the back of this card

I have to put a note about it in Google calendar straight away. I don't want to have a starved-to-death python on my conscience.

I power the Mac up, click on Firefox and put Matilda in the diary, a week from today. I add a few exclamation marks to her name and extend the duration of the appointment, so it stretches across half a day. It probably won't take that long, but it'll be more difficult to miss it this way.

My phone vibrates somewhere at the bottom of my bag and I remember I put it on silent before the concert. I fish it out and check the screen. Five new texts and three voicemails. OK, texts first. Rupert lets me know he's dropped off their keys. Delete. Jason wants me to call him. I have to give it to him, he is persistent. Delete. The next text is from Sophie.

I need to talk to you.

Shit. She knows.

I put the phone down, go to the kitchen and open the drinks cupboard. At the very back of it there is a large bottle of mescal which Anton and I dragged all the way from Oaxaca in Mexico. I shake it to wake up the *gusano rojo*, the red worm floating at the bottom of it. I need your strength, brother, I think as I take a swig straight from the bottle. Its musty and peaty taste burns my throat and its warmth spreads in my stomach instantly. I take a couple more swigs and put the bottle back in the cupboard. I don't want to get drunk, I just need liquid courage to deal with what's unavoidable. I'll have to speak to Sophie, I can't keep putting it off any longer.

While waiting for the mescal to do its job, I pick up the phone again and check the rest of my messages.

Back in town, fancy a bevvy?

That's from Erin and I'm glad she's got in touch. She's one of the few people who'd understand what's going on in my life. And I might need a friendly shoulder to cry on very soon. The last message stops me in my tracks.

Let's talk.

It's from Marcus.

I'm in trouble. If both sides of a couple contact you independently wanting to talk, the news is always bad. I find that couples tend to present a united front when they have something positive to announce. But when things go to seed, everyone goes it alone. I'm in trouble, no doubt about it, the question is how *big* is the trouble? The two independent messages, from Sophie and from Marcus, suggest it's of titanic proportions.

To delay the inevitable, I check my voicemail. A message from Vero makes me smile. Apparently Pixel got into some serious mischief right after my departure. It involved Vero's Kashan rug, but she doesn't go into details. Anyway, it turns out Fly is allergic to cats and Pixel's seaside holiday will have to be cut short. Vero and Fly are coming to London tomorrow to a special screening of the Final Cut of *Blade Runner* (not to be confused with the Director's Cut) at the NFT and will drop

Pixel off before the show. Vero has her own set of keys to the loft, so they'll let themselves in even if I'm not here. The little fur-ball is coming home.

The second message is from PC Singh. Through the mescal haze I listen to her reciting the words in a matter-of-fact, professional tone. *Coroner's decision. Inquest not necessary. Death by misadventure.* I stare at the phone's cracked screen in disbelief. And that's it? *Death by misadventure?* What about all the unanswered questions? What about the drugs in his system? CCTV footage? His missing laptop and bike? I can't believe they've just swept Anton's death under some bureaucratic rug! And then it hits me: that scoundrel Lionel and his cold fish of a lawyer. That's what they wanted all along. No inquest. No scandal. There, done and dusted. As if Anton had never existed . . .

I bite back the tears as I let the third voice message play out.

'Kris, it's Sophie, please call me when you get this message. I'm . . . Yeah, just call me, please, doesn't matter what time, I'll be waiting.'

Shit. I take a deep breath and touch Sophie's name in the Contacts list. She answers on the first ring.

'I need to see you.'

'Right now?' I glance at the clock on my Mac. It's 10.30 p.m. 'Sure . . .'

'I'm at the Four Seasons in Canary Wharf.'

'Canary Wharf?' What on earth is she doing there? It's an awkward schlep and I don't want to drive with mescal in my veins. But going to see her is the least I can do, under the circumstances. 'Of course, Soph, I'll be there as soon as I can.'

'I'll be at the Quadrato Lounge.' She disconnects.

I suppose I deserve short shrift.

I bring up the Uber app on my phone and am swiftly connected with my driver, Serhan, who'll take me to Canary Wharf. He is a chatty Turkish chap, who spends the journey telling me in great detail the story of his hip replacement surgery. He shouldn't be driving yet, but desperate times call for desperate measures. I know exactly what he means. I'm grateful for his amusing monologue that keeps my mind off PC Singh's revelation. The calculated iciness of Anton's brother doesn't bear thinking about. We arrive at the Four Seasons and I get out of the cab, breathing in the damp, slightly musty smell of the Thames. The hotel is perched on the riverside, its warm lights reflected in the water. It could be an idyllic picture, but it's not.

It's time to pay the piper.

I walk in through the glass door. Sophie is pacing nervously in reception, her hand to her mouth. As I approach her I can see she's biting her fingernails, a habit she kicked years ago when we were both students. She looks tired and pale and there are dark mascara smudges under her eyes.

What have I done to her?

She notices me and she throws me a wan smile.

'You've come.'

I nod, unsure what to say.

'They closed the lounge five minutes ago. Let's go up to my room.'

'You're *staying* here?'

She shrugs. 'I have a business account with Four Seasons.'

'You do?'

She ignores my question as she turns towards the lifts. I trot behind her, trying to understand what's going on.

Her room is on the seventh floor. It's spacious and elegant, in the style Anton called 'cosy corporate'. Its best feature is a massive window behind which stretches the most magnificent panorama of the Thames with the lights of the City shimmering in the distance.

Sophie goes straight to the minibar and takes two Johnny Walker Black Label miniature bottles out. She pours the whisky into heavy crystal glasses and hands one of them to me. She takes her glass to the armchair by the window and sits down with a sigh. I perch on the edge of the king-size bed.

I feel like asking her what's going on, but I know it would be duplicitous.

'I've left Marcus,' she says at last.

Oh no, here we go. The pounding of my heart is so loud I'm sure she can hear it.

'I checked in here last night. I've given him till the end of the week to move out of the house. I just can't stand being under the same roof with him . . .' Her voice catches.

I should say something now. I should try to apologize.

'Soph, I'm so sorry, I—' I break off, unable to find the right words.

'I've found a good divorce lawyer. She thinks there might be a slight complication with the division of the company assets, but apart from that it should be pretty straightforward.'

'You're getting a divorce?' God, what a mess.

'I can't imagine spending one more day with him. The lawyer says that, with adultery as grounds, it's going to be really quick. A clear-cut case, she reckons. He isn't even denying it.'

If there was a way of melting into the carpet and dropping down straight to hell, I'd choose it right now.

'Soph, I don't know what to say . . .'

She drains her glass in one gulp.

'I mean . . . I'm as mortified by the whole thing as you are
. . .' I cringe at my own words.

She jumps up from the armchair with a scream and hurls
the glass at the wall.

'Fucking idiot!'

I freeze, not recognizing the Sophie I know. Wild-eyed, she
stares at the broken glass, then slumps down to the floor, sobbing.

'Soph?' I put my glass down and kneel down by her.
Cautiously, I touch her arm. 'Soph?'

She abruptly turns towards me and for a moment I think
she's going to hit me. Instead, she leans forward and puts her
face in the crook of my neck. I put my arms round her and
rock her gently until her sobbing subsides.

Eventually she pushes herself up and goes to the minibar
again.

'We've run out of whisky. It'll have to be Jose Cuervo this
time.' She drops a mini-bottle of tequila in my lap.

This will go down a treat with all that mescal I had earlier.

She settles back in the armchair and takes a swig straight
from the bottle.

'Marcus and his fucking Lust Junction . . .' She chuckles
humourlessly.

'His *what?*'

'Lust Junk-shion.' She pronounces it in a slow, exaggerated
way.

Lust junction? Is that what he called our pitiful fumble?

'What do you mean?'

'Lust Junction dot com. It's one of those "infidelity websites".'
She makes quotation marks in the air. 'You know, like the one
that got hacked some time ago. Ashley Madison or something.
Life is short. Have an affair – that was their motto. So . . . it

turns out he's had his profile up for *four years*. Can you believe it? *Four fucking years* of us living together, working together, sleeping together . . .' She retches and covers her mouth with her hand.

'*What?*' I stare at her, dumbfounded.

'For all I know he could've had hundreds of encounters . . . I'll have to get myself tested for all the STIs.' She shakes her head. 'And HIV.'

I know I should be sorry for my best friend, I know I should be shocked by Marcus's transgression, but all I can feel right now is an overwhelming sense of relief. Relief that I, total bitch of a friend that I am, haven't been rumbled.

I take a deep breath and plod on in my newly discovered guise.

'But how . . . how did you find out?'

'This is the weird thing.' She takes another swig of tequila. 'This woman gets in touch with me out of the blue – oh, wait for this, she calls herself Anastasia – and she says she's been Marcus's lover for seven months . . .'

'Did she email you?' My alarm bells are ringing.

'No, she actually called me. At first I didn't believe her, I mean, fifty fucking shades of doolally or what, but she told me to check Marcus's profile on Lust Junction, because this is how they apparently met. So I go onto the website and bingo!'

'But why would she tell you all this?'

'Because . . .' she looks at me, pausing for effect, and I can see how drunk she is, 'because he's been cheating on her with other women on Lust Junction!' She screeches with hysterical laughter.

There is a quiet knock on the door and Sophie totters to the small hallway. I guess from the polite tone of the short conversation that it's official hotel business. She comes back to the room, kicking off her heels as she walks.

'There's been a complaint about the noise in this room. Some wanker thought we were having a fight . . .' She giggles and throws herself on the bed. 'I've asked for more booze.' She slurs her words and I'm sure she must've started her drinking binge long before I got to the hotel. I've never seen her in such a state. Tipsy – yes; wasted – never.

She begins to snore almost immediately, but when I approach the bed to cover her with a blanket, she opens her eyes.

'Why did you do it?' she whispers, looking straight at me.

I gasp and step back from the bed. Sophie closes her eyes and starts snoring again.

Stifling a whimper, I grab my bag and run out of the room.

28

She knows.

My brain seems to be locked in a loop, repeating the same thought over and over again.

She knows.

I find myself walking aimlessly around the hotel lobby, not knowing what to do. Eventually the night porter approaches me and enquires if I need a taxi. Yes, a taxi, that's what I want. It arrives almost immediately, shiny black and immaculate. I give the driver my address and curl up in the back seat.

She knows. I replay our conversation in my mind. She'd known all along and she played me, waiting for me to come clean. And I didn't.

'You come here often?' The driver is looking at me in the rear-view mirror.

'What?' I don't want to engage in chit-chat. 'No, never.'

'Interesting place, Canary Wharf.' He seems undeterred by my unwillingness to talk.

I stare out of the window, pointedly ignoring him.

She waited for me to say something, she gave me plenty of opportunities to be honest with her, and I sat there like a spineless, lying cow and said nothing.

'. . . the sea trade from the Canary Islands . . .' the driver drones on.

What kind of a person am I? Obviously a person who, having slept with her best friend's husband, doesn't have the guts, or the decency, to face the consequences.

'. . . dog in Latin. The Dog Islands and the Isle of Dogs – geddit?' The driver chuckles with pride at his own erudition.

That thing with Marcus and Lust Junction. Could it be true? Or was it just a ruse to get me talking about him? Marcus and porn dating sites? I've known the man for years and this is the most preposterous thing about him I've ever heard. It's totally *not* Marcus. The whole story could've been taken straight from the *Jeremy Kyle Show*. But, on the other hand, Sophie never lies.

'. . . canaries by boatloads. They used to take them straight to coal mines and miners would carry them in cages down to the tunnels. If a miner saw his canary drop dead he'd leg it straight back to the surface, because it meant the whole tunnel was full of methane or carbon monoxide. Think of it as a canary alarm.'

Despite my reluctance, I find myself listening to the driver's monologue. I wonder how many other London stories he has up his sleeve. Having charged me a fare that seems to include on-board entertainment, he deposits me right outside my front door and waits until I get inside. I slowly climb the stairs, breathing in the familiar smell. The pungent mix of old cooking and dried-up pee wouldn't kill a canary, but it does make me nervous. My loft used to be my sanctuary, but it doesn't feel like a safe place any more. Whoever has invaded my life has also poisoned my home.

I guardedly unlock the door, bracing myself for yet another

nasty shock. But the place is empty and quiet, it doesn't smell of gas and there are no drones hanging around outside the windows. I tiptoe to the kitchen and pour myself a glass of water. As I drink greedily, my anxiety level seems to drop.

Why am I tiptoeing, for God's sake, it's my own house!

I turn the light on and rummage through the cupboards in search of something to eat. I find an old packet of Dr Karg crispbread. It tastes a bit stale, but it'll do. Crunching on an organic seed cracker, I climb into bed and pull my MacBook towards me. Yes, I know, Fly's warned me against using it until he's swept it for bugs, but I don't care any more. I need to get to the bottom of it all.

Sophie knows about my episode with Marcus. Well done, Kristin. In one fell swoop you got rid of your best friend and created a new, fitting persona for yourself: a selfish conniving bitch.

He must've told her, there is no other way she'd find out about it. The question is *what* did he tell her? The 'poor, lost Marcus seduced by a predatory friend' version of it? Or the truth, about my accident and him coming to the rescue? The fact that I was shaken and doped up on painkillers doesn't make me any less guilty: I made no effort to stop him when he touched me.

But something in the whole Marcus/Sophie story doesn't add up. Is Marcus a harmless loser emotionally abused by his bossy wife? Or an insatiable lech with an active account on Lust Junction dot com? Neither persona seems to be the Marcus I know. But the same could be said about Sophie. Who is she? A ruthless businesswoman or a betrayed wife? Whose story am I supposed to believe? They can't both be telling the truth, which means one of them is lying. The question is who and why.

I click on the Firefox icon and type in LustJunction.com. And there it is, just as Sophie said, a whole page of cosy stock photos of embracing, happy couples, interspersed by testimonials promising a fulfilling sex life. As you scroll down, the corporate images are replaced by stamp-sized, home-made pictures uploaded by the users. The few smiling faces disappear in a sea of gaping vaginas and ejaculating penises. It's quite some lust junction.

It turns out that in order to be able to browse the selection of, well, members, one has to sign in and upload a profile. I quickly choose a close-up of a shrivelled old man from a stock-photo library, fill in a membership questionnaire with wildly bogus data and I'm in. *Hi, my name is Curious Glance.* I wonder how many people do what I've just done out of curiosity, never bothering to make actual physical contact with the other users.

Now, how do I find Marcus? The free membership I've opted for offers limited search possibilities. But I can set my search criteria according to sexual orientation and preferences, various fetishes, S&M, voyeurism, swinging, group sex, water sports, cross-dressing. There's a whole subsection for Rubber/Latex/Leather and another one for Role Playing. Blimey, how do I find Marcus in all this? Thankfully I discover I can also narrow my search to a location. I try East London, and then even tighter, within five miles of Roman Road. This would give me an approximate location of Soph and Marcus's house. I'm not sure it's the brightest idea. If I were a Lust Junction Romeo I'd set my location as far from my own house as possible. East Dulwich or Richmond in Marcus's case, but then who'd fancy a trek to the other side of town for a shag? Well, perhaps I'm underestimating the Lust Junction members' libidos.

I scroll through the multitude of mugshots and dick-shots, finding the process increasingly tedious. And then – Marcus's moody face in black and white stares at me from the screen. 'Gaius Ceasar'. Not far from Roman Road, after all. At least he's spared his potential dates the image of his penis. I click on his 'Profile Highlights'. 'Gaius Ceasar' is a few years younger than the man I know and is a musician (well, he *used* to be). He is also a 'cunning linguist'. *Good grief, Marcus!*

Is it possible that the real Marcus is behind all this? I push my MacBook away in disbelief. I shudder at the thought of Sophie reading his profile. It must've been awful for her. I can't blame her for not wanting to have anything to do with him any more.

Is this really happening? I lie back on the bed and close my eyes. I'm tired. And not only because it's nearly three in the morning. I'm tired because my life doesn't seem to fit me any more. Or is it the other way round? I don't fit my life. It's as if someone else, not me, has taken over and has been pushing me where I don't want to go. I don't like the new direction. I can't recognize my friends any more. I can't recognize myself. And every time I try to get my life back on an even keel, it slips out of control again. I'm tired.

29

I'm woken up by the ringing of my phone. Without opening my eyes I let it ring until it goes to voicemail. But a few minutes later it rings again. Who the hell is calling me at the crack of dawn? As I crawl out of bed in search of my bag I realize it's not early at all. It's dark in the loft only because of the red paint covering the windows. I manage to dig my phone out just as it goes to voicemail again. Two missed calls from Anna. Well, if she has something urgent to tell me, she'll ring again.

And she does, just as I'm mulling over my encounter with Sophie and waiting for the coffee machine to fill my mug.

'Hello, Kristin, I'm so glad I've caught you. There is something I have to show you.'

'Show me?' I grab the mug and sit down at the kitchen table.

'A picture has just come in. I've been approached by a new artist . . .'

'Anna,' I interrupt her. 'I don't think I'm in a Saatchi mood at the moment . . .'

She ignores my feeble joke.

'Kristin, you need to see it.' She sounds dead serious. 'Can you come into the gallery?'

'Right now?'

'Now would be good. Please come. I'll be waiting for you.'

She disconnects.

What is going on with her? I don't know Anna well, but she's never seemed like a person who'd get wound up easily. I finish my coffee and get up. I might as well go and see what it's all about. A short bike ride might do me good anyway.

It's hot and humid outside, another sizzling heatwave as the tabloids hysterically call it, and by the time I get to Sclater Street I'm covered in sweat. I lock my bike to the railings outside the gallery, noticing all the new street art that has popped up on the walls since my last visit here.

Anna appears to be waiting for me and she ushers me straight to her office. Without a word she points at a large, unframed picture leaning against her desk. As I come closer I can see it's a square photograph, probably 150x150cm, printed directly onto a thick sheet of aluminium. It's a stunning piece, layers of paint giving it an unusual texture, accentuating its edgy, industrial look.

It's a photograph of Anton's paste-up that I saw in Hackney Wick.

'Reena Acker.'

'Sorry?' I look at Anna, too shocked to concentrate on what she's saying.

'Reena Acker,' she repeats. 'Do you know her?'

'No.'

'Apparently it's her work.'

'What?'

Anna flinches at my raised voice. 'I received it this morning.'

'But it's—'

'I know. It's Anton's piece and it's your face. That's why I called you.'

'I've *seen* it, Anna! In Hackney Wick!'

'When?'

'Yesterday! I mean, it's brand new, Anna! It's Anton's *new piece!*'

'Oh . . .' It's her turn to look surprised.

In my agitation I take a step backwards and land in Anna's reclining armchair. She stares at me in silence, then turns to her filing cabinet and takes out the bottle of red wine. She raises it in my direction and, when I shake my head, pours herself a glass. She takes a sip and sits down behind her desk.

'This is interesting,' she says at last.

'Who is Reena Acker?' I've calmed down enough to speak quietly.

'I don't know.' She takes another sip. 'She contacted me via email. She said she had a couple of pieces that might interest me. I normally don't accept unsolicited work, but when I saw it I recognized Anton's style . . . I replied to her saying it's an unusual piece, who is the artist, where is it, the usual stuff. She couriered it to me overnight even though I didn't ask for it.'

'So you haven't met her?'

'No. She's based in Germany, I think, Berlin if I'm not mistaken. I've seen her website though.' She shrugs. 'It's pretty good stuff, mainly urban photography, but Anton's piece stands out, obviously. You say it's his new paste-up in Hackney Wick?'

'I *think* it's new . . .' I'm beginning to feel silly for making a fuss about it. 'I was on a recce in the Wick yesterday and wham! I ran smack into it. It's in an immaculate condition, as if it was done a couple of days ago.'

'But it could've been done a couple of *weeks* ago? Or last month?'

'Yes, I know, he could've pasted it up before his death.'

'It's definitely his work?'

'He took the picture of me when we were in Argentina.'

'I see.' Anna takes another sip of her wine.

'What about that woman, Reena? Did she claim it was her artwork?'

'No, she said the *photograph* was hers. She didn't say anything about the author of the paste-up.'

'But she *stole* Anton's image!'

'It's not as straightforward as it seems.' Anna sighs. 'You could argue that she's made Anton's piece a focal point of her photo and therefore infringed his copyright. But if there was someone standing in front of the paste-up in her photo, for instance, it would be perfectly legal. Either way, it's very difficult to enforce the copyright. Unlike in France and Belgium, we have Freedom of Panorama in this country. It's the unrestricted right to use photos of works of art or architectural pieces in public spaces without infringing the rights of their authors.'

'So this woman can take snapshots of other people's art and no one will bat an eyelid, as long as she's not doing it in front of the Eiffel Tower or the Manneken Pis?'

'She can take as many pictures as she wants, but she may have a problem with selling or publishing them.'

'You're not going to put this picture up for sale then?'

'No.'

'Thank you.' I feel a tearful wave of gratitude towards her.

'You have nothing to thank me for, Kristin. I run a business and I don't take decisions that might jeopardize it or cause problems. It's as simple as that. But I do appreciate how upsetting it must be for you to see Anton's work being used in such a way by another artist.'

'It is. Coming across his paste-up in the Wick, the paste-up I knew nothing about . . . it hurt. This' – I point at the picture – 'is just rubbing salt into the wound.'

'I know. It must be very painful now that Anton's gone.' Anna gets another glass out of the cabinet, pours some wine into it and offers it to me. This time I don't turn it down. Fighting back the tears, I take a few big gulps. The wine's dark-berry warmth and smoky finish spread on my palate. It's mellow and soothing.

'I'm so sorry, Anna. I didn't mean to—'

'It's all right. Really.'

'My life is such a mess at the moment. Anton's death has knocked me for six, but there's all that other stuff. I can't seem to break out of this evil, vicious circle. I don't remember how it feels to be calm . . . carefree.'

'That stalker of yours still giving you grief?'

I look at her, surprised by her question, then remember I told her about it when she received 'In Bed With Anton'.

'Yes. No. I mean, someone did spray my windows with red paint.'

'Kids?'

'I don't think so. My loft is on the top floor and whoever did it used a drone.' I don't feel like telling her about 'Exposure 4' and the message I deciphered in the paint.

'Wow. The work of a sophisticated vandal then.'

'I live in Hoxton, after all.'

We both share a joyless chuckle, then continue sipping the wine.

'I've slept with my best friend's husband. And she's just found out about it.' It comes out so easily, all that drama packed into a couple of short sentences.

'Ouch.' Anna puts her empty glass down.

'They've split up now. Two fucked-up lives for the price of one stupid slip-up.'

'I'm sure you're not the only one to blame.'

'Apparently not. He was up to some weird shit, online dating and stuff, but it doesn't change the fact that I allowed it to happen. I betrayed my best friend because I felt needy, lonely and hard done by. And it's not the only thing I feel guilty about in my past.'

'We all make mistakes when we feel vulnerable.'

'But it was so . . . accidental, so throwaway.'

'Most of our mistakes are. It's the consequences that take us by surprise, especially when they take on a life of their own.'

'You sound like you know what you're talking about.'

'Oh, I do, believe me . . . More wine?'

'No, thank you, I better get going.'

I suddenly feel self-conscious, divulging my shameful secrets to someone who's practically a stranger. I put my glass down and get up, a pleasant buzz in my head.

'Sorry for pouring my heart out like this. I seem to be doing it every time I come here.'

'No need to apologize, honestly. I know how it feels, I've been there myself. Oh, and don't worry about this.' She waves at the picture. 'I'll write to Reena Acker, whoever she is, and suggest it'll be in her best interest to withdraw this image from her portfolio.'

'Thank you, Anna.' I reach out spontaneously and hug her. 'I do appreciate it.'

She returns my hug, and we embrace a moment longer

than necessary. She smells of some musky, oriental perfume and red wine.

I get on my bike, pedal for a few wobbly seconds and jump off. I'm too pissed to cycle. I realize I've left my bag and my phone at home, so I ask a cool-looking Japanese girl with blue hair for the time. It's nearly one. Wow, I can count the few occasions I was drunk at midday on the fingers of one hand. I decide to walk and push my bike along; it's not that far, anyway.

I like Anna. A strong, independent woman with a somewhat sordid past that she likes to hint about, but never goes into details. What was it? Some people died because of her? I wonder what happened. A car crash most likely – she doesn't strike me as a serial killer. Whatever it was, it's made her into a bit of a car wreck herself, a drinker who starts her afternoon with a glass of Malbec, but runs a successful business. A high-achiever who only drinks expensive wine. A functioning alcoholic, who manages to stay in control of her life. I've noticed she always asks me to come and see her at the gallery. I've never met her outside, in a public place. It actually makes sense, as our meetings have always been art-related, but I wonder if there's more to it. The Fugitives is *her* space, safe and quiet, with *her* bottle of Malbec in the filing cabinet. Am I reading too much into her addiction? Maybe. Whatever her problem is, I still like her.

As I open my front door I'm greeted by a ball of fur that throws itself at me, purring and weaving around my legs. Pixel's back! On the kitchen table there is a large platter covered in cling film, filled with crescent-shaped pastries. Aunt Vero's *rugelach* croissants! She hasn't baked them for years. She really is pulling all the stops out for Fly. I'm glad she's found him.

She was getting a bit dispirited with Bridget and Midget as her closest companions.

Vero and Fly have come and gone and I'm sorry I've missed them. But the plate of *rugelach* on the kitchen table and Pixel's presence have lifted the mood in the loft. I drop a fresh capsule in the coffee machine and take the cling film off Vero's platter. The *rugelach* are just as I remember them, their chocolate and walnut filling melting in my mouth. Malbec, *rugelach* and good coffee for brunch, I could get used to this.

Munching the sweet pastry, I check my phone, which I'd left on the kitchen table. A text from Vero:

Njoy *ruglch* n Pxl. TTYL. Xx

Wow, if Fly's influence continues, she'll be winning speed-texting competitions next. There's a text from Heather too, saying she likes the photos from my recce and asking when we can schedule the shoot for. I'll get on it straight away, I just need to do one thing . . .

I open the MacBook and google 'Reena Acker'. I instantly get a link to what appears to be her professional page, ReenaAckerPhoto.com. Disappointingly, it's in German only, but it does tell me she *'ist eine deutsche Fotografin'*. It's divided into three different sections, *Grossformat, Panoramen* and *Bilddatenbank*. As I click on Large Format, I'm presented with three subsections, *Bauwerke, Lanschaften* and *Industrie*. I browse the folders, looking through moody photographs of buildings, landscapes and industrial sites. She's actually not bad. In fact, some of her pictures of street art are quite impressive. But one image is missing: Anton's paste-up. I go through all the photographs twice to be sure, but it's definitely not there. Perhaps she's taken heed of Anna's warning and removed it from the website already. Wise move.

There is a short entry about Reena Acker on Wikipedia, both in German and English. She was born in Frankfurt in 1980, studied photography at City College of New York and the Royal College of Art, has had exhibitions in New York, Berlin, London, Geneva and Shanghai, and her work has appeared in various art publications. All in all an interesting person I wouldn't mind bumping into if she hadn't pissed me off by stealing Anton's image. But having seen her work, I'm prepared to give her the benefit of the doubt: she may have genuinely thought that photographing an urban landscape decorated with a mural was fair game. She should've known better but, hey, we all make mistakes.

On an impulse I pick up the phone and dial Erin's number.
'Ryder!'
'Wow, I was expecting your voicemail.'
'Would you rather leave me a message?'
'No,' I laugh. 'I'll take my chances with the real person.'
'What's up, babe?'
It's so nice to hear her voice. I suddenly realize how much I've missed her larger than life presence.
'It's been quite horrible lately . . .'
'Oh God, I'm so sorry. I've read about Anton in the paper. I wanted to call you but – honestly – I didn't know what to say. I'm hopeless when it comes to handling grief. How are you coping?'
'I'm managing, I think. It's actually a relief to be able to talk about something else. I wanted to pick your brain about something . . . Is this a good moment to talk?' I can hear some traffic noise in the background.

'It's fine, what is it?'

'Does the name Reena Acker mean anything to you?'

'Reena Acker?'

'A German photographer, apparently.'

'Acker . . .' she repeats. 'It does ring a bell – I just can't place it. Why?'

'You sure you have time to listen to all this?'

'Go on.'

Trying to be as brief as I can, I tell her about Anna's phone call, the photograph and Anton's paste-up in the Wick.

'Did the gallery ever consider putting it up for sale?'

'I'm not sure. The owner recognized Anton's image, so she knew from the start there was something dodgy about it. She rang me straight away.'

'That's very decent of her. More than you'd expect from an average gallery owner.'

'It was. Especially as the photo's quite good.'

'Is it?'

'I'd put it up for sale myself . . .' I laugh self-deprecatingly.

'Well, you do have a stake in it.'

'As far as I know Anton's brother Lionel is the beneficiary of his estate.'

'But it's your face.'

'My face?'

'Anton has used a photo of you in the paste-up, hasn't he?'

'Oh, I see what you mean.'

'If you really wanted to make a nuisance of yourself, you could sue this Ackerman woman for using your image without your permission.'

'That's really far-fetched . . .'

'Did she ask you to sign a release form?'

'Obviously not.'

'And I bet Anton took that picture of you in a private space.'

'In our hotel bed in Buenos Aires, actually.'

'There you go. The public versus private space is a very important distinction. She had no right to use your private photo. There is an expectation of privacy every court would have to protect.'

'I'm not going to take her to court.'

'You could threaten her. No one wants a lawsuit, so she'd probably offer to settle.'

'I'm not going to do it, Erin.'

'Why not? Everyone's doing it. You know Shepard Fairey's painting of Obama? *Hope?* It was based on an AP Press photo of Obama at some public event. So all good here, Obama wouldn't sue him because of the public space bit. But AP did – claiming Fairey infringed on its copyright and demanding money from him! And they probably need cash less than you do . . .'

'Just drop it, will you?' I'm suddenly feeling annoyed by her insistence.

'Just sayin' . . .' she drawls.

'Then don't.'

'I'm sorry, Ryder.' She drops her mock-American accent. 'I didn't mean to upset you.'

'It's OK. Let's not talk about it.'

'Sure,' she says lightly but lets the silence drag on.

'I'm sorry, Erin, I've overreacted. It's just that since the revelation about Anton's brother taking over his estate, all this copyright shit is making me sick.'

'Of course, I understand. Listen, I have to go now, but let's have a drink soon. I'll text you with some dates.'

'Definitely, let's do that.' My enthusiasm sounds as insincere as hers.

I hang up, restless and unhappy. I wish I hadn't been so brusque with her. I don't know what possessed me, she was just trying to be helpful. But her suggestion of suing Reena Acker has made me feel really defensive. Is it because she implied I needed money? That I'm a strapped-for-cash loser, who'll never achieve anything under my own steam? That my only way of squeezing some dough out of someone is by suing them over a copyright of a picture that isn't even mine?

I *am* overreacting. I'm projecting my own insecurities on a successful friend who's only offered advice because I asked her for it. I realize how much I've always valued Erin's opinion of me and how much it hurts to even think that she might pity me. No, she doesn't *pity* me, she just doesn't think we're in the same league any more. And I can't blame her. I *am* a miserable plodder, while she is at the very top of our profession. That is the sad truth, Ms Ryder. Long gone are the golden days of Cubic Zirconia when we were on the same professional level, young, talented, hopeful. I fucked it up. Now she's jetting around the world, while I traipse all over Hackney Wick in search of some piss-alley for a second-rate shoot.

She's got what it takes and you haven't.

With a groan, I take a swipe at the *rugelach* platter, sending it crashing to the floor. Fuck all this.

Out of the corner of my eye I see a dark shadow pass along the wall of the loft. I turn abruptly with a scream, only to see Pixel's furry silhouette disappearing under the bed. Poor cat, he'd be so much better off at Vero's. I slide along the wall to the floor. I'm losing it. It's like someone wants me to lose it.

I should see a doctor. Get some antidepressants. Balance

the chemicals in my brain, fine-tune those neurotransmitters, because they are not working as they should . . .

My phone begins to ring and I ignore it. If it's Erin, I don't want to speak to her right now. If it's someone else, I don't want to speak to them either.

I crawl towards the smashed pieces of Vero's platter, mixed with broken-up *rugelach*. I pick out bits of the pastry with my fingers and stuff them in my mouth. Their taste reminds me of the first time Vero baked them, right after I moved in with her and Stella, a gangly teenager on the warpath with my parents. My mum, a housewife, and my dad, a dentist with a local practice, were adamant I should get a 'proper' education. For them the idea of their daughter studying art was simply un-acceptable. But I wanted to be like Aunt Stella, strong, free-spirited, in charge of her own life. When Stella and Vero took me under their wing I realized that being independent was no picnic. It was tough and challenging. It was also loads of fun.

So what has happened to the fun bit of my life? Where has it disappeared? When exactly did I change into this pathetic failure, unable to go through a single day without some crisis or disaster?

The phone rings again and this time I force myself to get up and answer it.

'Found the *rugelach* yet?'

'Vero! Yes, I'm actually stuffing my face with them right now. They are delicious!' I hope I sound upbeat enough. 'How was *Blade Runner*?'

'Oh, the screening isn't until midnight. We're at the Replicant Inception now.'

'The *what*?'

'The Replicant Inception Convention. You know *Blade Runner* is set in November 2019, but we've already started syncing with the storyline. So 2016 is the year of incept dates for the renegade replicants. Roy's incept date was in January, Pris's in February, Zhora's last month . . .'

'Pris! I loved her. It was Daryl Hannah's character, wasn't it? I wanted to look like her.'

'Yes, I remember your studded biker choker and the black mesh blouse.'

There's some clapping and cheering in the background and Vero gets distracted for a moment. It seems the *Blade Runner* worshipper-base is still going strong. And to think I was six months old when it was first released . . .

'Kristin, sorry about that. They were just announcing the winner of the best replicant replica. But the reason I'm calling is that while we were at the loft, Fly had a look at your Mac.'

'He *what?*'

'I know, that was exactly his reaction, but I convinced him you'd be absolutely fine about him checking the "Exposure" email. He didn't do anything else, I swear, I was watching his fingers on the keyboard all the time.'

I'm so taken aback I don't know what to say.

'OK, so here's what he told me, I wrote it all down. You can't trace the sender of the email. His guess is it applies to all the earlier ones as well. They were all sent via an untraceable remailer that forwards emails on anonymously. It's based in Singapore, apparently. Untraceable remailers don't keep records of their users, so a reply is not an option. The images you've received – they were all stripped of metadata – so no luck here either. Fly also said that your "Exposure" troll is using Tor and, wait, I have to read it to you word by word – "You probably wouldn't be able to peel back the layers of Tor even with Egotistical Giraffe". Don't ask me what it means, he said to give him a call if you want to know. He actually used the word "obfuscation". Not bad for a second-language speaker, eh?' Vero chuckles. 'I have to go now, honey. I hope you don't mind me unleashing Fly on your computer. I was really hoping he'd find something that would help us nail that bastard . . . It was worth a try, wasn't it?'

She's gone, back to her replicants. I stare at my MacBook incredulously. *Egotistical Giraffe?* I can't believe she's actually let some Chinese hacker touch my computer! It's like allowing a rogue surgeon to operate on your brain. Or giving your bank details to a stranger in the street. But I can't be angry with Vero. She's always had my best interests at heart and I know she was trying to help. Oh well, let's hope Fly and his pet giraffe won't abuse my vulnerability.

With a sigh, I open the MacBook and look at the screen. It's the usual busy mosaic of open folders, photos, Stikies notes and a multitude of open tabs in the Firefox browser. I'm a messy Mac user, rarely bothering to close all the apps and tidy up the screen. But it's my mess and I know how to navigate it. I'd always thought that if someone were to break into my computer I'd notice it straight away. I was certain that just as I'd notice an overturned chair or a lamp moved by a burglar in my house, I'd see something out of place on the screen. I couldn't have been more wrong. There is absolutely no evidence of Fly's presence on my Mac.

30

I've tidied up the loft, fed Pixel, taken a long shower and rung Heather to arrange the shoot. I'm feeling much better for it. Perhaps I can manage without Prozac, after all. Now for the digital side of my life. I sit down in front of the Mac and look at its untidy screen. Let's begin by closing all the open Firefox tabs. As I click on the tiny grey crosses, closing all the web pages one by one, I'm astonished how many of them I'd kept open simultaneously. I know, it's a bad habit and it slows down the browser unnecessarily, but I'm faithful to my bad habits. I imagine Fly wasn't impressed with it. The Lust Junction home page flashes up on the screen and I wonder if he noticed it. Oh well, there isn't much I can do to salvage my reputation in the eyes of a sapiosexual.

The sharp sound of my door buzzer tears me away from the computer screen.

'Hi, I'm looking for the occupier of the top flat . . .' The man sounds professional and polite. The police again?

'That would be me.'

'That's great. My name is Tony and I'm from Wall 2 Wall cleaning company. We're about to get rid of the paint on your windows.'

'On a Saturday?'

'We work 24/7. If there were any more days in a week, we'd fill them as well. You have no idea how many dirty walls there are in London. Would you mind if I just popped upstairs for a second to make sure all the windows are shut and secure?'

'Sure.' He seems genuine enough. I buzz him in. For once I'm impressed with the efficiency of the building's managing agent.

The man who appears on my doorstep is drop-dead gorgeous. A tight navy T-shirt with a yellow Wall 2 Wall logo accentuates his beautifully sculpted chest. He is tall, tanned and has a sweet smile to boot. I let him in and watch as he checks the locks on all the windows. Everything about this man is perfect, his long legs, his tight buttocks, his incredibly narrow waist and muscular, wide shoulders. And then there is his deep voice . . .

'. . . superheated water cleaning equipment. And don't worry, all our paint-stripping products are non-toxic and biodegradable, so both you and your kitty will be perfectly safe . . .'

That traitor Pixel, who normally hides at the sight of a stranger, is rubbing himself against the man's legs, purring.

'That's great, thank you.' I touch my chin to check I'm not drooling. 'How long will it take?'

'Oh, we won't be long . . . a couple of hours at most.'

'But how will you get out there?' I wave at the windows.

'Our high-level access vehicle is right outside.'

I look out through a gap in the red paint and see a huge cherry picker with the Wall 2 Wall logo parked in the street.

'So it is . . .' I want to kick myself for sounding like an idiot. 'So you won't need to go through my loft?'

'No, thank you, it'll all be done from the outside. We won't disturb you. Please make sure you keep your windows shut while we're out there.'

He gives Pixel one last pat, flashes another of his sweet smiles at me and is gone.

I sit down at the kitchen table, flushed and confused. If not for the massive cherry picker outside I'd have thought it was a kissogram visit from a rogue member of the Chippendales cast. But of course it's not. It's not my birthday and the very few friends I have don't do kissograms. It would've been totally inappropriate after Anton's death, anyway.

But still, I get up and tiptoe towards the window. The man – what was his name? Toby? Tony? – is already downstairs and putting on a yellow hi-vis jacket and a hard hat. Surely this is too much of the Diet Coke break cliché to be true . . . I'm almost expecting Etta James's smoky voice to blast out of the cherry picker's bucket. Instead I see another man, also dressed in hi-vis clothes, appear from behind the truck. He is short and bald, and carries his beer gut in front of him with an air of self-satisfaction. No, these guys are for real. Soon the cherry picker's long arm begins to unfold, carrying the bucket with the two men up. I step away from the window.

This is ridiculous. I'm in a flutter about some muscled hunk cleaning my windows. I'll be inviting the milkman for a coffee next. What on earth is wrong with me? It hasn't even been a week since Anton's death, for God's sake! I jump as a jet of pressurized water hits the windows. It *must* be hormonal, this is not my normal behaviour.

I force myself to go back to the computer. But my mind is out there, floating above the street in the cherry picker. As the layers of paint begin to disappear and the loft becomes brighter, an idea forms in my head.

*　*　*

My windows are spotlessly clean and the Wall 2 Wall guys are beginning to pack up when I dash downstairs with my Canon, a tripod and a digital camera mount.

'I was wondering if I could ask you a huge favour.' I'm addressing Toby/Tony, fluttering my eyelashes and making my voice higher-pitched. 'I'm a photographer and I've been *dying* to take a panoramic picture of the neighbourhood, waiting for an opportunity . . . and here you are, with this *wonderful* piece of equipment . . .' I wave in the direction of the cherry picker.

'Erm . . . we're not allowed to let anyone unlicensed onto the work platform . . .' The Diet Coke man's charming smile is gone.

'*Please* – it wouldn't take long . . .'

'And our parking dispensation is running out. We're blocking the road.'

'Just a few minutes . . .' I know it'd take a bit longer.

'Sorry, no can do.' He turns his gorgeous back to me.

'What's that thing then?' His beer-gut companion is pointing at the digital rig.

'Oh, it's a GigaPan. You mount your camera on it and program it to take loads of photographs which you can then stitch together to create an amazing panoramic picture. They use the same camera mounts on the Mars Rovers.'

'Really?' There is a sparkle of curiosity in the man's eyes.

'Yep, they developed the technology with Mars exploration in mind.'

'Blimey, it must've cost a few bob . . .'

'Wait till you see it in action.' I try my most seductive smile.

'Yeah?' The beer gut is hesitating. He looks at his watch. 'How long did you say it'd take?'

'Ten, fifteen minutes, tops.' I'm crossing my fingers behind my back.

'Go on, then.' He wipes his bald head with his hand. 'Hope I'm not gonna lose me job over this . . .'

'Thank you!' I feel like giving him a hug, but the sight of his beer gut stops me. Out of the corner of my eye I see Toby/Tony angrily throw his hi-vis vest to the ground. But my guy ignores him.

'You'll need to wear a hard hat, though, and I'll have to strap you in a harness. Shane's the name, by the way.'

I'd agree to anything to go up with my GigaPan. Shane climbs into the bucket with surprising agility. He hands me a hard hat and straps me in.

'Your colleague doesn't seem very happy . . .' I look at the Diet Coke guy, who is leaning against the truck looking handsomely pissed off.

'Tones?' Shane clips his harness in. 'Ignore him, he can be a right tosser sometimes.'

I forget 'Tones' as soon as we start going up. Never mind the fear of heights, this is fantastic. We swiftly climb to the level of my floor and I look in through the spotless windows. The loft looks unreal, more of a set in a dollhouse than my own home. I can see the messy kitchen with my Mac on the table, my clothes scattered around, Pixel sitting on the bed licking his paw, Aunt Stella's art deco mirror reflecting the warm, afternoon sunlight. I feel a strange sense of detachment, as if I am a spectator, not only outside my house, but also outside my life. The disturbing feeling disappears as we keep moving higher, the magnificent panorama of East London and the City opening before our eyes. The closest view is messy: flat warehouse roofs interspersed with brown-brick Victorian mansion blocks. An occasional flash of green announces the area's latest fad, roof gardens. Beyond the Shoreditch roofs stretches the shimmering monolith of the City. If London was a face, this is where its teeth would be.

'So tell me how it works.' Shane points at the rig and I'm reminded of the reason we're up here.

As I fix the camera to it and run the initial calibrations, I describe the beauty of the GigaPan to him.

'It's basically a very precise robotic mount that lets you divide any view into a multitude of single shots. What's special about it is that you can use a telephoto lens and create a large image out of extreme close-ups. Once you've got all the shots, its software stitches all the images into one massive mega-high-resolution panorama. It's essentially billions of pixels and hundreds, even thousands of photos combined into a single image. I'm not going to go for something that big, but the detail and resolution will be stunning, anyway.'

It turns out Shane is a keen amateur photographer with a special interest in astrophotography. He watches me set all the functions and is impressed when I'm able to preview the four corners of the intended panorama. Once all is set, I click on the 'OK' button and the GigaPan begins its laborious shoot. We both watch its progress in silence, keeping still, trying not to rock the platform. There is hardly any breeze, the hot London air isn't moving and for once I'm happy it's listless.

Exactly seventeen minutes later the shoot is complete. I pack up my toys as we majestically sail down. We land with a bump and are greeted by Tones' silent disapproval. Ignoring him, I thank Shane and try to offer him a couple of twenty-pound notes. He tells me to put the money away and wishes me luck with my picture. I promise to send him a link to the final panorama and dash upstairs to upload the photos onto the Mac.

I take the flash card out of the Canon, slot it in the card reader of my portable photo-data storage drive NextoDI and press the 'Copy' button. As the red light begins to blink, I go to the kitchen and make myself a coffee. Sipping the hot Java, I look around the loft, which seems much brighter now. Life isn't so bad, after all.

When the NextoDI announces the end of copying with a bleep, I take out the flash card and plug the drive into my Mac. It's the fastest way of dumping photos from the card and once I'm done with my coffee they have all been uploaded. I'm ready to launch the panorama-maker software. The Mac begins to crunch the pixels, estimating a waiting time of ten minutes. Enough to put an overdue load of washing into the machine and empty the fridge of all the mouldy smellies. To complete my cleaning fit I wipe the kitchen worktop with an antibacterial spray and go back to the computer feeling positively virtuous.

The panorama is done. Except for a few minor glitches that can easily be straightened out, it's perfect. The power of GigaPan panoramas lies in their mega-high resolution that allows one to zoom in and see things we wouldn't normally see in a picture. Try zooming in on an ordinary holiday snapshot and all you'll see is a blur. Not in my photo. I click on the screen and, using the stylus, scroll through the image. I can see every brick in the nearby houses, every small detail of the cityscape, things I wouldn't see with the naked eye. I keep zooming in and out of the picture, playing with it like a child. I'm not sure what I'll use the image for, but seeing it with such sharpness is exhilarating.

If only I could zoom in and out of my life like this and see what's going on with such clarity! Wouldn't that be nice . . .

I scroll down and see the roof of my building and, underneath it, my loft. Again, the sharpness of the image is incredible. I can almost count the whiskers on Pixel's nose. I keep rotating the picture until the building opposite comes into view. Feeling like a spy, I peek into Patrick Ewer's loft, which is disappointingly dark and empty. I suppose with his busy concert schedule he doesn't spend much time in London. A tiny flare above his loft catches my eye and I move the image to have a closer look.

Right above Ewer's loft there is a narrow recess, which hides a shaded window. A loft above the loft? I crank up the brightness of the picture until the darkened window reveals more detail. As it dawns on me what I'm looking at, cold sweat begins to trickle down my back. The flare that has caught my eye is a reflection of light in the lens of a telescope. I can just make out the name Bushnell on its side, right next to an attachment that holds what looks like an iPhone. The telescope is not pointing at the stars. It's looking straight into my loft.

I drop the stylus and turn away from the computer screen to face the windows. The sun's gone down now and the building opposite looks dark. But I can see the narrow recess above Ewer's loft, an architectural quirk I'd never noticed before. From this angle it's hard to imagine that the shadowy niche hides a window. But now I know it does, and in that window there's a powerful lens trained on me.

As I get up from the chair I realize I'm trembling. But it's anger, not fear, that is giving me the shakes. I grab my keys and storm out of the loft, slamming the door behind me. I charge down the stairs, the adrenaline in my body making me feel invincible. I'm going to get the bastard who's doing this to me. This has to end, right now.

It's quiet and dark outside, too late for the locals to be out, too early for the transient party animals. I sprint across the street and check the door to Patrick Ewer's building. It's locked, of course. I try the buzzers on the entryphone, starting from the top, all the way down. *Someone* must be in. No answer. I try again, keeping my finger on each buzzer until my arm goes numb. How is it possible that in a five-storey building in the centre of London there is no one to answer the door? The back door. There *must* be a back entrance. Tripping on the slippery cobblestones, I run along the front of the building. A couple of doors with black shutters down, an industrial rubbish bin, a wide, painted-over shop front reinforced with thick iron bars, but no visible access to the back.

I turn the corner and hit a brick wall. As I stumble backwards, the wall in front of me transforms itself into a big guy in a dark T-shirt and low-slung black jeans. His face is partially covered by some kind of respirator mask. I step back with a gasp.

The guy raises his arms in a placating gesture.

'Wow, you gave me a fright.'

'I gave *you* a fright?' I'm still trying to catch my breath.

'You OK?' He pushes his mask further up his forehead, staring at me. I can now see cans of spray and a ladder leaning against the wall. A tagger.

'Was someone chasing you?'

'What? No, I was just . . . jogging . . .'

'Ohh-kaaay,' he drawls incredulously.

'Yeah,' I try to sound casual. 'Sorry, I should've slowed down . . .'

'No worries.' He turns back to the wall and picks up a spray can.

'Well, I'd better get going.'

'Sure. Enjoy your jog, yeah?' I can't see his face, but I can hear a smirk in his voice.

I slowly retrace my steps, reach my front door and sit down heavily on the stairs outside. I can't face going up to the loft. The adrenaline rush from a few minutes ago has suddenly faded. I take a deep breath and look up, suppressing a sob. The walls of the buildings on both sides of the street form a shaft capped with the bleached darkness of London's night sky. It seems still, almost serene. But it's not. Because I know that somewhere in that darkness there is someone who watches me, someone who wants me to be scared. And I don't know why.

'Kristin?' I flinch at the sound of my name.

'Heather?'

She crosses the street towards me.

'What are you doing here?'

I force a grin. 'I'm having . . . a moment . . .'

'Are you all right?'

'I've been better,' I sigh.

'Can't you get in? Have you lost your keys?'

'My mind, more like.'

'What's going on?' She sits down on the step beside me.

'Oh, nothing.' I don't feel like telling my only employer that I'm cracking up. 'I thought I'd sit here for a while and enjoy the night. What are you still doing here?'

'Bubbles and Browse open evening. I've just closed the shop.'

'Busy night?'

'Free champagne always brings in a crowd.' She chuckles.

'And when people are tipsy, they are more likely to be creative with their money.'

'Heather, do you know if there's another flat above Patrick Ewer's loft?'

She looks at me, surprised by the sudden change of subject.

'Well, there is an attic space there . . . why, are you interested in renting it?'

'No, I thought I saw someone there earlier today. I never knew there was anything up there.'

'It's just an empty space, no utilities. It actually belongs to Patrick's loft, but has a separate entrance. He's been letting it out as an artist studio.'

'Do you know who rents it?'

'Not sure . . . Actually, he might have mentioned a photographer. Yes, I think there's a darkroom up there. Which reminds me – are we still on for our shoot next week?'

'Absolutely. Hope the weather holds.'

'Rain or shine, my dear, I need those photos.'

'And you shall have them.'

'Great.' She gets up and yawns. 'I'm off, my bed is calling me. Cheerio, lovely, don't stay out here too late.' She wiggles her turquoise-tipped fingers at me and toddles off down the street.

31

When I eventually get back to my loft I'm chilled to the bone. It always surprises me how the temperature can drop so dramatically at night, even though it's the middle of the summer. Without turning the light on, I grab a blanket from the bed, wrap it round myself and sit down in front of the Mac. As I move the cursor, the panorama lights up the screen. It's mesmerizing. A familiar warm feeling spreads inside me. I get it each time I manage to create something aesthetically pleasing, something that could be called art. This is not art, it's just a product of advanced technology, but it could be a start . . .

It's so quiet in the loft that the ping of a new email hitting the inbox sounds like a gong. At this time of the night it has to be junk. But out of habit I minimize the panorama and click the 'Mail' icon. Yes, on top of the list sits a new message announcing that 'English Bespoke Tailors are visiting UK'. How very nice of them. I click the 'Delete' icon and look at the long list of unread emails with a sigh. I'll have to tackle it, sooner or later. I scroll through the messages, looking at senders and trying to separate junk from the real stuff. Thankfully there are no new 'Exposure' messages. There is, however, a cluster of four emails from Marcus, sent at more or less the same time this morning. What now?

I click on the first of them and stare at the screen, perplexed. The message contains just one short line of text.

I'm sorry.

No 'Dear Kristin', no signature, nothing else, just these two words. How bizarre.

I click on the next email from him. And the third. And the fourth. The message they all carry is the same.

I'm sorry.

I look at the four identical emails, trying to understand. What is he apologizing for? Our embarrassing clanger? Why now? Or is he feeling guilt-stricken about Lust Junction? He should be apologizing to Sophie, not me, about it.

If it is a digital atonement, he could've chosen a more personal, and civilized, method of making amends. To be fair, he did try to get in touch, rang me a few times, and I hadn't returned his calls. OK, so he's sorry. Fourfold sorry. Is he expecting an answer from me? All's forgiven, Marcus, it was as much my fault as it was yours. Now go away and try to sort out your life, and I'll try to sort out mine.

Why has he sent the identical message four times? Perhaps it's just some weird email glitch? I look at the time of the emails. They were all sent around 8 a.m., within a few minutes of each other. It could be an email outage, like the one that flooded some poor guy's Hotmail account with thousands of messages.

There is something desperate, almost unhinged, about the four identical emails. Is he losing it because of the split-up with Sophie? It must be hell for both of them. But that stuff with

Lust Junction, it was such an unexpected, unlikely revelation. Marcus and lust . . . it almost seems like an oxymoron. Marcus, the dependable, if not a little boring, best friend's husband. A hazy, neutral figure hovering on the peripheries of my friendship with Sophie. She never spoke about their sex life, but over the years I got the impression it wasn't earthquakes and fireworks. More of a Sherlock Holmes/Dr Watson marriage of the minds. The mousy, self-effacing Marcus with his 'Kiss the Cook' apron and lazy sperm. And Sophie, a fashion-flower-turned-entrepreneur. I'd always thought I knew them well; now I'm not sure any more. What other skeletons are they hiding in their cupboard?

On an impulse I type her name into Google and get a handful of articles related to her online catering business. Good write-ups on TripAdvisor, the *TimeOut* page and a few foodie websites. An interview with Sophie Adler-Smith in the *Hackney Gazette* and the *Metro*. A nice photo and an article in the *Evening Standard*. All good stuff and nothing out of character. Phew.

I type in Marcus Morton next. He's on Facebook and LinkedIn, just like most of the people I know. No sign of the Lust Junction page, and I'm not surprised. If I really wanted to dig out some sordid stuff about him, I wouldn't be going on Google. How *does* one dig out dirt about people? I'll have to ask Fly next time I see him.

A link at the bottom of the page catches my eye. It's to today's local news section on the BBC London Live website. Feeling a stab of apprehension, I click on it.

HAMMERSMITH & CITY, DISTRICT AND CENTRAL LINES DELAYS: MAN HIT BY TRAIN AT MILE END TUBE STATION.

EXPOSURE

I skim through the text, my anxiety growing.

> A man is fighting for his life after being
> hit by a train at an East London station.
> Mile End station in Tower Hamlets was
> temporarily shut following the incident,
> which also closed other Hammersmith & City,
> District and Central stations.
>
> One witness said: 'I was in the first carriage
> when it happened. It was horrific. People were
> screaming. They had to walk us off the train,
> with London Underground staff blocking the
> view to the tracks. But we could see paramedics
> attending and there was a lot of blood.'
>
> Police confirmed that the man, Marcus
> Morton, 37 . . .

Oh God. I grab my phone and dial Sophie's number. It goes straight to voicemail. I look at the clock. A few minutes past midnight. I go back to the web page.

> Police confirmed that the man, Marcus
> Morton, 37, from Bow, East London, was
> taken by the London Air Ambulance to the
> Royal London Hospital. He is believed to be
> in a critical condition.
>
> A spokesman for British Transport Police
> said: 'We are investigating the incident.

We are studying the CCTV footage and
interviewing witnesses to understand exactly
what happened. The safety of our customers
and staff is our top priority.'

The Royal London in Whitechapel. I should go there. Be with them.

I grab my bag and car keys and dash for the door, then stop, my hand on the door handle. Would Sophie be there, by his side? And would she want me there after what's happened? What should I do? Call the hospital? I doubt they'd give me any information over the phone. No, I have to go there. Even if Sophie kicks me out, at least she'll know I'm there for her if she needs me.

It's raining outside and the streets are shiny and deserted. It takes me less than ten minutes to get to Whitechapel. I try to find a parking space, then give up and leave my car on the double yellow line outside the hospital. I run into the bright reception. A young woman in a headscarf at the information desk stops me with a polite question. How can she help? Chaotically, I ask her about Marcus. Am I next of kin? No, but I'm a close friend and I'd really appreciate any information she can give me. Yes, he's here, in the Adult Critical Care Unit, which is a restricted access ward. No, I can't go up now. The visiting hours are between 2 p.m. and 8 p.m., but most patients in ACCU are not up to social visits anyway. Is he going to be OK? She doesn't know, but I could try to get in touch with the next of kin who's been nominated to receive information from the care team. But I need to know. Is he going to make it? Reluctantly, she picks up a receiver.

Marcus Morton is critical, but stable. He's out of surgery,

but is still heavily sedated, so his brain function can't be properly assessed. He isn't out of the danger zone yet, but there hasn't been any further deterioration.

It's clear I'm not going to get past this woman and I won't get any more information out of her either. I thank her and leave. It's stopped raining and the air outside is heavy with moisture. I walk slowly back to my car, which miraculously hasn't been ticketed or clamped. I get in and suddenly a wave of extreme heaviness overwhelms me. I lean my forehead against the steering wheel, forcing myself to take a few deep breaths.

Where is Sophie? I pull my mobile out and dial her number. It goes to voicemail again.

'Hi Sophie, it's Kristin. I've just found out about Marcus. I'm at the Royal London right now, but they haven't let me into the ward. I just wanted to say that . . . I'm here if you need me . . . if Marcus needs me . . . if there's anything I can do. Please call me.' I disconnect, angry with myself for not being able to come up with something more eloquent.

Was it an accident? Or was he trying to kill himself? The two questions keep spinning in my head as I drive back home. What really happened on that platform? The article said the police were 'investigating the incident'. I don't remember the usual line about it 'not being treated as suspicious'. Which means there is some doubt, some uncertainty about what happened. Could someone have pushed him? Accidentally or on purpose? Was he standing too close to the edge? Perhaps he dropped something on the tracks and leaned forward to retrieve it? What was he doing at a tube station anyway? He prides himself on shunning public transport and getting everywhere on his bike.

When I get home I go back online and google 'man under train in Mile End'. I find news items on *Metro*'s website, as well as the *Daily Mail*'s page and London24.com. But they don't add anything new to what I've found out from BBC London Live. I try Sophie's phone again, but don't leave a message when it goes to voicemail. Where is she? Why isn't she answering? I look at the time. It's half past one in the morning. *That's* why she's not answering. I suddenly realize I'm shaking with exhaustion. I should probably get some sleep as well. There is nothing I can do at this very moment to help Sophie and Marcus.

I grab Pixel and climb into bed, snuggling next to him for warmth. But I can't sleep. I toss and turn, unable to switch my brain off. Pixel graciously purrs for a while, then slithers out of my desperate embrace and disappears, probably looking for some peace and quiet. But I can't find peace. After what seems like an eternity of sleepless torment, I get up, wrap myself in a blanket and sit down in front of the computer again.

What is the significance of the emails from Marcus? Why did he choose to send them to me yesterday, just a few hours before his accident? Surely, he didn't feel *that* guilty . . . What if he did? What if he tried to kill himself because of what happened between us? It was so *insignificant*. But once Sophie found out about Lust Junction, his shame may have pushed him over the edge. God, it's all too awful.

Bleary-eyed, I look at the four blue highlighted message headers. *From:* Marcus Morton. *Subject:* blank. *Date received:* yesterday. They are exact copies of each other, differing only by the time they were sent.

08:02. 08:05. 08:13. 08:18.

Why would he wait to send them at intervals of a few minutes each time? Why not send them all at once? And why *four* times? Deep in thought, I scroll down the mailbox. As if the answer is there . . .

And there it is, staring me in the face.

Subject: Exposure 4. *Date received:* 18 August.

My heart pounding, I scroll down looking for the other 'Exposure' emails, then remember they'd all disappeared. When did I receive 'Exposure 3'? The day I threw Anton out, hours before his death. The day I'll never forget. The thirteenth of August. 'Exposure 2'? The day I lost the Serpens job. I scroll down and find the last email from Zoe. The fifth of August. 'Exposure 1' is a no-brainer. I remember looking at it in the dark car park of the film studio with a vague sense of dread, as if subconsciously anticipating the nightmare that was just about to begin. It was the day of the shoot with Jason, the second of August, according to my Google calendar.

I rummage through the mess on the table for pen and paper, the long-forgotten buzz of excitement I used to feel as a teenager about number puzzles making my hands shake. I write down the dates chronologically:

02/08. 05/08. 13/08. 18/08.

Underneath, I write down the times of Marcus's emails:

08:02. 08:05. 08:13. 08:18.

My hand shakes so badly when I pick up the piece of paper that I can't read my hasty scribbles. But there they are, giving me two sets of four pairs of exactly the same numbers.

This cannot be a coincidence.

I get up abruptly from the computer table and go to the kitchen. Without turning the light on, I fill the kettle and wait for it to boil. With a hot cup of tea warming my hands I go to the window and look out. The building opposite is dark, the street below empty. It seems peaceful and quiet. But in my mind it shouldn't be. It should be collapsing around me, turning into clouds of dust.

Because my world is collapsing.

Everything I've taken for granted, everyone I've known, has been tarnished by disbelief and mistrust.

Marcus as my 'Exposure' troll? I can't believe it. And yet, the evidence is there, on my computer, his digital confession in the same twisted style of all the 'Exposures'.

I take a sip of my tea, trying to calm down.

Is it really possible that he's been behind the campaign of hatred directed at me? If so, *why*? Why would he hate me so much? I've known Sophie and Marcus for years, gone for holidays with them, had fun together . . . why would he turn against me? What have I done? The only thing I can think of is the fact that he's always been on the margin, on the outer edge of my relationship with Sophie. But it was his personality, it *was* him, the nice, quiet guy pottering in the background. Soph had been my original bosom pal anyway. Marcus came into the equation later, when she started dating him and dropped out of college. He was different then, fifty pounds lighter, with a wild mass of black curls, a Daft Punk leather jacket and his own band.

His band . . . Marcus did use to be a musician. He'd know what a violin bridge is. But he was a bass player, not a violinist! Surely there is no connection between him and a Czech serial killer? Why did he send me the crime-scene photo then? Just to spook me? What about the 'In Bed With Anton' photos? What was that about? Bigger penis envy? Perhaps he hated Anton? Enough to push him off a building? It doesn't even bear thinking about. His connection to the final two 'Exposures' is tenuous at best. Marcus hacking into my computer or flying a drone? Nah . . . It simply doesn't make any sense.

But what if he wasn't acting alone? What if Sophie was part of it?

Sophie? My best friend?

Well, yes, the same Sophie whose husband I let go down on me because I was feeling a bit under the weather . . . God, what a mess.

I put the empty mug in the sink and go back to the computer.

The four emails from Marcus still sit in the inbox, the proof of his guilty conscience. Why now? Why did he suddenly feel the need to apologize? I think I know the answer. It's because Sophie's found out his dirty little secret and his life started to fall apart, just like mine. It's not much fun being on the receiving end of someone's resentment, is it, Marcus? I shouldn't be feeling like this, not when he's fighting for his life in hospital. But I do. I'm not able to generate much compassion for him right now.

The troll who's been poisoning my life has come clean and apologized. No more 'Exposures'. Why am I not happy, or at least relieved?

I don't know.

32

I'm a train driver, but the train I'm supposed to be in charge of is driverless. I desperately search for the controls as it hurtles along a track resembling an amusement park ride. But I can't find the brake and it's accelerating, its wheels screeching and the smell of hot metal filling the cab. I know I'm approaching a station and I need to stop to avoid a terrible disaster. I can already see the crowded platform, with people literally spilling onto the tracks, unaware of my train speeding towards them. I realize with horror I won't be able to stop the train in time. I have to warn them. 'Get out of my way!' I scream. My voice is like the buzzing of a fly, trapped in the sealed capsule of the cab. 'Get out!' The front of the train ploughs into the mass of bodies, rises and seems to surf on something slippery and soft . . .

My own scream wakes me up, a hair-raising gurgling howl. I'm curled up at the foot of the bed, hugging a pillow like a long-lost friend. My heart thumping in my chest, my T-shirt wet with cold sweat, I lie motionless, too scared to move. Gradually the feeling of panic subsides. I slowly push myself up and look around.

It's another sunny day outside. The loft is bathed in a soft light, warm, bright, peaceful. Distant sounds of a Sunday in the city seep in through the closed windows, the background music to urban life. I take a deep breath and put my feet down on the floor. The smooth, oiled wood feels solid and cool. Pixel trots towards me, his soundless, ballerina steps like a mute dance. He nudges me with his nose, purring.

Life goes on. My nightmare is over.

But another nightmare is just beginning. How do I deal with Marcus's revelation? Part of me still doesn't want to believe he is my 'Exposure' troll. But if he is, how am I supposed to react to it? Tell Sophie? That would be one hell of a conversation. But I can't just ignore it. I can't do *nothing*.

His accident. *Was* it an accident? What if it wasn't? Only Marcus knows that. What if he's going to die? God, I really need to get hold of Sophie.

Just as I'm reaching for it, my phone chimes with a new text message.

It's from Sophie.

I need to see you. 1pm at St Pancras Old Church?

I stare at the text incredulously. She wants to meet *in a church*? Whatever next? Sophie is the most non-religious, atheistic person I know. Going to a place of worship, any worship, would be for her as out of character as going to a cricket match or a snooker game for me. Why this church in particular? The one in St Pancras Gardens, adjacent to the mortuary I frequented in my crime-scene days?

The mortuary . . . Oh no, Marcus . . . Is he dead? I sit motionlessly, trying to process the thought. He *can't* be. She would've said something. She wouldn't be so casual in her message. And the Royal London has its own mortuary with a post-mortem room, anyway. There wouldn't be any reason to transport him all the way to St Pancras if he'd died. And it's Sunday, anyway – the mortuary is closed. I breathe a sigh of relief, thankful for my old knowledge of London mortuaries.

There must be another reason she's picked the church as our meeting place. Does she want us to pray for Marcus? Sophie? I shake my head and text her back.

OK. See you at 1pm.

Just to make sure, I power up the Mac. There is nothing new in the local media about Marcus's accident. This is surely good news. If he'd died, they would've said something about it. They always do. He isn't dead.

I can't stop thinking about Sophie's text and by 11.30 a.m. I'm ready to leave home. I won't be cycling to King's Cross, though. I'll take a bus.

The 205 comes along as soon as I get to the bus stop. The traffic in Pentonville Road makes me regret not taking my bike, but eventually I reach King's Cross. It's as busy and congested as ever, its usual commuting crowd replaced by weekend visitors. To escape the hustle and bustle of Euston Road I cut across the station concourse and head towards Granary Square. The memory of the weird encounter with the Budnitz biker gives me a shiver, but I relax as soon as I reach the Grand Union towpath. This could easily be my favourite stretch of water in London. I have enough time to walk by St Pancras Lock, flanked on the opposite side by a tangled mass of urban wilderness. It's peaceful here, despite it being surrounded by the throbbing metropolis. The picturesque narrowboats at the Cruising Club basin rock gently as the Eurostar trains whoosh on the tracks above them. A couple of moorhens, or maybe coots, flap about against the backdrop of the ghostly white roof of St Pancras station.

'Excuse me!' a sweaty cyclist roars at me from under his racing helmet.

'Sorry!' I pack all the London passive-aggressiveness into my voice, begrudgingly moving out of his way. Pedestrians have priority on this path, so what's *his* problem?

I emerge from the tunnel under the railway tracks, climb the steps to street level and turn right into Camley Street. It takes me straight to the gate of St Pancras Gardens, right by the entrance to the mortuary. I know these narrow steps well, but I ignore them this time and go through the wrought-iron gates to the gardens. It's an amazing enclave of peace which I used to appreciate a lot in my forensic days. Flanked from one side by the old walls of St Pancras Hospital and shaded by mature trees, it has the hushed air of a sanctuary. It *is* a sanctuary. It used to be a graveyard, pushed out of existence by the nineteenth-century railway boom. Now the old headstones are stacked like slides in the drum of a projector around an old ash tree. It's the Hardy Tree, as it was none other than a young Thomas Hardy who was given the unenviable task of overseeing the moving of tombs.

Why would Sophie want to meet here, in this beautiful but eerie place? As I continue to stroll around the gardens, I'm drawn to the familiar pink building tucked away in the corner, a white sign above its entrance.

ST PANCRAS PUBLIC MORTUARY

I used to come here in my white Peugeot packed with forensic gear. I used to run up these steps, always rushed, always tired, numbed by the tragedies enclosed in these walls. And then I'd briefly step out into the sanctuary of the gardens for a quick cigarette, before going back to ugly reality.

As I stare at the square windows, a sudden realization hits me. I stumble backwards, leaning against the park railings.

This is where they would've brought Anton's body.

This is where I refused to come when they asked me to identify him.

This is where he lay on a stainless-steel table, waiting for someone to claim him.

And I never did.

A wave of grief knocks me off my feet. I slide down along the railings to the ground. Sobbing comes as a relief. I cry for us, Anton and myself, for what we could've had, but somehow never bothered to really try. *I miss you, the larger-than-life, outrageous, beautiful giant of a man that you were. OK, a lying cheat who couldn't keep his dick in his pants, too.*

I wipe the tears off my face with the sleeve of my T-shirt. Oh, Anton, none of this would've happened if you hadn't decided to go on some stupid recce at a building site. I would've forgiven you, like I always did. Your death has deprived me of the chance of making that generous gesture. Of feeling good about us again. They say death is supposed to bring resolution. Yours hasn't. It's brought chaos and pain.

But I have to go on. And now I have to deal with a friend whom I've betrayed. Sophie knows about me and Marcus. She knows about his double life. But does she know he's been hounding me for days, poisoning every bit of my life? Does she know he's the 'Exposure' man?

I check the time on my phone. It's 1 p.m. exactly. I force myself to get up and walk towards the church, passing John

Soane's telephone-box-like tomb on the way. This is such a strange location to choose as a meeting place. What was Sophie thinking?

The heavy wooden door to the church is open, but the quaint parish room is empty. With its mock-Tudor ceiling, a busy noticeboard and cosy table lamps, it looks more like an entrance to a pub than to a place of worship. It's my second church in the last week and the irony of it doesn't escape me. For a firm non-believer I seem to be spending a lot of time in places of worship. But as I go through the second pair of doors into the church, I'm struck by how simple and intimate it seems. There is no one inside. I take one of the plain wooden chairs at the back and let the peaceful atmosphere sink in. I'm beginning to understand why Sophie wanted to meet here. The place exudes calm and dignity. A handful of votive candles flicker in the small rack below the shrine of St Pancras, a strapping young lad, holding a model of a church in his right hand and a palm branch in his left. I must find out what his story was.

Through the middle of the church, all the way to the altar, runs a path made of old headstones, worn by hundreds of years of foot traffic. I lean over, trying to decipher the one closest to me.

Here lyeth þ body of
Katherine daughter of þ above
Who departed þ life
þ 21 August. 1716
Aged 34

She died exactly three hundred years ago. And she was exactly my age. A shiver runs through me.

Suddenly the church turns chilly and dark, as if someone pulled heavy curtains around it. My sweat-dampened T-shirt sticks to my back like a wet rag. I can hear the desperate buzzing of a fly somewhere above. I'm not enjoying the moment any more.

Where the hell is Sophie anyway? Why isn't she here?

I jump at the sound of the door opening with a creak behind me.

Sophie sits down next to me and puts a slim black briefcase on the chair in front of us. She's wearing a tailored trouser suit with a white blouse underneath. I've never seen her looking so, I don't know, official.

'Thanks for coming.' No hug, no kiss, none of the usual displays of affection.

'That's all right . . . How is Marcus?'

'Oh.' She seems surprised by my question. 'He'll be fine, I think. They are keeping him in a drug-induced coma to protect his brain. So the next few days will be touch and go, but the prognosis is moderately good, considering.'

'What happened?'

She shrugs. 'It seems he had a little run-in with a train.'

'A *run-in*?'

'He met it head-on, apparently.'

'Are you *serious*?' I'm beginning to suspect she's lost her mind.

'Oh, I'm serious.' She looks at me without a smile. 'I've never been so serious in my life.'

'What's going on, Sophie?'

'I'm leaving.'

'You're leaving Marcus . . . ?'

'No, I'm leaving all this.' She makes a sweeping gesture with her hand.

I stare at her, unsure what to say.

'I've sold my business. I'm moving to France. I've just signed a *promesse de vente* on a property in Dordogne, not far from Bergerac.' She nods at her briefcase. 'A nineteenth-century chateau. Two towers, south-facing gardens, its own *pigeonnier* and all. It needs a bit of work, new kitchen and bathrooms, but it's purely cosmetic. I've always wanted to have my own vineyard and this one has nine hectares of well-maintained vines that produce an excellent AOC Bordeaux wine. It's perfect.'

I listen to her, hardly recognizing my friend. She exudes confidence, contentment and something else I can't quite put my finger on.

'What about your house?'

'It's on the market. Open day is next Saturday. The agent tells me it should go like hot cakes. And I'll still have some change left after I buy the chateau.'

'And Marcus?'

'Marcus?' She looks at me, unblinking. 'You can have him, if he ever wakes up.'

Speechless, I realize what the third new quality is I've noticed about her. She's as cold as ice.

'Well, must dash.' She picks up her briefcase. 'Oh, I nearly forgot.' She opens it and takes out a set of keys. 'Your keys.' She throws them on the chair in front. 'By the way, don't try to reach me.'

She gets up and brushes a speck of dust off the sleeve of her jacket.

'Sophie?' I can only think of one pitifully unimportant question. 'Why here? Why did you ask me to come here?'

'Here?' She looks around as if seeing the church for the first time. 'Oh, I had a meeting up the road at the Renaissance. It was convenient. Ta-ra.'

She turns and leaves, her high heels clicking on the stone floor.

I sit in my chair staring at the simple altar, unable to form a single coherent thought. It's as if all the energy has been drained out of me. I have no strength to move or think, or to be shocked.

When I eventually get up, the church's interior spins around me and I have to grab hold of a chair in order not to fall. I slowly make my way into the brightness outside, shuffling like an old woman.

Who was that cold, hard person I've just met? Where is *my* Sophie?

The sunlight hits me and I stop, shading my eyes with my arm, unsure where to go, what to do next.

'Excuse me?' A voice behind me. I ignore it.

'Excuse me? Are these your keys?'

I slowly turn round and see a man, Sophie's set of my house keys in his outstretched hand.

'Yes, thank you.' I reach out to get them and the world around me spins again.

'Whoa!' The man catches my arm and steadies me. 'Are you all right?'

'I'll be fine . . .'

He leads me to a wooden bench and sits down next to me.

He takes a small bottle of water out of his bag and hands it to me.

'Have a sip.'

I do as I'm told. The water is cool and has a faint metallic taste. I gulp it down greedily.

'There, that's better.' He smiles at me.

I *am* beginning to feel better.

'Thank you.'

I take in his black trousers, plain black long-sleeved top, neatly cropped hair with a few specks of grey.

'Are you a priest?'

'Who, me?' He grins. 'Did you think it was my franchise?' He gestures at the church. 'For all I know they have a lady vicar here.'

'Sorry, I thought . . .'

'It's fine. Although no one has ever taken me for a man of the cloth before. Perhaps I should reconsider my vocation.'

I can't help but laugh at the way he says it. He joins in with a wholehearted chuckle. Now I notice a discreet HBA logo on his plain jersey top. A priest wearing a Hood By Air top at £280 a pop? What was I thinking? I know how much they are because I splashed out on one for Anton in a moment of amorous generosity.

'Welcome back to the land of the living.'

'Did I look that bad?' I give him back his bottle.

'As if you'd seen a ghost in there.' He points at the church with his thumb.

I take a deep breath and let it out slowly.

'I did, of sorts . . .'

'Want to talk about it?'

'Not particularly.'

'Haven't you heard of the stranger-on-a-train phenomenon?'

'The what?'

'We are wired to disclose deeply personal information to people we don't know and won't see again. It's been documented by psychologists.'

'Are you a psychologist?'

'I'm a writer. I'm writing a book about ghosts.'

'Are you?'

'I'd like you to tell me about your ghost.'

'You're not really a writer.'

'No, I'm not. Sorry.' The mischievous glint in his eyes has been replaced by something more sincere. 'But I still would like to hear about your ghost.'

I'm tempted. Wouldn't it be liberating, almost cathartic, to spill my guts to a complete stranger? A complete stranger who seems interested and, well, let's admit it, quite hot?

'Tell me who you are first.' I'm playing for time, trying to make my mind up.

'Ahh . . . but that would destroy the beauty of us being complete strangers, wouldn't it?'

'Not if we promise never to see each other again.'

'What if I don't want to make that promise?'

Here we go. I feel a familiar flutter of excitement in my stomach. And to think I was bawling my eyes out for Anton a few minutes ago. I know I shouldn't be feeling like this. But it's so refreshing, exhilarating.

He has kind eyes and a self-effacing Ryan Gosling smile. I can't take my eyes off his lips, full and claret red, and I realize I want to kiss him. God, I've forgotten how much *fun* this can be. I smile back at him, a non-committal but gently testing kind of a smile. Almost imperceptibly, he shifts towards me and his hand casually resting on the bench touches mine. I start at the unexpected contact and something inside me snaps. The buzz of attraction turns into panic.

'My boyfriend's dead,' I blurt out, almost involuntarily.

A tiny part of me expects him to take me in his arms now, console me. But he flinches as if slapped across the face, then tries to cover his reaction with fake concern.

'I'm sorry . . .' He's searching for something to say. 'Is that why you've come here?'

'No. I was meeting a friend. An ex-friend, actually. She's just un-friended me.'

'Oh . . .'

'That's after I slept with her husband and he fell under a train.'

The guy is staring at me, obviously trying to figure out if I'm serious or not.

'He may have jumped, but it's possible he was pushed.' I'm on a roll now. 'My boyfriend was pushed too, I'm pretty sure of that, although the police think it was misadventure. *Misadventure*, huh?'

'Have you tried to get help?' he says quietly.

'What kind of help?'

He thinks I'm crazy.

'I mean . . . the police, for instance, they have that non-emergency number . . .'

'But this *is* an emergency! It's been an emergency for *days*. And I can't take it any more!'

I jump up from the bench. He gets up too, keeping his distance.

'Look –' I turn to him – 'I'm sorry. I'm not in the right

headspace at the moment . . . Thank you for the keys, and the water, but I have to go now.'

'Will you be OK?'

'Yes, yes, I'll be fine.'

'Take care of yourself, won't you?' He doesn't insist on helping me, in fact he's relieved I'm going and I can't blame him.

'I will.'

I turn and run away from him because I'm convinced something bad will happen if I stay here even a minute longer.

It's the noisy chaos of Euston Road that slows me down eventually. To escape the din I dive into the British Library courtyard and perch on the stone stairs. My whole body is shaking. I take a deep breath and hold it, one, two, three, four, then slowly release it, one, two, three, four. Then I hold my breath for another count of four and repeat the cycle once more. 'Tactical breathing' – Anton taught me the trick he learnt from his 'special forces' mate. It helps. My heartbeat slows down and my grey cells regain their grip on reality.

What the hell happened back there, outside the church? Why did the encounter with that man freak me out so much? He was nothing but sweet and considerate. Should I go back and apologize? Even if he's still there, which I doubt, he probably thinks I've slipped out from St Pancras Hospital's mental ward.

What is wrong with me?

Have I turned into a paranoid recluse scared of even the most innocuous emotional connection with another human being? A twitchy weirdo jumping at someone else's touch? I stare at the people milling around in the courtyard. They don't scare me. What is it then? Had the shock of Sophie's revelation shaken me so badly I rejected a genuine offer of help from a kind stranger? It *was* genuine, wasn't it?

My heart begins to beat faster again. What was he doing there? Oh my God. Perhaps he's a journalist. One of Mindy's minions. And I just spilled my guts to him . . . I replay the encounter in my mind. He found my keys. It means he was inside the church. But I didn't see anyone there when I was talking to Sophie. No, it *is* possible he walked in as I was rushing out, noticed the keys, guessed they might be mine, grabbed them and followed me out. It's the most likely scenario and there is *nothing* suspicious about it. I could've just thanked him and walked away. But I didn't. He noticed I wasn't feeling well, sat me down on a bench and gave me some water. The water. I drank it from a bottle offered to me by a total stranger. I remember its strange metallic taste.

My heart is pounding now. My legs feel heavy and my hands have gone numb. I try to force my breathing back to a slow, 'tactical' rhythm, but end up gasping for air. Rohypnol. He'd spiked the water with Rohypnol.

I lean forward and put my head between my knees. Any minute now I'm going to pass out. But at least I'm in a public place and not a deserted churchyard. I'm safe with strangers around me. But what if he's followed me here? I need to run. But I can't move. I sit motionlessly waiting for the darkness to fall.

33

The darkness hasn't fallen. I feel the warmth of sunshine on my neck. I raise my head cautiously, blinking in the bright light. The courtyard looks the same, full of movement and noise. No one has taken any notice of me and I'm glad of the invisibility. *It was just water, you silly-billy.*

I push myself up and slowly walk towards Euston Road. There is no one following me. Everything seems to have gone back to normal. *Everything except my life.*

Absent-mindedly, I join a queue at the bus stop. I need time to think. I board a bus going towards Angel and go straight upstairs. The seat at the front is empty and I automatically make a beeline for it, squeezing myself in next to a teenager engrossed in something on her mobile phone. Old habits die hard – I used to love the front seat when I was her age, a bit of a freak even then, an arty loner with blue hair and no friends. Not much has changed then.

My thoughts go back to St Pancras Church. Sophie. She must really hate me. I know, she has every reason to be pissed off with me. But it was the intensity of her hostility that shocked me. The pure, cold fury, which is much worse than someone throwing a tantrum. I'd much rather she called me a slut and spat in my face. But that icy detachment, the cool contempt, it hurt. How is it possible that the Sophie I've known for nearly twenty years, the affable, delightful, dependable Sophie, has turned into an unrecognizable monster? The way she discarded Marcus, *you can have him, if he ever wakes up*, that was brutal. Yes, his Lust Junction antics were disgusting, he did betray her in the most nauseating way, but to throw him under the bus like this . . . Oh God. Did she have something to do with his accident?

'No, no, no,' I say out loud and the teenager next to me throws me a quizzical glance.

Sophie attempting murder? Absolutely and categorically not. She may have turned into a cold bitch, but she is not capable of killing anyone. Though how can I be sure of it? As it turns out I don't know her at all. She had my keys. She had access to my loft. What if she was my stalker, not Marcus? But *why*? And more to the point, *when*? Sophie's always been so busy with the running of her business that I don't think she'd have the time or the inclination to stalk anyone. Stalking is a lonely business, it's a loser's pastime. Sophie is not my stalker, she is just furious with me. And I can't blame her. I can't blame her for leaving London, Marcus and myself.

Marcus. What will happen to him? I realize my anger towards him has dissipated. I think of him as a grotesque troll now, pitiful rather than menacing. He must've been a very unhappy man. If he pulls through, he'll be a very lonely, unhappy man. With Sophie gone, I'll be lonely too. But not lonely enough to ever want to see him again.

The bus feels claustrophobic all of a sudden. It rocks to a stop and I dash down the stairs and jump out of the closing door to the driver's irritated 'Oi!'. It takes me a while to get my bearings. I'm in Angel. I turn left off the main road and reach the entrance to the Regent's Canal towpath. It's a relief to descend into this haven of tranquillity after the urban ruckus of King's Cross.

The path along the water is almost deserted, with just an occasional dog owner strolling at the sedate dog-walking pace. I walk briskly, unable to shake off the feeling that someone's following me. You're paranoid, I try to reason with myself. Your life's a mess. You've lost a lover, your best friend and a job. No wonder you're overreacting.

But my amygdala knows better. I'm scared and I want to run.

As I pass the Narrow Boat pub I remember Rupert and Daniel. I mustn't forget to feed Matilda. Once I've sorted out what's left of my life . . .

I go through the tunnel under New North Road and emerge onto street level, stopping briefly to get some milk at the Co-op in the Gainsborough Studios. I remember coming here with Aunt Stella and Vero to see Ralph Fiennes in the Almeida Theatre production of *Richard II*. I must've been seventeen or eighteen, not long after I moved in with them. Now I can buy milk at the same spot.

As I cross Shoreditch Park my anxiety dissipates enough for me to become aware of the life around me. Young mothers with their babies, a gaggle of rowdy teenagers, a couple of weathered guys in denim, a hipster nursing his non-Starbucks flat white, a hippy dog walker with three Chihuahuas and two Pomeranians attached to her belt. The dog walker has probably lived here all her life, but the Chihuahuas and Pomeranians are a recent addition, as are their owners. As the new Shoreditch tries to cosy up to the old, the locals fight off private equity and are being 'means tested'. Perhaps this is where I should be with my camera, documenting the dance between altruism and greed, capturing the moment that will soon be gone? Could I pull something like this off? Or is it just another of my pipe dreams? Let's face it, I'm a washout and I'll never be able to come even close to what Erin and I once had. The Cubic Zirconia days are over.

I turn left towards Hoxton Square and stop abruptly, staring at the building in front of me. It's one of the lovingly cultivated stretches of murals on a brick wall, with a monochrome paste-up of a child by Swoon and Stik's sleeping stick person. Next to the familiar images there is a new piece of graffiti. It's nothing spectacular, in fact it's rather naive and kitschy, but I'm rooted to the spot, unable to take my eyes off it. It's a big silver heart outlined in black, with a simple caption inside. *RIP Savage*, it says.

I approach the wall and touch its smooth surface. I'm not quite sure if I should feel moved or alarmed. Whoever made it must've known Anton lived round the corner. But there's nothing menacing or boasting about it. It's just a sweet, simple gesture. A street-art tribute to Anton.

At the very bottom of the heart, right by its cusp, someone has added a small yellow tag in a different font. YOLO it says. YOLO, Anton's favourite acronym, the one he'd occasionally incorporate into his murals.

You Only Live Once.

Is that what he's trying to tell me? That I should seize the day and follow my instinct? 'Be yourself and do what feels right,' he used to say to me. But I don't even know who I am any more! *Damn it, Anton, I miss you!* I cross the street and walk into the shade of my building.

My phone rings just as I'm opening the door to the loft. Vero.

'You back in Whitstable?'

'No, actually, that's one of the reasons I'm calling. There's a seminar on the legacy of science-fiction cult movies tomorrow lunchtime at the Hackney Picturehouse, and Fly and I thought we might check it out before we head back. But we don't fancy another sleepless night, so I was wondering if we could crash at yours.'

'Of course, Vero, you know you can stay here anytime you want. It's yours and Stella's loft anyway—'

'Don't be silly. It's your home and we wouldn't want to intrude.'

'You won't be intruding, honestly. I could really do with company. Vero –' I hesitate, unsure if I should tell her now – 'I know who my stalker is.'

'You do?'

'It's a long story. He's out of action, anyway.'

'Come on, who is it?'

'I'll tell you all about it tonight. You have the keys, so just come anytime.'

Vero suggests they bring a takeaway selection from Busaba Eathai, knowing full well I'd never say no to a nice Thai curry. It sounds like a perfect plan for the evening. I put the phone down, overwhelmed by Vero's restored joie de vivre. If only I could have even one tenth of it . . .

But the prospect of their visit spurs me on to some house cleaning. I tidy up the general mess, mop the floor and attack the bathroom with Flash. I even do the washing-up. I rinse out Pixel's bowls and put the kettle on. There, I'm ready for the guests.

Exhausted by the cleaning outburst, I sit down at the kitchen table and open the MacBook. It springs to life with its usual agility. I google Bruce Gilden, one of my favourite photographers specializing in ordinary people's portraits. His images stare at me from the screen, tough, ugly, confrontational. They are all close-ups, extreme both in their proximity to the subjects and the unforgiving in-your-face nature of the shots. This is life at its most brutal and honest, scars, warts, bad teeth and all. Would I have the courage to do what he's done, put my camera literally in the faces of people who've been bruised and crippled by life? Do I have what it takes? Or should I forget it and stick to taking pictures of toys and dildos? What did Professor Stein call it? Easy mediocrity.

A new email pings in my mailbox and my chest tightens with anxiety. I know I have no reason to react like this any more, but the sound still fills me with dread. I click on the mailbox icon and stare at its contents in disbelief.

'Exposure 5'.

My worst nightmare isn't over, after all.

I could ignore it, I could delete it, but I know it will appear again. And again. I also know there is no point in trying to trace its sender. The person who has sent it doesn't want to be found and isn't interested in my answer.

I take a deep breath and click on the attachment. It's a photograph this time and it's mesmerizing. I've seen something like this before. It seamlessly blends two images, the one of the view outside and that of the inside of a room. The image of the exterior is projected on the back wall of the room and is upside down. I rotate the picture on my computer screen and take a closer look. It's a section of an urban riverbank, a uniform row of solid four- and five-storey houses, perched in a neat line above the dark water. The brown and beige brick mass is interrupted by splashes of colour, marking the developer's frivolous idea of painting some of the tiny balconies white or blue. A modern addition breaks the brick monotony, an incongruous cube of glass and steel crowned with a 'For Sale' sign. Below, the river has left its mark on the mixture of rotting wood and concrete with a vibrant green bloom of algae clinging to the man-made walls. My heart begins to pound when I realize the view looks familiar.

I know where the photo was taken.

I rotate the image back and concentrate on the interior. It's someone's bedroom, dominated by a large bed. The heavy wooden frame fills the picture, its carved antique headboard clashing with the image of the exterior projected over it. The bed is unmade, a mess of pillows and a duvet entangled with sheets that are dark red, almost crimson. A small bedside table on the left, with an unlit brass lamp on top of it. Some books scattered on the floor, mostly large format, hardcover art albums. I find my eye keeps coming back to one spot in the image, a body on the bed. The woman is partly covered by the crimson sheet, her dark hair spilling over the edge of the mattress. One of her arms is twisted at a weird angle, revealing a small tattoo on the inside of the forearm, just above the wrist. I recognize the image. And I can tell the woman is dead.

I close the attachment and get up from the table, away from the computer. I feel dizzy and faint, my skin clammy, the thin shirt I'm wearing drenched in cold sweat. No, I can't let panic get the better of me. I have to think and act. I go to the sink and pour myself a glass of water from the tap. I drink it greedily, spilling some on the floor. It helps a little, but the choking sensation in my throat persists as I go back to the Mac and click on the attachment. I force myself to look at the image again. Yes, there is no doubt about it. I am the dead woman in the photograph. And I know who my killer is.

34

I'm going to confront him. I can't let him go on doing this to me. It has to stop. He is blocking my attempts to challenge him in his cowardly electronic way, so I'm going to do it face to face. I'll go to his house and knock on his door. We'll see who's the coward then.

I'm relieved it's not Marcus. I wouldn't know how to deal with him unconscious in his hospital bed. How do you exact revenge on someone who can't defend himself, who isn't even aware what's going on? No, I feel Marcus has already paid a high price for his misdemeanours. I'm glad I can let go of my vision of him as my stalker. Now I can direct my anger at the real culprit. I welcome the feeling building up inside me. I'm no longer scared of him, I'm furious. How dare he poison my life like this! *Him,* of all people!

I know where you live. For the first time the common phrase sounds like music to my ears. Because I *do* know where he lives and I'm going to make good on the implied threat. I'll ridicule him, demand an apology. It's time the shoe moved to the other foot.

I drop my phone into my bag, grab my keys and rush out of the loft, propelled by my growing hatred towards him. I storm down the stairs, nearly knocking my neighbour the florist off her feet. She groans from behind a huge bouquet of white lilies.

'Where's the fire?'

'Sorry, Susan, on my way to sort my life out.'

'Good luck with that!' I hear her cackle behind me just before the front door slams shut.

I trot, almost breaking into a run, to Shoreditch High Street, then spend ten excruciating minutes at the bus stop. A 78 comes along at last, swallowing the small crowd gathered at the kerb. It's stifling hot inside. Well, it's summer in London. I stay on the lower deck to avoid the oven temperature upstairs.

Shouldn't I be calling the police? Perhaps it would make sense, now that I know who my stalker really is. He *is* a stalker, isn't he? I rummage through the inside of my bag for my phone and google 'stalking'. The Crown Prosecution Service website lists a number of behaviours associated with stalking: *contacting, or attempting to contact, a person by any means*, yes; *publishing any statement or other material relating or purporting to relate to a person*, yes; *monitoring the use by a person of the internet, email or any other form of electronic communication*, yes, yes, yes; *watching or spying on a person*, YES. My stalker is a bona fide stalker.

I go to the 'reporting the crime' section of the CPS website. *In an emergency you should phone 999 and ask for the police.* Well, it's not exactly an emergency. *In non-emergency situations you should contact your local police station by phone or go to the nearest . . .* Try explaining what's been going on to some bored PC at the front desk. No, it wouldn't work. The website tells me I could also report it anonymously to Crimestoppers. But I don't want it to end up as an anonymous complaint. I want to be involved, I want to be able to watch him squirm . . .

Forget the police, I have to face him on my own. What is he going to do, kill me?

The bus reaches the Tower of London, then crawls at walking speed across Tower Bridge. The views are stunning along this stretch of the Thames, but I'm not in the mood for sightseeing. It's my stop. Tower Bridge Road is full of traffic and noise. I breathe in the smell of the river mixed with car fumes and take the stone steps down to Shad Thames. It looks a lot cleaner and posher now, but still feels familiar. I used to come here a lot years ago, running down those steps, eager, inspired, hopeful. Naive.

And there it is, right in front of me. Sprawling, imposing, rich with history. Butler's Wharf.

I've always been fascinated with the place. Originally a Victorian riverside warehouse built to accommodate shipping trade goods: sugar, spices, tea. Closed at the beginning of the 1970s and promptly adopted, and adapted, by craftsmen, performers and artists, Derek Jarman among others. It eventually succumbed to the redevelopment craze of the eighties and was converted into luxury apartments, office spaces and posh eateries. So much for the free, alternative spirit of the place. But, even though it's all City bankers and tourists now, it still holds some attraction for me. After all, this is where we used to come, an earnest and opinionated bunch of art students, to discuss burning *issues*. It all felt so important, cutting edge. Our fire stoked by our admired host, the beloved mentor, a legend of a man.

Professor Robert B. Stein.

The smooth cobbles of Shad Thames under my feet, I stop and look up. Even though it's a sunny day, the narrow street flanked by tall brick warehouses is shaded in semi-darkness. Old industrial winches and cast-iron walkways criss-crossing overhead look almost black against the intensely blue sky. A shiver runs through me. Somewhere up there, on the sixth floor of the monolith of Butler's Wharf, is Professor Stein's coveted apartment. It's probably worth at least a couple of million now, but it was pretty spectacular back then, when we were his guests, gasping at the river view, overwhelmed by his art collection, drunk on ambition and expensive wine. This is where Erin and I hatched up Cubic Zirconia, this is where we used to come to celebrate our first tentative triumphs.

And this is where he must've been plotting his bizarre campaign against me. This is where he created 'Exposure 5', the amazing collage of reality and fiction. It was the view that gave him away, the urban riverbank of St Katharine Docks on the other side of the Thames, just east of Tower Bridge. The view that has burnt itself into my mind because it's always been synonymous with art and success for me. With being Professor Stein's protégée.

What now? Do I go up and confront him? Try to find out why he's been doing this? I'm suddenly overcome by doubt and apprehension. What if he denies it and laughs in my face? I'd be finished in his eyes and the eyes of his coterie. I realize I still care about what he thinks of me. Not to mention the fact that he is still a powerful man. His inner circle, the in-crowd, continues to rule the London art scene. He says a word and I'm simply wiped off the map. *Kristin Ryder? Nah, never heard of her.* But if I don't challenge him now, he'll just continue harassing me, he'll keep sending me those ridiculous 'Exposures'. Damned if I do, damned if I don't.

Just as I'm about to turn, the heavy entrance door swings open and a well-groomed man in a suit emerges onto the street, talking loudly on his mobile. I catch the door before it closes and slip inside, unnoticed by the man who seems to be single-handedly taking credit for the Dow Jones being up by 320 points. I'm in and the concierge desk is empty. It must be my lucky day. I cross the lobby and get into the lift conveniently waiting on the ground floor. I press the button for the sixth floor and lean against the cold, metal wall, remembering to breathe. When I visited Professor Stein for the first time I was convinced I could still smell the spices which were originally stored here, vanilla, cinnamon, anise, a touch of clove. I can almost smell them now, but it's probably just the Dow Jones guy's aftershave.

'Sixth floor, door opening,' announces a warm female voice and the lift's doors slide open.

I can still turn back and leave.

But I know I won't, because I have to find out the truth.

As in a horror movie, I watch my own hand rise and knock on his door. Silence. I grit my teeth and knock again. There, I can hear some movement behind the door, the sound of a mortise lock turning. My heart pounding, I watch the door handle move. *Hello, Professor, do you remember me?* The silly line knocks around inside my head. What on earth am I supposed to say?

The door opens and I stare at the tall figure in front of me, incredulous.

'Erin?'

'Welcome to the party!'

She grabs me by the hand and pulls me inside. I hear the door click shut behind me.

'What party? What's going on?'

But she has already turned and is walking towards a drinks cabinet by the large windows overlooking the river. A wave of nostalgia mixed with awe washes over me. Everything is as I've remembered it. The subdued elegance of the vast space, the sublime artwork on the walls, the amazing view.

'Drink?'

'Sure. Anything.'

As she busies herself with bottles and ice, I perch myself on the arm of a black leather sofa, trying to understand what is going on. Is this the professor's idea of a student reunion? A shindig for old times' sake?

And suddenly I know. The Light Vault! That's what it is! He's invited his former students he wants to include in his show.

'It's the Light Vault party, isn't it?'

'Well done, you've figured it out at last.' Erin hands me a large tumbler.

She raises her glass towards me and we both take a sip. The G&T is cold and strong. All is forgiven, Professor Stein, as long as my name appears in the Light Vault catalogue. The sudden release of tension is making me light-headed.

'Did you get his weird invitation?' I lower my voice. 'The "Exposure"?' I make quotation marks in the air. 'From the master of convoluted messages . . .'

'I thought it was quite brilliant.'

'Well, in a very creepy kind of way. Cheeky of him to ask you as well. I thought the show was for his lesser stars . . .'

'I wouldn't miss it for anything.'

'So great you could make it. You shooting in the UK at the moment?'

She shrugs with an air of nonchalance. 'Just finished a royal commission.'

'What? As in Kate and William? And George and . . .' I'm searching for the name of the youngest royal offspring.

'And Charlotte. That's right. As in the Duke and the Duchess of Cambridge.'

I nearly choke on my G&T.

'Wow, that's amazing! The ultimate family portrait!'

'They wanted to break away from the traditional heavy-lit portraits and do something lighter, more relaxed and intimate. You know, smiles, sunshine, cocker spaniel puppies . . .'

Gobsmacked, I listen to Erin talking about a series of sessions, at Kensington Palace and the gardens of Sandringham House. This is every portraitist's dream, the pinnacle of a photographer's career. And to think she had time to come here, to mingle with us, the mediocre lot!

But as Erin goes on describing her shoot, the use of controlled lighting and desaturated colours, something uncomfortable begins to stir at the bottom of my mind. Kensington Palace, bright summer light, a cocker spaniel puppy . . . I've seen it before. It was Jason Bell's famous photograph of the royal couple with their son, framed by an open sash window of the palace. I remember it, because it struck me with its casual air, so different from the usual official portraits. The desaturated colour palette – that was also something Bell introduced in his photographs of the royal family. And as for the frolicking in the gardens at Sandringham – wasn't that Mario Testino's shoot?

I stare at Erin, barely listening to her monologue. What's going on? I've never had any reason to doubt her career, but this sounds delusional. Would she really be offered a shoot of this calibre? Well, why not? As far as I know she's taken pictures of everyone, from Desmond Tutu to Kathryn Jenner. Has she? Of course she has, I've seen quite a few of her portraits in *Vogue* and *Vanity Fair* over the years. Not recently, though.

Her delusion or my paranoia?

I put my tumbler down on a glass bar surface and look around uncomfortably. Why are we here alone?

'Erin? Sorry to interrupt . . . Where is the professor?'

'Robert? He's running late.'

'How come you're here early?'

'Oh, he lets me use his space when I'm in London.'

'What about your penthouse?'

I've been to it once, her penthouse in Southwark, minutes from the Tate Modern, an amazing space with floor-to-ceiling windows and a huge terrace overlooking the river and St Paul's Cathedral.

'I've let it out. I was hardly ever there.'

'What time does the party start?'

She looks at her black Hublot watch and I catch myself wondering if it's a knock-off.

'Soon. Want another drink?'

'No, thanks, I'm fine. It's gone to my head already.'

This feels wrong. A couple of hours ago I didn't even know I'd be coming here, so unless Professor Stein is a clairvoyant, he wouldn't have been able to predict my visit. A coincidence? I don't believe in them any more. How would all the earlier 'Exposures' relate to this, anyway? There won't be any party. 'Exposure 5' was not an invitation.

'Erin? What's going on?'

'What do you mean?'

'Why are we here?'

'Well . . .' She takes time pouring herself another drink. 'Robert wanted to talk to you about your art.'

'Really?' A part of me desperately wants to believe what I'm hearing, but deep down I know it isn't true.

'He wanted to discuss the possibility of resurrecting Cubic Zirconia with both of us.'

'Are you serious?' Oh God, *please* let it be true.

She nods and takes a sip of her G&T.

'I think I'll have that drink, after all.'

She smiles and reaches for my empty tumbler.

My every brain cell is screaming not to believe a word she says. But my heart wants it to be true so badly . . .

I gulp down nearly half of my drink and it tastes like pure gin this time. It packs an immediate punch and I have to sit down on the leather sofa in order not to fall. I'm suddenly very drunk and confused. This isn't really happening. I have to call a cab and get out of here. I rummage in my bag for my phone, but it's not there. Shit, I must've left it on the bus.

'I've lost my phone,' I tell Erin, hearing myself slur the words. 'I have to go and find it.'

It takes a monumental effort to hoist myself up. I take a few wobbly steps towards the front door and notice a bicycle leaning against the wall in the hallway. It's a Budnitz. As I turn in slow motion to ask Erin about it, I hear a strange sound, a quiet ticking, as if a rattlesnake has suddenly woken up somewhere behind me. And then all I feel is pain followed by darkness.

35

The pain has gone and I'm floating on something soft and warm. My arms and legs are heavy, but it's the pleasant kind of dreamy languor one feels just before waking up. Maybe I am asleep. Whatever it is, I don't want it to end. There is only one thing disturbing the peace – a quiet, regular clicking noise I'd recognize anywhere – the shutter of a camera. It's a sound worth waking up for. My eyelids feel like lead, but I force my eyes to open.

The semi-darkness around me is lit by moving, multi-coloured patches of brightness. It's someone's bedroom and I'm lying on a large bed, propped up by a pile of soft pillows and covered with a red linen sheet. Have I been asleep? The room feels familiar, but I don't know where I am. It's dark, so it must be night-time. What have I got myself into? My mind scrambles for answers, but fails to produce anything sensible. I blink a few times, trying to focus. As my eyes adapt to the peculiar lighting in the room, I'm beginning to see more detail. A dark wall in front of me is not a wall: it's a large window covered with a black plastic sheet. There is a tiny hole in the sheet, right in the middle of it, letting rays of light in. It's still bright outside.

The persistent clicking of the shutter draws my attention to the right-hand corner of the room. I can just make out the shape of a tripod with a small camera attached to it. Click. A few seconds pause. Click again. Someone is making a time-lapse video. It takes me a while to understand the significance of the camera pointed at the bed. Someone is making a time-lapse video *of me*.

But *why*? What is going on? I try to push myself up, try to get up, but my limbs feel heavy, almost paralysed. Maybe it's better to stay put in this nice bed, where I'm comfortable and safe. Actually, I do feel like having a nap. I'm so tired. All that running around . . . what was that about? My eyes close again and I begin to surf the slow wave between being awake and asleep.

A change in light wakes me up. For a moment it's bright in the room, then it goes dark again. Blinded by the sudden flash of light, I squeeze my eyes shut and see bursts of colourful phosphenes inside my eyelids. Funny, I remember the word *phosphenes* but don't know where I am or how I got here. I cautiously open my eyes again and see movement behind the camera. There is someone in the room.

'Hello?' My voice sounds hoarse.

'Ryder. You're awake.'

'Erin?'

She comes out of the shadow into a pool of light by the bed.

'I had to tase you.'

'You *what*?'

'I had to stun you with a taser. Klonopin wasn't working.'

'What are you talking about?' The shock jolts me out of the pleasant stupor. I suddenly remember being in Professor Stein's apartment, having a drink with Erin. I remember 'Exposure 5'. 'Is it some kind of a joke? Did he put you up to this?'

'Robert? He's been in a nursing home for months. Totally gaga.'

'Professor Stein has dementia?'

'Completely *non compos mentis.*'

Oh well, so the whole idea of resurrecting Cubic Zirconia was a hoax, after all. But wait a minute . . . what about the 'Exposures'? If he hasn't been sending them, then who . . . ?

'How do you like my camera obscura?' Erin points at the plastic sheet on the window.

Of course, that's what it is. A camera obscura, the most basic and brilliant of optical devices. Erin has made it out of Professor Stein's bedroom by blacking out the window and cutting a small hole in the makeshift blind. The aperture lets in an inverted image of the view outside and projects it on the objects in the room, the wall at the back, the bed, me. The technique that worked so well in – 'Exposure 5,' I blurt out.

'Well, think of it as the first draft.'

'It was *you*? You? You . . . ?' I'm too shocked to process the news.

'Why, you thought it was someone else?'

She looks at me, a contemptuous smile on her face.

'This is insane!' Propelled by a sudden flash of anger I throw the red sheet off and move to sit up, but something jerks my arms back, stopping me.

Both my wrists are tied with black nylon restraining cords, attached to the bed's heavy oak headboard. I've seen them being used by the police. They are cheap, practical and unremovable, thanks to their one-way locking mechanism in the toggle.

'What the fuck? Erin!' I pull at the restraints.

'Shhh!' She puts her hand on my forehead and pushes me

back against the pillows. 'Remember from our police days? The more you struggle, the more they'll hurt.'

Speechless, I lean back and notice something that escalates my horror even further.

I'm naked.

As much as the restraints let me, I grab the red sheet and pull it up, trying to cover myself.

'Where was I?' Erin goes back to the camera on the tripod. 'Ah, camera obscura. The dark chamber . . .' She makes quotation marks in the air.

'Erin, for fuck's sake! Let me go!'

' . . . Invented by the ancient Chinese, studied by the Greeks, described by Leonardo, utilized by Vermeer, revived not long ago by the Hockney–Falco thesis, and perfected by *moi*, Erin Perdue.'

'Erin, listen to me. This isn't funny any more.'

'*This*,' she looks at me, her smile gone, 'was never meant to be funny.'

This is not the Erin I know. There is something unhinged but at the same time detached about her, as if she's tripping on some hallucinogen. I can feel drops of sweat running down my forehead. Despite the heat in the room I'm shaking.

'Erin, why are you doing this to me?' I try to keep the trembling out of my voice, but it's there, betraying my fear.

'You *still* don't know? Despite all the clues I've given you, despite all the effort?'

'You mean . . . the "Exposures"?'

'*Yes*, the "Exposures"! I've been waiting for you to bloody wake up for weeks! But no, Miss Sleeping Beauty here has been positively comatose. God, you've been so *thick*!' She kicks the base of the bed.

I stare at her, unsure what to say, afraid to stoke her anger. *Wake up from what?* She paces up and down the dark room, sighing and mumbling to herself. The camera on the tripod keeps clicking away in its steady, unrushed rhythm. Erin stops suddenly, shakes her head and leaves, slamming the door behind her.

I check the restraints on my wrists. They are too tight to slip them off. I bring them to my mouth. That's no good either. The nylon they are made of is impossible to bite through. I turn my head to look at the way they've been attached to the headboard. The knots look solid, professional. The headboard doesn't even budge when I tug at the restraints with all my strength, cutting the skin on my wrists. Damn. I have to get out of here, but how?

I glance around the room. Apart from the camera and the bed, there isn't much hiding in the shadows. It seems almost empty. A simple bedside table, a brass lamp, some art books scattered on the floor . . . Just like in 'Exposure 5'. But this is not a photograph, this is real life. And it's getting darker. The image of the outside world projected through the aperture of Erin's camera obscura is beginning to fade; the patches of light on the bed and the wall behind me have lost their intensity and soon will disappear. Night is falling. It must be nine, maybe ten in the evening. Vero and Fly are probably at my loft already, wondering where I am. Will they raise the alarm if I don't come back for the night? No, probably not. Vero is used to me disappearing without a word. But they'll try to reach me on my phone. My phone, God only knows where it is by now . . .

I must've fallen asleep because I jump with a start when Erin opens the door again. She drags in a large tungsten lamp and plugs it in. I turn my head away as its bright light hits my eyes.

'Erin? Can we please stop this? It's gone beyond a joke . . . Erin?'

She doesn't reply, fiddling with the camera controls.

'Can you untie me, so we can *talk?*'

Without a word she leaves the room, but the door remains open. She comes back with a large bottle of Bombay Sapphire and takes a swig from it.

'You want to talk? Let's talk then.'

She waves the bottle at me, but I shake my head.

'Go on then, talk.' She looks at me, challenge in her eyes. 'Tell me what this is about.'

'This?' I look around, playing for time. What do I say in order not to spark her fury again? 'If I've done something wrong, something to upset you, I'm sorry.'

'You're sorry.' She laughs, but it's not a pleasant laugh. 'Kristin Ryder is sorry. Let's drink to that.' She takes another swig from the bottle.

'Erin . . .' My eyes are burning with tears. 'What is this all about?'

She carefully puts the bottle down on the floor, approaches the bed and raises her closed fist in front of my face. I instinctively move my head back, expecting a blow. But she opens her fist to reveal a small, beautifully cut gemstone nesting in the palm of her hand.

'A diamond?'

'Cubic Zirconia, you idiot!' She throws the crystal against the wall. It bounces back and clatters somewhere onto the floor. '*This* is what it's about! *Cubic Zirconia!*'

'But why now, after all this time . . . I don't understand . . .'

'*Of course* you don't! You stupid, ignorant bitch! And to think I was hoping we could work together again . . .'

'You wanted to *revive* Cubic Zirconia?'

'Shut up! You're not worthy of even saying the name.'

She paces the room again, swigging from the bottle.

'Cubic Zirconia was our chance, our future, it was everything. We were set to become the biggest artists of the decade, of the new millennium. Hirst, Hockney, Gormley, Riley . . . they'd be so *tiny* compared with us, so insignificant.'

She stops right in front of the bed and turns towards me, her eyes glassy and bloodshot.

'And you destroyed it. You just walked away from it with that fucking French dickhead of yours as if it was some picnic in the park. How I hated you, with all your insecurities, your misgivings . . . your *blandness* . . . You *killed* it. And then you forced us into that stupid forensic job, made sure there was nothing left of the joy, the creativity, the ambition . . . the *hunger* we used to feel. And *why*? Because you couldn't cope with the limelight, because you were *afraid* it wouldn't lead anywhere, because what Anton had to offer was so much better, because, because . . . You've *ruined* my life.'

I stare at her, speechless. She turns away and laughs, a bitter, cackling sound.

'But, Erin . . . you're the one with the career, fame, money . . . It's worked out for you.'

'Being at the beck and call of every fucking celeb who wants to have a pretty picture? You call *that* a career?'

'Most photographers would kill to be in your shoes. I spend my days taking pictures of kids' toys and dildos.'

'And that's supposed to make me feel better about myself?'

'Well, yes . . .'

I wish there was something I could say to pacify her. I'm desperately searching for the right argument, that one thought, one word that would change everything. But it's not a dream in which one magic word has the power to end a nightmare. This is really happening to me.

'You could've continued without me . . .' I'm trying a different tack.

She stares at me as if I've said something preposterous.

'Without you? There was no Cubic Zirconia without you. Do you get the irony of it? You betrayed me, abandoned our project, chose that fucking French *bobo* over Zirconia and me. You destroyed my life and I *still* couldn't do it without you. And I was reminded of it every day, when I watched you, "the hip Krissy", the *enfant terrible*, wasting her talent on mediocrity, bumbling along from job to job with Anton. The self-absorbed prick. Only two things mattered to him – his dick and his ridiculous paste-ups. He was the easiest pick-up of my life. He practically dragged me to your loft. I played him like a . . . violin.'

As she smirks, amused by the innuendo, I can feel my panic grow. So she was the woman in the 'Exposure' video, fucking him in my loft. She gave him the violin bridge. It was probably supposed to be another message for me. Oh, Anton, you gullible idiot! But I haven't been much smarter . . . There is something else stirring at the bottom of my mind. A picture of the Budnitz I saw earlier in the hallway flashes through my head. Anton's bike. Oh my God, she isn't responsible for Anton's death as well, is she? No, no, no, this can't be true. I have to stop this horrible train of thought. But I can't . . . I have to know . . .

'It was you he arranged to meet that morning in King's Cross . . .'

'He was stifling you. I've done you a favour. '

She's not a killer. She's drunk and she doesn't know what she's saying.

'You kept running after him, wasting time, wasting your energy, because of his pitiful attempts to conquer the world. With what? Lazy wallpaper he called street art? Mind you, his last piece, the one in the Wick, is a different story.' She has that smirk on her face again.

'You've seen it?'

'It wasn't difficult to imitate his style. Think of it as a gift from me.'

'*You* made it?' I don't believe her. 'But . . . you couldn't have known I'd be there to see it.'

'Oh, I made sure you'd see it. Remember Reena Acker?'

I stare at her, speechless.

'Reena . . . Erin . . . Acker . . . hacker, get it?

'But . . . I've checked her out on the net. She has her own website. And an entry in Wikipedia.'

'Oh well, if she's in Wikipedia, she must be real.'

'But . . . *why* would you do all this?'

'I wanted for you to see how redundant he was. Him and his derivative, insignificant attempts at art. Pathetic, empty bubble. That's what you dumped Cubic Zirconia for.'

I shake my head in disbelief. This is *not* happening. I must be asleep, having a nightmare.

'But I have to give it to you, "In Bed With Anton" is one of the best things you've ever made. Thanks to you, not him, obviously. It's raw, erotic, beautifully executed. But of course you kept it under lock and key. Typical you, your best work sits on some old drive at home.'

'It was personal.'

'Show me art that isn't personal. It was *good*, Ryder, and you didn't have the guts to let the world see it.'

'So you did it for me . . .'

She shrugs.

'Another wasted effort. All the "Exposures" were wasted on you.'

'What do you mean?' If I keep the conversation going, perhaps she'll wake up from this psychotic trance. Perhaps I'll wake up.

'I put a mirror to your life, exposed your biggest triumphs and failures, and you still didn't see it. This is how blind you are. Even your cat is more self-aware.'

'You broke into my computer.'

She rolls her eyes.

'You've been spying on me.'

'I've been keeping an eye on you.'

'That studio above Patrick Ewer's flat . . .'

'I like Patrick. He insisted I take over the space and he wouldn't accept any money for it. Sweet man. And his new chamber piece . . . it's sublime.'

Violin-Land.

'Violin-Land,' she says, as if on cue. 'I suggested the title to him. Very apt, don't you think?'

I say nothing, shaken to the core by the revelations that keep coming at me, thick and fast. Everywhere I turn, I see Erin in my life.

'Do you remember it?'

Of course I do.

It was during the heyday of Cubic Zirconia, the crazy, intense period of our collaboration when we used to work, eat, sleep and dream together. Sex was a release, a relaxation, it cleared our heads and gave us a boost of much-needed dopamine. Neither of us made a big deal out of it, it just felt right at the time. Whenever we had a break in our schedule, a moment to ourselves, we'd sneak out to Violin-Land. It was our code word, taken from my favourite book, something no one else would understand. Our perfect little fling.

'Violin-Land.'

She sits down on the bed next to me and leans forward. Up close her eyes are like a cat's, ocean green around the pupil and sandy yellow near the edges of the iris. Her pupils dilate as she looks at me. She smells of gin and Patchouli Absolut. Something stirs inside me, a flicker of the old attraction. For a moment it looks as if she's going to kiss me, but then she puts her hand on my chest, pushes me hard against the headboard and gets up.

She *must* be feeling what I've just felt. This is my chance, maybe she'll change her mind.

'Erin, let me go.'

'I can't.'

She's fiddling with the camera again, but I sense her hesitation.

'We could start all over. We could relaunch Cubic Zirconia . . .'

'Shut up!'

'Untie me, please.'

'I need you.'

'I won't go anywhere, I promise.'

'You don't understand. I need you for the "Final Exposure".'

36

She's gone. She checked the camera and left the room, quietly closing the door behind her.

How long is she going to hold me here? Until I slowly wilt and die? Well, people do take time-lapse photos of dying flowers, why not of a human? It would certainly be ground-breaking.

All the things she's said keep coming back at me, despite my efforts to block them. I try to be logical, cold, keep panic at bay. But I can't stop thinking about it. If what she said was true . . .

If what she said was true, she is a dangerous psychopath. She's been stalking me for months, if not years, she broke into my computer, pillaged my private files, insinuated herself into my life . . . She might have killed Anton.

No, I can't believe it. I used to know her so well, she was my friend, my kindred spirit. Is it possible she's changed that much? What has happened to her?

What is the 'Final Exposure'?

A shiver runs through me. What is she plotting in her sick mind?

I'm shivering because I'm scared and cold. I'm thirsty and my bladder is full. In fact, 'full' is an understatement. It's absolutely bursting and if I don't go to the loo soon . . .

'Erin! I need to pee!'

There is silence beyond the closed door. Where is she? Has she gone out and left me? It's still dark outside, but the quality of light coming through the camera obscura aperture has changed. The inky gloom of midnight has given way to oyster twilight. It must be early morning, probably around five. Where the hell is she?

'Erin! Erin! I need the loo!'

Maybe someone will hear me if I keep shouting.

'Erin, let me go!'

Maybe an irate neighbour will complain about the noise.

'Erin!'

Maybe they'll call the police.

'Help!'

My voice bounces off the thick walls like a ping-pong ball. This is a solid brick Victorian warehouse, not some plasterboard shack. No one's going to hear me.

I lean back on the pillows, stifling a sob.

Has she left me to die? She'll be back for her camera. But when? How long will she keep me here, tied to the bed?

The pain in my bladder is excruciating. I try to shift on the mattress in order to relieve the pressure, but no matter how I position myself it hurts. I cross and uncross my legs, raise my hips, take deep breaths. I hum to myself, try to count clicks of the shutter, but nothing helps. I think I'll have to wet the bed. This is such a cliché, the ultimate indignity of a prisoner. Maybe she'll come back. She *has* to come back. I must hold out for a bit longer. But I can't.

The warm wetness spreads under my buttocks and the relief is immediate. I moan with pleasure, luxuriating in the sudden absence of pain. It feels great for a few minutes. But as the warmth evaporates all that is left is a patch of uncomfortable wetness. As I wonder how long it'll take before it starts to smell, I detect an unpleasant odour lingering in the air. But it's not the wet mattress, not yet anyway. It's me. Every time I move a strong, almost animal-like stench of sweat wafts from under the red sheet.

I stink of fear.

If there was ever a hope of getting out of here by seducing Erin, I can forget it. She wouldn't touch me with a barge pole now.

I must've fallen asleep because when I open my eyes again the room is full of movement and light. The wall behind me, the bed and myself in it, are bathed in patches of colour, green, blue, white. I sit up and turn my head to get a better look. It's the view from 'Exposure 5'.

As light from the outside goes through the camera obscura aperture, it flips the image upside down, just like the lens of a camera or a human eye. A brown and beige row of houses perched on their roofs is projected across the bed's headboard, the pillows and my body. The sky is below, on the floor, and the Thames runs above me. I lean back and look at the ceiling. The river is quite busy already. A squat barge filled with yellow containers crawls slowly from left to right, towed by a small tug boat. It's being chased by a red-and-white City Cruiser, its tinted windows reflecting the sun. Mesmerized by the upside-down spectacle, I momentarily forget where I am.

My brief reverie is interrupted by the sound of the door being opened. Erin's back. She drags a large Manfrotto tripod in and stops abruptly, blowing the air out with a frown. It must stink in here.

Without a word she sets the tripod at the foot of the bed, then leaves again to return with a camera. Yep, it's a Hasselblad H5D-60 medium format digital camera that would set you back more than a brand new Audi A5. And that's *before* you fork out on a lens. I feel a ridiculous stab of envy. I watch Erin as she sets up the camera, quick, efficient, focused. She looks so professional, so . . . normal. But as I observe her closely I begin to notice a slight tremor in her fingers, a few beads of sweat on her forehead, the jerkiness of her movements.

'Erin?'

She hushes me with a raised hand, totally absorbed in what she's doing.

'Erin, we need to talk.'

'Not now, Ryder.'

'Erin, you *have* to let me go.'

She ignores me. Fear tugs at my empty stomach.

'Erin, what the hell are you doing?'

She carefully makes the final adjustment, then looks up.

'I am creating a masterpiece.'

'No, you're not. You're holding a hostage in a room that stinks of piss.'

'You don't get it, do you?' She stares at me with her scary, empty eyes, tapping her foot impatiently. 'This,' she points at the bed and the wall above me, 'is going to be one of the most famous images of the twenty-first century.'

God, she *is* mad.

'It'll push the boundaries of art. Instead of being a reproduction of reality, it'll *be* reality.'

'You don't need me for this . . .'

'Oh, I do. We used to work together, remember? This is going to be our final piece. The ultimate triumph for Cubic Zirconia.'

'But you already have "Exposure 5". It's good, by the way, very good. I actually thought it was me in the picture. Down to the tattoo.'

She slides her sleeve up to reveal the tattoo on the inside of her forearm, just above the wrist. It matches mine exactly.

'Fire. Remember when we got them?'

'I'll never forget it. It hurt like hell.'

She actually smiles. Maybe if I keep chatting with her, she'll abandon whatever she's planning to do and let me go.

'Listen, I've pissed myself. And now I'm sitting on a soggy mattress smelling like granny's knickers. Let me go to the bathroom, clean myself. You don't want to work with me like this . . .'

'That's precisely what I want.'

The smile is gone. It's as if her human side shuts off, leaving the psycho shell.

She leaves the room. This isn't going well. I look around in desperation. I wish there was something I could use to cut these bloody restraints. She is not going to let me go, so I need to find a way of getting out of here, by hook or by crook.

If I could slide down on the bed as far as I can, maybe I could reach the tripod with my foot. And if I kick it . . . Knocking a forty-thousand-dollar camera to the floor may not be the cleverest idea, but it's all I can think of. It'll provoke her, elicit some kind of unplanned reaction, force her to change her plan. She won't be able to shoot the 'Final Exposure', whatever it is, on her Hasselblad, so maybe she'll abandon the project altogether. She's always been a perfectionist . . .

Propping myself on an elbow, I shift my buttocks off the wet patch. I can do it. I put my arms above my head so the restraints don't stop my slow progress and keep moving towards the foot of the bed. I'm nearly there when the door opens again.

She's back, twitchy and keyed up. She puts a small metal tray on the floor, then approaches the bed and pulls on my restraints. They cut into the skin on my wrists.

'Ouch. It hurts.'

'Move back.'

'It's wet there. I was trying to find a dry patch.'

'Move back.'

There is something in her voice that makes me do what she says without another word. Satisfied with my position, she goes back to the tray. As she picks it up I notice its contents. A syringe and a small glass vial with a green top.

'Erin, what the fuck . . .' My heart is pounding.

'Shhh . . .' She shakes the vial.

'Erin, what are you doing? What is it?'

'Ketamine. I could've chosen something much more painful.'

Ketamine. The same drug they found in Anton's blood after his death.

'No! You can't!' I'm yanking on the restraints, trying to move as far from her as I can.

'You'll be gone in thirty seconds.'

'No, I don't want to . . .' I'm thrashing around in panic.

'I'm afraid what you want or don't want is no longer relevant . . . Actually, let me tell you what *I* want.' She puts the tray down. 'It's going to be a triptych. Three camera obscura images linked together by their common object, you. And their common subject, death. Think of it as a twenty-first-century altarpiece. Left panel – waiting for death. I'll have to be snappy with this one. Death in a Ketamine overdose is apparently quite quick. Central panel – death. The moment your heart stops beating. Right panel – after death. Victorians called it "memorial portraiture". I'll have to wait for this one until the light outside is right. Very à propos, don't you think? Considering it was you who had the brilliant idea of making us do post-mortem photography for a living . . .'

I stare at her, speechless. In her twisted mind she's confusing killing me with art. This *can't* be happening . . .

She picks up the Ketamine tray again.

'Erin, wait. You can't do it. It's murder. You won't get away with it. You'll go to prison and no one will buy your art. They'll ban it . . .'

'You're wrong. Notoriety sells.'

'But you won't be able to enjoy it.'

'I'm enjoying it now. In fact, I'm loving it.'

She pierces the vial's top and pulls on the plunger.

'Fuck! No!'

I kick, aiming at her hand with the syringe. My foot misses it by inches.

'Bad girl.'

'Don't come near me! I won't fucking let you come near me!'

'Then I'll have to tase you again.' She puts the syringe back on the tray. 'I was hoping we'd avoid it. It might spoil the composition. You're being so *difficult!*'

'Erin, *please!*' My last-ditch fury from a moment ago has been replaced by despair. 'You're *my friend*. You can't do this to me . . .'

She's not listening. She places the Ketamine tray on the floor away from the bed and leaves the room. She is going to kill me and there is nothing, absolutely nothing, I can do to stop her. I'm choking on my tears.

An unexpected noise penetrates my anguish and I hold my breath, trying to suppress the sobbing.

Someone's knocking on the front door.

I'm imagining it. No, there it is again. Oh God, please let it be true.

'Help!' I try to shout, but I barely manage a whimper.

Someone is banging on the door. I can hear muffled, raised voices.

I've been saved. I'm not going to die.

There's more noise outside and suddenly Erin is back in the room. She kicks the door shut behind her and turns towards me. She is shaking and her face is a pale mask twisted in anger. She points a black and yellow object at me.

A gun. No, a taser.

'Erin, wait . . .'

I hear the familiar clicking. I want to say it's too late, I want to tell her all will be forgiven if—

Pain. And then nothing.

37

My body is heavy. My head is throbbing. My eyelids refuse to move. I can feel the restraints on my wrists.

Damn. I'm still on the fucking bed. Nothing has changed. But I'm alive.

It takes effort to open my eyes. I close them immediately, blinded by the brightness in the room. Where is Erin's camera obscura? Where is she? I must've passed out, but what happened before that? I can't remember.

'Kristin?'

The voice sounds familiar. Erin has never called me Kristin. I crack my eyes open again. Short grey hair, bushy dark eyebrows, big brown eyes magnified by stark glasses in a black frame.

'Vero? What are you doing here?'

'Waiting for you to wake up.'

'But how . . .'

I look around the room. I'm not at Professor Stein's apartment. What I thought was a restraint on my wrist is a catheter attached to a drip.

'Where am I?'

'The Royal London.'

That place again. Marcus's hospital.

'Why am I here?'

'You've had a bit of a shock. Literally.' Vero smiles. 'Erin tased you for a bit longer than necessary.'

'Erin . . . where is she?'

'It's OK, Lily Liver.' Vero pats my hand gently. 'Don't you worry about her now.'

'Can we go home?'

'As soon as the doctor says yes.'

It turns out the drip in my hand is there to treat dehydration, but the good news is my fluid volume is almost back to normal. A young doctor with bloodshot eyes and heavy five o'clock shadow talks loudly about 'possible scarring' after the removal of taser darts and how lucky I was to avoid 'ventricular fibrillation'. Satisfied with 'my responses', he signs a discharge note. I'm free to go.

'This is the best cup of tea I've ever had.'

It's strong, milky and very sweet, and I'm drinking it at the kitchen table in my loft.

Vero and Fly have evidently made themselves at home here and it's fine. It's actually great to have them around, especially as we still have a lot of catching up to do.

'How did you know I was at Professor Stein's flat?'

Fly shoots Vero a worried look. She clears her throat.

'Well . . . I was a bit naughty. You'd actually got me worried with all your stalker stories and I asked Fly to find a way of keeping an eye on you . . .'

'You *spied* on me?'

They both look rather sheepish.

'Well, no . . . yes . . . it wasn't like that . . . Fly, you explain it . . .'

He sneezes and blows his nose noisily.

'Sorry, it's the cat . . .'

'Come on, Fly.' Vero glares at him. 'I saw you take your antihistamine this morning.'

'OK.' He sighs. 'We planted a Tile in your bag.'

'I was walking around with a *tile* in my bag?'

'It's not a "tile" tile. It's a Bluetooth lost-item tracking device.'

'You've lost me already.'

'OK. It helps you find misplaced things using a smartphone. The Tile I put in the side pocket of your bag was linked to my iPhone.'

'Thank heavens I had my bag with me.'

He smiles. 'Yes, that was lucky. Especially as you'd left your mobile phone on the bus, so we couldn't use it to locate you.'

'How do you know I left it on the bus?'

'It was found by an honest person. She looked up recently dialled numbers on your phone and got through to Vero. She dropped it off here this morning.' Fly points at my phone sitting on the table, then puts a small square object next to it. 'This is your Tile.'

I pick it up and turn it in my fingers. It's light, made of glossy white plastic, smaller than a flat paper matchbox.

'You said it was linked to your phone by Bluetooth. But Bluetooth has a range of a couple of hundred feet. I was on the other side of the town. How did you find me?'

'Ah, this is the beautiful part.'

I can see a twinkle of geeky excitement in Fly's eyes.

'It has a Community Find feature. It automatically connects with all the other users who have their Tile app open and creates a large network that amplifies the Bluetooth radius.'

'So the more people have the app running, the bigger the network?'

'That's right. Incidentally, Butler's Wharf seems to be full of Tiles.'

'I'm not surprised. So, you tracked me down to Butler's Wharf, but how did you get in?'

Fly looks at Vero expectantly.

'OK, I'd better come clean.' She takes a deep breath. 'I got worried when you didn't come home for the night. Especially as you knew a curry from Busaba Eathai was waiting for you. So I asked Fly to check your MacBook. We found the email with "Exposure 5". I recognized the view and when Fly managed to pinpoint your location we knew you'd gone to challenge whoever was behind all the "Exposures". It could only mean trouble. So first thing in the morning we set off for Butler's Wharf. We still didn't know where exactly at the Wharf you were, but it all clicked into place when I saw Robert's name on the buzzer.'

'You know Professor Stein?'

'Robert is an old friend. I knew he was your lecturer. Poor sod, he hasn't been doing great lately. He's in a nursing home in Surrey. I should go and visit him.' She shakes her head with sadness. 'Anyway, we decided we had to get into the apartment, so . . .' She coughs and busies herself with her silver E-cig.

'So Vero rang the police pretending she was Mrs Stein!' Fly finishes the sentence for her.

'You said you were the professor's *wife?*'

'Well, yes. But all I said was that I couldn't get into the apartment and I was worried because he had dementia . . .'

'You didn't! Aren't you in trouble, wasting police time and all that?'

'Well, as it turned out I wasn't wasting their time, was I? I just chose the fastest way of making them smash that door down without having to go into the whole story about you and your stalker. A very sweet sergeant gave me a tiny slap on the wrist, but even she acknowledged that under the circumstances my actions were justified.'

'My God, Vero . . . Fly . . . you've saved my life . . .' I feel a tearful wave of gratitude coming on.

'Let's drink to that!' Vero raises her mug and we all sip our tea in silence.

'Erin – where is she?' I don't want to think about her, but I have to know.

Vero and Fly exchange a quick glance.

'Kristin . . .' Vero puts down her mug. 'Erin is dead.'

I stare at her, dumbstruck.

'There was a commotion when the police entered the apartment, she was out of control in some drug-induced frenzy, waving the taser around, shouting something incoherent, and then . . . she jumped.'

'She jumped?'

'She threw herself out of that blacked-out window. It happened so fast . . . you were there, tied to that bed . . . I didn't even know if you were alive . . .'

'It was total mayhem . . .' Fly joins in.

'One second she was there, screaming at us, the next she was gone, broken glass everywhere.'

'She threw a tripod at the window. With some big-ass camera attached to it.'

'Her Hasselblad,' I whisper.

We all sit in silence, looking into our mugs. Vero and Fly are clearly reliving the scene; I'm digesting the shocking news.

She's gone.

My creative soulmate turned my tormentor is dead. Perhaps I should be rejoicing over the fact but all I feel is overwhelming sadness.

'What about the other camera? The one she was shooting the time-lapse on?'

'We couldn't get to it . . .'

Vero silences Fly with her stare. 'I guess the police have it. It contains evidence, doesn't it?'

I groan and put my face in my hands. I can't bear the thought of anyone watching the most humiliating episode of my life, even though it's only time-lapse.

'Talking of the police . . . A cute policewoman popped in when we were waiting for you to wake up at the hospital. PC Singh?'

'Anu,' I nod.

'Yes, she said you'd remember her. She wished you a speedy recovery. Oh, and she asked me to tell you that in the light of new evidence they'll be reopening the inquiry into Anton's death . . .' Vero throws me an anxious glance.

I close my eyes, thinking of the Budnitz bike in Professor Stein's apartment. I know what they'll find out. But it won't bring Anton back.

'There is one more thing . . .' Vero sounds suspiciously contrite.

'What?' I open my eyes. I'm not sure I can take any more news.

'Erm . . . while we were at the apartment I accidentally swiped Erin's MacBook . . .'

'You accidentally did *what*?'

'Well, as Fly said, it was total mayhem, the paramedic was

there with you, and we were told to leave the scene, and as we were leaving I noticed this MacBook and for some reason I thought it was yours – I completely forgot yours was back at the loft. So I just slipped it into my bag . . . I didn't want it to get lost . . .'

'You removed evidence from the crime scene?' I can't believe her stupidity. Or brazenness.

Vero and Fly exchange a guilty look. This is bad. Tampering with evidence is a crime. But on the other hand . . . finders keepers?

'Do you still have it?'

'Yes.'

'And has Fly had a look at it?'

'Yes.'

'OK then, tell me what you've found.'

'Erin *was* your stalker.'

'I know.'

'She'd been spying on you for months. There are hundreds of photographs, emails, documents . . .' Vero hesitates. 'About you *and* Anton.'

'I know,' I whisper. It feels as if all the energy has drained out of me.

'Fly's had a little poke around in her files. She was quite a hacker, you know. I think Fly was a tiny bit impressed.' She grins at him, then continues. 'It appears she'd somehow managed to insinuate herself into Robert's life. Fly's found some correspondence with Robert's nursing home signed "Erin Stein". She might have been pretending she was his daughter. She hadn't worked for months. She booked herself into The Priory last January. She was out in February and by March her flat in Southwark had been repossessed. She was heavily in debt. She was spending money on two things: online dating sites and pharmacies. Prozac, Xanax, Klonopin, Ketamine, Mephedrone, you name it. She wasn't well, Kristin.'

I'm too shocked to say anything.

'There is quite a lot of her art on that computer as well. Some amazing photographs and drawings. Fly and I thought you might want to have a look at them . . .' Vero throws me an anxious glance. 'Whenever you're ready, obviously . . .'

I nod in silence.

Maybe one day, in the distant future, I'll be able to face Erin Perdue again.

Epilogue

I can't find any more tidying up to do. Once Vero and Fly left for Whitstable, I hoovered, dusted and scrubbed, although nothing in the loft needed cleaning. When everything smelt of bleach and furniture polish, I spent an hour playing with Pixel and his new catnip toy from Vero.

The washing machine is chugging away through its 'Mixed Items' cycle. Pixel's asleep, snoring softly on the bed. I don't fancy another cup of tea and I can't think of another displacement activity I haven't tried yet.

Erin's MacBook is sitting on the kitchen table, an innocuous lump of metal and dormant electronics. I should pass it on to the police.

But I won't. I can't bear the thought of anyone opening this Pandora's Box again.

I dig a black rubbish bag from under the sink and wrap the computer in it, sealing the parcel with gaffer tape. I then stuff it in the utility cupboard, behind some battered suitcases and Anton's old rucksacks. It fits snugly in a dusty, dark corner I never look into.

Perhaps I can manage one more cup of tea, after all. I put the kettle on and sit down in front of my MacBook.

I open the mailbox and let the cursor hover above the

'Exposure 5' email. And then I click 'Delete'. I find it in 'Trash' and click 'Delete' again. There. It's gone.

I'm staring at the screensaver on the Mac when the phone rings.

'Hey, Kris.'

'Jason. Sorry I haven't been in touch, I've been a bit preoccupied.'

'I know, I've been trying to get hold of you for ages. Is everything all right?'

'Everything's fine.'

It feels strange to hear myself say it. Perhaps if I keep repeating it, I'll believe it eventually.

'Great. Listen, not sure you'll be interested, but I might have a job for you . . . A friend of mine runs a travel company, one of those exclusive outfits that cater for the rich and bored. You know, tailor-made trips to South America, the Bahamas, Bali and such. They've recently started offering a new service they call "Shutterbird". Basically they include a professional photographer as part of the cost of the trip. Apparently it's the latest fad. All you'd have to do is tag along and take some snaps of the rich and bored which they'll able to post on Instagram or Facebook as their own.'

'You're joking . . .'

'No, I'm dead serious. I know it's not a creative challenge, but the money is good and I thought you might fancy a break. The next trip they need a Shutterbird for is to Necker Island. You know, Richard Branson's home? I would've taken the job myself, but I've got too much on, the family and stuff . . .'

'I'll take it.'

'You sure?' He sounds surprised.

'Absolutely. When is the trip?'

'In a couple of weeks.'

'Perfect.' It'll give me time to do Heather's shoot and pack.

'Fantastic. I'll let him know and he'll be in touch.'

I put the phone down.

Everything's fine. Well, if it isn't yet, it will be in a couple of weeks.

There is one more thing I need to do. I pick the phone up again and speed-dial a number.

'Vero, I need to speak to Fly.'

'Sure. You OK?'

'Yes, I have a question for him.'

'Hold on, he's right here.'

His 'hello' is full of apprehension.

'Fly, you said Erin was addicted to dating sites. Do you remember which ones?'

'Erm . . . definitely the one that got hacked last year, Ashley-something, and some others, Match, I think, and something with fish in the name, Fishpond, no, Plenty of Fish, that's it, oh, and Lust Junction . . .'

'Lust Junction, are you sure?'

'Yeah, the name reminded me of Clapham Junction for some reason. It was the one she used most, I think . . .'

'Thanks, Fly, you've been really helpful. I have to go.'

I disconnect, my heart pounding. Erin was familiar with Lust Junction. *It was the one she used most*, he said. Is it possible she faked Marcus's profile and invented the whole 'Marcus the sex addict' scenario? Something about the story didn't ring true from the start. The phone call from 'Anastasia', Marcus 'the womanizer', the four strange emails from him . . . Was Erin behind all this? Is it possible she saw Marcus with me at the loft? That stupid, forgettable fumble I should've never let happen.

Was Erin capable of involving an innocent couple and wrecking their already rocky marriage in order to hurt me? I lean back in the chair and close my eyes. Snippets of our camera obscura encounter pop up in my mind. Yes, she was. She'd taken Anton away from me. But ultimately I'm to blame for what happened to Sophie and Marcus. They would never have ended up in the cross hairs of Erin's vengeful crusade otherwise.

I get up and go to the window. There are people milling around in Patrick Ewer's flat, champagne flutes in their hands. I wonder what the occasion is. For a split second I feel the urge to join the party, chat amiably with strangers, away from my loft, away from my life . . . But I have to stick with it, try to undo the damage.

It won't be easy. I'm not sure if I'll ever succeed. But I have to try. Small steps, Aunt Stella used to say, small steps take you in the right direction. I hope it's not too late. I hope Marcus wakes up from his coma. I hope Sophie will want to speak to me at some point. Perhaps one day she'll understand my side of the story. Maybe we'll be friends again. Small steps.

I notice an art nouveau card standing on the kitchen counter next to a set of keys with a small grey fob. I grab the keys and the card and head for the door.

Downstairs I nearly collide with Susan, barely visible from behind a bunch of tall sunflowers.

'Rushing off to sort out your life again?'

'Not today, Susan.' I hold the door open for her. 'Just popping out to feed a python.'

Acknowledgements

Thank you to the fantastic team at Pan Macmillan, my editor Trisha Jackson in particular; my wonderful agent Jane Gregory; Sandra Skibsted for sharing her fascinating knowledge with me; Basia Chomski and Philippa Patel, for being my faithful readers; and to Jola, for showing me what art and photography are about. Erin's final camera obscura piece was inspired by a series of stunning camera obscura 'roomscapes' by photographer Abelardo Morell.